LOCK
THE
DOOR

ALSO BY JANE HOLLAND

FICTION

The Queen's Secret (as Victoria Lamb)
Witchstruck (as Victoria Lamb)
Wolf Bride (as Elizabeth Moss)
Miranda
Last Bird Singing
Girl Number One

POETRY

Camper Van Blues

LOCK
THE
DOOR

Jane
HOLLAND

THOMAS & MERCER

Text copyright © 2017 Jane Holland

Published by Thomas & Mercer, Seattle

www.apub.com

Amazon, the Amazon logo, and Thomas & Mercer are trademarks of Amazon.com, Inc., or its affiliates.

ISBN-13: 9781503941786
ISBN-10: 1503941787

Cover design by Mark Swan

Printed in the United States of America

For my readers

Prologue

'The test results are in.' Dr Shiva checks a document on her desk, then looks up at us; her brief smile is sympathetic, which fills me with dread. 'I'm afraid it's bad news. You need to prepare yourselves.'

I clutch Jon's hand, glancing sideways at him. He's staring straight ahead, rigid in his seat, but his fingers squeeze mine in return.

'No,' I hear myself say, automatically denying the words she has not even spoken yet. There must be a mistake, I'm thinking. The wrong test results. A mix-up in the lab. Some overworked junior doctor sleepily typing the wrong surname . . .

But of course there is no mistake.

I see my husband's face begin to close in as Dr Shiva continues, her soft voice filling in blanks we had hoped would remain empty forever.

'No,' I say again.

I glance down at Harry, fast asleep beside us. He looks so peaceful, tiny wrinkled hands curled into fists on top of his blanket. He didn't wake up even when Jon unbuckled the seat belt and carried him into the hospital, still cradled in his car seat. He had his last feed only an hour ago.

A thin, grey rain begins to fall outside the window.

After all the information and support leaflets have been duly handed over, Dr Shiva rises to shake our hands on the way out, diminutive and professional in a golden-brown dress and black boots, noisy bangles on her wrist. I still don't quite believe her. But her immaculate white coat and name label are unassailable.

'I'm so sorry, Mrs Smith,' she keeps saying. 'I'm so sorry, Mr Smith.'

And she probably is.

I wonder how many other people she will have to apologise to this morning, shaking their hands with just the right amount of professional concern.

Harry is still asleep.

The car seat handle crooked over my arm, I carry him out of the consulting rooms. I look at the others still sitting in the waiting area with its plastic seating and toy table, their expressions patient and distracted, one woman watching a toddler play, another reading a magazine, untroubled by having to prepare themselves for bad news, and wonder how many of them . . .

The hospital corridors are impersonal and overheated, the bright fluorescent lighting somehow intrusive. There are lines painted on the wall with smiley faces and arrows to help us escape the maze of departments.

PAEDIATRICS

OUTPATIENTS' RECEPTION

WAY OUT

We run through the car park in the rain, my coat over Harry to keep him dry. I keep my face politely blank until I'm back in the car. Back in its rain-streaked little cave, looking out at the world.

Jon does not notice. Or ignores my heaving chest. He secures Harry's car seat in the back, then goes to pay for the parking ticket. When he gets back, he's soaked, swearing under his breath.

Rain is falling more heavily now. I look round at Harry, but he is lying still, as pale as his blanket. Apart from a tiny yawn as we left the consulting room, he has not stirred.

'Here.' Jon hands me the ticket for the exit machine, flicks the windscreen wipers on, then concentrates on backing out of the narrow space.

I clutch the parking ticket and watch the wipers swing back and forth. So pointless, wiping away rain that returns a split second later. Almost before the wiper has completed its arc.

Jon stops backing, partway out of the space, and stares at me helplessly. 'Meghan, for God's sake . . .'

But I don't care who sees me crying. What does it matter? What does any of it matter? From today, nothing will ever be the same.

I look round at Harry again, nestled so cosily in his car seat. Oblivious to his condition, his future. I wish now that I had chosen to ride in the back beside him, to hold his tiny hand, to watch him even as he sleeps.

'Our perfect boy,' I cry, and hear my husband cry out too, like a wounded animal.

Imperfect, as it turns out.

Our perfectly imperfect boy.

Chapter One

I have a tiny fleck of grey at my temple. I noticed it last night in the bathroom and was shocked, though I didn't say anything to Jon. I am only twenty-five.

In the supermarket aisle, I turn over the packet of hair dye, check down the list of instructions. They don't look too complicated.

Test patch first for allergic reaction . . .

This might be a good time to go blonde. I'm finally starting to settle into a treatment routine with Harry, and I've always been dissatisfied with my brown hair. It's not exactly mousey, but blonde seems more exciting than chestnut. Camilla next door is a blonde, and she and her husband, Treve, have such a great relationship, I really envy them. Besides, I went blonde once as a teenager, for the last summer of sixth form, and got far more attention from boys that term. Quite the head-turner.

I put the product back on the shelf, though it promises one hundred per cent grey coverage. Stupid idea. Jon would call it a waste of time and money. I already know what he'll say. 'It's one strand, Meghan. What's all the fuss about?'

And what is all the fuss about?

One grey strand of hair. That can happen sometimes before you hit your thirties. It doesn't mean anything. Except that I know how ambitious Jon is, and how hard he works at the law firm, and I don't want him to feel embarrassed that his wife is not as young and exciting and energetic-looking as he might like. Not that Jon would comment on my appearance. Some days he does not even seem to notice me. But I'm uneasily aware that I don't make as much of an effort as I used to. Not since the birth.

'Come on, Harry.'

Harry does not answer. Still asleep, hopefully.

The doctor said to treat him like any other child. Easy for her to say. Some nights I feel like he's made of glass, especially when I undress and bathe him before bed. As though he might shatter at any minute.

Seven months old this Saturday.

I'm getting used to the buggy and basket routine. The trick is not to hurry. And at some point, I suppose, he may be strong enough to ride upfront in the little plastic trolley seat.

As usual, my mind shies away from anything that involves the future. 'What a gorgeous little boy,' women exclaim over Harry in the street. 'He'll be a heartbreaker when he grows up!'

He's a heartbreaker now, I think, but say nothing.

What is there to say, after all?

The first few weeks after he came home from the hospital, I saw parents out with those sling things, baby snug against their chest, and asked Jon if we should try one. But he wasn't impressed. 'New Age nonsense.' I wasn't so sure. You never saw those babies wriggling or screaming. But it was certainly true what Jon said, that we had paid a huge amount for the buggy and its accessories and ought to get some proper use out of them before Harry . . .

A woman drops a family-size shampoo bottle further up the aisle, spattering cheap red shampoo everywhere. The loud crack wakes Harry; his eyes spring open in his flushed face. His legs jerk first, then his chest heaves, and he cries out, sharp and plaintive.

'There, there.' I bend to comfort him, and tidy the blue fleece he's kicked off. 'Hush, it's okay.'

The woman looks at me apologetically. 'Sorry,' she mouths before fleeing the scene of her crime.

Harry looks up at me accusingly, but settles down after a few thin, disgruntled cries. He only recently had his feed, and it's obviously an effort for him to keep his eyes open.

'Checkout next, I promise,' I mutter.

I grip the basket firmly and manoeuvre the buggy past the staggered splatters of red shampoo. It looks like strawberry jam without the bits. I see another woman up ahead browsing the medication shelves; a fifty-something in a tired-looking suit and heels, her head is almost entirely grey.

Abruptly, I decide to go back for the hair dye. It can always go into the bathroom cabinet for later. It may be one grey hair now, but who knows what's coming next?

I glance back down the aisle.

Do I really have to turn the buggy in this tight space, and then negotiate my way back through the red spillage, as if performing a slalom?

It's only a few yards.

Leaning forward, I check Harry. He's already asleep again, looking angelic. It's a risk. But it's only, what, ten or eleven steps there, plus the same back again?

I let go of the buggy handles.

My heart beating fast, I walk-run back to the hair dye shelves.

Quickly, I locate the dye and turn to see a middle-aged woman in glasses bending over the buggy.

Bending over Harry.

I'm too shocked to react at first. Like my brain can't quite decipher what my eyes are seeing. She's broad-hipped, with smooth black hair – falling to mid-way down her back, a suspicious lack of grey for her age – and thick ankles. Flat shoes and opaque black tights. Dull skirt and blouse under a duffel coat; an odd combination, especially in such warm weather.

Then I see her finger extend towards my boy.

Touching him?

'Hey, what are you doing?'

The woman straightens at once, looking blankly in my direction.

I run back and drag the buggy away, waking Harry again. I glare at her as he starts to cry. 'Did you touch him? Did you touch my baby?'

'No, of course not,' she insists, her eyes widening.

She has a strikingly broad Cornish accent: *carss* for course. A local, then. Dark-brown eyes and thick-rimmed, rectangular glasses that look slightly too large for her face. She has thin lips, the hint of a moustache above them. Older than the perfectly black hair suggests, I realise. This woman obviously has no problems using hair dye.

I don't trust her.

'I saw you. It looked to me like you were touching him.'

'No,' she repeats, backing away.

'He can't be touched. It could be dangerous. He's not well. He . . . He gets infections very easily.'

'Didn't touch him,' she insists. 'Never touch them.' Again the strong Cornish accent, the words slurred together, not quite clear.

At first I am inclined to believe her. But her gaze grows restless and shifty, moving past me as though to check who else might be listening, and something clicks in my head. What does she have to hide?

Other shoppers are staring now. A member of staff who was walking past the head of the aisle stops and comes towards us, his expression concerned. He has a phone in his hand and is speaking into it.

I look down at Harry who has woken up and is yawning delicately. He'll need changing soon. I've already been out of the house too long. I should get him home.

'I don't let anyone touch my baby,' I tell the woman vehemently, anxiety fuelling my panic.

She blinks at me as if confused, though she understands me well enough. It's an act, I'm sure of it now. The countrified innocence, the surprised expression. Her voice is high and breathy, a touch of genuine indignation behind the denial. 'I come round the corner and he was just sitting here, all on his own. So I thought . . .'

The member of staff comes to a halt beside the buggy.

'Ladies?'

He's wearing suit trousers and a smart lavender shirt with matching tie. The badge on his shirt says JERRY: ASSISTANT MANAGER. He notices the shampoo mess on the floor first, a frown tweaking his brows together. He looks down at Harry, and then at me, and lastly the woman in the duffel coat. The phone is still in his hand.

'Is there a problem, ladies?' he asks, carefully not directing the question at anyone in particular. 'Can I help?'

The woman turns to him at once, a note of outrage in her voice. 'Yes, actually, you can help.' Her voice grows stronger as his gaze sharpens on her face. 'I want to make a complaint. This woman's mad. She just accused me of touching her child. I did no such thing.' The strong accent intensifies. 'Left him alone in his buggy and walked away, she did. I thought the poor little thing was going to cry. I was just saying hello to him when she charged up and—'

'You touched him.'

'No, I didn't.'

I stare at her, and feel my face begin to burn.

'Well, I'm not going to stand here arguing,' I tell them both. 'I have to take my baby home. He needs changing.'

I wrench the buggy round, the metal shopping basket banging against the handles. Make a complaint against me, indeed. I'm feeling murderous now, which is why it's best for me to leave.

The assistant manager pauses to speak to the woman as I wheel Harry hurriedly away, then follows me through the narrow aisles. I do not look back at him.

'Excuse me, madam?'

I pay no attention.

'Let me help you with that,' he insists, and I stop, reluctantly letting him take the heavy basket. The crook of my arm hurts from where it's been hanging. I would have used the tray under the buggy, but that's already full. 'Go on, I'll carry it to the till for you.'

'Thank you.'

I keep pushing Harry towards the tills.

'Do you want to pursue this matter any further?' the assistant manager asks, glancing back over his shoulder.

I look too, but the woman in the duffel coat has disappeared.

'What do you mean?'

'I wouldn't normally suggest this, but under the circumstances . . .' He hesitates. 'We could inform the police. Though only if you genuinely feel your child has been threatened.'

I am relieved he does not think I was exaggerating. He has nice eyes too, warm and concerned. But the mention of police only increases my anxiety.

'Thank you . . . Jerry.' I make a point of glancing down at his name badge. 'But it's not important. Looks like she's disappeared now anyway. She got the point. I don't like people touching him.'

'Of course. That's only natural.'

'He's special, you see.' I smile down at Harry, who is gurgling now and twisting his fist in his mouth. 'A special baby.'

The assistant manager smiles as though he understands, but he doesn't. Not really.

I've noticed that before, since bringing Harry home from the hospital. When they see a woman out with a baby, people always nod and smile, and think they know what's going on, what your life must be like. They only see what's on the surface, never what's hidden. How could they, after all? Like an iceberg, there's always more underneath the waterline, concealed in frozen darkness.

More than anyone could possibly imagine.

Chapter Two

I stop by the supermarket's spacious baby-changing room on my way out and investigate Harry's nappy. To my surprise, and concern, it's dry.

Instantly, I'm scared.

I stare down at the nappy, then pat it tentatively with the back of my hand. Definitely dry. That was not what I was expecting. Harry fed normally this morning, the nappy should be wet by now.

I struggle to remember the danger signs, but my brain is closing down in panic. Dry nappy, listless behaviour, weak cry . . . and fever.

I feel his forehead with the back of my hand.

A little warm, perhaps.

Hurriedly, I fumble for the digital thermometer in my emergency pack, and check his temperature for fever. Waiting for the beep that shows it's finished taking a reading seems to last forever.

36.2 CELSIUS

That's easily within the normal range.

Harry kicks his stubby legs, blowing bubbles while he watches me refasten his nappy and striped navy-blue sleepsuit. *Flaky mummy*, he's probably thinking. *Getting all uptight over a tiny change in routine.*

'That's a good boy,' I tell him, smiling. 'You're wondering what all the fuss is about, aren't you?'

I bundle him back into the comfortable buggy and tuck the covers round him, trying not to worry. One dry nappy is not necessarily a sign of anything amiss.

But when I turn to wash my hands, automatically checking my reflection in the mirror above the sink, I look stressed. Chestnut hair in a too-tight ponytail, bags under my eyes, only the sketchiest attempt at make-up after a troubled night, and the remains of a flush from that unpleasant encounter.

Outside the supermarket, the clouds have finally blown away across the wide-flowing River Truro and the glorious May sunshine makes Harry blink. I try to walk in the shade as far as possible, but sometimes we have to turn into the sun to cross the road or avoid people on the pavement.

'Sorry,' I mutter, turning the buggy abruptly into somebody's path to sidestep a particularly bright patch of sunshine.

Truro is always popular with shoppers, which is why I prefer to walk into town when I can. So much less stressful than battling in with a car and a baby. Today is a Friday, a major shopping day, and although it's not quite lunchtime yet, the place is already thronging with people.

I make my way through the busy car park towards the underpass, heading for the main shopping streets. Seagulls call to each other overhead, heading inland from the broad, dazzling waters of the River Truro. Some days we take the walkway that meanders on stilts above the water, and I crouch down occasionally to point out a seabird or a passing boat to Harry, but not today.

Today I need to stay focused.

The three spires of Truro Cathedral look beautiful this morning, rising high above the narrow streets of the medieval city centre. I have never set foot inside the cathedral, though I did glance briefly through the vast double doors once. Carved statues, stained glass and echoes. And the fragrant scent from all those burning candles.

I stop in front of an expensive jewellery store not far from Jon's offices and study the watches in the window display. The black-and-white-striped awning flutters in a warm breeze that blows in off the nearby river.

It's our third wedding anniversary today, and I've arranged a small dinner party at home with some of our friends. Nothing too elaborate, though I know Jon is counting on me not to mess up tonight. I don't want to let him down, especially in front of his friends. Jon warned me not to buy him anything for our anniversary, and it's true that we are on a budget these days. But I could use my credit card.

I am so engrossed in the display of watches that I jump when someone touches me lightly on the shoulder.

'Anniversary present for Jon?'

It's Simon, one of Jon's colleagues; he'll be coming to dinner tonight with his partner, Emily. He's a lovely man, friendly and attractive, about Jon's height and always smartly dressed. Today it's an expensive pinstripe suit and very elegant shoes. Italian design? Jon once described him to me as 'the perfect lawyer', and was delighted to land a job at the same Truro law firm as his friend. 'Son of one of the senior partners. A great guy too. I could learn a lot from him.'

'Simon,' I say, my heart racing. 'You surprised me.'

'Sorry.' He grins, clearly unrepentant, and runs a hand through floppy blond hair. 'Look, I'm glad I ran into you. Emily's got a doctor's appointment later today. We might be a teensy bit late. That a problem?'

I shake my head. 'I'll be rushing about, trying to get dinner ready in time. Come when you can.'

'Thanks.'

'Nothing serious, I hope? You wouldn't prefer to cancel?'

'No, it's an ongoing thing. She's switched to working part-time while she gets over it.' Simon hesitates, then makes a wry face. 'Besides, Em's looking forward to meeting Harry for the first time. Wouldn't miss tonight for the world. She's very broody, you know.'

'Perfectly natural.'

He glances down at Harry. 'And how is this little chap? Goodness, he's big now. Jon brought him to the office last month, but I swear he's doubled in size since then.'

Harry is actually underweight for his age, which is a worry, but Simon's comment was meant to be a compliment. I smile and pretend to agree.

'Yes, he's growing fast.'

Simon's gaze seeks mine, and I notice a flicker of something unexpected in his eyes. Concern? The possibility embarrasses me. 'I know they kept Harry in hospital for quite a while after the birth. The intensive care unit? Jon was close-mouthed about it, of course, and we didn't like to pry. Family is family. I assume everything's okay now?'

'Absolutely,' I lie.

'That's great. And how about you, Meghan? How are you coping?'

'Me?' I stare then, taken aback. 'I'm fine.'

'You look flushed.'

'Oh, some nonsense in the supermarket. A woman upset me.'

He frowns. 'Upset you how?'

I worry that I will sound foolish if I tell him. Perhaps even hysterical. But Simon has such an encouraging smile, I feel I could tell him anything. 'It was nothing, really. She was going to touch Harry, and I – I—'

He nods sympathetically. 'Please, no need to explain.'

'The classic overprotective mother, that's me.' I shrug, feeling sheepish. 'You know, before the birth I thought I'd go mad, stuck at home all day with a baby. But there's so much to remember, the days go by so quickly and there never seems to be enough time.'

'Hence the need for a new watch?'

I am confused, then realise he means the diving watches in the window display. 'Oh yes, ha ha.' I turn away from them resolutely. 'No, actually, I was window-shopping. Daydreaming, really. Jon told me he doesn't want an anniversary present this year.'

'Men always say that,' Simon assures me, leaning forward conspiratorially. His hand brushes my shoulder, then is gone. 'I'm sure he'll be thrilled if you get him something.'

I am suddenly anxious. 'You won't mention to Jon that you saw me, will you?'

'Of course not,' he says smoothly, 'if you'd rather I didn't.'

But I can see he is surprised behind that lawyer's well-practised smile. Some explanation is required.

'I don't want Jon to know I was in town this long,' I elaborate carefully. 'I texted him when I set out this morning, and he probably thinks we're back home by now. Harry tires so easily, he'd only worry.'

Simon bows his fair head. 'In that case, mum's the word. Though Jon's not in the office at the moment anyway.'

I am confused. 'Really?'

'I think Susan sent him on some kind of errand too. You know what Susan's like when she's cracking the whip. He went out before lunch and hasn't got back yet.'

I say nothing.

'I would chat longer, but my desk is creaking under the weight of unread files. I'd better get back before it collapses.'

He walks away with an easy stride, hands in his suit trouser pockets, aware of his own good looks but not arrogant with it.

'Come on, Harry, time to pick up some flowers.' I push the buggy quickly towards the main shopping centre. 'Then home, and pop this food into the fridge.'

But I wonder where Jon has gone, and am brooding over Simon's mysterious comment too. *Men always say that.* Have I misunderstood again? The diving watch is beyond my pocket; that was a reckless thought. But should I get Jon an anniversary present anyway, in case he is secretly expecting one?

I decide on a new tie, and stop to choose one at a men's clothes shop in the main shopping street. It's a bold choice for a lawyer, broad and electric blue, and I regret the purchase as soon as I've accepted the gift-wrapped box from the sales assistant. But at least I won't be sitting there empty-handed tonight if Jon suddenly produces a surprise present for me. Which would be very like him.

I stop at the small corner shop near our house to pick up a copy of the local paper along with some flowers for the dinner table. Harry is asleep and the aisles are cramped, but I bring the buggy in anyway. The woman behind the counter looks at me disapprovingly.

I study the front-page story for a moment.

'Oh God, not again,' I mutter.

My pulse is racing.

I glance down at Harry, who does not stir, oblivious to my concern. My hands are sweating as I chuck the newspaper into the crowded tray under the buggy, and keep pushing, the headline still dancing in front of my eyes.

WHO SNATCHED BABY TOM?

Chapter Three

On the way home, my phone begins to vibrate.

I fumble it out of my pocket and stare down, uncomprehending, at the flashing word on the screen.

ALARM

It's almost as though the phone is responding to my mood, like we're psychically linked. I can't breathe, staring down at the word. Alarm, indeed. Then memory abruptly returns, and with it some semblance of normality. I remember setting the alarm when I left the safety of the house this morning, and what it's for.

Harry's medication.

I turn off the alarm, and shove my phone back into my handbag. But my hands are shaking as if I've been in an accident.

Adrenalin rush.

'For God's sake,' I mutter to myself.

I've been under a lot of stress since the birth, and it's starting to affect my judgement. I need to relax, to take it easy. Maybe I should be thinking about counselling. It would be good to have someone to talk to about all this, about the changes I've had to make in my life.

Back home, I unlock the door and wheel Harry inside. It's not safe to leave him outside. Not even for a moment, not even while I carry in the shopping. The house smells of flowers already. Yesterday's freesias, unseen, in a vase on the kitchen table. I inhale, enjoying the lovely scent and the silence. We've been living here since we were married three years ago. Jon insisted on buying a house as a wedding present for us; we had been renting previously, but his father had died earlier that year, leaving him a substantial inheritance. A generous gesture, and one that I was sure he must be regretting now. Making the mortgage repayments on two good incomes had been easy; now though, it is increasingly a struggle.

'Home again, darling,' I murmur. But when I look, Harry's still asleep, his face so peaceful and relaxed it seems a shame to wake him.

I double-check that the door is locked behind me, then stand in the narrow hall and listen to the silence for a moment.

'Jon? Are you home?'

No answer. The house is quiet. The only thing I can hear is the steady hum of the fridge. There's a scattering of junk mail on the mat. I shove it to one side with my foot. One message flashing on the answerphone.

He's not here. So where on earth is he?

Susan sent him on some kind of errand.

My skin prickles with foreboding, and I shrug it off impatiently. There were a few bad moments early on in our marriage when I felt Jon might be the sort to stray. He does love attention from women. But he's my husband and the father of my child. I have to trust him more, to give him the benefit of the doubt. If Simon says he went off on an errand, then there's nothing more to it.

I wheel the buggy further down the hall, kick off my shoes and tiptoe back to the answerphone. Maybe Jon has left a message.

I hope he's not going to be home late. Not tonight.

I turn down the volume, so as not to disturb Harry while he's sleeping, and then play back the message. Only it's not Jon.

It's my mother.

'Hi, Meghan, it's me again. Just ringing to check how you and Harry are getting on. It's so hot here in Spain, I'm having trouble sleeping at night.' A long pause, despite the cost of the phone call. Mum sounds a little flustered, like there's something on her mind. 'Your dad's not been well this week. No need to worry; it's just his angina playing up. You know how he is; he's never learnt to relax. Look, I hate these machines. Call me back sometime soon, okay? It would be lovely if you could fly over and stay with us for a few weeks, since you're not working. Maybe in the autumn, when the weather's cooled down a bit. I know you said Harry wouldn't be able to take the heat out here. Bye then, love.' Another pause. 'Give my love to Jon too.'

I smile.

Mum doesn't like Jon, and isn't very good at concealing it. But she means well, trying to like my husband for my sake. And my son's.

It would be nice to visit Mum and Dad in Spain; they have such a lovely, spacious apartment, right by the sea. After Dad retired, they decided to move abroad, hoping the change in pace would be good for his heart condition. I've only visited them once, but I have a memory of immense heat and a glittering bay of deep-blue water. It would be cooler there in autumn, that's true. I'm not sure how Harry would respond to air travel though. And what about his meds?

Worried about the chilled food, I remove my shopping from the three-wheeler buggy and put it in the fridge. Jon already put several bottles of champagne into the fridge to chill, so I don't need to worry about that. The kitchen is spotless, just as I left it this morning. Mentally, I tick off the hall, the lounge, the dining room. All clean and ready for our guests this evening.

I drop the newspaper on the kitchen table, then glance again at the photograph of a sleeping newborn baby below the headline WHO SNATCHED BABY TOM?

Unable to help myself, I scan the first few paragraphs.

Parents of a seven-week-old baby boy who went missing in Truro two weeks ago spoke of their despair at a press conference yesterday. 'The police have been working very hard, but they seem no nearer finding our son,' said Jack Penrose, 43, from the Carnon Downs area. 'We are now asking members of the public to help with the search. If you have any suspicions at all, please report them in confidence to the police.'

His wife also made an emotional appeal to the public for information. 'Our lives have been torn apart,' said Serena, who has been suffering from depression since her son's abduction. 'We are not looking to punish anyone. We just want Tom back where he belongs.'

A police spokesman admitted they believe that Tom's disappearance is linked to the abduction of two other babies in the Truro area over the past three months by the so-called Cornish Snatcher, but that they are no nearer to discovering the kidnapper's identity.

Parents of young children and babies in Cornwall are being urged to be extra-vigilant and never leave a child unattended in a public place.

The newspaper report goes on to name the other two missing babies, along with how and when they were taken. A sidebar details the police hotline to call with any information.

The Cornish Snatcher.

I close my eyes, my heart pounding, and hate myself. It's ridiculous to be so obsessed with this ongoing news story. But how would I feel if it was Harry who had gone missing? I find it hard to imagine why anyone would want to steal a baby, let alone three. It's too horrific. I hope they catch this Cornish Snatcher soon, and the babies are safely returned to their parents.

I shudder, and return to Harry in the hallway. He needs his meds. The doctor told us not to mess the timings up if we could avoid it, that it could cause complications if he missed an injection.

'Come on, sleeping beauty.'

I scoop him up and carry him upstairs to his nursery. He barely stirs. The trip into town seems to have worn him out.

Before I left the house this morning, I removed one pre-filled syringe from the mini-fridge in the nursery and left it beside his cot. The medicine needs to come to room temperature before it can be administered. I lay Harry in his cot, then nip into the bathroom to use the loo. Afterwards, I wash my hands assiduously, the way the specialist nurse showed me when they let us take Harry home, then dry them on a fresh towel.

Harry is beginning to fuss by the time I return. He's woken up hungry; I recognise the signs. He's got one small fist stuffed into his mouth and is gurgling quietly, both legs kicking against the blanket. I've been trying him on solids for the past month, just a few spoon-fuls of apple and banana purée, and baby rice occasionally, but he still seems most satisfied by breast milk.

'Medicine first,' I tell him soothingly. 'Then a feed.'

Glancing out of the bedroom window as I prepare the syringe, I study the cars parked up and down the street. Plenty of gaps during the day. There's only one car I don't recognise. An old Volvo, faded gold. It looks like there's someone behind the wheel, but I can't be sure; it's facing away, parked a few doors down on the other side.

Probably someone stopping to check their satnav or answer the phone. That happens all the time on our street. People use it as a convenient rat-run between two main routes into Truro, so we get cars going past at all hours.

Harry starts to cry, frustrated by the long delay. I pick him up and carry him to the waist-high changing station next to the mini-fridge where I keep all his medicines neatly stored and labelled. He cries even harder when I lie him down gently on his blue padded mat, his face screwed up with fury.

'Hush,' I tell him, though it's pointless to try to pacify him in this mood.

Harry's been the same ever since he came home from the hospital. He likes to have his screaming fit for about fifteen or twenty minutes, then will collapse afterwards, limp in my arms, perhaps take a short feed, and eventually fall back to sleep. We used to take him out in the car at night, to give the neighbours a rest from the screaming. Everyone we know swears by a car trip for calming a crying baby. It's never worked for Harry though.

'Colic,' my mum said, diagnosing him over the phone, and suggesting various old-fashioned solutions. None of them worked. Because it's not colic, Jon says. It's pure temper. I don't agree though. It's more likely he's almost constantly in some kind of discomfort, due to his condition. Except the poor child can't tell us about it yet.

'Mummy's here, it's okay.'

Jon hates it when the baby screams like this. He does not understand Harry like I do. But then, how could he? He's not with Harry all day, every day like I am. And, to be honest, I'm not sure how well he would cope if he was.

I check the wall chart. Right buttock this morning. Left thigh this afternoon. We have to rotate injection sites during each medication cycle, Dr Shiva said, to prevent any unnecessary damage.

I remove the needle cap from the pre-filled syringe, clean Harry's thigh with an antiseptic wipe, and pinch his skin to plump it up. Then I hold my breath and slide the needle smoothly into his chubby leg.

Harry goes puce, and erupts into screams.

'There, there, poor darling,' I say helplessly, pushing down on the plunger and watching to make sure all the medicine gets pushed through before I remove the syringe. As soon as it's out, I feel the most tremendous sense of relief. 'See? Mummy's all finished with that nasty needle. What a brave boy you are, Harry.'

I give his thigh a brisk rub with a fresh wipe, then throw the used syringe into the sharps' bin beside the changing station, taking care not to touch the needle.

Harry is still flushed and damp-cheeked, staring up at me accusingly.

I bend over and kiss his forehead. 'I'm sorry, darling. But we're halfway through the course now. Only another ten days to go.'

After he's had a play, and been bathed and fed, I put him back in his cot to sleep and fill out the medication wall chart – time and site of injection, how much, etc. It's a little over-fussy of me, I suppose. But my life has become so chaotic since Harry's birth, I would never remember otherwise.

It's still bright outside. I glance down the street as I turn back to close the blinds above Harry's cot.

The Volvo has gone.

Chapter Four

Since Harry is asleep, I decide not to wait any longer to take a shower. Wherever he is, and whatever he's doing, Jon may be running late, but I can't afford to.

I strip off and hop under the drumming cascade of hot water.

It is hard to hear anything under the deafening water. But through the frosted glass of the shower door I see a shadow enter the unlocked bathroom.

The shadow of a man.

I hold my breath, watching the figure come closer. He moves slowly and hesitantly towards the cubicle, as though searching for something.

I rinse the soap out of my eyes. 'Jon?'

Who else could it be?

The shadow comes nearer, not answering, and suddenly I feel uneasy. I find myself backing up against the wet tiles of the shower wall, staring.

'Jon? Is that you?' My heart begins to thud. 'Please stop playing games. You're scaring me.'

A hand closes round the handle to the shower door, and it creaks slowly open. A man's face looks in at me.

'You bastard!' I splash him with water. 'I thought you were . . .'

Jon grins at me. 'Thought I was who? A burglar? They don't tend to creep up on women in the shower.'

He reaches for my wet, naked body, and I shy away instinctively.

Jon frowns, and stretches past me for the controls. His blue shirt sleeve turns dark with water as he turns off the shower. 'Hey, come here. Sorry if I scared you.'

'You didn't. I'm just jumpy today. I don't know why.' I smile when his arm comes round my slippery waist, adding, 'You'll get soaked.'

'I don't care.'

I laugh, incredulous. 'What's brought this on?'

His voice is instantly defensive. 'What, I can't kiss my own wife on our anniversary? I heard the shower running, and thought . . .' He looks me up and down, hunger in his eyes. 'Well, you know what I thought.'

I feel heat in my cheeks. 'I'm sorry, I didn't mean to upset you.'

'It doesn't matter.' He reaches for me.

'Wait, did you check on Harry?'

I see a flash of impatience in his face. 'Of course. He's fast asleep.'

'Okay, then. But clothes off first.'

Jon makes a face, but he strips off his expensive shirt and trousers. He drapes them over the towel rail, then hurriedly jettisons the rest and climbs into the narrow cubicle beside me. There isn't really enough room for both of us, and the structure groans alarmingly.

I remind him, 'We've got guests tonight.'

'Then we'd better be quick.'

Jon draws me close, smiling down into my eyes. His desire is unmistakable. 'Happy Anniversary.'

'Happy Anniversary, darling.'

We kiss in the dripping silence of the cubicle, and I close my eyes, letting it happen. I'm taken aback by his unexpected spontaneity. Here in the shower too. Jon has always been a strictly-in-bed man since our marriage. But maybe this is what I need to calm my nerves.

Besides, there's no big hurry. Simon and Emily are going to be late anyway and the food will not take that long to prepare. And it's been such an age since we last made love. I think the last time he touched me was when Harry was about three months old. But it was a rushed event, very unsatisfactory, and Jon had been out that evening and came home late, wild-eyed and a little drunk.

The time before that, I was in the middle months of pregnancy. And he had been very careful with me, almost too careful, and kept saying he wasn't really in the mood. Frankly, he hasn't been in the mood for months. In fact, just recently, I have begun to think our love life may be over.

So this is a surprise. Though a pleasurable one.

He lifts me against the frosted panel of the cubicle with both hands, grabbing at the wet flesh of thighs, buttocks, seeking a firm grip.

'No,' I whisper as the panel creaks ominously. 'You'll break it.'

I see his look of frustration, and worry he may change his mind and walk away. But he grunts and swivels ninety degrees, taking me with him.

'Yes,' I hiss.

He kisses me fiercely, then buries his face in my shoulder. 'Meghan.'

I don't know why, but I encourage him to push boundaries this time. Our bodies slam against the tiled wall of the bathroom. My breasts are sore and swollen, and not just with milk for the baby. I can't remember feeling so desperate for him before. I cry out and hope the neighbours cannot hear. Then he whispers something I don't catch, and clamps his hand over my mouth.

I suspect he is leaving bruises, and do not really care.

Afterwards, he turns on the shower again and we stand beneath its cooling stream together, panting, dumb as animals. Thoughts still incoherent. My skin tingles and smarts with pleasure and it's hard to think ahead to the dinner party, to what is ready, what still needs to be done.

'I bought you an anniversary present.'

He strokes my back. 'So did I.'

'You want it at dinner?'

'Later.' He pauses. 'In bed, when they've all gone.'

The thought of us together in bed, exchanging intimate anniversary gifts, makes me happy.

Jon lifts his head to peer down at me, perhaps sensing that my mood has changed. 'Getting cold?'

'And wrinkly.'

'We can't have that. Skin like a rhinoceros.' Lazily, he nuzzles my cheek, his hands still resting lightly on my hips, our bodies close. I cling on to that comforting warmth for a few more seconds.

Then he sighs, and lets me go. 'Come on, better get ready for our guests.'

The evening is still fine outside, so I decide we should dine al fresco.

Jon looks in on Harry, and tiptoes out, saying he's still asleep.

'With any luck,' I say optimistically, 'he'll sleep right through dinner, and I can feed him when they've gone.'

'How has he been today?'

28

I hesitate. 'Fine, though he's got a red patch on his hip. It wasn't there this morning, I'm sure of it. I hope it's just the nappy rubbing. Not the start of a rash.'

He nods, looking sombre.

We both know how dangerous a rash could be. Any kind of infection.

'Don't worry, I'm keeping an eye on it,' I tell him. 'In case it spreads.'

Reassured, he goes outside and drags the large table and chairs out of the shed, cleans them off, then positions them under our pergola. The climbing roses are not yet in bloom – it's too early in the season – but there are buds and plenty of fresh leaves, and the growing tangle of clematis provides enough coverage for it to look a touch Mediterranean. The winters are always mild in Cornwall, so we can afford to grow less hardy plants.

Preparing the first course to the backdrop of a static hiss from the baby monitor, I look out of the kitchen window. I'm pleased to see how exotic the table and chairs look, our small ornamental pond beyond them with its young, broad-leaved gunnera and floating water lily pads. Our garden is looking pretty, though it's not a patch on next door's.

Treve, our neighbour, is a self-employed electrician by trade, but quite a keen gardener; I often see him outside at the weekends, not simply keeping his lawn trim but weeding the beds and planting up annuals. He has a large shed too, wired up for electricity, of course, and occasionally spends time in there during the evenings, working on small items of furniture and other DIY projects; he made an impressive pine coffee table last year, and donated it to the local hospice.

The doorbell rings at a little after seven-thirty.

Jon answers the door, and shows our next-door neighbours, Camilla and Treve, into the lounge. I listen to their voices and laughter as I sort out the food.

Once the first course is sitting on the kitchen table, covered with cling film, ready for serving, I quickly check everything looks ready outside, then wash my hands and join our guests. Nothing worse than a hostess who spends the whole evening busy in the kitchen. But I listen for a moment by the baby monitor before leaving the kitchen.

Nothing.

I hesitate, frowning. Then I hear a faint, familiar rustle as Harry turns over in his cot, and smile.

He's fine.

In the lounge, Jon is pouring a glass of Australian red wine for Camilla. Treve has chosen a chilled beer from the selection on the table.

'I absolutely adore the Shiraz grape,' Camilla is saying.

There's a note in her voice that I don't recognise. A slight quiver of emotion, not quite hidden beneath the layers of significance she puts on every word. I wonder if she and Treve have argued tonight, for her husband has turned his back, looking out of the window at his own front garden. It's only a tiny patch of lawn, like ours, with a few shrubs for privacy. But he takes excellent care of it.

'Too much wine is bad for you, of course,' she adds. 'But drunk in moderation, it can help you live longer.'

Usually, I see her out of the front window when she's coming back from her work at the local leisure centre. A fitness fanatic, Camilla has the body of a teenager, and teaches aerobics and Zumba as well as several popular yoga and meditation classes. So I'm used to seeing her in yoga pants and leotard, her blonde hair caught up in a glossy ponytail, a slight sheen of sweat on her forehead.

Tonight, her hair is worn down, a pair of silver earrings adding to her air of glamour. She's more elegant than usual too, in a red-and-white polka-dot dress, drawn in tight at the waist, with a wide white belt that matches her patent white stilettos.

Suddenly, I feel underdressed and under-made-up.

She smiles at me, glowing with perfect health and well-being as always. 'Hello, Meghan,' she says brightly.

'How are you, Camilla?'

'I feel absolutely wonderful,' she says at once, showing us perfect white teeth. 'It's this new rainbow diet Treve and I have been following. Super-detox foods. They clean you out, make you feel incredible inside.'

'I hope tonight's dinner won't break your diet,' I say, suddenly anxious. I realise that I didn't ask any of our guests what kind of food they would prefer.

'I'm sure it will be fine,' she says, then adds smoothly, 'If there's anything I can't face, I'll just leave it on the plate.'

I don't know what to say to that.

Jon turns his back on her, and winks at me. 'Red wine for you, darling?'

'I'd better stick to fruit juice.'

'Of course.'

Jon unscrews the lid on a bottle of fresh orange juice, then pours me a large glassful. 'Meghan is still breastfeeding,' he explains to the other two, his tone indulgent as he hands me the glass. 'She has to be careful how much she drinks.'

Treve turns, his smile warm and relaxed. Perhaps I imagined the quiver in Camilla's voice. He kisses me on the cheek. 'How are you, Meghan?' he asks in his deep, sing-song voice.

There's a powerful Cornish accent there; Treve has occasionally mentioned a family in the wilds of Cornwall, somewhere near the Atlantic coast. He's only a little shorter than Jon, but more sturdily built, with strong thighs and a broad chest like a pit pony, and very short, dark hair – a perfect foil to Camilla's blonde looks. I've never asked, but I'd guess both he and Camilla to be in their early thirties, and a very close-knit couple. He's not my type, physically. Too muscular and thick-set. I like them long and lanky, in general, not to mention blond. But he's a nice guy.

I smile back in response. 'I'm very well,' I tell him. 'Thank you.'

Camilla looks me up and down. 'Lovely dress,' she says. 'Kind of a Victorian feel to it. Is that new?'

I nod.

It's a silky, deep-blue material with buttons down the bodice, flaring out into a below-the-knee skirt that hides my post-baby bump nicely. It fits rather more tightly than I had hoped, but Jon seemed to like the way it hugs my figure so I did not send it back. I've worn black heels with it, not too high, but high enough to make me feel elegant. If that is possible when I'm still a little overweight from my pregnancy and have breasts that seem to leak milk at the worst moments.

'It doesn't quite fit though,' she adds, frowning slightly.

'It's a tight fit now, but I'm hoping to slim into it.'

'Hmm,' is all Camilla says, but her eyes say it all. After a pause, she adds, 'You should sign up for one of my Zumba classes.'

I glance at Jon, and he winks again. He seems very relaxed tonight.

'Your outfit is amazing,' I tell her.

Camilla smiles. 'Thank you, darling. That's very kind of you.' She glances at the men, then does a little twirl in her polka-dot dress. 'Retro fashion is all the rage, of course. But not everyone has the figure to carry it off.'

'Well, you certainly do,' I say.

'So sweet.' She comes over and air-kisses me, for which I'm secretly grateful; her lipstick is a violent red that matches her dress, and I don't want it staining my cheek.

The doorbell goes again.

'Excuse me.'

I open the front door to Simon and his girlfriend, Emily.

Simon kisses me on the cheek, then hands over a large bunch of red and white roses wrapped in pink tissue paper. 'Happy Anniversary to you and Jon. Three years. Not bad going for a lawyer.'

'Flowers.' I accept the bunch of roses, and bury my face in their heady aroma. 'They smell gorgeous, thank you so much.'

Simon and Emily are an odd couple, but hugely likeable. I only know him through Jon, but the two men have been friends for years. They tend to socialise in the pub after work, sometimes quite late into the evening after a big case, and Simon has been to the house a few times to watch football over some beers.

Emily I don't know as well. She always looks a little dowdy and unkempt, her shoulder-length brown hair straggly, like she's not terribly aware of her appearance. But tonight she's made some kind of an effort. Her eyes are heavily made-up behind her glasses, and she's wearing deep-green culottes with a creased, high-necked white blouse decorated with huge red poppies and tiny yellow buttons. The colour clash is striking and a little uncomfortable.

Her smile is endearingly shy though.

'Hello,' she murmurs, embracing me awkwardly in the hall. 'I'm sorry we're late. Doctor's appointment.'

'Not a problem.' I close the front door behind them.

Camilla appears in the doorway to the lounge, wine glass in hand. She studies Emily. 'Oh, what a fabulous ensemble,' she says appreciatively. Treve comes up behind her, smiling at the newcomers, and wraps his arm about her waist. She relaxes back against him, her smile broadening. 'I *adore* the colour combination. So bold and original. Don't you agree, Treve?'

Treve makes a sort of soft grunting reply, and Emily looks at them both uncertainly.

'You four already know each other, don't you?' Jon asks, smoothing over the difficult silence with his usual charm. 'Treve lives next door at number nine, and this is his wife, Camilla.' He turns to them both. 'This is Simon, who works with me. Do you remember the Christmas party? I'm sure you all met that night.'

He smiles, adding quickly, 'And this is Emily, of course. Simon's partner.'

The men nod to each other. Emily manages a thin smile for Camilla, who is still clearly amused with herself for the catty remark about Emily's outfit.

'Is Harry upstairs?' Emily asks, glancing at me as I hand the flowers to Jon.

I nod, smiling. 'Fast asleep.'

'And long may he remain that way,' Jon says drily, as he carries the flowers through into the kitchen.

Everyone laughs.

'I suppose he must be awake more now he's getting older,' Emily comments, looking curious. 'What is he now?'

'Seven months, nearly. And yes, he's sleeping less and less these days. I actually get to play with him now.'

'I was so pleased when Simon told me he had come home from the hospital. Forgive me for being nosy, but why was he . . .?'

'Nothing serious, just a few complications from the birth,' I lie easily, and catch Jon frowning at me as he returns from the kitchen. Hurriedly, I change the subject. 'We're eating al fresco tonight.'

'That's a great idea,' Simon says at once. 'Sorry to interrupt the baby talk. I know how you women love it, but any chance of some wine? Emily's driving tonight, so I can go wild.'

'Of course.' I grin at Emily. 'We can talk about Harry later, if you like.'

'Definitely.'

Once everyone has a drink, we shepherd them out into the garden. I ask Jon to put the baby monitor on the table in front of my place setting, hoping I'll be able to hear it above the conversation that way.

Camilla raises her eyebrows, bending to listen to the faint hiss of the baby monitor. 'What an intrusive thing. Like listening to white noise. Is it strictly necessary at the dinner table?'

'Yes,' I tell her firmly.

She smiles, straightening. But I can see she does not understand.

It's not dusk yet, but the sunlight is starting to fade. The generous six-seater outdoor table has been covered with a white damask cloth, then laid with cutlery and glasses and thick white cotton napkins. Along the top of the pergola Jon has strung little fairy lights, which are now glowing softly. The whole place is beginning to look magical.

'How beautiful,' Emily gasps.

Jon pulls out a chair for her. 'Please, everyone, sit, make yourselves comfortable. I hope you'll forgive us both for disappearing, but I've promised to help Meghan carry out the starters.'

Camilla laughs. 'You mean hors d'oeuvres, don't you?'

'Starters, hors d'oeuvres. It's all the same to me.' Jon grins at the other two men, and they smile back.

'I thought it was pronounced horses' doofers,' Simon says glibly.

More laughter.

Treve stands by his seat, hands clasped behind his back. He has a kind smile. 'Do you two need an extra pair of hands? I'm very skilled at carrying dinner plates. And not dropping them.'

'Thanks, no, it'll only take a moment,' Jon insists.

Simon draws out the chair opposite Emily, sits rather unsteadily and throws the cotton napkin across his lap.

'I'm starving,' he says plaintively, looking up at the fairy lights with interest. 'Talking of horses' doofers, I could certainly eat a horse. But maybe not a doofer. Whatever the hell that is.'

Shooting him an irritated look, Emily hesitates, not sitting down yet. She peers first at Jon, then looks round at me, as though deciding I'm the weaker link. 'Meghan, I know you must be busy with dinner, but I had hoped . . .'

'Yes?'

Her eyes seem very large behind the big-framed glasses, staring at me fixedly. 'I don't want to be a pest, but would it be possible to take a quick peek at Harry before we eat?'

Chapter Five

'Harry?' I hesitate, taken aback by her request. 'You want to see Harry? Right now?'

'Well, only if it's convenient. Just a quick peek round the door. Three minutes, that's all. Sorry, I do love babies.' Emily glances at Simon, who makes a face and averts his eyes. 'We hope to have kids. One day.'

Jon lights the citronella candle that forms part of my table centrepiece and is also supposed to discourage insects. I watch him, but he says nothing. The evening light is thickening and softening, the flowers less visible now, nightfall creeping up on us as we stand about the table under the faint glow of the fairy lights.

'Maybe we could bring Harry down after we've eaten dinner?' I tell Emily, my tone light and non-committal. I point to the monitor. The row of lights on the front show a steady green. No cries, no snuffling noises. 'He's asleep at the moment. And he can be difficult in the evenings. Grouchy, you know. I don't really want to wake him until it's time for his next feed.'

'Of c . . . course,' Emily stammers, and sits down.

Jon looks at me sideways. 'Darling, I don't see what harm it would do.'

I stare at him.

'Look, why don't I bring the little man down for five minutes? Just so he can say hello. It's a warm evening; he won't catch cold.' He ignores my quick shake of the head, and smiles at our guests instead. 'Then everyone can see how much he's grown.'

Emily says, 'I'd love that.'

'There you go, see? Emily would love that.' Jon puts his arm round my waist, his expression cajoling. 'Come on, darling. I'll get the baby, you get the dinner. And if he cries, I promise to do my penance and look after him.'

I say nothing, but smile. What can I say, after all?

'She's a bit twitchy, isn't she?' Jon murmurs on our way back into the house. 'Simon says she's obsessed with having a baby, never stops talking about it. But I don't see what harm it does to show Harry off to them. And I rather like the idea. The proud father, and all that.'

'Of course.' I force myself to smile. But inside I'm worried. 'I wanted him to sleep as long as possible though. He may need a feed again soon.'

'I'm sure it'll be fine, especially now you've started him on solids.' Then he frowns. 'When was his last injection?' I tell him, and he shrugs. 'He won't need another one until tomorrow morning, then. Twice a day, isn't it?'

Reluctantly, I nod.

Inside, Jon heads straight towards the hall, leaving me to cope with the plates on my own. Then he looks back round the kitchen door. 'Do you think this dinner party might have been a mistake?' He's grinning, enjoying being the host. 'Simon has obviously been drinking since the end of work, Emily keeps looking at him like she hates him, Camilla is in one of her infamous moods, and we haven't even eaten yet.'

I take a deep breath. 'They're here now. Too late for regrets.'

'We could always run away. Leave them to it.' He blows a kiss at me. 'Barricade ourselves into the bedroom for the evening.'

I shiver deliciously at the suggestion, but shake my head. 'You know we can't. Maybe later though. If Camilla starts throwing food?'

'It's a deal.'

———————

While Jon's upstairs, I start ripping cling film off the cold hors d'oeuvres. It's only orange-fleshed melon slices decorated with mixed fruit and mint leaves, but I really did not have time to be more creative.

Jon has still not come back down by the time I'm finished. Probably changing Harry's nappy. I go to the foot of the stairs, and nearly call up. But then I realise how much he would resent my interference. I can't wait for him any longer though, so decide to carry the melon slices out on my own.

I make my way to the back door, laden with precariously balanced plates, and find Treve standing in the doorway. He seems to take up the whole space, I notice.

'No Jon?'

'He'll be down soon. Harry probably needed a nappy change.'

His ironic gaze meets mine. 'Babies, eh? So much trouble.'

'But where would we be without them?' My arms are aching now. 'Sorry, have you come to help?'

Treve smiles, and holds out his hands. 'Allow me, Meghan.'

He helps me carry the melon slices out to the others. The garden looks marvellously peaceful now, an orange-streaked dusk beginning to settle about the city. Camilla and Simon are deep in conversation.

The monitor is surprisingly silent, green lights holding steady.

I chew my lip, considering it.

What's going on up there? There's a changing mat in the bathroom, though I usually change him in the nursery.

'I'd better see where Jon's got to.'

Treve stops me. 'Let me,' he insists, and takes the empty bottles with him, tucking them under his arm as he disappears into the house.

I sit at the head of the table, slowly turning the plate of melon slices to face me so the arrangement is how I intended it to look.

Jon will be fine, I keep telling myself.

I worry too much.

Treve comes back from the house only a few minutes later. Behind him is Jon, carrying a sleepy-looking Harry in his arms.

Emily has been rummaging through her bag. She produces a small pill bottle, then glances anxiously at the empty water bottle. 'Is there any more water?' Then she sees Jon, with Harry, and jumps up from her seat. The chair falls backwards with a clatter as she gasps, 'Oh, how gorgeous. Look at those eyes. Simon told me he was a beautiful baby, but I didn't realise just how . . . Meghan, you are so, so lucky.'

'Thank you.'

I get up too, and hold out my hands for Harry. But Jon ignores me, cradling his baby son with every evidence of paternal pride.

'So here he is, guys,' he tells us, looking down at Harry with a fond grin. 'Getting big, isn't he?'

While the others exclaim over him, I meet Jon's gaze. 'You took a while.'

'Dirty nappy.'

'I told you to let him sleep.'

'It wasn't a problem. I'm not helpless. I can handle a few stinky nappies, you know.' He lets Simon take Harry, despite my instinctive protest. 'That's right, keep one arm round his back, just like that. Hey, you're a natural.'

Emily is staring wide-eyed at the baby in her partner's arms. Her face is flushed, her mouth slightly open. I feel a little sorry for her; she is probably imagining how things would be if they too had a child.

Perhaps I was wrong to try to stop Jon from bringing Harry down to the dinner party. They do seem pleased at the interruption, and he's well wrapped up, a cosy blue blanket tucked round his sleepsuit for extra warmth.

Even Treve is leaning closer, tickling Harry's cheek with a work-roughened finger. 'Ah, he's a stunner. Proper job, you two.'

Jon grins at me over Simon's shoulder. 'Proper job' is a very Cornish phrase, and one he often likes to mock in private. I only hope he won't do so tonight and spoil the atmosphere.

'Why not let Emily hold him for a minute?' I suggest to Simon, who turns at once so she can lift Harry carefully out of his arms.

Emily's face is beatific as she holds my baby. 'So gorgeous,' she repeats, and breathes in his scent, kissing the top of his head. 'Darling little thing. I'm not surprised you don't want to go back to work, Meghan. If I had a baby, I'd probably never work again.'

Simon looks round at us, his brows raised. 'And there's an excellent argument for birth control, right there.'

The men all laugh.

Camilla makes a snorting noise, then takes another long swallow from her wine glass. I realise belatedly that she is the only one who did not stand up when Jon brought Harry outside. But I suppose she is not the maternal type.

I catch Treve looking at her a little sternly. I expect he wants kids, but Camilla doesn't. Maybe that's part of the tension I've been sensing between them lately.

Harry sucks his fist thoughtfully, staring round at us all with wide blue eyes. I am a little concerned that he'll need a feed earlier now that he's awake.

'Right,' I say, 'I don't want to spoil anyone's fun. But we need to eat, and Harry should probably go back to bed for now.'

Jon nods, taking Harry back from Emily's arms. She does not protest, but I catch a stricken look on her face as she watches the baby being carried back into the house.

'I do envy you,' she tells me as we sit down again, her tone wistful. 'To have such a lovely baby.'

I wonder how much she would envy me if she knew all the worries and stresses we have to contend with on a daily basis. But I say nothing, just smile. Jon is obsessed with the idea of people judging us in some way if they knew about Harry. As though his condition is our fault, which is absurd. But I have promised him not to talk about it.

I listen on the monitor as Jon lays him back to sleep in the cot, murmuring something under his breath. Before leaving, he turns on the musical mobile. Harry makes the soft cooing noises he always does as he watches it spinning above him.

Jon comes back a moment later, still grinning. 'Our little star is back in bed,' he says, and bends to kiss me on the mouth. There's real warmth in his kiss, and I recall how we made love in the shower earlier. Maybe our relationship is on the mend after all.

'Oh, you wanted some water, Emily.' I start to push back my chair, but Simon is already on his feet.

'I'll fetch some,' he says. 'Tap water?'

'There's Perrier in the fridge.'

Emily looks round, still in a kind of trance. 'I'd prefer tap water,' she insists, and nods at Simon.

He disappears into the house.

'So Harry settled again okay?' I ask Jon, though we can all still hear the tinkling music from Harry's cot mobile coming out loud and clear via the monitor, and there is no sound of any whinging or crying.

'Good as gold,' he assures me.

Simon comes back out, whistling. He hands the tumbler to Emily. 'Here's your water, darling,' he murmurs before sitting down.

Camilla watches with undisguised interest as Emily takes two pills, putting each on the back of her tongue, then knocking it back with a gulp of water. 'I can't take pills like that. I prefer to pop them on the tip of my tongue. My mother-in-law's a nurse. She always tells me off about it,' she says, then adds with a slight edge to her voice, 'though we don't see much of her these days, thank God.'

Everyone looks at Treve.

He puts down his wine glass. 'A retired nurse,' he corrects her. 'And she means well.'

Simon looks from one to the other, his face wry. 'Do I sense some tension here? You don't like Treve's mother, Camilla?'

'Apparently, I'm not Cornish enough to be Treve's wife,' she says tartly, and we all laugh. 'My mum's Welsh and my dad's from Launceston, only just inside the border.'

'I love Wales,' Emily says.

Camilla studies her, but says nothing.

In the silence that follows, I ask Emily, 'Where are you from?'

'Oh, here, there and everywhere.' She cleans her glasses with her napkin, then puts them back on and looks round at me. 'My family are kind of . . . nomadic.'

'So mysterious,' Simon says, laughing, and ducks when she tosses the napkin across the table at him.

'Can we eat yet?' Camilla asks plaintively.

'Of course,' I say.

'Well, I didn't want to be *rude* and start too soon.'

The way she emphasises the word *rude* makes me deeply uncomfortable. Camilla finishes her glass of wine, and then pours herself some more from the bottle beside her. I look away, suddenly awkward.

Maybe it's not Treve that's put her on edge tonight. Maybe it's me. At any rate, I feel as though I must have upset her in some way, or been a bad hostess. Only I can't put my finger on what I've done wrong.

In the silence that follows her remark, Treve picks up his fork. 'Meghan, you've surpassed yourself. This looks amazing.'

Thankfully, everyone seems to have relaxed by the time dinner is almost over and the dessert course is being served. The alcohol, presumably. Though Emily does not touch any, I notice, and joins me in drinking fruit juice and sparkling water instead. I wonder if she is unwell. After all, she arrived late because of a doctor's appointment, and she looks pale, even by the flickering yellowish light of our citronella candle.

I place a small glass bowl on every place, bursting with cream and meringue and raspberries. 'Eton Mess.'

'Mess is right,' Jon says, poking it with his spoon. Then he grins up at me. 'It smells delicious. I can't wait.'

I sit down, trying not to let my hurt show. I don't want to seem needy. But my mouth aches from smiling, and I know I'm only partially successful when I start chatting lightly with Treve and see him glance between me and Jon.

Does he have to make fun of me?

'I'm sorry,' Emily suddenly says, standing up. 'Not your fault, Meghan. The food has been lovely, but I have to leave. I don't feel so good.'

Simon stares up at her, clearly bemused. 'Darling?'

'My head, sorry.' She makes a face, and adjusts her glasses, as though they are part of the problem. 'I tried. I really did. But it's aching so badly . . .'

I get up too. 'Can I get you anything? A headache pill? Some more water?'

'Honestly, I just need to go home.'

'Of course. Let me find your coat.' I glance at Simon, but to my surprise he does not move. 'Simon?'

'How bad is it, Emily?' he asks, frowning.

She hesitates, then forces a tight smile. 'I can run myself home if you want to stay.'

'I would prefer that, if you're sure you're okay to drive.'

Emily nods.

He pushes the car keys across the table to her. 'I'll grab a taxi home.'

Jon pours his friend some more wine, spilling a little on the tablecloth. 'No, you won't. You can stay the night.'

'Thanks.'

Emily looks from Simon to Jon, then raises her gaze to mine. She does have that wan, heavy-lidded look that I associate with a gathering migraine. 'Well, that's settled. I'm so sorry to have upset your dinner party, Meghan.'

'Nonsense, you haven't upset anything.' I escort her back inside. 'I'll see you out. I like to keep the door locked while we're in the garden.'

At the front door, I hesitate. Emily does not look up to driving herself home; her skin is pasty, her eyes rather wild behind her glasses. 'Look, wouldn't you rather I call a taxi for you? It's no bother.'

45

'I'll be fine.' Emily turns on the front step to kiss me on the cheek, which surprises me. 'You have a lovely house, Meghan, and an even lovelier baby. Take good care of him, yes?'

I smile. 'Absolutely.'

I think losing poor Emily partway through dessert is going to be the only blot on an otherwise perfect dinner party. There's worse to come though. The three men carry the dessert dishes and used glasses inside while I organise the coffee, but as soon as we sit down again to drink it, I hear an odd rustling sound from the baby monitor. Harry turning over in his sleep, maybe. I feel my breasts tighten and tingle in response, suddenly uncomfortably full, and glance down at them.

Camilla spots the tiny movement and stares too, then exclaims, 'Oh no! Did you spill something on your dress?'

There is a dark spreading stain on my right breast. It must be over four hours since he was fed.

I stand up, guilty and stirred by some age-old need to return to my child. 'Harry,' I murmur, looking back at the house.

Camilla is horrified. 'Is that . . . milk? How disgusting.'

'Camilla!'

I look back quickly. Treve is staring at his wife. She shrugs and turns away, making a face. Too much wine, I think, and try not to be offended.

'I'd better go in and feed him.' I fold my arms across my breasts, though it's uncomfortable to do so.

I force myself to smile at Camilla. Jon is always urging me to be more polite to our friends. 'Would you like to come too, Camilla?'

To my relief, Camilla grimaces. 'Not really my thing, babies.' Then she goes back to what she was saying before, which is explaining to Simon how flexible she was in sixth form, while her husband watches from across the table.

Treve looks sleepy, but his hand on the table top is curled into a fist.

I cannot tell if he is annoyed that his wife is flirting with another man, or merely checking that she does not make a fool of herself. Nor do I care. My mind is entirely focused on my son and his needs.

Back inside the quiet house, I tiptoe upstairs.

It's dark on the landing. I grope for the light and switch it on.

To my surprise, Harry's door has been left slightly ajar. I stand outside the nursery, head tilted to listen, but cannot hear any sounds from within.

I push the door to the nursery open and peer inside the darkened room.

'Harry?'

The cot is empty. The room is silent.

Harry has gone.

Chapter Six

I burst out through the back door and into the garden. I've lost one of my heels; I'm limping, and under my bare sole is the damp, slightly prickly feel of dewy grass. It's almost night now; the stars are beginning to come out, though it's hard to see them with the faint city glow.

In my mind's eye is the empty cot. The covers, rumpled, still warm from his body. The faint depression from an absent head, a strand of hair left behind on his blue flannel sheet.

Part of me is still hoping it's a mistake. That I will find him outside, cradled in his father's arms, perhaps, or peering up at Simon or Camilla with his big blue eyes.

I know there would be no logic in finding him out here, but my brain is so desperate for him to be delivered back to me, it tries to defy the facts, to return everything to the default setting. Which is Harry safe and well, wide awake, ready for his feed and his medicine. Or maybe Harry weeping and griping, his cheeks flushed, his high-pitched voice raised in protest at the emptiness of his stomach.

Harry is not here though. His father's arms are as empty as mine, and there is no sign of a baby at the dinner table or anywhere in the darkening garden.

Jon has turned his head to stare at me. The others look round too, their expressions surprised, even shocked. Camilla is smiling incredulously.

That's when I realise that I've been shouting.

'He's gone.'

I hear the words from a great distance, as though someone else is saying them. I'm panting like a sprinter at the end of a race. My gaze is fixed on my husband's face as my chest heaves. I must look wild, almost insane.

'He's gone,' I repeat stupidly, all other ideas temporarily lost to me. 'He's not there, Jon, he's gone.'

They stare at me. Their baffled silence makes me want to scream and tear at my hair. But what good would hysteria do?

Camilla frowns. 'What are you talking about?'

I force the sickness down, and concentrate on my husband's face. It is important to be clear. Our child's life could depend on it.

'Harry.'

As soon as I say his name, my voice does not sound like my own anymore. Perhaps because I cannot connect my words with the reality of my life.

'I went up to feed him but he wasn't there. He's not in his cot.'

'*What?*' Jon is on his feet now.

'I don't think he's even in the house.'

He looks into my face, frowning heavily, as if he's in court, gauging the veracity of what someone is saying. Then he hurries past me into the house.

Standing up, Simon starts after him. He pauses beside me. 'You're sure he's definitely gone?'

'Of course.'

His lawyer voice too, sharp and incisive. 'Did you search everywhere?'

'No, but—'

'So you could be wrong?'

'I'm telling you, he's not there.'

He glances back at the other two: Treve, on his feet now, down-ing the last of his coffee; Camilla, still in her seat, staring at us with a frozen expression on her face.

'Right, we'd better form a search party. Just to be on the safe side. Treve, Camilla, you check the gardens. Front and back. I'll do a sweep of the downstairs.' Simon hesitates, looking at me. 'I was going to suggest you search the upstairs rooms with Jon, but you don't look too good. Are you okay, Meghan?'

'Where is he?' I ask helplessly. 'Where's my little boy?'

'I don't know, but we'd better make sure he's not in the house. That's the first order of business. Then we'll have to call the police and get a proper search organised. If Jon hasn't already called them, that is.'

Call the police and get a proper search organised.

I say nothing, but I remember the newspaper report and feel sick.

The Cornish Snatcher.

I think of those missing babies. Their frantic parents. The gen-eral bafflement of the police. I'm still hoping it's a mistake.

There must be another explanation. Maybe I didn't look in the cot properly. It's just possible, isn't it? Perhaps Harry was crying and wriggled down inside the covers, and I just didn't see him when I glanced in. It sounds unlikely. But it's less fantastical than assuming that my child has been stolen by the Cornish Snatcher. That's like thinking the bogeyman took him. And yet those missing babies are real. They were taken, and have not yet been found.

And now Harry is gone too.

I imagine Jon coming out into the garden with our baby, laugh-ing at me for being such a fool. But a part of me knows that is not going to happen.

Simon disappears into the house. I see my shoe on the grass near the back door. It looks so forlorn, abandoned, lying there on its side. Like an open mouth, gaping with tragedy. I limp towards it over the damp grass, and bend over to pick up the shoe. Light-headed, I feel myself overbalance.

Treve catches me by the shoulders, brings me upright again, steadies me. 'It's going to be fine, Meghan. You hear me?'

I nod, but in a perfunctory manner. I can't speak anymore. I can't meet anyone's gaze. I can't even focus on what's happening around me.

He glances back at Camilla, who is still sitting motionless at the dinner table. 'Jesus wept.' I've never heard him blaspheme before and it shocks me vaguely, even though I am not religious. But from him, it sounds like an explosion. 'Help Meghan, would you? She needs to sit down. Maybe have something hot and sweet for the shock. I have to search out here for the baby. If you won't come with me, then at least make yourself useful.'

Camilla sounds resentful. 'Why on earth are you searching the garden? He's only seven months old. He can hardly have crawled downstairs and out the back door under his own steam.'

'Camilla!'

'Well, it's ridiculous.' But she leaves her half-empty glass of wine and comes over to us. I don't resist when she puts an arm around my shoulder. 'Anyway, it's almost dark, you won't be able to see anything.'

'There's a torch,' I say, 'hanging from a hook behind the back door.'

Treve nods, and goes to fetch the torch.

'All right, then.' Camilla's tone is cajoling and a little world-weary, as though she does not believe any of this is worth her time. 'Come inside, and I'll make you some tea. Though, frankly, I'm sure someone's just playing a trick on you.'

'Who would play a trick like this?'

She shrugs.

'Wait,' I say faintly.

I struggle to put my shoe back on, then walk slowly with Camilla back into the kitchen. Treve is already swinging the torch beam around the garden, parting shrubs with his foot, and bending to search along the dark paths, as though hunting for clues rather than a baby. It's good of him to make the effort, but Camilla is right. Harry is not going to be in the garden. He's not going to be in the house either.

WHO SNATCHED BABY TOM?

What if I'm right and this is another baby abduction like the ones in the newspaper report?

Again, I stop myself from pursuing that thought.

It's too terrifying.

I wander into the kitchen, shaking violently. I wish Emily had not gone. I don't know her very well, but she has such kind eyes.

'I'll put the kettle on,' Camilla says, and suddenly I am grateful that she is there at least. That I am not alone.

Jon comes downstairs at a run, and I hurry to meet him, thinking it's over, that he's found our baby. But he stops at the bottom, staring at me. His eyes are wide and blank. 'Not there,' he says shortly. 'I emptied the cot. Even looked underneath and down the sides in case he had somehow . . .'

'But where is he? How is it possible that . . .'

His voice is bitter. 'I don't bloody know. All I know is that he's gone.'

Simon comes out of the lounge. His face looks very sombre. 'The front door wasn't locked,' he says quietly. 'I checked. First thing I did. It was left on the latch.'

He looks at Jon, then away again, as though uncomfortable at being the bearer of bad tidings.

I stare at them both, piecing together what he is insinuating. 'But I always lock the door. I'm sure it was locked. I . . . I locked it after Emily left. I made a point of . . .'

Simon shakes his head.

My mouth is having trouble forming words properly. 'You mean, while we were out there . . . having coffee . . .'

I'm slurring my words like I'm drunk. Am I drunk? No, I haven't been drinking. It's the shock, that's all. The shock of losing my baby.

He is nodding. 'Anyone could have walked in off the street, taken Harry out of his cot, and left the same way without us even being aware of it.'

I feel physically sick. 'Oh my God.'

'Hey, come here.' Simon puts an arm around me, hugging me close. 'It's okay, it's not your fault.'

I gaze at Jon, longing for some physical comfort from my husband, something to reassure me that things are not as bad as they seem, but he's not looking at me anymore. His face is abstracted. He's gone inside his head to find a solution, I realise. To work the problem. Like it's a puzzle he could solve if only he can figure out how all the pieces fit together.

Treve comes in from the garden. His shoes are damp from the grass. 'No sign.' He looks grim. His gaze seeks out Jon's. 'You've run out of options, mate. Next step, ring the police. Let them take over.'

Jon nods.

'But where is he?' I ask nobody in particular. I simply can't believe what is happening to us. I'm caught in a nightmare, and I keep wishing I could wake up. That it will all turn out to be a bad dream. 'Where is Harry? I don't understand.'

'The police will sort it out,' Treve reassures me.

The police.

I fumble for the phone handset and nearly drop it. Jon takes it away from me. 'Go and sit in the lounge,' he tells me firmly. 'I'll ring the police.'

'I want to hear what you're going to tell them.'

'You know what I'm going to tell them.'

'No, I don't.' I try to snatch the phone back, suddenly frightened. 'I need to do it. You won't say it right.'

He looks at Simon, who steers me away.

'Sorry, so sorry.' I'm babbling but can't seem to get myself under control. I look up at the man who's trying to get me into the lounge while I'm trying equally hard to stay in the hall. 'I'm sorry, Simon.'

My husband sits down on the first stair. His face is pale but determined. 'Meghan, I want you to go and drink . . . I don't know, some brandy. Something to calm you down.'

He starts to punch the number keys. Three numbers only.

I say, 'No.'

'Let me do this,' he insists, not looking at me.

'But what will you say?'

'That while we were having dinner outside in the garden, our seven-month-old baby son disappeared from his cot upstairs.' He listens to the ringtone. His tone is heavy, curt, bordering on the dismissive. 'That's all I can tell the police, Meghan. Because that's all I know.'

Chapter Seven

The space between Jon's calm, level-toned call to the police and the arrival of the first car with its blue flashing light is only about ten minutes. Yet it feels much longer in my head. It's as though an eternity has passed while I sit in our lounge, flanked by Simon, who insists on holding my hand – largely to stop me getting up again, I begin to suspect – and Camilla, who has helped herself to a large glass of brandy too and collapsed on the sofa beside me.

Treve has been standing by the window, watching. 'They're here,' he says flatly, and leaves the room.

Everything seems to happen in slow motion from that point. Perhaps it's the blue strobe effect of the light from outside, flashing off the walls of neighbouring houses, that makes it feel so strange. But when I get up and stare out of the window, I see Jon and Treve approaching the police. They seem to walk jerkily, like the marionettes in *Thunderbirds*, and I hear their voices echoing along the street but cannot catch a word they are saying. Except that I keep hearing my own name.

Meghan.

I wonder what the neighbours are thinking. I see a few curtains twitching.

'I can't stand this,' I mutter.

I want to go outside too, to hear what the men are saying to the police, but when I go to the lounge door, Simon touches my arm. 'Better wait here,' he says, and I hear Camilla mutter an agreement from the sofa. 'Come back and sit down. Let the police come to you.'

'But I need to talk to them. To give them a statement. Don't you see? I need to do something. I can't just sit around . . .'

The door to the lounge opens, and it's Jon. He's accompanied by a well-built man who looks to be in his thirties, tall and clean-shaven, his face very earnest. One of the police, I presume. As he turns towards me, I see he has a scar on his left cheek, running from his eye to the corner of his mouth. It's deep but old, not a recent injury, fading to silver. I wonder how he got it.

The officer smiles. 'You must be Meghan.'

I break away from Simon at once. 'Yes, that's me. I'm Harry's mother.' I'm talking too quickly again and try to slow myself down. 'Have you . . . found him?'

'I'm afraid not.'

I stare at the policeman, and feel despair at those words. A despair that drowns me in a sea of hopelessness, that leaves me no hope of reprieve.

He comes further into the room. 'Perhaps you'd better sit down.'

'I don't want to sit down,' I tell him defiantly, though my legs are unsteady. 'I want to find my son. I want him back.' I blink away tears. 'I want an explanation.'

Another police officer comes in after him. A woman this time. She's about my age, blonde and very slender. Dressed severely in black, with one of those hourglass figures men seem to love. The policeman nods to her, almost imperceptibly, and she comes towards me, smiling, holding out her hands.

I back away but she catches hold of my arm. 'Here,' she says, pulling me down on to the sofa beside her. 'Let's sit you down, Meghan, get you comfortable. Then we can go through all the details. These things can take a while.' She turns to Camilla, who has shuffled along the sofa to avoid being crushed. 'Sorry. Are you family or friends?'

'We're the next-door neighbours,' Treve says from the doorway, standing just behind Jon. 'She's Camilla. I'm Treve, her husband. We live at number nine, that side.'

He points in the right direction for their benefit. Then folds his arms across his broad chest, his gaze returning to my face. He looks like a rock of dependability, like he would do anything for me in that moment.

'You okay, Meghan?' he asks. 'We're here for you.'

'Thanks,' I manage to say.

The policewoman smiles winningly at Camilla, and receives only an irritated look in return. 'Any chance of a cup of tea, Camilla?'

'I suppose so,' Camilla says, looking resentfully at her as she gets up and leaves the lounge. 'I could do with a hand though.'

Treve glances at me.

'It's all right,' I tell him. 'I'm sorry about this. You'd better go. Jon and I need to . . .'

My voice tails off.

I cannot believe my baby is gone.

Treve catches a look from Jon, and follows his wife out of the lounge. Simon looks at us hesitantly, though trails out after them. There isn't really much room for everyone anyway, the room is too small. Jon pushes the door shut, but leaves it slightly ajar. Outside, I can hear more police arriving, orders being given, the tinny chatter of police radios. More blue lights flash in the street.

Without my friends, I feel abruptly bereft. As though it's only now coming home to me what has happened, that my boy is gone.

The earnest policeman introduces himself as Detective Sergeant Dryer, and the female officer as Detective Constable Gerent. She smiles and takes out a notebook.

There's a strange whirring sound in the distance. A helicopter? It grows louder as it approaches, then is suddenly deafening, hovering above the house. Why on earth do the police need a helicopter to find a lost baby?

I wonder if the local newspaper is still in the kitchen.

I left it there for Jon earlier. Did he see it on the kitchen table when he came home? Did he stop and read the headline before coming upstairs, before climbing into the shower with me? Before we made love?

WHO SNATCHED BABY TOM?

I can feel myself trembling, my teeth close to chattering, like someone suffering from hypothermia. Emotions crash back and forth inside me, and thought has become impossible. My head is full of white noise. I clasp my hands together, focus on what the police are doing and saying, try to regain control. But it's like trying to hold back the tide, and I know if this goes on much longer I'll simply drown.

DS Dryer looks up out of the window, craning to see. 'Excellent, air support is already here. We've got the dog handlers en route too.'

'Oh God,' I murmur.

He looks round at me, his face carefully blank and professional, then turns to Jon. 'I think we got most of your son's details on the phone.' In contrast to DC Gerent's gently sympathetic air, his tone seems brisk, almost matter of fact. 'We'll need to go through it all again, of course, just to make sure we haven't missed anything. A forensics officer will be here soon too. I expect he'll want to do a thorough examination of your son's room, and perhaps look at the stairs and front door as well.'

He pauses. 'But before we do that, maybe you could tell us everything that happened tonight?'

'What good will that do?' I demand, my voice small and shrill. 'Someone has stolen our baby. You need to be out there, looking for him, not standing about here.'

'And we will be, don't worry. But first, you may know something useful without being aware of it. So from the beginning, if you could, and as quickly as possible. For instance, we'll need the names and addresses of your guests.' He is still looking at Jon, not me. 'I presume they're all still here?'

'All but one.' Jon hesitates. 'Emily. She came with my friend Simon, but left early.'

'Why was that?'

'She wasn't feeling well.'

'I see.' He nods to DC Gerent, who scribbles something in her notebook. 'We'll need to talk to her too. Tonight, if possible.'

'Talk to Emily?' I stare up at him. My voice is shaking but I can't seem to control it. 'I don't understand. You think one of our *friends* might have taken Harry?'

'It's nothing like that, Meghan,' the detective says soothingly, giving me a quick, reassuring smile. 'Your friend Emily may have seen or heard something when she was leaving that could help us locate Harry. Even if she's not feeling well, we'd still like to speak to her without delay.'

Jon nods. 'I'm sure Simon can give her a call.'

'Thank you. In our experience, the first few hours after a child goes missing are often the most vital.'

I exchange a glance with Jon.

DC Gerent moves discreetly aside as my husband comes to sit next to me on the sofa. Jon looks at me sideways, takes my cold hand in his, squeezes it comfortingly. It is the first time he has touched me since before the dinner party.

I can feel his hesitation. But it's time, and we both know it.

'Detective,' he begins in a low voice, 'there's something I didn't mention on the phone earlier. I wanted to keep it private, but I realise that's not possible anymore. It's something you really need to know.' His face is haggard as he turns it towards the police officer. 'Something about Harry.'

Chapter Eight

Auto-immune neutropenia.

I do not blame the police for looking blank when we try to explain, in a fumbling way, what's wrong with Harry. Six months ago, I would not have had a clue what those words meant either. Now though, auto-immune neutropenia is a massive part of our daily lives. It's a phrase that stops and silences us, that reminds us that our beautiful little boy is mortal.

'Not all doctors agree on what it is,' I tell them shakily, 'which makes it hard for us to be completely specific. But it's a rare condition that hits very young children and babies. The immune system in kids with neutropenia is seriously compromised, which basically means Harry can get sick very easily. He has to be protected from germs and bacteria. We have to keep everything immaculately clean. You see, the slightest contact with germs and he can become dangerously ill within hours.'

DS Dryer frowns. He glances at the constable, who is busy scribbling in her notebook. 'Getting him back quickly is a priority-one issue, then. We'll need the name of his doctor too, and any specialist care workers.'

'Dr Shiva is the hospital consultant in charge of his case,' Jon says quickly, always more confident when dealing with hard facts. 'I expect she'll have all the details on file.'

'That's very useful, thank you.' He looks at his colleague. 'Constable, could you see if we can get hold of the doctor? I know it's late, but as soon as possible, please.'

Gerent nods and leaves the room. I hear her quiet voice on the radio outside the door. At least they seem to be taking his illness seriously.

DS Dryer continues, 'Is Harry on any medication for this condition?'

I glance at Jon.

Jon nods. 'He's in the middle of a course of Neupogen to improve his immunity to germs. It's a strong drug. Twice-daily injections. It's vital that he doesn't miss any. The doctors take a frequent blood count to see how well his immune system is working, and when his count is low, he has to take a course of Neupogen to improve his . . . chances.'

The detective frowns at this hesitation. 'Of survival?' he asks bluntly.

I let go of Jon's hand and cover my mouth. My hand is shaking.

'I'm sorry, Meghan,' DS Dryer says. He crouches before me, looking into my face. 'I have to ask these things, I'm afraid. We need to know what we're dealing with, how dangerous this break in medication could become for Harry.'

'It's not so much missing the injections that could have repercussions,' Jon tells him, his voice suddenly unsteady, 'but the fact that his ANC may drop without them.'

'ANC?'

'Absolute Neutrophil Count,' I manage to say, finding my voice again. 'That means Harry's immune system would be severely compromised and at risk from any infections he encounters, however slight. Simple exposure to the common cold, or just touching a dirty toy, could potentially . . .' I swallow. 'It could kill him.'

DS Dryer nods slowly, his gaze locked on my face. 'I understand. And when is Harry due another of these injections?'

'8 a.m. tomorrow.'

After a two-hour interview with the police during which we try to remember as much as we can about the dinner party, who went where and for how long, how unusual it is for us to leave the front door on the latch, that it must have been a mistake, until I am exhausted and barely able to speak anymore, the sergeant finally nods to his constable, and the two police officers stand up.

'Thank you,' Jon says, sitting forward on the sofa, slightly apart from me. At some point during the interview he let go of my hand and shifted into professional mode, his voice no longer hoarse and emotional, discussing Harry's disappearance as though it is a legal case he is dealing with. I suppose that makes it easier for him. 'I'll look out those hospital letters for you, let you have copies.'

'That would be helpful,' Dryer agrees.

Jon stretches wearily, reaches for his cup of tea and puts it down again without drinking any. It's his second cup of tea since the long interview started, and is probably cold by now. I must remember to thank Camilla for being so kind, hanging on in the house long after Simon has been questioned and allowed to go home, and making several rounds of tea for us all. I wonder if the police were able to speak to Emily tonight too. But I suppose they would have told us if she had seen anything useful.

'Thank God it's Saturday tomorrow.' Jon pauses, thinking. 'Should I take Monday off work, do you think? Maybe several days?'

He frowns, considering it. 'That could be complicated though. Somebody else would have to take over my case load.'

I wonder how he can even ask.

'You must do whatever feels right for you,' Dryer tells him.

'Simon's pretty snowed under at the moment, but he might offer to . . .' He glances at me, then shrugs. 'No choice, really. I need to be at home with Meghan. Just in case.'

I ponder those words, the odd hesitation after them, almost as though Jon had intended to say more, but then caught himself up at the last second.

Just in case.

Then I realise what he means. Just in case they find Harry – and he's dead.

I stand up and wander to the window to stare out. Everything aches, especially my heart. I don't know what lies ahead for us, just as I don't know where my son is, and it's the *not knowing* that is driving me crazy.

I lean my forehead on the cool windowpane. If only something would happen, I think, or one of the police would show a flicker of emotion. Then perhaps I could get a sense that progress is being made.

But everyone is so calm and professional. While we have been talking, other officers have wandered in and out with written notes and whispered comments, brief phone calls have been made to those searching, communications on the radio have crackled and buzzed, and the helicopter has swung around and away, then returned to hover above our street. I've heard ominous bangs and thuds from around the house as a team of officers have searched our property thoroughly, looking in every tiny space, even climbing up into the attic, with no result. Things seem to have quietened down now. The blue lights are still flashing out there, but there are fewer than before, and the ambulance that had been mysteriously called glides silently away into the night.

The helicopter is still on patrol though.

'What exactly are they doing up there?' I ask into the silence, lifting my head to stare up at the misty white beam of the helicopter searchlight as it touches the roofs opposite.

'Searching the area around the house.' DS Dryer comes to stand beside me. 'They use thermal imaging cameras,' he explains, watching the helicopter too, 'to see if there's anyone hiding out in any of your neighbours' back gardens, plus all the back alleys, cut-throughs and streets adjacent to this one. If they see anything suspicious, an officer will go in on foot to investigate.'

I am shocked. 'You think Harry might be in one of my neighbours' gardens?'

'Not necessarily. But we have to check. It's standard procedure.'

At that moment, the helicopter swings away and disappears swiftly across the rooftops, its searchlight beam wavering and then rising. Within less than thirty seconds, I can barely hear its whirring rotor blades anymore.

Dryer grunts. 'Nothing.' Then shoots me what is presumably supposed to be a reassuring look. 'The helicopter is just stage one, don't worry. The dogs are still out, and there'll be house-to-house enquiries first thing in the morning. In fact, we should have a clearer overall picture tomorrow. If we haven't got him back by then.'

'Is that a possibility?'

The policeman hesitates. 'Best not get your hopes up, Meghan. I'm going to leave an officer outside tonight though, in case of further developments.' His tone softens. 'Meanwhile, you both look shattered. Probably a good idea if you try to get some sleep, impossible though that probably sounds.'

Jon gets up and starts to collect the dirty tea mugs together. The constable offers her mug with another of those sympathetic smiles she does so well, and some murmured comment, but he takes it without responding. Now that the interview is finally over, his shoulders have slumped and he's shuffling about the room like an old man. I've never seen him like this, so drawn and beaten down.

I watch him anxiously. Even when Harry got his diagnosis, Jon seemed to handle the bad news better than I did.

It makes me fear the worst.

'So you've got all the information, everything we could tell you.' Jon pauses at the door, mugs in hand. 'You've searched the house, the street . . . What happens now?'

'There'll be a press release early tomorrow, letting people know what Harry looks like and how to contact us if they see him.'

'Do you think it's this snatcher that's taken him?' I ask abruptly. 'The one they were talking about in today's newspaper?'

Dryer grimaces. The scar across his cheek twitches. 'Too early to tell. Not the same MO as the others though. You know, it doesn't follow the same pattern.' He shrugs. 'But obviously it's one of the possibilities we're considering.'

Jon nods slowly. 'How can we help?'

'You've given us enough to go on for now. If we need any other information, or if you want to add something or make a further statement, someone will call round. Tomorrow, you should be allocated a liaison officer to keep you informed of our progress.'

'In other words, it's out of our hands.'

Dryer looks at us both, not unkindly. 'That's how the system works, I'm afraid, and it's usually a pretty efficient machine. All you need to know right now is that we're going to do our absolute best to get your baby back safe and sound. Goodnight, Jon, Meghan.'

He nods to me, then the two police officers leave.

I watch from the window as they confer with their colleagues outside, then gradually get back into police cars and drive away. The forensics officer, a thin young man with several briefcases under his arm, has been and gone. One police car remains, no flashing light, tucked in discreetly down the road amongst our neighbours' cars, about a hundred yards from the house.

I wonder who drew the short straw to keep watch over us all night. It's a warm evening, but it must be a lonely job.

Jon looks at me. 'Oh God.'

I take a few steps towards him, and my legs fail entirely. I wobble and then collapse, like a newborn calf trying to walk, ending up on my knees on the wooden floor.

Chapter Nine

Jon makes a grab for me, falling to his knees too. His arms come round me, hands clutching at my back, holding me tight. We grip each other without passion, just desperation.

'I locked the door,' I insist. 'I'm sure of it.'

'It's okay.'

'I'm sorry, so sorry.'

'I can't believe this,' he mutters against my throat. His voice is cracked, unfamiliar. 'Where the hell can he have gone? He was there, I checked on him. Then he just . . . disappeared.'

I can't find my voice for several minutes, but hang on to him instead, mutely thankful for his presence. This man is not just my husband now, but my life raft; I could not possibly face this storm on my own. And though the warmth of his body can no longer comfort me – I am not sure anything will ever comfort me again except the safe return of my baby – it does at least steady me enough to be able to carry on. By which I mean survive.

Anything more than mere survival is beyond me right at this moment. I feel like an overstretched elastic band, too slack and exhausted to do anything but balance there on my knees, waiting for the next blow.

Minutes pass like that; I'm not sure how many. The two of us clinging together, speechless, staring at nothing, trapped in the inertia of bewilderment.

Finally, the door to the lounge creaks open.

It's Camilla, peering round curiously.

'Oh, I'm sorry,' she mutters at once, no doubt shocked to find us both on the floor, on our knees, and begins to close the door again.

'No,' I say, finding my voice at last. 'Please, Camilla, come back. Thank you so much for staying.' Jon releases me and I stumble to my feet, light-headed. 'I didn't even realise you were still here. It must have been hours since . . .'

'It was no trouble,' she insists.

Jon gets to his feet, thrusts his hands into his jeans pockets. His face is darkly flushed. The stress, I realise. I'm not the only one here suffering.

'Where's Treve?' he asks.

'Gone home.' She glances at the clock on the mantelpiece. 'About forty minutes ago. He was getting tired, has to be at work early tomorrow morning, or he would have stayed too.' Camilla looks tired herself, I notice; dark circles are showing through her usually immaculate make-up. 'My first class isn't until noon.'

'Well, thanks for staying,' he says.

I look at him.

Camilla hesitates, then nods. 'Right, I'll be off, then.'

She looks back at me, very directly. I can see the concern there, and it warms me to her at once. She was a little self-centred at the dinner party tonight, but I could see that she had argued with Treve, and I understand how that feels, even in company.

She adds, 'No . . . news, I take it?'

I can almost see the word hanging in the air between us, carefully unspoken. Like it would be a breach of good manners to say his name aloud.

Harry.

'The police are out there now, looking for him,' Jon replies for me, not looking at her but bending to rearrange the scattered cushions on the sofa. His tone comes across as tense, almost hostile, which surprises me. 'That's all we know. They said they'd be in touch again tomorrow, give us a progress update.'

She nods again, her face shuttered, then slips out.

Once she has gone, I study Jon's averted face, watching as he tidies the room in a mechanical fashion, straightening the magazines on the coffee table, tightening the screw tops on the spirit bottles.

It is not like him to be rude, even when under pressure.

'You weren't very nice to her,' I comment.

'I don't need their pity,' he tells me brutally. 'She and Treve were only hanging around so they could watch what was happening. It's ghoulish. We see people like that all the time in the courts. Pretending to be sympathetic, but actually enjoying other people's misfortune.'

'That's unfair.'

'Is it?' He straightens and stares at me. 'Camilla can be a spiteful cow at the best of times. But she was so rude to you tonight. Why the hell do you put up with it?'

He is looking at the milk-stains on my dress. I have been uncomfortable for hours, but have pushed it to the back of my mind while struggling to answer the policeman's questions.

'Poor Harry,' I say, distracted. 'He must need his feed by now. He'll be distraught. I hope whoever . . . Oh God. They will feed him, won't they? Whoever took him. They'll have to give him bottled milk.'

'Meghan,' he begins, but I'm no longer listening.

'Harry's never had a bottle. He won't know how . . . He won't be able to feed. And they don't have his medicine. It's still all here, waiting for him.' I start to cry, and my milk comes, responding to my emotion. The front of my dress grows wetter, and I tear at the buttons to release it, dragging it up and over my head, not caring that the lounge curtains are still partly open, that the lights are blazing, that people passing by outside will be able to see in. I sob uncontrollably, 'He's going to die. He's going to die.'

Jon stares, saying nothing, his face still flushed. Then he wrenches the lounge curtains together and stands there, his back turned to me, head bowed. His hands are still clutching the curtains.

'Please, stop it,' he says thickly. 'Let's . . . Let's go to bed. Maybe in the morning we'll get good news.'

'Go to bed?' I am astonished by this suggestion, which seems insensitive in the extreme. I wipe my eyes on the back of my hand, saying, 'I won't be able to sleep. How on earth could anyone sleep with this hanging over them?'

'Well, I'm going to bed,' he says, and walks out of the room.

I can't believe he's left me to go to bed. I stand for a long time, staring at the closed door, listening as he locks up the house, back and front, and treads heavily up the stairs to the bedroom. But yes, he's gone.

Harry has gone.

Now Jon.

The house grows still and silent. I am alone at last. I hunt for a tissue and blow my nose. Belatedly, I think of our anniversary dinner party. The table outside was left strewn with dirty coffee cups, dessert bowls, soiled napkins. I should pull my dress back on and go out there. Camilla and Treve have probably cleared it though. Now that I think about it, I caught the soft whoosh of the dishwasher earlier while talking to the police. Camilla again, I guess.

And I expect the two men will have helped. Such good friends, all of them. Yet we barely spoke to them after the police arrived, we don't really deserve their kindness. I didn't even say thank you, except to Camilla, and she seemed so horrified when she left, her face turned away, that I doubt we'll see her again for a while.

Between my wild behaviour and appearance, and Jon's hostility, she must have wondered why she bothered staying to help out.

She was so rude to you tonight.

Was she?

I can't recall a word of our dinner conversation now, though I know we talked for what must have been well over an hour after I served that first course, maybe even two hours. How strange. It's as though Harry's disappearance has wiped everything else from my mind. Like there was a before and an after to this evening, and after is the only part that exists for me now.

I don't even know who nipped in to visit the loo or to fetch another bottle of wine, nor how many opportunities I had to check on my baby after Jon took him back to bed, yet wasted every one of them. All I can think is how selfishly I behaved tonight, how irresponsible I was, how unfit to be a mother. I have always been so careful with Harry, never missed a feed, never missed his medication times, never left him wet or hungry or to cry. But I neglected him tonight – and fate was watching.

I have been justly punished for my neglect; I see that now. But does Harry have to pay as well? That seems too cruel for words.

I curl up on the sofa in my knickers and bra, covering myself with my dress, and hug myself into a tight ball. The overhead light burns into my eyes, so I bury my head under a cushion. My breasts throb, and I long for the release of feeding, for the cool touch that has gone, tiny fingers clenching and flexing against my skin, intent blue eyes staring up at me.

'Harry . . .' I whimper.

Chapter Ten

The police are back at the door early next morning.

I am ready for them. At about five o'clock in the morning, I dragged myself wearily off the couch and crept upstairs for a quick shower. Then I slipped into our bedroom for clean clothes. Jon was still asleep – or pretending to be. Either way, I could see the top of his head poking out from under the duvet, but he stayed motionless while I opened and closed drawers as quietly as possible, gathering underwear, clean jeans, T-shirt and a thin cardigan.

Once dressed, I spent several minutes in the nursery, just staring into the empty cot. It's almost as though I can't believe he's gone without constantly reminding myself, without seeing the evidence first-hand.

In my panic and hysteria last night, I did not notice that my medicine chart is also missing. The chart where I have been meticulously listing all Harry's injections, times and sites. This morning, I looked blankly at the tape marks left on the wall where it appeared to have been torn down, then searched the room in case the chart had been thrown under the cot or changing station.

There was no sign of it.

But I cannot seem to think clearly enough to work out whether its loss is significant or not. All I know is that I have to remember to mention it to the police. It's as though my fear is consuming my brain to the point where it's all I can do to survive from hour to hour. So by the time the police arrive, I've been watching the road for several hours. Eager for news, I jerk the front door open before the detective even has a chance to ring the bell.

It's DC Gerent and DS Dryer again, accompanied by a third, older man in a black coat. He looks me up and down with a careful, assessing gaze. I guess he must be another plain-clothes police officer. Perhaps a specialist in abductions.

'Well?' I gaze past them, wide-eyed, staring up and down the quiet suburban street. I know I must sound hysterical, but cannot seem to control myself. 'Have you found him?'

DS Dryer shakes his head.

'Nothing?'

'I'm sorry.' He glances at his colleagues. 'May we come in, Meghan? We have some more questions about Harry.'

'Of course.'

I struggle to sound welcoming, to smile as they enter the house, wiping their feet on our doormat, making their way into our lounge. These are the officers who are going to help us get Harry back, after all. But the little hope that's been burning in my chest all night, the hope that I would wake up in the morning and discover that my ordeal was all over because he had been found safe and sound, begins to waver and look thin. Much more bad news, and it will go out completely.

I cannot let that happen. I have to believe that we will see Harry again.

'Early days, I suppose.'

DC Gerent smiles at me comfortingly. 'Exactly. And once you've answered these questions, and we've got the press release out there, we may see more movement.'

I have followed them into the lounge. 'Please, sit down.'

The third officer sinks into Jon's favourite chair. The other two hesitate, then sit together on the sofa.

I stand near the window, my gaze occasionally wandering to the street. 'Movement?'

DC Gerent says helpfully, 'When people see a child abduction on the news, dozens tend to phone in sightings and suspicious activity.' She opens her notebook and flicks through to a blank page. 'Mostly mistaken information. But one or two of those calls may yield something useful. So yes, we do sometimes get movement after a press release.'

'But not always,' the new officer says.

I look at him directly. 'I'm sorry, I don't think . . .'

Dryer makes a noise under his breath. 'Apologies, that's my fault. I forgot you haven't met Detective Inspector Pascoe yet.'

I study the new officer more carefully. 'Detective Inspector Pascoe,' I repeat.

I am pleased the police are taking it so seriously. But my heart gives an odd little jump, like it's hopped sideways in my chest. Does this mean they think Harry is . . . But I shut down the thought before it can go any further. I must not think like that.

'It's good to have so many people looking for Harry,' I say.

He is older than the other two, probably in his late forties, with bushy, silver-flecked eyebrows and moustache, a thickening body and the beginnings of a paunch. Too many good dinners, I think.

'Please try not to worry, Meghan. We're going to do our best to get your son back as soon as possible,' the inspector assures me.

'Thank you,' I tell him.

'I'm only here for a few minutes, I'm afraid. I have to go and prepare the team for the door-to-door.'

'You mean, question my neighbours? Do you really think someone in this street might have—'

'Not necessarily. It's all part of our standard procedure for lost or missing children. Press release, appeal for information, plus door-to-door enquiries . . . We ask if anyone's heard or seen anything suspicious, especially around the time of the actual abduction, then pool the resulting data.' Pascoe smiles thinly, showing yellowing teeth. A smoker? That would explain the faint whiff of tobacco smoke I keep catching. 'Like a fishing net, trawling for information. As the constable here said, there can be a lot of irrelevant sightings and claims the first few days of an operation like this. But we'll follow up all the positive leads, speak to as many people as possible, and somewhere in there hope to find whoever took your son.'

My gaze wanders back to the street. 'Good,' I say absently, and move the curtain aside slightly to see the parked cars a little better.

Gradually, I sense his gaze on my face and look round. All three police officers are watching me. I muster a smile, and let the curtain drop.

'Did you manage to talk to Emily last night?'

Pascoe glances at Dryer, who raises his chin and says, 'Emily? Yes, indeed. She gave us a full account of her movements yesterday evening, but we didn't see anything suspicious or unusual.'

'Well, I found something suspicious here,' I tell them. 'I kept a medication chart on the wall next to his cot, a daily record of Harry's injections. The doctor told me it might be useful for their records, and would also remind me not to inject him in the same place twice. I went back into his room this morning, and that's when I noticed.'

'Noticed what?' DS Dryer prompts me.

'That it's gone,' I explain. 'Torn off the wall, by the look of it. I think whoever took Harry must have taken the chart too.'

Dryer is frowning. 'That would suggest they know about his condition.'

I stare at him.

'Where's your husband this morning, Meghan?' DI Pascoe asks. He sounds impatient. 'I know it's early, but I had hoped to meet him too.'

'Jon's still asleep. I can call him, if you like.'

'Please.'

I go to the bottom of the stairs and listen, then call upstairs. 'Jon?' There is no answer. I raise my voice. 'Jon?'

It's still early, a little before eight o'clock, but I am sure Jon must be awake. Though if he had a night as rough as mine, he may not want to get out of bed yet.

There's a noise from above. Jon comes to the head of the stairs and looks down at me, still in his dressing gown. I can tell from his face that he has been suffering all night too. 'Who was that at the door?'

'It's the police.' I lower my voice. 'They want to speak to both of us, together. Get dressed and come down, would you?'

I can see that he does not like my tone.

I soften my voice. 'There's going to be a press release. They just need to ask a few more questions.'

The door to the lounge creaks.

I turn, seeing DI Pascoe in the doorway. The inspector comes to the foot of the stairs, looking up curiously at my husband. 'Morning, good to meet you. I'm DI Pascoe, in charge of the investigation.'

'Hello,' Jon says, very stilted, not moving.

'A terrible time for you both.'

Jon remains silent.

'Well . . .' Pascoe nods, a little awkwardly, then turns to me. 'I'm afraid I need to be somewhere. I just wanted to say how sorry I am about this whole business, and that I'll be giving it my full attention. Now I must be on my way.' The inspector thrusts out a hand, and I shake it, studying him uncertainly. 'Don't worry, you're in excellent hands with Detective Sergeant Dryer. One of our best, in fact.' He heads for the door, already checking his phone. 'Hope to catch up with you both later. I can let myself out.'

I glance up at Jon. He looks at me, then turns and disappears back into the bedroom.

My breasts tingle, hard and uncomfortable. But it's not as impossible to bear as yesterday, nor is it leaking more than the pads can manage to absorb. This is Nature responding to Harry's absence with age-old pragmatism, I realise. Half a day without feeding, and milk production is already beginning to lessen.

Wearily, I head for the lounge, and stop dead.

DC Gerent is blocking the doorway.

I meet her level gaze, surprised, and she steps aside.

'Is he coming down?' she asks.

'He's getting dressed.' I smile in a chilly fashion, and hope it's the truth. I go back into the lounge and sit in the chair the inspector vacated. The cushion still holds a slight, residual warmth. 'He won't be long.'

I feel like crying again, but cannot. Not in front of the police. They might misinterpret it. But I did not recognise the expression on Jon's face just now. It was like looking at a stranger.

I'm scared. Not simply over Harry's disappearance, but of the change of mood I am sensing in my husband. I saw it last night after the police had left, that sudden, inexplicable withdrawal of affection. Our marriage has not always been smooth. But why this new, disturbing silence?

Dryer is looking at me expectantly.

'Can I offer you a drink?' I ask belatedly. 'Tea? Coffee?'

Both officers politely decline.

'Tell me about yesterday,' Dryer says.

My gaze flies to his. 'Yesterday? Didn't we cover all that last night?'

'You were a little sketchy on some of the details.' He has his own notebook, I realise, and has bent his head, glancing through it. 'Lots of information about the dinner party, your guests, what you ate, where everyone was when you discovered Harry was gone.' He pauses. 'But almost nothing about earlier in the day. You went to the supermarket, is that right?'

'Yes, shopping for dinner.' My skin prickles. 'Sorry, how is that relevant? Harry didn't go missing until—'

'We like to get a fully rounded picture of the parents' daily routines, in cases like this.'

In cases like this.

I imagine my son's name and date of birth on a file, tucked away in some dusty folder in a police archive twenty-five years from now. CHILD ABDUCTION: UNSOLVED.

'How many do you get back?' I ask.

'Sorry?'

'Missing children. How many are ever found?' I swallow, my throat so dry it's almost closing up. 'Alive, I mean.'

DS Dryer glances at his colleague. There's a kind of regret in his face. 'We're going to do everything we can, believe me.'

The door opens.

Jon, at last. He's showered, and had a close shave, and is looking far more like himself. Jeans again, I notice, but his best ones, straight from the drawer and still neatly ironed, a thick leather belt with a metal clasp threaded through the loopholes. He has chosen a blue shirt today, open collar, and draped a thick cream woollen jumper about his shoulders, sleeves tied together to hold it in place.

Even after three years, I'm struck by how sexy he is. How, every time he walks into a room, I instinctively smile and think, this gorgeous man is my husband. It's like a reflex action, something I can't control.

Today, Jon manages a smile for me too. A smile that does not quite reach his eyes. I wonder if it's for the sake of our guests or if he really wants to make up after our fight last night. He kisses my cheek, and I catch a hint of warm, citrus aftershave. Only his face gives away his lack of sleep, two dark smudges below each eye.

'Darling,' he murmurs, turning immediately to the police, 'have you offered these detectives a cup of tea?'

'We're fine, thank you,' Gerent says at once. 'I hope you both managed to get some sleep last night.'

'Some,' he agrees.

She leans forward to shake his hand, studying him as she did last night, then sits down; she's wearing trousers but she smoothes an invisible skirt behind her. The gesture catches my eye as Jon reaches past to shake Dryer's hand.

The formalities over, Jon comes to stand behind me. The policewoman keeps her eyes on his face. Not suspiciously but with interest. She is smiling faintly.

I suppress a ludicrous quiver of jealousy.

Now that Jon is downstairs, the whole thing feels very calm and professional. Except for the earliness of the hour, we could be two couples meeting to discuss the sale of a house. The clock on the mantelpiece ticks relentlessly, and I glance at it. Nearly twenty minutes past eight; I probably only had two or three hours' sleep, or it certainly felt that bad. I look at the sunshine starting to creep across the window frame. It's going to be another warm day.

The house is very quiet, I think.

Too quiet.

'Did you manage to speak to Dr Shiva?' Jon asks.

DS Dryer nods. 'Yes, she was very helpful. I think we've got a pretty good idea of Harry's condition now, and the medication he needs. Actually, I was just asking your wife about her movements yesterday.' He produces a pen from inside his jacket, tests it on the paper, then looks up at Jon. 'And we'll need to hear yours as well.'

'Me? Oh, I was in the office all day,' Jon tells the policeman, and then smiles at him in that charming, self-deprecatory way he has with strangers. 'I'm in the office all day most days. Meghan is always complaining about the long hours I work. But now she's not working, someone has to pay the bills.'

I keep my gaze on the patch of sunshine beside the sofa. I can see dust spinning in it. Does he resent having to work while I stay home with Harry? I thought we had decided that was best for now, until we know more about how to cope with his condition. It's a little alarming to think he may be harbouring some secret resentment. Then his actual words go round inside my head, and I listen more carefully this time.

I was in the office all day.

I remember staring into the jeweller's window, studying rows of expensive watches and gold-plated clocks, and seeing Simon's reflection in the glass beside me. I asked him not to mention to Jon that I was in town, and he denied that Jon was even in the office yesterday afternoon.

Susan sent him on some kind of errand.

I don't look at him. He is my husband; I would not dream of giving him away. But my hand clenches slowly into a fist. He was not in the office all day. Simon told me as much when I saw him.

Why is he lying?

Chapter Eleven

'Right.' Dryer is scribbling all this down in a hurry. He is left-handed, I realise, watching his hand curve across the notebook. Then he looks up at me, taking me off guard. 'And you went shopping in the supermarket, I think you said? You did mention it briefly last night, but we didn't go into details.'

'I took Harry in the buggy and walked into town,' I tell him. 'It would have been late morning by the time we left, after his medication and feed. It's not far to walk, about fifteen minutes at a good pace. And I had plenty of things to do yesterday, so I don't think I dawdled.'

'You said you have a car though, didn't you? A Ford Focus.'

'Meghan prefers to walk,' Jon says before I can answer. He puts a supportive hand on my shoulder. I want to look round at it, at him, but keep my eyes fixed on the police. 'Since Harry's birth. It's a cheap and easy form of exercise. She's trying to lose weight, you see.'

DC Gerent turns her incisive gaze on me, as though hunting for rolls of flab. Her smile is sympathetic.

My cheeks grow hot, but I say nothing.

'Very well, tell me more about this supermarket visit,' Dryer says to me, not looking at Jon.

With gratitude I refocus on him.

'The supermarket,' I say slowly, thinking.

I remember the black-haired woman bending over Harry. My angry questions, her aggressive response, the way the other shoppers were staring at us.

I don't want Jon to hear about that embarrassing incident. Or the police to think I'm flaky. I'm already worried that they suspect me of something, the way they keep asking about what I did yesterday, the times and details, as though I'm hiding something.

'There's nothing to tell, really. Harry and I went round the aisles, did some shopping, mostly for the party, then walked home. It was such a lovely day.' I hear myself give a little gasp at the end. It's hard to keep control. I am remembering Harry's flushed face in the sunshine, his small, compact body, the way he gurgled and kicked as I changed him in the supermarket baby-changing room. My empty arms yearn to hold him, to grab him up and breathe in his delicious baby scent, to feel his warmth against my chest. 'Harry likes being outdoors. He was content.'

Jon's hand tightens on my shoulder. I look up at him, and see that he is suffering too. He's pale again, his lips drawn back slightly from his teeth, eyes narrowed.

I remember how we made love in the shower after he came home from work yesterday. How his touch and kisses made me feel like I was boneless. Everything seemed so perfect at that moment. Like nothing could touch us.

'What about the woman?'

I look back at Dryer. 'Sorry, what woman?'

'The woman in the supermarket.' He consults his notebook again, frowning. 'DC Gerent spoke to the supermarket manager before coming here, to check what you told us about your movements yesterday. He told her there was some kind of misunderstanding in the shampoo aisle. That you had an altercation with another woman.' He glances at Gerent. 'That's right, isn't it?'

'Yes, sarge,' she agrees. 'The assistant manager remembered her from the photo I showed him.'

Jon is staring at me now. He releases my shoulder. The absence of his hand is somehow more disturbing than its weight.

'What other woman?' he repeats, directing the question at me. His voice is sharp, almost suspicious. I cannot imagine what Jon has to be suspicious about, and turn my head, looking up at him in surprise. 'Meghan? You didn't mention any of this to me. Who was this woman?'

I do not know what to say. I look from one face to another, and see nothing there to make me feel better. 'Nobody. It was just a misunderstanding.'

'The manager said you claimed the woman touched Harry. Maybe tried to take him out of the buggy?'

'No, no,' I stammer. 'She . . . I didn't see exactly . . .'

'Meghan?'

I do not look at Jon again, but fix my gaze on DS Dryer's face. Like I'm drowning and he will save me.

'I made a mistake,' I tell him urgently.

'Did you know her?' DS Dryer raises his eyebrows when I don't reply. 'This woman, did you know her? Recognise her, maybe?'

I shake my head.

He consults his notebook again. 'This woman said she wanted to make a complaint against you. But when the assistant manager went back to speak to her, she had left the store. Apparently didn't even buy any shopping.'

Jon is disturbed. I can hear it in his voice. 'What kind of complaint?'

'She accused your wife of erratic behaviour, I believe.' Dryer looks down, then reads out loud, '*Mad.* That was the word she used to the assistant manager.'

Jerry. I remember looking at his name badge.

'She was going to touch Harry. I told her not to, that's all. Then I left.' My voice sounds very high in the silence. 'There was nothing else to it.'

'And you didn't know this woman?'

'No.'

'Can you describe her?'

'Glasses,' I say, thinking back. 'Black hair, probably waist-long. Quite a big woman too. She was wearing a duffel coat, which struck me as odd.'

'How so?'

'Well, it was a very warm day.' I bite my lip, remembering the glorious weather and how happy I was in the sunshine, pushing my son in his buggy. 'I'm really sorry, I can't remember much else about her.'

Dryer nods. More scribbling in his notebook. 'Don't worry. We've asked to look at the supermarket camera feeds. I'll send DC Gerent over later.'

'She had a Cornish accent too. For what it's worth. I remember thinking she must be a local.'

'Thank you, that's helpful.'

It's important to me that they understand what happened. 'I didn't mean to lose my temper with her. She didn't do anything wrong, now I think about it. But it's hard work, shopping with a baby. Very stressful. I only left him for a few seconds—'

Sharply, Jon exclaims, 'What?' and I feel my cheeks flare with heat again under his accusing stare. 'You left Harry alone in the supermarket?'

'I had to go back down the aisle, that's all. A few steps. He was asleep; I didn't want to turn the buggy.' My eyes pleading, I turn to DS Dryer again. 'Do you have children, Detective Sergeant?'

'A boy and a girl. Both teenagers.'

'Then I'm sure you remember how difficult it can be, trying to shop when they're so very young. If he had started to cry . . .'

'Of course. Nobody's accusing you of anything.'

I look at Jon, thinking bitterly, *he is.* But I manage a smile for the policeman's benefit and say merely, 'Thank you. Anyway, it was a mistake. Nothing that has anything to do with Harry's disappearance, I'm sure. She was a woman in the supermarket who stopped to admire Harry, that's all.' I swallow, then add humbly, 'I overreacted.'

'You do that a lot,' Jon mutters.

'But in my defence,' I continue, not looking at my husband, 'there's a baby snatcher out there.' I close my eyes, feeling the hot tears come suddenly and without warning. My last words are a choking stammer, 'And I was right to be c . . . c . . . cautious, because someone's taken him, haven't they? My baby's g . . . gone.'

Jon sits on the arm of the chair, hugs me silently. I suppose he does not want to look too unforgiving in front of our guests.

Thankful for his support, I nuzzle against his side, looking away from the police. I'm the victim here, surely? Yet their questioning makes me feel like I'm a criminal, like I have something to hide.

It's not true though. *I have nothing to hide,* I tell myself fiercely. *Nothing.*

Dryer says, more gently, 'We may need some of Harry's things at some point. Not immediately, but if you could provide a small selection, it could prove useful later. Forensics last night said they'd finished with their examination, but it's probably best not to tidy his room for the time being. Don't clean it, you know.'

Jon queries, 'Things?'

'Maybe a baby toothbrush? Some of his hairs, if you have any. In the cot, perhaps. A used nappy.'

I stare. 'Why on earth—?'

A phone begins to ring, shrill and disturbing.

Dryer hooks a mobile out of his jacket pocket, then grimaces down at the screen. 'I have to answer this, sorry.' He gets up and leaves the room, pulling the door shut behind him. We hear his voice in the hall, deep and murmuring.

Gerent closes her notebook and puts it away. Her smile is bland as she surveys my face, and the ring I'm twisting round and round on my finger.

'Don't worry, Meghan. I expect it's just something to do with the press release. DS Dryer is supposed to be coordinating that.' She turns her attention to Jon. It is definitely not my imagination that her smile broadens and grows warmer. 'This is a lovely house. Have you lived here long?'

'Three years.' His arm tightens about me. 'We moved in after the honeymoon. It was a stretch for us financially. But it seemed like a good way to start married life.'

'And you're happy here? Nice neighbourhood, good people?'

'You get one or two that cause trouble, but overall . . .' He looks down at me, and I meet his gaze. 'Yes, we're very happy here.'

'My uncle lives a few streets from here. You can see the cathedral from his house.'

Jon smiles back at her easily. 'Sounds idyllic.'

The door opens again. It's DS Dryer, and he's looking very sombre. He nods to his constable. 'Time to go.' He shakes our hands, managing a smile for me. 'Thank you for your hospitality. Someone will be in touch later.'

'What is it?' I can't help asking as the two police officers head for the door. 'What aren't you telling us? Is it the door-to-door enquiries? Have you found Harry?'

But he does not answer, striding from the house in a hurry, leaving DC Gerent to look back at us apologetically.

'I promise,' she insists, following her boss rapidly to the car, 'as soon as we know anything concrete, you'll know too.'

The car engine revs loudly, then they drive away, Dryer at the wheel, staring straight ahead. There's been some urgent development that we are not permitted to know about. What other explanation can there be?

Left alone, we stand on the doorstep in the sunshine, watching the car head to the corner at speed, then disappear. I reach for Jon's hand, and he accepts it.

'I wish I knew what's going on,' I say.

On instinct, I glance down the street. There is still a police car parked a few doors down, the dark blur of a uniformed officer behind the wheel, watching us in his turn.

We are not quite alone, then.

Behind us, in the hall, the telephone begins to ring.

Chapter Twelve

Jon gets there first, and lifts the handset. 'Hello?' His voice is cautious, almost wary. He pauses, frowning, then says more naturally, 'Yes, speaking.'

I stand beside him, waiting while he listens to whoever is on the other end. It's difficult to be patient. I cannot hear the caller's voice; the front door is still wide open, and there's a faint noise of traffic as a car slows down outside. Cars often slow down when passing our house, probably in anticipation of the speed bumps at the other end of the road. But this driver stops right outside and sits there, engine running noisily.

I go back and shut the front door, muffling the sound of the car engine.

'What?' Jon exclaims suddenly, and I look at him in surprise. His brows jerk together. He listens some more, and his eyes widen. 'When?'

I know better than to interrupt Jon when he's on the phone – he hates that – so try instead to gauge what is being said by his facial expressions. At first I think he's angry. Then I realise it's a look of horror. His mouth flattens to a straight line, then abruptly he ends the call and thrusts the handset back into its charging cradle.

My heart begins to thud. 'Who was it?' I ask urgently. 'The police? Was it about Harry? Have they found him?'

He looks at me strangely, then turns and strides into the lounge.

I remain where I am, staring after him. What the bloody hell is going on? Why won't he talk to me? For a moment I want to go upstairs and pack a bag, get the fuck away from him. But that would be ludicrous. It's the situation I can't handle, not him. I'm behaving childishly and I know it.

I take a deep breath and follow him into the lounge.

He's turned on the television and is flicking rapidly from one news channel to the next, as though searching for something.

'Jon? Talk to me. Who was that on the phone?'

He stops on one news channel and stares. Then presses the volume button until the sound is right up.

'For God's sake, turn that down. Have you gone mad? What are you doing?'

Silently, Jon points with the remote, and I turn to look at the television screen, wincing at the high volume. Then I stop worrying about the sound, and focus instead on the picture and what is being said.

The news presenter is a middle-aged woman in a mustard-coloured blouse with gold buttons. Her face is immaculately made-up, her hair perfectly coiffured. She has kind eyes, but a calm, matter-of-fact tone that undermines any impression of empathy.

To the right of her head, in a square screen insert, one segment of film is playing over and over.

I study it wordlessly.

It's a loop of footage taken in a narrow country lane so generic, it could be anywhere in rural England. The road itself is cordoned off with ribbons of yellow-and-black POLICE DO NOT CROSS tape, two police cars parked aslant the road with flashing lights, one male officer directing drivers away from the scene. Beyond them, through a half-open five-bar gate, several people in white forensic suits are crouching over something in a muddy field. Something too small to be seen from that distance.

As one of the forensic team straightens, the film snaps back to the beginning, to the officer bending to speak to a driver through his open window. Then loops through it again. The segment itself lasts maybe thirty seconds.

Frowning, I watch it through twice before I begin to fully comprehend what I am seeing.

'The body, wrapped in black plastic, and believed to be that of a young baby,' the news presenter is telling us in her mild, dispassionate voice, 'was found by a local resident earlier this morning while walking his dog. Police at the scene, which is a rural location only a few miles outside Truro, have so far refused to comment on speculation that the body could be one of three young infants reported missing in recent weeks from that area. Our reporter understands an official statement to the press will be made later today.'

The news presenter pauses there before adding, with a slight softening of her voice, 'It is believed the families of the missing children have been informed of this discovery. Now, in international news, the summit meeting has—'

Jon mutes the sound, throws the remote aside and walks to the window. The television report continues in silence behind him. He has not said a word since putting down the phone.

'Oh my God,' I say, my voice thick with terror, unrecognisable. I sink numbly on to the sofa, still staring at the screen. 'No, no.'

Jon makes a noise under his breath.

'It's not Harry, Jon. It can't be Harry.' I repeat this several times, round and round, like the looping segment of film we saw. 'The police would have said something if they thought . . .'

But the words sound horribly thin and false, like I've been asked for my name and given someone else's instead. I fall silent, remembering instead the people in their white forensic suits, stooping to look at something on the ground. Something nobody but them could see. The police cars with their blue lights flashing. The cordoned-off road. The clinical impersonality of it all.

I hear myself say, 'That poor, poor baby. Poor little soul. But it's not Harry. It's not *our* baby,' and feel immediate guilt.

Because it's somebody's baby, isn't it? Somebody's child has died and been left in a field for men in white suits to pick over.

Jon runs a hand abruptly over his eyes, then turns to face me, his face ashen but surprisingly composed. 'You're right, of course,' he says briskly. Trying to make me feel better, I think. 'It can't be Harry. Still a shock though.'

I look at him closely. A memory breaks through the deadening fog of denial and disbelief. 'Who was that on the phone?'

'Some reporter,' he says dismissively.

'Shit.' I stare at him. 'The papers know? They know already?'

'Apparently so.'

I look back at the television screen, as though drawn to it magnetically. The report has moved on. Now we have various heads of state in some lavish meeting room, smiling at each other, shaking hands around a table. I can name our Prime Minister, and recognise a few other familiar faces, but the reason for their big summit meeting is lost to me. Global warming? Terrorism? Something to do with Europe? I lost interest in following current affairs around the time Harry was born. There are only so many hours in the day.

I feel again the emptiness, the terrible yawning absence of Harry at the centre of my life, like a black hole sucking everything of light and joy and hope into it.

I begin to panic.

'So it wasn't a television reporter, then?' I ask hurriedly, gripping on to the known, on to what's next, desperate to avoid the chaos in my head.

'I think she mentioned a newspaper,' he says vaguely, then shrugs. He thrusts his hands into his jeans pockets. 'One of the tabloids. I don't care which one, frankly. I'm not interested. Bloody vultures.'

'But what did she want? What exactly did she say?'

'God, I don't know.' He blinks, then looks blankly at the television too, as though it will help him recall the phone conversation. 'Okay, she started off with her name, something Irish-sounding like O'Riley, then asked did we know a body had been found, that it was on the news?' He grimaces. 'Before I could even process that, she started making us an offer. For an exclusive. That's when I hung up.'

'Jesus.'

I think of the police, the phone call that came for DS Dryer before they left. 'How the hell did a journalist know about us? Or our phone number?'

'I don't know,' he repeats wearily.

Tears spring into my eyes again, but this time it's anger, not grief. A deep, pounding anger that shocks me, that makes me want to smash something – or someone. I can't believe it's my precious boy they've found in some dirty patch of mud out in the back of beyond. I refuse to believe that. It's the only way I can keep sane. But that does not mean we should have been kept in the dark over this poor child's death. Our baby is missing too; we have a right to know everything that happens, and that means before the newspapers. We also have a right to privacy, to go through this agony without the eyes of the world on us.

'I blame DS Dryer. Why didn't he tell us what was going on? He got that phone call. Then both of them fucked off without another word. I bet that call was about the dead baby. That poor dead baby. What else could it have been about?'

'Meghan.'

'No, listen.' I am ranting, my voice high-pitched, yet cannot seem to control myself. The tears are flowing freely now. 'The police must have known what they'd found in that field. We should have been told. But they said nothing; they deliberately kept us out of the loop. They let us find out on the news, for God's sake, like everybody else. Like ordinary people.'

'I know.'

'But why did they do that? It's appalling. They're treating us like—'

'Suspects,' Jon supplies flatly, and I stare at him, uncomprehending.

Jon sighs and reaches for the box of soft white tissues on the table. He drags out a generous handful, and passes them to me.

'That's what we are, Meghan,' he explains gently. 'I've seen it from the other side, remember, as a lawyer. Most murders are committed by someone close to the victim. Fact. Most children who are murdered are killed by one of their own parents. Fact. The police are simply doing their job by restricting information until they know for certain what's going on here.'

'Are you serious?'

'I know you're upset, and you have a right to be. But you have to look at this from their point of view. We're not just parents of a missing child. Not anymore.' He looks at me, and I hear something indefinable in his voice. Something that chills me. 'We're suspects.'

The doorbell rings.

'Stay here.' He leaves the room. I wait, listening, and hear some kind of altercation on the doorstep. I get up and stare round the door. There's a man, looking in past Jon's shoulder.

'Meghan,' he shouts as soon as he sees me, holding up a phone. Presumably he's recording the whole thing on it. 'Who do you think took your son last night? Is it his body out at Billing's Farm?'

'I'm sorry, but we're not answering any questions from the press.' Jon is trying to stay cool and professional, but I can hear the anger in his voice. 'And I would appreciate it if you could respect our privacy—'

'Why did you leave your baby unattended?'

'He was not unattended. He was in his cot, here in our own home,' Jon tells him sharply. 'Now I'd like you to leave. There's an officer parked down the road. I can summon him if you won't leave.'

The man's tone turns aggressive. 'No need to be like that. I spoke to one of your neighbours this morning. She says you left the front door unlocked last night, that you didn't check on the baby for hours, that you could be arrested for negligence . . .'

'Get lost!' Jon sounds furious now. 'You're trespassing.'

I come further into the hall, not sure if I should lend a hand or not. The way the journalist is grinning makes me hate him. Vile man!

Suddenly, a few feet behind him, a second man appears out of nowhere, as though he has been hiding, waiting for his chance. A man holding something up over his colleague's shoulder.

I blink as a flash goes off, illuminating the hall and presumably my startled face too. A photographer, I realise too late.

Jon wrestles the door shut, then shuttles the chain across. 'Bastards!'

'They took a picture of me. Oh my God. For the papers.'

'It's not important.'

I stare at him, suddenly cold. 'Jon, they must know something. Something about that body. Why . . . Why else take a photo of me?'

He takes me by the shoulders, looks into my face. 'I told you, it's not important. If it was Harry, we would know by now. You heard the news report. The families of the missing children have been told.' He pauses significantly, holding my gaze. 'We haven't been told though, have we? So they can't think it's Harry.'

I lean my forehead on his chest, listen to the rapid thud of his heart. He's as wound up as me, I realise.

'I love you,' I say brokenly.

His arms come round me. 'Meghan, darling,' he says deeply. 'You're upset, and no one blames you for that. But we've got to hold it together. For Harry's sake, yes?'

I think about what he's said, then nod. 'For Harry's sake.'

'That's my girl.' He tips up my face, a finger under my chin, then kisses me briefly on the lips. 'Now I have to ring Sue about taking Monday off.'

'Do you think he meant it?'

'Did who mean what?'

'That journalist. He said we'd been negligent. That we left Harry alone too long, that we could be . . . arrested.'

'He was trying to get a rise out of us, that's all.'

'You really think so?'

'Of course. Look, while I call work, why don't you go upstairs and put some of Harry's things together in a bag, like DS Dryer asked?'

'I want to meet the other parents,' I whisper. 'The other parents whose babies have been abducted.'

'That doesn't sound like a good idea. You'll only get upset.'

'I want to meet them,' I insist.

He closes his eyes briefly, then nods. 'I'll mention it to DS Dryer. Though there's no reason to think the cases are related. Not until the police tell us they are. Now up you go, and let me make my call to the office.'

Numbly, I go upstairs and he watches me go.

I stand outside the closed door to Harry's nursery for a long time, then finally find the courage to turn the handle and go inside.

The forensics officer has not moved anything, as far as I can tell. Yet somehow I can still tell that people have been in here: walking about, studying the store of pre-filled syringes in the mini-fridge, touching Harry's cot and his changing mat and his brightly coloured mobile, looking at his belongings, maybe checking the wall for fingerprints where the medication chart was ripped away.

The nursery feels both invaded and horribly empty at the same time. My gaze keeps being drawn back to the cot, as though I may suddenly see Harry lying there, as though it's possible all of us somehow failed to spot him during the search. The human mind is a peculiar machine, I think; so good at self-healing, it keeps attempting the impossible again and again, even when hope is gone.

I stand there silently. I can hear Jon on the phone to Susan downstairs. He sounds almost relieved to be talking to his boss instead of me, back to professional mode, his voice calm and even, discussing with the senior partner how long he may be away from the office, how things should be handled in his absence.

I was in the office all day.

That was what he had told DS Dryer. Only he wasn't, was he? He lied to the police. He was not in the office yesterday afternoon because, according to Simon, 'Susan sent him on some kind of errand'.

Stop it, I tell myself sternly. Running an errand for a senior partner is part of his job. So in Jon's mind, he probably considers that as having been at work all day. And if I ask him directly about it, it will only cause another argument.

I bend and rifle through the fridge, counting how many syringes are left, taking some comfort in the monotonous task until I stop, frowning.

I do a more careful recount.

Same result.

There seems to be less medication in the fridge than there should be.

I rub my forehead, stressed.

I ought to know, but I can't remember exactly how many syringes we had at the start of this course or how many should be left in the fridge. But then, I kept the chart on the wall precisely so I would not need to remember. Maybe Dr Shiva will know how many pre-filled syringes were prescribed for this most recent course of medication, and how many should be left. Though, of course, it hardly matters now. Harry's not here anymore, and he's already missed this morning's injection. Then he'll miss the next one, and the one after that . . .

Suddenly, I shake the fridge violently, tipping it forward so that the door tilts open, throwing its contents to the floor. I am breathing hard, my chest heaving.

I bite my lip, struggle to hold my breath.

Stop it, stop it, stop it.

Several moments pass while I stand there, staring blindly at the fallen fridge, and the jumble of syringes and other packets on the floor. There seems to be some significance in the scattered mess, like it's a metaphor for what's going on inside my head.

I love you.

I stoop and tidy up the mess I've made, then restock the fridge with the remaining syringes and reposition it on the cabinet.

Thankfully, it still seems to be working.

I'm not surprised the mother of that other missing baby has become depressed. I have not been myself since the birth, often muddled, sometimes miserable or stressed, even hysterical at times, and now this. *Our lives have been torn apart.* Yes, I think, looking around the silent room once more before I leave. It feels like my heart has been ripped out, and I do not know how I am going to survive. Not like this, not on my own.

I love you.

Jon did not say, 'I love you,' in return, did he?

Chapter Thirteen

When I finally come downstairs again, I find Camilla and Treve sitting together on the sofa in the lounge, talking to Jon in low, concerned voices. All three look round when I walk in, and their conversation dies away to silence.

It's hard not to feel awkward as I meet their stares. Clearly they were discussing me in my absence, and not in a positive way. They could not have made it more obvious if they had tried, I think, but restrain myself from demanding to know what has been said. That will only make them all the more convinced of my fragility.

Camilla looks beautiful in a striking Japanese top, decorated with red flowers and worn loose over white leggings. Her neat feet are encased in white ballet pumps, her make-up light and perfect, hair hanging smoothly golden. Beside her slender figure, Treve looks almost overweight, yet somehow healthy at the same time; he always reminds me of a rugby player, large without looking unfit, his eyes watching kindly as I hesitate in the doorway.

'Hello,' I say, and have to suppress an impulse to burst out in laughter at how ridiculously inadequate that greeting has become.

Jon would understand. But our glamorous next-door neighbours would not.

Hello, I am broken. *Hello*, my life is a howling pit of despair. *Hello*, my gorgeous baby boy may be dead, and I do not know where to look or how to speak or even if I shall ever be whole again.

Camilla jumps up from the sofa first. 'Darling,' she says, and hugs me tightly. I glance at Jon over her shoulder, but he's turned away, looking out of the window. His profile is tense, mouth compressed. 'I saw the news this morning, and knew we had to come round. How are you?'

'It's not him.'

She steps back, studying my face. 'The police have been in touch, then? Jon said . . .'

'It's not him,' I insist.

Treve stands up and hugs me too. 'So dreadful, Meghan. I can't begin to imagine how you're feeling,' he tells me, his Cornish voice rumbling against me. 'We're both very sorry. Very sorry indeed. How are you coping?'

I manage a shaky smile when he releases me.

'Oh, you know . . . Surviving.'

'Aren't we all?' he quips, but his answering smile is warm and understanding. 'Now listen, if there's anything you need, anything either of us can do, you only have to ask. Isn't that right, Camilla?'

'Absolutely,' she agrees.

'Thank you.'

I feel a little weepy faced with such kindness, and have to battle the temptation to dissolve into tears again. It would be so easy to give up and cry on their shoulders. To let tears be my habitual expression from now on until the worst possible news arrives, the words I never want to hear. Nobody would blame me, everyone would understand.

But I've made my decision.

I say to Jon, 'I want to go and speak to that officer parked outside. I can't sit here uselessly anymore. I need to know.'

Without even waiting to hear his response, I turn and leave the room. Jon will be furious, of course. His instinct is always to behave conservatively, and he will not like me approaching the police instead of waiting for them to come back to us. But a wild impatience has got its teeth into me, and I find myself marching down the street in the spring sunshine, my arms folded, my face set.

I hear Jon's voice behind me and ignore him.

The police officer is a dark-haired man, gazing down at his smartphone, his expression distracted as he flicks from one screen to another. He's not one of the team DS Dryer introduced us to last night, so I don't know his name. I do have a vague memory of seeing him on the front path though, talking to DS Dryer, probably somewhere around midnight. I wonder if he was on the night shift too, or if someone else has recently handed over to him.

He looks round, startled, when I rap sharply on the passenger window.

'Hello? I'm Meghan Smith,' I say through the glass. 'I need to talk to you. Or to DS Dryer. It's important.'

The policeman gets out of his car immediately, coming round towards me. The sun is dazzling off the windscreen, but I squint at him, arms still folded.

'Is there a problem?'

'Much good you are, sitting here,' I say accusingly. 'We had a newspaper reporter round the house just before, and a photographer. He got a picture of us before Jon closed the door.'

The man looks worried. 'I wasn't aware of that, I'm sorry. I had to take a call from the station a short while ago. That could have been why—'

'Was it about my son?' I interrupt him.

Jon has come up behind me. He tries to pull me away, making some apologetic noises at the policeman, but I shake off his hand.

'The baby they found in the field,' I insist, my voice rising. 'Whose baby is it? Do they know yet? Why haven't we been told? I saw on the news just now that the families of the three other missing babies had been informed about the . . . the body.' I swallow hard, my voice breaking on that word. I force myself to continue though. 'But nobody's saying a word to us.'

'Meghan, please.' Jon is angry. I can hear it in the way he says my name. 'Look, come back inside. This isn't doing any good.'

'I want answers.'

'And you'll get them,' the police officer assures me, but he is looking at Jon over my head. Like a silent conspiracy, man to man. 'Though I think it would probably be a good idea to continue this discussion inside your house.'

'I agree.' Jon smiles. 'Sorry, I don't think I know your name.'

'PC Turner. Or just plain Pete, if you prefer.' He turns to lock the vehicle. 'I'm happy to wait inside with you, if you like. Or just outside the front door, if you'd prefer to have privacy. I'm very sorry about the journalist and photographer; I'll make sure that doesn't happen again. If you give me their names, I can report them for misconduct.'

Jon shakes his head. 'They didn't give their names. Couple of freelancers, I expect. Hoping for a story to sell to the nationals.'

'Excuse me,' I say sharply as they turn towards the house.

Both men look round at me, surprise in their faces.

'Do you mind speaking to me, not just to my husband?' I ask, my voice shaking with annoyance, and wonder if I've gone too far when I see Jon's brows jerk together. 'I exist too, you know.'

PC Turner hesitates, his gaze searching my face. 'Of course you do. I'm very sorry if you thought I was ignoring you, Meghan. Do you mind if I call you Meghan?' Without waiting for an answer, he gestures me to walk ahead of him. 'Shall we go inside?'

I hate the silence now that Harry isn't here.

Just walking into the empty house reminds me of his absence. For months now, my entire life has revolved around Harry: his feeding times, his bath times, his medication and special care, only a few snatched moments on my own while he was sleeping, to put on a wash or sit down with a coffee. Even before he came home from the hospital, the nurses set up a trestle bed for me beside his cot, I was there so often, every day, most nights, Jon unable to make the time as frequently as I could.

Now, I feel lost and directionless, my mind constantly groping towards the next task, only to remember with a jolt that there is nothing to be done. No baby to feed or change or bathe, no medication to administer, no alarm to set on my phone.

The cruel empty hours stretch away in all directions like the spokes of a giant wheel, and I no longer have the faintest idea how to fill them.

I walk into the lounge to find it empty. Treve and Camilla have left. I suppose they think I've gone mad, charging out without explanation. Maybe they're right.

'Tell us about the baby the police have found,' I say, turning to the policeman as he and Jon follow me into the lounge. 'And no more stalling. We've got a right to know.'

An empty cereal bowl is on the table. I glance at it, temporarily bemused. Jon never usually eats breakfast in here. He must have grabbed something while I was upstairs in the nursery. I realise I have not had any breakfast. I'm not hungry though. In fact, I feel vaguely sick at the thought of food.

'I can't help you, Meghan,' the PC says, his tone apologetic. He looks from me to Jon, then adds, 'Even if I knew something, which I don't, it's not within my power to discuss the case with you.'

'For God's sake!' I explode.

Jon looks at me disapprovingly, as though pained by my outburst. 'Meghan, please.'

'But I can certainly put in a call to the station,' Pete continues, 'explain the situation, and ask DS Dryer to get in touch with you. How does that sound?'

I sink on to the sofa, staring blankly at the wall opposite. There's a framed photo on the wall: Harry as a newborn, red-faced, wrapped in a white blanket, little crocheted woollen cap on his head.

'Thank you, Pete, we'd appreciate that,' Jon is saying smoothly. The lawyer's voice again, firm but fair, almost dispassionate. 'It's not very helpful being kept out of the loop. As you can see, that news story on the television has left my wife quite shaken.'

'Understandably so.'

'So the sooner we can get our questions answered, the better for her. For everyone, really.'

'Of course.' Pete nods, looking across at me with an air of professional sympathy, but it's obvious he's not keen. Maybe DS Dryer left a standing order not to be disturbed. Maybe he's a difficult boss. Nonetheless, he fumbles with his radio, then hesitates. 'I'll have to make the call outside. Five minutes, okay? Then I'll be back with some news.'

He leaves, and we hear him a minute later in the front garden, speaking quietly to someone on his radio.

I hug my chest, remembering the last feed he took, Harry's little hands grabbing on to me, the smell of his soft flesh against mine, then I push the memory aside. I dare not go down that route. I can't allow myself to think about Harry, just in case . . .

'You weren't very friendly to PC Turner,' Jon remarks.

'I just want the truth.'

'Don't we all?'

I bend my head, staring at the floor. The patch of sunlight is moving closer to the sofa. 'What does that mean?'

Jon has been watching the policeman out of the window. Now he comes towards me. I keep my head bent. His trainers stop in front of me, and I study them, not speaking.

'Do I need to call the doctor, Meghan?'

I shake my head.

'Good,' he says, and then leaves the room. I hear his feet on the stairs.

My mobile pings. Notification that a new text message has arrived. I turn over my phone to check it, and frown. The message is from Emily.

Just seen the news. If there's anything you need, you know where I am. xxx

Oh God.

I stare at the misty screen, tears in my eyes, then text her back with fumbling fingers.

The police aren't telling us anything.

I hesitate, biting my lip, then add four more words.

What do you know?

Rather less than five minutes later, PC Turner is back. He looks round for Jon and sees only me, still sitting on the sofa. I can tell from his expression that 'Pete' has pegged me as trouble and would rather not speak to me alone.

'Is your husband about?'

I stand up, aching but too restless to sit any longer. 'I think he's gone upstairs. Did you manage to get in touch with DS Dryer?'

'I left a message for him. He's out at the . . .' He stops himself, then looks at me awkwardly. 'Detective Sergeant Dryer will be back at the station in about an hour or so, I'd expect. Best to sit tight until he calls.' He manages a thin smile. 'And don't turn on the telly, yeah?'

'Where is that place?' I ask, picking up my handbag and rummaging through it for my hairbrush. I give my hair a quick brush. 'Where they found the . . . the remains?'

He says nothing for a moment. Then clears his throat. 'I'm not sure. Off the A30 somewhere.'

'It looked like one of those little lanes out beyond Treliske . . .'

'Something like that.'

I smile. He's a nice man. But I have no intention of sitting tight.

'Tell Jon not to worry, would you?' I collect my handbag and car keys from the coffee table. 'I'll be back soon. I just have to go out for a bit.'

PC Turner stares, following uncertainly as I leave the house. 'Meghan, I really think you should wait here until DS Dryer—'

'No need.'

It's so bright outside, I suddenly wish I'd brought my sunglasses with me. They are in the kitchen though and I am not going back inside for them. The car is parked a few doors down. Far enough to make me nervous. I don't run, but I don't hang about either. The last thing I want is for Jon to realise I've gone and come after me before I can get away.

The suburban street is very quiet, nobody in sight. I notice that Treve's work van has gone from outside next door. Camilla must still be at home.

The car makes a high-pitched beeping noise as I unlock it.

I glance back over my shoulder.

Jon is standing at the window of Harry's nursery, the blinds drawn up to let the sunshine in. My heart gives a violent jolt. Has he seen me?

My hands shake as I drag the driver's door open and throw my handbag on to the passenger seat. To my relief, Jon is looking the other way, studying the street. But then his head turns and he sees me.

Too late.

I look back at the policeman with a hurried smile before getting into the car. He still has that uncertain look on his face. 'Thanks for your help, Pete.'

Chapter Fourteen

Just beyond the city of Truro runs the A30, the busy main road in and out of Cornwall, an east-west axis that is sometimes single, sometimes dual carriageway, and opens out into unpretentious countryside as it heads further into rural Cornwall. Low dry-stone walls border roadside dwellings, occasional laybys proclaim NO LITTERING beside overflowing bins and plastic bags caught in the hedgerows, and the white cross of the Cornish flag flies proudly above a few tree-shrouded roofs.

At the roundabout, I merge on to the crowded single carriage-way with the rest of the traffic, heading slowly west towards Redruth, Camborne and, eventually, Penzance. Rough hills and fields stretch towards the restless grey-blue glint of the sea on my left, miles in the distance. Row after row of vast, long-legged wind turbines stand on the hilltop there, graceful and sinister at the same time, their vast blades slow-moving this morning.

In my mind's eye, I see again the news report on the television. The five-bar gate, the muddy field beyond, the forensics' team bending over something. My hands tighten on the wheel.

I know the place; I am sure of it.

But what will I find when I get there? And if it's a crime scene – I force myself not to dwell on what may have been found there – will the police even allow me to stop and get out of my car?

Jon must be absolutely furious. I remember his face at the window, the abrupt turn of his head. He will have run downstairs at once, seething with rage, taking the stairs two at a time, determined to stop me. I try to imagine his expression when the policeman gives him my message, then wish I hadn't said anything.

There's nothing he can do about it, I tell myself firmly. But I am still nervous, my body humming with uncertainty.

My palms sweat on the wheel, and I have to wipe them on my jeans, one at a time. It's possible I have done the wrong thing. But I could not contain myself any longer; I had to do something.

The sun bouncing off oncoming windscreens is blinding. I lower the sun visor, shield my eyes from the migraine I can feel building.

I keep flashing back to Harry's nursery.

His empty cot.

The appalling silence.

With an effort, I push that memory away. But perhaps the constable was right. Perhaps I should have waited for DS Dryer to return with news. What if the police find Harry, and I'm not there to take the call?

The traffic queue moves on again on my side, a few cars at a time.

Suddenly, I'm there.

It's a narrow country lane off to the right. An obscure Cornish village name on a dirty road sign. I miss the name as I signal and get into position to turn. Pen-something, probably. Plus other signs for a campsite and a tourist attraction a few miles on.

A police car is parked across the mouth of the lane, lights flashing. Police officer in uniform beside it, watching the traffic pass.

No time left to change my mind.

I pull in alongside his patrol car and put down my window. The police officer assesses the car, my face, then bends to speak to me. 'Resident?'

I nod silently, hoping he does not ask for an address or any kind of proof.

'Nothing to worry about.' His smile is reassuring. 'There's been an incident about half a mile down, and the road is partially blocked. We're only stopping large vehicles.'

'So I can go through?'

'Of course.' He pats the car, and then steps back. 'Not too fast though. Mind how you go.'

I thank him, put the car into gear, and pull away.

As I recall from a failed shortcut we took once, struggling to find a local hotel with a wedding exhibition, the lane is deep and narrow. It twists and turns for the first quarter mile, then opens out briefly. High wild hedgerows cut off my view on either side, punctuated by sporadic gates that lend fleeting views of the Cornish landscape. Green pastures, yet more green pastures, and then the faint yellow splash of rape fields in the distance.

I drive slowly, staring about, my heart still thudding. The hedgerows are bristling with lush spring growth, occasional white pinpricks of flowers among the sharp tangle of hawthorns. It would be an idyllic scene if it were not for my knowledge of what was surely left here to rot, of the desecrated, muddied remains of a young life.

Less than a minute later, I turn the corner and see them.

Police cars, other vehicles, and a large police van parked up on the verge. Officers in uniform standing about, one looking my way. There's no sign of the forensic team now. The gate has been left open, the field itself cordoned off.

It looks like the scene from the television report, but colder, clearer, somehow more real. The field standing muddy, its entrance crisscrossed with tyre marks and boot prints. POLICE DO NOT CROSS tapes fluttering in sharp gusts blowing across fields from the sea. A man in a black leather jacket packing cases and zip-up bags into the back of the police van. Some people with tripods and camera equipment – reporters? – standing further away on the other side of the road, huddled together in the windy sunshine.

And DS Dryer in the midst of all this activity, his face tense, brows drawn together, talking to one of the uniformed officers.

I pull on to a narrow strip of verge maybe fifty yards shy of the field entrance, and sit there a moment, listening to the engine ticking as it cools. Why did I come here? It seemed like the obvious thing to do when I was at home. The only thing, in fact.

But now, with Dryer heading towards me down the lane, a frown on his face . . .

I get out and stumble across the uneven grass. 'Hello.'

'Meghan?'

'I had to come. I need to know—'

'PC Turner called to let me know you might be on your way.' DS Dryer is trying to steer me back towards the car, like I'm an errant sheep. 'I'm sorry you've wasted a trip. There's nothing to see.'

'They said on the news . . .' I feel sick, but force myself to say it. 'They said the police had found a baby.'

'Please, Meghan. This isn't a good idea.' He turns, signalling to one of the uniforms standing by the police cars. 'Let me get one of my officers to drive you home. Your husband is beside himself.'

'I don't give a fuck what he thinks!' I explode, and then bite my lip in consternation when he stops, staring at me. 'I'm so sorry, I didn't mean . . . Look, Detective, please can't you just . . . ?' The words tumble out like vomit, horrible, impossible to hold back. 'Was it Harry's body in the field? Have you found Harry? I can't stand not knowing; it's driving me mad. Please, can't you just tell me the truth?'

The uniformed officer has arrived, a man about Jon's age. He smiles at me, then looks at DS Dryer for instructions. 'Can I help, sir?'

'Yes, would you escort Meghan to—' DS Dryer stops, staring down the lane. A police car is edging its slow way down the lane towards us. 'Hang on, this looks like PC Turner and her husband arriving now. Doesn't matter, Constable. You can go back to what you were doing.'

'Yes, sir.'

I turn back towards my car, hurrying, my head down. I can't face Jon. Not right now. At the car, I drag my phone from my pocket and check it again.

Still nothing.

No reply from Emily.

I double-check, but my previous message mocks me on the screen, unanswered.

What do you know?

I nearly drop the phone, trying to force it back into my pocket. I can't seem to focus on what I'm doing. The simplest tasks feel beyond me today. I fumble in my pockets for the keys, but can't find them. They must still be in the ignition.

'Meghan, wait.'

I am opening the car door when Dryer catches up with me, one hand grabbing at my elbow.

'Get off,' I say thickly.

'What's the matter?' he asks, frowning down at me. 'I know this must be a very upsetting experience, but you need to calm down, take things more slowly.'

'Was it Harry?'

'No,' he says quietly, and I almost collapse against the car with relief. Dryer glances over his shoulder. I can see Jon bearing down on us, his face grim, the constable a few steps behind him. Dryer lowers his voice, bending towards me. 'Look, I shouldn't say this.

Frankly, I could be reprimanded just for discussing it with a member of the public. But the remains we found today . . . They couldn't be your son.'

'How can you be so sure?'

Dryer hesitates. 'Because this was not a recent death, according to the police surgeon.'

I close my eyes briefly in horror, then nod to show I've understood. It isn't Harry. It can't be Harry. There is still hope.

'Thank you.'

'Now please, go home.' He straightens, turning to my husband. 'Jon, good to see you again. Thank you, Constable.' He shoots me a glance. 'I think Meghan is ready to go home now. Aren't you?'

I want to say no. But I dare not.

'Of course,' I agree limply, and do not resist as Jon guides me round to the passenger seat of the car.

He helps me into the car, his hands gentle and solicitous. But I see the look in his eyes, and know I have not been forgiven.

He does not speak until the police have been left far behind and we are back on the A30, heading for Truro. Then his hands relax on the wheel and he asks, 'Okay, so what was all that about?'

I do not reply, staring out of the window at the countryside flashing by.

'Talk to me, Meghan.'

I shut my mouth tightly, folding one lip over the other.

Jon waits, then gives a short, unpleasant laugh when I remain silent. 'Very well,' he says lightly, then adds a moment later, 'Don't ever do that again.'

The warning in his voice is unmistakable.

Chapter Fifteen

Later that afternoon I get a notification of a new text on my mobile at last. I open it in excitement, but it's not from Emily. It's from my mother, randomly asking if we've decided what we're doing for a holiday this summer.

Only then do I realise that I have not yet phoned my parents and told them about Harry's abduction. I had to give their names and addresses to the police, though I was assured they would not be contacted, that it was just protocol 'at this stage'.

Guilt floods me.

DS Dryer has left a message on our landline answerphone, asking about the possibility of us appearing at a press conference on Monday. My parents buy British newspapers occasionally out in Spain, and I know they often watch UK news on satellite television. It would be awful if they had to find out about Harry second-hand because I hadn't got the courage to ring them.

I make the phone call sitting on the third stair up with the front door partially open, letting in sunlight.

Jon is outside in the front garden, mowing the unruly strip of lawn in front of our low hedge. 'I might as well do something useful while we wait and get the mower out,' had been his reasoning when we came home. But I'm certain that Jon, like me, is groping about for something to do, for tasks to fill the ever-widening space in our lives that Harry's loss has created. The passing to and fro of the mower is loud and mind-numbingly domestic, and I listen to it for several minutes before dialling my parents' number, somehow comforted by its familiarity.

I know Treve and Camilla are home, because both their cars are parked outside. Besides, I saw Treve out the back when we got home, picking leaves out of their small ornamental pond. He lifted a hand when he saw me at the window, and smiled. I waved back, but my return smile did not quite happen.

I dial, and listen to the ringtone, and wonder what Treve and Camilla must think, seeing their neighbour out there in the sunshine, casually mowing his lawn while his baby son is missing. As though we have shrugged and moved on in less than a day.

Not that it matters what they think. None of that matters anymore. But my head is full of so much noise . . .

The rotary mower makes a sudden crunching, whirring sound. The blades must have hit a stone hidden in the grass.

The engine cuts off.

I see Jon's shadow through the frosted glass of the front door as he bends over the mower to investigate.

The phone is going to ring out. They must not be in, I decide. I am just about to give up when my mother's voice breaks into my thoughts.

'Hello,' she says breathlessly.

'Hi, Mum, it's Meghan.' I try to sound bright, unconcerned.

'Meghan? What's wrong?'

Obviously I am not very good at sounding unconcerned.

'Is . . . Is Dad in?'

'Gone to the shops. He should be back in about half an hour. Sorry about the long wait to answer the phone, by the way. I was

outside, hosing down the patio, and couldn't hear it ringing at first.'
She pauses. 'Why?'

I hesitate, wishing Dad was there too. He's always been the
sensible one and I know he would keep Mum calm. But there's no
way I can escape an inquisition if I try to ring off now, so I plunge
in anyway.

Briefly, or as briefly as is possible with my mother, I explain the
situation. Harry's disappearance. The police involvement. Today's
horrific find in the field. That it was not Harry's body, that was certain. But given this new development, we should probably prepare
ourselves for the worst.

I knew this phone call would be a strain. Nonetheless, I had
intended to remain calm if possible. But my mother's exclama-
tions of distress, her constant cries of, 'Oh no, poor baby!' and 'Not
Harry! Please God, not Harry!' bring me to tears before I've even
finished explaining.

'That's it,' she says. 'I'm flying straight home to be with you.
I'll call your dad. Assuming he remembered to take his mobile this
time.'

I wipe my eyes with the back of my hand. 'No, Mum, please. I
can't . . . The house is upside down. I need space to . . .'

'You need someone to look after you, that's what you need.'

'Honestly, we're coping.'

'It doesn't sound like it. You're in floods.'

'Obviously I'm upset.'

I rummage in my pocket for a tissue, and try to discipline
myself to stop crying. Or at least not to sound like I'm crying. I
can't tell her what I'm feeling inside, the confusion in my head, the
agonies I'm crawling through like barbed wire just to make this
phone call; it's too awful, too unbearable to articulate. I don't want
her to worry about me at the same time as worrying about Harry.

'But it's such a long way. I don't want you to come if there's no need.'

'No need? Now you're just being silly. Of course you need us, Meghan. You must be beside yourselves, poor things, and now Jon's lost both his parents there's only us.' My mum takes a deep, quivering breath. 'Now, listen to me—'

Suddenly, Jon is there, blocking out the light from the outside, plucking the handset away from me.

'Hello, it's Jon,' he says into the phone, then listens. 'Yes, I know. Thank you. But it isn't a good time for you to visit right now. No, I'm sorry.' He looks at me as he listens again, his expression unreadable, then repeats into the handset, 'It's not a good time, Rose.'

'Give me back the phone,' I insist, but he ignores me.

'I'm sorry you feel like that, but can Meghan call you back tomorrow?' he asks smoothly, and does not wait for a reply. 'We have to keep this line free in case the police need to get in touch. Thanks, Rose, speak soon.'

He clicks off the call, and hands the phone back to me.

I stare at him. 'Why did you do that? That was my mother.' My voice rises. 'Oh my God, what possible right do you have to—?'

I stop as he holds up a syringe.

'What was this doing in the garden?' he demands instead of answering my questions. 'I just ran it over with the mower.'

I rub my eyes with the tissue, my head throbbing with pain. This bloody migraine. 'What?'

'You heard me.'

I do not understand. 'So you found that in the garden . . . So what? There's no need to look at me like that. I didn't put it there.'

'But it's one of Harry's syringes, isn't it?'

He hands the cracked syringe to me. The needle cap is missing. It's damp and bent out of shape, presumably by the mower, and a little grass-stained. It could be one of Harry's. But then again, all syringes look alike.

'Maybe. I'm not sure.' I turn it over, examining it gingerly. I don't want the needle to scratch me. 'It could be any syringe. Perhaps someone walked past and threw it over the hedge into our garden.'

'What, you mean, like a drug addict? Here? In suburban Truro?'

I look up at him, perplexed by his accusatory tone. 'Well, I don't know where it came from. What on earth makes you think I do?'

'You're sure you didn't drop it yourself?'

'In the front garden?' My voice is high, incredulous. 'Is this why you hung up on my mum? Because you found this in the grass and wanted to tell me off about it?'

'Not tell you off. Just ask you about it.' His face is grim. 'You've been in such a daze lately, Meghan. I simply thought perhaps—'

'Jon, I don't know what you're talking about. I've never even taken Harry on to the front lawn, let alone given him his injection out there. I follow the procedure the hospital gave us. What kind of mother do you think I am?'

I wish he would stop being so cold with me. I can't help feeling he blames me for Harry's abduction. But he was the last one to see him before he went missing.

I hold the broken syringe back out, my palm flat.

'Careful,' I tell him. 'Don't touch the sharp end.'

He takes the syringe back, but stares at me moodily. 'I'd better tell the police.'

I'm startled, not sure what to think as Jon picks up the handset and bends to check the notepad beside it. The mobile number DS Dryer left us is still on the top sheet, scribbled in the policeman's hurried scrawl.

'Tell them what?'

'About the syringe, of course.'

Of course. The syringe.

'If this syringe does turn out to be from the nursery, and you didn't leave it in the front garden,' he continues, still watching me, 'then it must have been dropped by whoever took Harry.'

Chapter Sixteen

DS Dryer arrives at about four o'clock in response to Jon's call, followed within ten minutes by a more surprising visitor: Dr Shiva. I am talking quietly to the detective when the consultant walks in and everything changes, the air subtly shifting around us. I had forgotten how much energy she seems to radiate just entering a room.

I stand up when Jon closes the door behind her, unsure what her arrival means. Beside me, the detective sets aside the album of photographs of Harry we had been discussing and stands too, right beside me. It feels awkward.

'Dr Shiva? I didn't expect . . .'

I stare from her face to my husband's. Did he contact her?

'Coffee, doctor?' Jon offers politely.

She smiles back at him, saying, 'No, thank you, I can't stay long,' then comes straight across to shake my hand. 'Meghan, how are you?'

Her grip is cool and oddly loose, as it was on the day she gave us her diagnosis of Harry's condition. Non-committal, I thought at the time. But I suppose she must shake lots of hands during the course of a day clinic at the hospital, so perhaps it's easier for her not to grip too hard.

I make some polite noises in reply, and she nods sympathetically.

She shakes DS Dryer's hand too, exchanging a few words with him, then turns back to me.

'How are you coping, Meghan?' She is the kind of woman you can't lie to easily, so I say nothing. 'Please, sit down. I'm sorry to turn up like this without checking first. Detective Sergeant Dryer asked if I could come over.'

I sit down again, but my nerves are on edge and I can't help myself. 'Are you here because of the syringe?' I ask the doctor.

'Syringe?'

DS Dryer holds up the transparent evidence bag in which he has placed the bent syringe.

'Jon found this in the front garden earlier,' he tells Dr Shiva. 'It appears to be one of Harry's syringes, but nobody knows how it got outside.'

Nobody meaning me.

'I'll be sending it off to the lab as soon as I get back to the station,' he adds. 'It could take a while to get the results back though. So if you could check the rest of Harry's medication while you're here, doctor, and let us know if any of it seems to be missing, that would be very helpful.'

'Of course.' The consultant peers at the bagged syringe without touching it, then shrugs. 'It could be one of Harry's disposable syringes, yes. Until the contents are analysed, it will be hard to tell for sure. But I'll certainly check how many of his pre-filled syringes are left, if it will help you.'

'Thank you.'

Dryer places the plastic evidence bag on top of the photo album, which is still lying open on the coffee table. I stare at it, and my hands clench into fists in my lap.

The bag is resting on a photo of Harry, taken when he was only three weeks old and lying asleep in his see-through cot in the ICU.

His tiny, twig-limbed body is obscured by the folds of plastic, but in my mind's eye I can still see his reddened arms and legs, his skin baggy and shrivelled like an old man's, as though he had been left in a bath too long, and his screwed-up face turned towards the camera, eyes closed, his body peaceful. Without all the machines wired up to his body, the soft, steady beep of the monitor, I might never have been sure he was actually alive.

'It's been almost twenty-four hours,' I say, my tone angry and accusatory. I look up at the detective. 'When are we going to hear something?'

'Meghan.'

I ignore Jon's quiet voice.

'This endless waiting . . . It's driving me insane.' I stand up, clasping my hands together, squeezing them restlessly. 'Sorry, I've tried to be patient. But I thought you would have heard something by now.'

'These things take time,' Dryer says.

'But the first twenty-four hours are the most crucial, aren't they? I read that on . . . on the internet.' I glance from him to Jon, then to the doctor's concerned face. 'If you don't get an abducted child back within the first day, the chances of ever finding him alive begin to . . . begin to . . .' I end on a gasp. 'Diminish.'

Dr Shiva comes to me, her hands warm, reassuring. 'Sit down, Meghan, please.'

'I don't want to sit down.' I break away from her and pace the room, breathing very quickly. There's so much to do, yet nobody seems to be doing anything. 'My son is out there somewhere,' I remind her, 'being kept in God alone knows what kind of conditions. How on earth can I *sit*?'

'But you will do yourself no good like this.'

I turn to stare at her. 'It's been nearly a day since Harry had his shots. You said they had to be administered regularly. That it could endanger his health even to miss one injection.'

She nods.

'So tell *them*,' I say, pointing to DS Dryer. 'Tell the police how important it is. Tell them he has to be found.'

'We know how important it is,' Dryer insists.

'Tell them my son is going to die if he does not get his medication.' I do not recognise my own voice. 'Tell them, tell them.'

The doctor catches at my hands as I swing past her, and I realise that I have been scratching at my face, driven by some deep, instinctual need to act, to do something, *anything*, even if it is just to punish myself.

'I have told them,' she assures me, her voice soothing. 'But I need you to sit down and stop hurting yourself. It is a very bad situation, I agree. But this behaviour cannot help Harry. It will only make matters worse.'

'How can they be worse?' I am almost screaming at her. 'He's gone. Someone took him. And nobody seems to care what they're going to do to him. Nobody but me.'

'What who is going to do to him?' DS Dryer asks.

'What?'

'You said, *they*,' he points out, his expression neutral. 'Do you know who took him, Meghan?'

'Of course I don't. How could I know that? Do you think if I knew I wouldn't say?' I turn to Jon, staring wildly. 'What have you been telling them?'

Jon does not reply, merely closes his eyes. As though he's sick of me. As though he wishes I was not his wife.

'What's going on here? Am I a suspect now?' I'm finding it hard to breathe. My fingers are tingling. I stare down at them. 'Fuck, fuck.'

I collapse on to the armchair, unable to stand any longer. There's a silence in the room, then Dr Shiva crouches beside me.

She rubs my back, bending me slightly forward. 'Head down,' she tells me, her voice infuriatingly calm. 'Try to breathe more smoothly. In, out, in, out.'

I shake my head. My whole body is trembling. Like I've got hypothermia.

I see DS Dryer's polished black shoes approach, and try to focus on them. He asks my husband, 'Would you happen to have a paper bag? Maybe in the kitchen?'

'A paper bag?'

'Your wife is hyperventilating,' the doctor explains succinctly, still rubbing my back. I hear her speaking, but for some reason the words do not register properly. Like a flat stone bouncing off water, then sinking without a trace further on. 'The detective is right, a paper bag would be useful.'

I'm gulping at the air now, barely able to catch my breath. My lungs hurt. It feels as though everything below my throat has been closed off.

Am I going to die?

I stare down at my hands. My fingers are stiff and outstretched, slightly turned up at the tips; I can no longer bend or relax them. Then I realise with a shock that my fingertips are starting to turn blue.

I struggle to speak. 'Wh . . . what's happening . . . to . . . me?' My voice sounds like air bubbling up from the bottom of a swamp, thick and incoherent.

'You're having a panic attack,' Dr Shiva tells me, no change of expression on her face, as though this is something she has to deal with every day. 'It's perfectly okay, just follow my instructions and you will be fine.'

Perhaps the doctor does see this kind of thing every day. But I have never felt like this before, never had my body refuse to do what

I tell it, and I am scared. Too scared to be able to listen properly, to process what she is telling me.

Someone hands her a paper bag. Jon, probably. I can't look up, focused on my stiff, blueish fingers. Dr Shiva shakes out the bag, blows into it, then fits it carefully over my mouth. It's not what I had expected; it's a simple white paper bag I folded and put away in a kitchen drawer a few weeks ago. It had contained cinnamon and sultana rolls from a baker's in town, and I thought it might come in handy.

Though not for this.

'Breathe,' she instructs me in that gentle, relaxing tone. 'You need to breathe. Nice and slow and easy.'

I struggle to obey her, but can't. She tells me again to breathe. My whole body is tingling now, and I can feel the two men staring, standing about uselessly while I am dying.

'Meghan, come on.' Her voice in my ear is like a hot needle now, piercing my brain. 'Just let your diaphragm relax and take a breath. Stop resisting, you can do it.'

'Look at her fingers!' Jon exclaims. 'Meghan, for God's sake!'

He is so angry. Angry that I am refusing to obey. I rock backwards and forwards, hysterical now, fighting against the paper bag. Does he think I am doing this deliberately? I want to live. I need to live, if only for Harry's sake.

'One more time,' Dr Shiva insists, relentlessly patient. I want to push her away but can't manage even that small effort. 'Try sitting up instead. Here, shoulders back. Relax your torso. Breathe into the bag.'

I fight to follow her instructions. Shoulders, torso, airway. My body rebels, first against the idea of drawing air into my closed lungs, then against the absence of oxygen. I thrash backwards, and the bag comes with me, held in place by the doctor. Her voice comes again from a distance, cruel, persuasive. She won't let me go, won't let me faint, won't let me die. The pain in my chest is building to a crescendo, my head spinning horribly. She tells me I'm going to be fine, and I almost begin to hate her.

'I'm calling an ambulance,' DS Dryer says.

At that second I drag in air, more like a violent hiccup than a breath. The air burns in my airways.

'That's it, good girl,' Dr Shiva tells me, warm approval in her voice, like I'm a ten-year-old, not a grown woman. 'And again.'

I gasp.

More air floods my lungs, and I choke on it, coughing.

The bag inflates, then is sucked flat against my face as I breathe in and then out, and then in again, suddenly hungry for oxygen. I smell the long-gone rolls, remember how they tasted, split and toasted, then buttered. The sweet spice of cinnamon, the rich sultanas, the luxurious melt of butter on the tongue.

'There now. Sit back, try to relax.'

Jon walks out of the room.

Dr Shiva settles me more comfortably on the armchair. 'She will be better soon,' she says, a note of satisfaction in her voice.

'Should I call for an ambulance anyway?' Dryer asks.

She hesitates. 'In my experience, there is rarely any point once the attack is over. There is nothing they would do at A&E except check her over.'

'So that's a no.'

She stands up, the two of them talking over my head like they're my parents. 'Yes, that's a no. But I do think a prescription would be in order.'

'Pills?'

'Meghan is clearly very distressed,' she says, rummaging in her large shoulder bag for a pen and prescription pad. I watch her, too exhausted to protest. 'And who can blame her? This must have been a very traumatic experience for her, and I doubt that Monday's press conference will be any easier to deal with.'

My breathing is becoming easier. I keep the paper bag against my mouth though, scared that if I remove it, the mindless panic will return.

Dr Shiva bends over me with a prescription. 'I've prescribed you a sedative, Meghan. One pill, three times a day at first, then dropping to two after a week if you begin to feel more able to cope. Do you understand?'

I nod.

'Should I give it to your husband?'

At that, I remove the bag. 'No,' I say hoarsely, and take the prescription from her. I push it into the front pocket of my jeans. My chest and throat have started to ache badly; they feel almost scorched, like I've been inhaling strong chemicals. 'Thank you.'

'You're welcome.' Dr Shiva notices me rubbing at my sore chest, and smiles. 'It will hurt for a while. But don't worry, you haven't done yourself any lasting damage. If you ever find it hard to breathe again, don't let yourself panic. Just use the paper bag like I showed you. Or cup your hands against your mouth like this,' she says, and demonstrates, her delicate gold bangles clashing together, 'and breathe into them instead. In and out, nice and slow.'

'Thank you,' I say again.

She smiles, then turns to the policeman. 'I'll go upstairs now and check Harry's store of medication. But after that I must go. I'm afraid I had to double-park outside. There were no spaces. But one of your officers is keeping an eye on my car.'

'You've been very helpful, doctor,' he says.

She smiles, glances down at me again, an assessing look, then leaves the room. I hear her a moment later talking to Jon in the hall. I wonder if he's still angry with me.

My whole body is trembling. I am so tired, I just want to crash out, get some sleep. But at the same time I am totally wired, on full alert. It feels like I will never be able to sleep again. Or not until Harry is back with me.

I had to double-park outside. There were no spaces.

A memory floats back to me.

'Detective?'

DS Dryer has been looking down at his smartphone, flicking through screens. He glances at me suddenly now, his eyes sharp and watchful. 'Yes?'

'There was a car parked down the road yesterday. When I got back from the supermarket. A car I didn't recognise.'

'What kind of car?'

'An old-style Volvo. A dull gold colour.'

He takes out his notepad and pen. 'Did you get the registration number?'

I shake my head.

'Pity.' He scribbles something down regardless. 'And you say you didn't recognise the car? Do you usually know all the cars parked on this street?'

'I don't *know* them, as in who they belong to,' I tell him, suddenly tentative, feeling my way carefully. 'But I tend to notice if there's one that's not normally parked here.'

'But it could have been an innocent visitor? Someone who'd come to see a friend in this street, perhaps?'

'Perhaps.'

Something is nagging at me, but it's hard to think clearly when my body is suffering. My chest is sore, and my legs still feel a little rubbery from the shock of not being able to breathe.

I hear Jon showing the doctor upstairs to check the contents of the fridge. The stairs creak under their feet, their conversation deliberately quiet, like they're talking about me.

'I was looking out of the window from Harry's nursery,' I say slowly, remembering. 'It was just after I'd changed his nappy. And this probably sounds strange, but I got the impression that, whoever it was, they were just sitting there in the car the whole time. Not getting out.'

His eyes narrow on my face, but he says nothing.

I hear feet on the stairs again. Coming back down this time.

'It's like they were waiting for something, or watching the street.' I pause, only now considering what I mean. My eyes widen, my voice dropping to a whisper. 'Watching us.'

The door opens.

It's Dr Shiva, with Jon behind her. 'I've counted how many pre-filled syringes remain unused,' she says, her air urgent, 'and by my calculations, there are at least six missing. Possibly one or two more.'

'You mean they took his medication too?'

'I would say whoever stole Harry not only knew about his condition, but how to treat it too. Either that or they made a very clever guess, perhaps based on the wall chart that Jon says was kept next to his cot.'

DS Dryer stares. 'So there are six syringes missing.'

'Maybe more.'

'How many days' supply is that, doctor?'

'Three,' she says firmly. 'Though if the syringe Jon found in the garden is part of that number, they may only have five.'

'True.'

'Well, let's say they have roughly six syringes in total.' The doctor counts on her fingers. 'Two a day, that covers Saturday, Sunday, Monday. So Harry should be safe for at least another forty-eight hours, assuming whoever took him knows how and when to administer the medication correctly.'

'That's a pretty large assumption.'

'Indeed.' Dr Shiva hesitates, shooting me a worried glance. 'And once the medication wears off, his ANC may begin to drop quite rapidly.'

'Meaning?'

'Within another three days, Harry's life could be in serious danger.'

Chapter Seventeen

Sunday is a dreamless blur, thanks to Dr Shiva's prescription of sedatives, which Jon had insisted on getting from the supermarket pharmacy as soon as Dr Shiva left. When I wake up on Monday, the first thing I do is throw the rest of the pills in the wastepaper bin. Harry is still out there somewhere, and he needs me awake and alert, not comatose.

I know Jon won't be happy about that, so I decide not to tell him.

Our press conference is scheduled for three in the afternoon on Monday.

Late morning, I am sitting cross-legged on the sofa, watching television, and picking at my toast and marmalade without any real appetite.

Day three without my son.

The doorbell rings.

I don't move. Jon is in the kitchen, working on something work-related at the table. He does not seem able to shut off from his job, even when he's not in the office.

Sure enough, I hear him get up and answer the door.

It's Camilla from next door.

'How is she?' she asks in a loud-enough-to-hear whisper.

A moment later, Jon comes into the room, followed by a smiling Camilla. 'Ah, there you are.' He turns off the morning news show I have been watching. 'Camilla has come to see how you're doing.'

Camilla is in her habitual yoga pants and crop top. Her skin is glowing with well-being. 'I can't stay. I'm on my way to give a new class. Eastern Meditation Yoga.'

Jon's lips twitch. 'Sounds good.'

She holds out a Tupperware box, and he takes it. 'I made a batch of wholewheat cookies with raisins. Too many for me and Treve. I thought perhaps . . .'

'That's very kind,' I say, and force myself to smile at her.

'If there's anything Treve and I can do,' she murmurs, looking from me to Jon with sympathetic eyes, 'anything at all, we'd be only too happy to . . .' She draws a sharp breath. 'Anything.'

Jon nods. 'Of course.'

There's an awkward silence.

I put down my plate of uneaten toast. It was cold anyway.

'Well, I'd better go.' Camilla straightens, suddenly brisk and business-like again. 'I'll be late for my class otherwise.'

'I'll show you out.'

'Thank you.'

Jon follows her to the door and into the front garden. I hear their voices at a distance outside, muted, indistinct. Talking about me, no doubt.

Catching my name, I wander out into the hall. The front door is ajar. I can see Jon on the garden path with his back to me, shoulders slumped, head bent, as he struggles to explain something to Camilla. Probably apologising for my offhand behaviour.

Then she hugs him.

I didn't get a hug. But I suppose she thinks he needs comforting more than I do. Because I'm such a flake.

My phone pings.

I return to the living room, studying the screen.

It's another text message from Emily, replying to my previous question.

I don't know anything. But would love to talk if you need it. Do you want to meet for lunch?

I consider the question for a moment, then text back:

Can't. Press conference at 3pm.

I close my eyes. Jon and Camilla are still talking outside. Somewhere overhead I can hear a helicopter circling the town lazily. The phone pings again almost immediately, as though she has been sitting there, waiting for my response.

Before the press conference. Noon at Wetherspoons, Lemon Quay. Bring Jon. Simon's coming too.

I hear the sound of a car starting up. Then Jon comes back into the room. He runs a hand through his hair, looking a little flustered.

'What's that?' he says, staring at the phone in my hand.

'I just had a text from Emily. She wants to know if we'd like to meet her and Simon at Wetherspoons for a quick lunch before the press conference.'

He looks amazed. 'Lunch? When?'

'Noon.' I swallow. 'I'm going to say no, of course. Going out with friends, behaving like nothing's happened. It doesn't feel right.'

'Noon?' He checks the clock on the mantelpiece. 'That's just under an hour away. I don't see why we can't make it.'

'Jon, our baby son is missing. Our desperately sick baby son. And you think it's okay to be going out to lunch with one of your work colleagues?'

'Simon's a good friend, not just a work colleague.' He looks offended. 'Besides, I thought you liked him. And Emily.'

'That's not the point.'

'Then what is the point? It's just lunch, for God's sake. Not a . . . a party.' His voice stutters over the last words. He covers his eyes with his hand. 'Jesus Christ, I don't fucking believe you.'

I open my mouth, then shut it again. I don't know what to say.

'I'm sorry,' he says, still covering his face. 'I just want to feel normal again. Even if it's only for an hour or two.'

Feel normal again?

My hands have tightened into fists, my whole body tense. But I know how this will play out if I do not stop it now. It will end in yet another fight. And I still have to face the press conference this afternoon.

'No,' I tell him with weary resignation. 'If you want to go, then we'll go to lunch with them, of course. I'll text her back. Say yes.'

Jon lowers his hand, staring at me. There's a dark flush along his cheekbones. Rage, I think, and try not to show what I'm feeling.

'You're sure?'

'Definitely.' I force a smile, adding, 'You're right, there's no reason why we should stay home for lunch. And we can make our own way to the press conference. The police have both our mobile numbers if . . . if there's any change.'

'That's exactly what I think,' he agrees, seeming to relax. He glances at my pyjamas. 'You'd better go and get ready, or we'll be late. I have a few work calls to make.'

He leaves the room, whistling under his breath.

It takes a minute to get my composure back. Then I uncross my legs and clamber off the sofa. As soon as my bare feet hit the rug, I feel unsteady and have to deal with vertigo. I count silently in my head, like waiting for a lightning storm to pass over. One, one thousand. Two, one thousand. Three . . .

Glancing down, I wince at the sight of my hands. Each palm is marked with a half-horseshoe of tiny, red marks where my finger-nails have dug into my flesh.

To avoid any hassle with parking, Jon calls a taxi to take us into central Truro. The drive into town brings back memories of my last visit there. Memories I would rather not have but cannot seem to push away. Harry in his buggy, the two of us walking through town, enjoying the sunny day. It is bright again today, just like Friday was, but with clouds threatening rain later.

The taxi driver drops us behind the department store, then we walk through on to the broad, paved pedestrian area of Lemon Quay, so popular with tourists. People are sitting on benches in the sunlight, or emerging from the stores with plastic bags, or watch-ing their kids on the carousel. I always used to stop a moment here to let Harry admire the merry-go-round with its mirrors and bob-bing horses and brightly painted signs. Today Jon and I keep walk-ing, though my head turns and my hungry gaze scours the buggies ranged around the carousel, as though looking for one particular fair-haired baby.

Stupid, really.

From the pedestrian underpass comes the strains of a guitar-playing busker, the low moan of his voice as he performs a Bob Dylan classic. 'It's All Over Now, Baby Blue', I realise, catching the ironical refrain, and wonder if the universe is mocking me.

'Feeling better?' Jon reaches out a hand and I mimic the move-ment with barely a second's hesitation. He links his hand with mine, smiling down at me, and I nod and smile back.

What else am I supposed to do?

As we walk across the square, hand in hand, a raft of pigeons rise as one into the air and flap noisily away, probably heading for the sunlit stretches of the River Truro.

I watch them fly, then hear him whisper in my ear, 'Hey, it's going to be okay. The police will find him.'

'How can you be so sure?'

'DS Dryer rang while you were in the shower. He wanted to be sure we were all set for this afternoon. He said they had some leads.'

'About Harry?'

He hesitates. 'About whoever took him.'

I do not want to be hopeful. The possibility of being mistaken is too painful. But I hear a slight catch in my voice, and know that I cannot help myself. 'Does he know who took him?'

'No,' he concedes reluctantly. 'But apparently they spotted something on CCTV from back when one of the previous babies was taken, some kind of clue, and it's being analysed at the moment. DS Dryer couldn't tell me what it was, but he said it's possible they may be able to identify the snatcher from it.' He squeezes my hand. 'So I don't want you to worry yourself to death over this. The police know what they're doing.'

'Of course.'

I can see Jon does not believe that, any more than I do, but is trying to reassure me. It's surprisingly sweet of him, especially given the terrible strain we've been under these past few days. I have to keep reminding myself that he is suffering too, that I am not the only one caught in this trap. His frayed temper is another sign of the strain he's under. I just wish he could direct it outwards, and not always at me.

A gritty wind suddenly gusts across Lemon Quay, blowing straight off the harbour, and my eyes blur with tears.

'Well, here we are,' he says, and drops my hand. We have reached the pub. 'And look, there's Simon and Emily. They're early.'

He waves as the couple glance towards us, and smiles. 'Brilliant, they've grabbed us an outside table.'

Emily is looking pale and upset. She kisses me twice, once on each cheek, and hugs me tight. 'I'm so sorry,' she says hoarsely. 'You must be going through hell.'

I can't find a reply, but nod.

'If you want to talk,' she adds in my ear, 'I mean, talk properly, just you and me, then let me know. I'm not ready for full-time work again yet, still feeling a little fragile. So anytime, just give me a call or text me.'

Simon has risen from his seat to greet us too. He shakes Jon's hand, then also hugs me, though it's a quick, almost brusque embrace compared to his partner's. 'Meghan. How are you?'

Jon puts an arm around my shoulders before I can say anything, answering for me. 'Bearing up. Right now, we're focused on the press conference this afternoon, hoping it could jog someone's memory.'

He sounds as though he's outside the magistrates' courts, giving a statement on some court case his firm has been handling.

'A brutal business,' Simon mutters, nodding, then pulls out a seat for me. 'Please, Meghan.'

'Thank you.'

I see Emily watching him, her eyes unhappy, shoulders hunched forward, and sense some kind of tension between the pair. I recall she said they had been trying for a baby, but unsuccessfully. Maybe that has something to do with it.

Jon hands me a menu, and I stare down at it blindly while he and Simon chat about work. I wish they had not chosen to sit outside.

The sun is too bright; it's hurting my eyes and making them tear up again.

'Meghan? Shall I just get you something simple?' Jon asks after a few minutes. From his tone, I get the impression it is not the first time he has asked me. 'How about a chicken salad?'

I nod, handing back the menu without having taken in a single item.

'I'll come with you, get the drinks,' Simon offers. He raises his brows at Emily, who shakes her head. Her white wine looks untouched.

I am still considering what I want to drink when Jon suggests a fruit juice for me, and the two men go off together, apparently satisfied by this.

I haven't been able to drink for months. First the pregnancy, then expressing milk for Harry when he was at the hospital, then breastfeeding once we got him home. Though I'm not breastfeeding now. Not anymore.

But I suppose that, if I were to order an alcoholic drink, it could be seen as having given up on getting Harry back. A symbol of defeat. A white wine instead of a white flag. That may be why Jon intervened. Because he saw me hesitate and read my mind.

Couples do that, don't they? Read each other's minds?

'I hope you didn't mind me texting you.' Emily is leaning across the table, keeping her voice low, as though she does not want anyone else to hear. 'Any news at all?'

'Not yet, no.'

'God, that's awful. I don't know how you're doing it.'

I hesitate. 'Doing what?'

'Staying so calm, of course.' She adjusts her glasses, her eyes wide, fixed on me. 'If it was my child who was missing, I'd be climbing the walls by now. A complete basket case.'

'Jon says the police may have some kind of lead on a suspect.' I shrug, helpless to elaborate. 'Meanwhile, all we can do is wait.'

'Well, I think you're incredibly brave. Both of you.'

139

'Thank you.'

'I hope they find him soon. Before . . .'

She gives a sharp sigh but does not finish, looking distraught on my behalf. An onlooker could be forgiven for thinking she is the bereft mother and I the comforting friend.

Jon and Simon return. They have been talking about me, I can tell. Simon shoots me a quick, assessing look as he places the fruit juice – a cloudy and astringent grapefruit, I discover – in front of me.

'Thanks.'

Simon meets my gaze. 'You're welcome.' He hesitates, then asks, 'Jon tells me you've been in touch with your parents. Are they flying over from Spain?'

'I don't know.' I feel rather than see Jon shift restlessly beside me. He does not like my parents, and I am sure he does not want them to visit. But I will need someone with me if the worst happens. 'Perhaps later.'

The unspoken words hang in the air between us like smoke.

If all this goes bad. If Harry never comes back. If Harry's found dead.

'I know you miss them badly. Emily misses her mum sometimes, having to live so far away.' Simon gives me his sympathetic lawyer look. Jon has one just like it, though he stopped using it on me soon after we married. I suppose it works best with people who do not know you intimately, which tends to exclude wives. 'But you've got enough on your plate right now without having to look after house guests. I perfectly understand.'

Jon has definitely been talking to him.

My head turns abruptly.

No, I was not imagining it. I can hear a baby crying somewhere.

It's a faint whine on the breeze at first, pitched high, more like a distant siren than a child. Then it drops and thickens into an angry wail that cuts across the tinkling music from the carousel and the low buzz of voices all around us.

An angry, hungry wail. The wail of a baby demanding to be fed, to be held close, to be loved.

It's Harry.

Chapter Eighteen

My body responds instinctively to that familiar cry, everything tingling and aching again, tightening with love.

'Oh my God,' I say without thinking, staring out across the busy square of shoppers. 'That sounds like Harry. I really think that's Harry.'

'What?' Emily sits up, looking at me blankly from behind her large-rimmed glasses. 'Harry?'

'Help me, help me.' I jump up, then look round urgently at Jon, who has his pint glass partway to his lips. 'Don't you hear him too? Please help me. Where . . . Where is he? Quick, can any of you see him?'

Nobody moves. They just stare at me.

I hear Harry again. That long keening wail when he's hungry.

'Please,' I moan.

I run from the table, knocking over my chair and struggling through the makeshift barrier that separates the pub's outside tables from the square itself. I can still hear that piercing wail somewhere ahead of me through the crowd.

But where?

There are people everywhere.

I stare helplessly, standing on tiptoe to see beyond them to the colour and noise of the carousel, then begin to weave and push between the tight-packed shoppers. But it's slow progress. I have to keep stopping whenever I see a buggy, just to bend down and check, just to be absolutely sure it's not my baby.

There are buggies everywhere, it seems, and parents frowning at me, pre-school kids with helium-filled balloons on ribbons tied round their wrists, old people leaning on sticks, others stopping every few yards to window-shop, a man selling copies of the *Big Issue* at the shadowy mouth to the underpass, a skinny mongrel loyal at his side.

'What the hell are you doing?' one mother accosts me when I turn, staring down at the bald, chubby-faced baby in her three-wheeler buggy.

I can't blame her for being angry.

'Sorry,' I mutter, and run on.

I hear my name called out behind me but do not stop. This is more important. I could lose him if I stop now. May already have lost him.

At the carousel, the crowd is thinner. I come to a halt, bending at the waist, breathing hard, then lift my head and scan all the buggies. Only a few babies the right age. Most of the kids are two and three-year-olds, all pre-schoolers out in the May sunshine. Mothers standing in groups look at me as I slip past. Some of them swear at me, others are frankly shocked when I pay no attention and bend over their prams and buggies, peering at babies' faces.

Then I see a woman crossing the road, pushing a red buggy.

And hear Harry again.

I break into a run once more, knocking into people, thumping my leg against benches and buggies, but by the time I have crossed the busy square and the road beyond, the woman has vanished, wheeling the buggy into the old indoor market along the block from the main theatre in Truro, the Hall for Cornwall.

I do not hesitate but plunge into the market too. The narrow network of aisles feels gloomy out of the sun, and people turn and stare, surprised to see this panting, red-faced woman run past. The way divides once, and then again, a maze of little wooden booths crammed with goods on display and boxes and sales posters, some narrow and pokey, others several booths long.

Numerous women with babies, which I eye from a distance. Not Harry. No sign of a woman with a red buggy either.

I close my eyes, trying to fix an image of her in my mind. Thickset, medium height, greying hair, fairly nondescript. She was wearing a light-blue jacket, and perhaps blue denim jeans, I'm not sure.

I choose one corridor at random and hurry down it, glancing all around in case she's stopped in one of the little shops. One booth-owner is arranging cheap trainers on a stand, and stares at me.

'Can I help you, love?'

'Yes, I . . . I've lost my . . . mother,' I lie, hesitating. 'Grey hair, about my height, blue jacket. With a buggy. Have you seen her?'

The man nods, and points on towards the next row of booths. 'Went past a minute or so ago.' He grins as I start to run. 'Sure I can't sell you some running shoes?'

That reminds me. I've left my handbag back at the pub. And my jacket. And my husband.

Jon will be furious.

I pause at the next intersection, peering along all the aisles, then catch a glimpse of light blue moving rapidly towards the exit into the next street that runs parallel with Lemon Quay. My heart thudding wildly, I take the nearest corridor, nearly knocking an old lady flying as she backs out of a booth entrance with her plaid shopping trolley.

'Sorry,' I shout over my shoulder, feeling awful, but I keep running. That woman's got my baby, and I have to catch her.

Nothing else matters.

Daylight is ahead, a tiled passageway, glass cabinets, books arranged on a stall. I stumble headlong down the steps, bursting out into the sunlit street, and almost collide with a white van pulling into a parking space. The driver leans on his horn, startling me, and I stare up into his angry, bearded face.

'Sorry,' I say again, gasping. 'Sorry.'

I stare about the street, searching every passing face, scouring the crowds for any sign of a greying head and blue jacket, that distinctive red buggy.

'No, no, no.'

I want to scream. I am on the verge of tears, my mouth a grimace, my heart hurting like I've been punched in the chest.

How could I have been so stupid? It was Harry in that red buggy, I'm sure of it. He was right here, within my grasp, and I was too slow. I didn't run fast enough. I didn't look hard enough. I let the woman get away.

I failed him again.

I turn round and round on the spot, looking everywhere, a blur of colours and faces, even staring back into the indoor market. But there is no one in the entrance now but a few astonished shoppers, who immediately look away and pretend not to be watching me. I must look crazed, I suppose. My face is hot, sweat on my forehead, my hair coming loose from my ponytail.

'I've lost him, I've lost him.'

I lean my forehead against the cool stone wall, feeling dizzy. I have no idea what to do now, where to go, who to tell. I have failed Harry again.

A hand on my shoulder makes me jerk violently. It's Jon.

'Meghan, thank God.'

I stare at him. 'I saw Harry,' I tell him desperately. 'I'm sure of it.'

'You saw him?'

I hate the incredulity in his voice. 'That is, I . . . I heard him. Heard him crying.' I see the flicker of scorn in his face. 'I know his cry. It was Harry. I'd stake my life on it.'

'So where is he now?'

I look around helplessly, and feel again the crushing weight of my own failure. The tears begin to come, burning my eyes. 'I don't know.'

'For God's sake, Meghan.'

'I *heard* him.'

He nods. 'You heard a baby. Not Harry.'

'No, I'm certain it was Harry. Some woman had him.' I try to picture her in my mind, but all I can see are a few tantalising glimpses of her greying hair and the blue jacket. 'I only saw her from the back. But I think she was middle-aged, maybe older. Sixty? We have to call the police, make them search the streets for her. She can't have gone far.' A thought hits me. 'What's DS Dryer's number? You need to call him right now.'

'Meghan, slow down. You're not making sense.'

'I'm making perfect sense,' I insist. 'I heard Harry crying. He was in a red buggy being pushed by a woman with grey hair. We have to tell the police.'

'Let me get this straight. You want me to ring DS Dryer, and tell him to arrest any grey-haired grannies he finds pushing buggies round Truro?'

I stare. 'You don't believe me?'

'I want to believe you. But that panic attack the other day, and the way you ran off just now without even a word, all this wild behaviour . . .'

'You expect me to be calm?' I raise my voice, perhaps more than I intend. 'Jon, someone came into our house and took our baby. Who in the world could be fucking calm about that?'

Jon looks at me intently. So intently that I take a step backwards, my back against the wall, suddenly uncomfortable.

'Meghan, have you taken your pills today?' he asks. 'The ones Dr Shiva prescribed for you? They seemed to be helping. You were so much more relaxed yesterday.'

'Yes, because I was totally stoned.'

I see the warning flash in his eyes. I had originally intended to lie to him about the prescription, to keep things calm between us for a little while, but now discover that I can't.

'Answer my question.'

'No,' I admit. 'I didn't take the pills. In fact, I threw the bottle in the bin.'

His mouth tightens as he studies me, then he says, 'You shouldn't have done that.'

I shrug.

'Right, come on.' He glances at the passers-by, as though aware that our argument is attracting some attention. 'I can't take you back to the pub in this state. We'll have to take a taxi straight to the press conference instead. If you're hungry, we can always grab a pizza on the way home afterwards.'

He steers me off the pavement and away from the indoor market.

I go with him, momentarily thrown by his forcefulness and unsure what to do. But the old road is cobbled and uneven, and one of my wedge heels catches between the stones.

'Wait,' I say urgently. 'My shoe.'

Jon stops, watching while I adjust my shoe. The heels are not high, only a few inches. But they are not made for crossing cobbled streets. He runs a hand through his hair, his tone distracted. 'I'll ring Simon in the taxi, give him our excuses.'

'But my bag . . .'

'I've got it,' he tells me, and holds it up. 'And your jacket.'

I think about Emily. She remarked on how calmly I was taking Harry's abduction. Now what will she be thinking? Simon had just bought me a drink too. Our lunches will be waiting.

'No,' I say again, more firmly, and straighten up. Our eyes meet. I see the angry jut of his chin and waver, almost giving in. Then I remember how he would try to railroad me into decisions before we were married, and only capitulate if I stood up to him. 'I want to go back to the pub and have lunch. I'm okay now.'

This time, standing up to him does not work.

'That's too bad,' he says curtly, and grabs my elbow, hustling me forward. His fingers hurt my arm, gripping me so violently, but when I make a distressed sound under my breath, he only pushes harder. 'Come on, stop fussing. There's a taxi rank five minutes' walk from here, not far from my office.'

We are halfway across the road, with a car heading towards us, when I stop dead.

'No, I'm not going,' I say.

'*What?*'

'I'm not going to the taxi rank with you,' I tell him breathlessly. 'I'm going back to the pub. I want to see Emily and . . . and talk to her.'

The car slows. The driver sounds his horn.

'Meghan, for God's sake.'

He tries to pull me forward. But I wrench my arm free from his iron grip and turn, fleeing back across the cobbles to the pavement, flushed and unsteady, not really looking where I'm going. The driver, who has tried to navigate round us, has to slam on his brakes to avoid hitting me.

I hear Jon swear, but keep running.

All I can think about is Harry. Jon can say what he likes about my state of mind, but I *heard* him, and I know it was my son.

Jon catches up with me on the narrow pavement a few feet from Lemon Quay. 'Stop,' he says furiously, and drags me round to face him. We are blocking the pavement and people have to step into the busy road to get past. 'You could have been killed back there. What the hell are you trying to do, Meghan?'

'Have lunch.'

'Don't be bloody smart with me, or I swear I'll——' Jon stops mid-threat, suddenly aware that we are being overheard, and takes a reluctant step back, releasing me.

A weathered-looking man of around sixty has hesitated in passing, glancing from Jon's face to mine, then stopped beside us. He is wearing a bulky fisherman's sweater and leaning on a stick, but not with his full weight. I expect he could use it as a weapon if he wanted.

'You all right, love?' the man asks, focusing on me, though I can see that he is very aware of Jon's icy glare.

He has smiling eyes, wrinkled around the lids, a grandfather type. I know he would protect me if I asked. But I can't drag a stranger into this. Especially someone well over twice Jon's age.

'Fine, thank you,' I tell the man, though it is obvious from my high-pitched voice that nobody here is fine. Taking a breath, I add more calmly, 'He's my husband.'

The man glances at Jon again, a very stern look on his face, then shrugs and moves on without saying anything.

I wait for the explosion. But to my surprise it does not come. Instead, Jon looks at me coldly. 'Go, then,' he says, and hands me my bag.

I do not move, confused. I blink up at him in the sunlight. 'What?'

Go, then.

For a few dizzying seconds I think he's leaving me. That he's finally had enough of me and this marriage. The worst thing is that I am almost relieved, until I realise that's not what he means.

'Back to the pub. For lunch with Simon and Emily. *My* friends.' Unsmiling, Jon nods in the direction of Lemon Quay. 'That's what you want, isn't it? So let's do it.'

I have never seen him like this before. There is something in his voice that terrifies me. But I turn and keep walking along the narrow pavement, aware of him a few steps behind me the whole way.

Go, then.

Chapter Nineteen

Simon has to get back to work after lunch but Emily volunteers to come with us to the press conference. By then my head is screaming and I am grateful not to be alone with Jon, even for a few minutes.

'Thank you,' I tell her.

'As long as I'm not intruding,' she says, and glances at Jon while he's talking to Simon. 'I just thought you could do with some support. All those cameras, you know. I expect it can be quite intimidating.' She pauses, then adds, 'Though I'm sure you'll be fine.'

Somehow her reassurance makes me feel more nervous. But I know she means well, so I smile and nod.

'Good luck, Meghan,' Simon tells me before leaving, and he bends to give me a warm kiss on the cheek, very near my lips. I am not expecting it, and look up at him, surprised. But his smile is innocent when he straightens, and aimed at both of us. 'If you need me later, for advice or whatever, just call.'

Once Simon has gone, Jon rings for a cab. 'Five minutes,' he tells us, a touch of strain in his voice, then disappears inside to the toilets.

I shiver in the breeze, and catch a hint of salt air. We are quite close to the sea here, something that always surprises me, because

Truro feels like an inland city when you're walking around it. I remember only last week, taking the path that runs alongside the river, trying to point out the seabirds to Harry as they swept over the long shimmer of water, and promising him we would go to the beach once the weather was warmer. I was never sure how much he was taking in on our walks, but his sleepy gurgles were always enough for me.

I miss him so much, it hurts to remember.

Emily finishes her drink, then looks at me compassionately. 'Are you feeling better now?' She leans forward to touch my hand. 'We were so worried. Did you really . . . I mean, you thought you saw Harry, is that why you ran off like that?'

I nod, and am relieved when she does not look pitying or tell me I must have been mistaken, merely accepting what I have said.

She rummages in her handbag for a compact, then checks her make-up in the mirror. There's an odd, contorted furtiveness about the way she applies fresh lipstick, bending almost into her bag, as though to conceal what she is doing. The shade is a very pale pink, almost translucent, so that it's not obvious she is wearing lipstick at all. But she smacks her lips together twice afterwards, and seems satisfied with the result.

Her flowery blue-and-white blouse is nothing I would ever wear, and it seems to be missing a button. But it suits her personality, I realise.

'You look nice,' I say.

Emily stares at me, then hurriedly throws her paraphernalia back into her bag and zips it up. As though she is ashamed. 'Thank you.'

'And it's very kind of you to come with us this afternoon. I must admit, I'm feeling a bit . . .' I struggle but fail to find the right word. Or one that won't make me sound like I need to be committed. 'It's been a very difficult few days.'

'I'm not surprised. If I had a baby, and someone stole him . . .' Emily's fists clench, perhaps unconsciously, and she stares across the square with a blank expression. 'I'd probably want to *kill* them.'

The venom in her voice makes me hesitate.

'I just want Harry back safe.'

She nods, her gaze snapping back to my face. 'Of course you do.' Then she asks abruptly, 'Do you like Camilla?'

'She's a good neighbour.'

'But as a person?'

I am unsure what she wants from me, and sense some underlying hostility. 'Camilla has a tendency to say things without thinking first. Especially when she's been drinking. But I don't think she does it deliberately to hurt people.' I frown, thinking back. 'Did she upset you the other night?'

She does not answer that, but says instead, 'It felt very deliberate to me.'

'She was drunk.'

She stands up. Jon is coming back from the toilets. 'Treve doesn't like her either,' she mutters.

'What?'

But she never answers, because Jon is there again, smiling in a false way, helping me gently into my jacket as if I'm an invalid, then handing me my bag with a murmured, 'There you go, darling.'

It's as though the row in the street never happened. As though he has wiped the whole terrible incident from his mind.

My arm still aches where he gripped me though, forcing me to go with him. I didn't imagine that, and I can't erase it with a smile and an understanding look. Not this time. I haven't had a chance to check, but I know there'll be bruises there by now, soft purplish marks springing up where his fingers touched.

He holds out his hand for mine, but Emily jumps in. 'Please, walk with me,' she says, and he hesitates, then steps aside, still smiling.

Emily points out the carousel. 'So pretty,' she says into my ear. 'But I hated them when I was a kid. It used to terrify me, all that spinning round and round. Like you're stuck on there forever, and everything outside is a blur.'

'Did you mean what you said about Treve and Camilla?'

She looks away, shaking her head, but I don't believe her. 'Pay no attention to me. I'm in a catty mood. Everyone's relationship is different, isn't it?'

I look at her, catching something in her voice, but she is smiling. We follow Jon, walking arm in arm through the square towards the waiting taxi. There's a fishmonger among the few stalls set out in the square; as we pass, I smell the fresh fish on his stall, and turn my head, catching a horrific glimpse of dead eyes, long rows of scaly bodies packed on ice, as the white tarpaulin flaps to and fro.

I stumble, suddenly nauseous. But Emily squeezes my arm, and I smile at her hesitantly. Yes, I need to focus on the press conference. Get through that and then . . .

Even if Jon disapproves, I need to tell DS Dryer what happened today. Though now, thinking back, I'm finding it harder and harder to believe my own account. How could I have been so sure that it was Harry?

It had sounded like my baby. But I could have been mistaken.

Above the city centre, the ornately carved spires of the cathedral rise into the blue; beyond them clouds are starting to pucker together, a darkening mass that threatens rain later. I stare up at the three famous spires. I don't believe in God, never really felt a need before now. But with Harry's disappearance, perhaps it would not do any harm to go into the cathedral and light a candle for him.

Desperation, that's what that would be. Sheer bloody desperation.

We're not there yet, I tell myself.

We squeeze into the back of the taxi together, smiling at each other like it's a pleasure outing, an entertainment. But my heart is thudding horribly now, and my palms are clammy, and all I can think about as the taxi pulls away from the kerb is that woman with the buggy, and Harry's high-pitched wail cutting above the rest of the noise. Why should I allow myself to feel like a fraud? It was him, it had to be him.

So why didn't Jon let me call the police? Why didn't I call the police myself? What kind of mother am I?

Everyone's relationship is different, isn't it?

Sitting on the top table at the press conference is a hellish experience: so many camera lenses focused on my face, so many faces turned in my direction.

DS Dryer begins to speak.

The mics set up in front of us are intimidating and slightly alien, not only a reminder that what we are about to say may be broadcast to the world, but also that we are out of our depth here. No previous experience has prepared either of us for this ordeal. Is it any wonder that Jon is on the edge of his temper all the time, that we can barely say a civil word to each other in private?

DS Dryer's voice is calm and level, though I catch a hint of fatigue in his face. He has not managed to shave today, so has a dark stubble-shadow about his chin and jaw, though clearly he has combed his hair back, probably splashed his face with water too. But before we were led into the room, he admitted that he had not been to bed last night, that he had spent the past twenty-four hours chasing various leads – with little success so far.

He's a good man. It's not his fault the police have so little to go on.

I listen as he explains the circumstances of the case so far, then outlines the steps they have taken during the investigation, and I think again of the dead baby they found, whose identity has not yet been confirmed by the police. I remember the muddy field and the pure white of the forensics suits, and feel my heart jolt as though crashing. It may not be Harry they found, but *what if it had been?* What if my baby son's body is the next one some rambler stumbles across in a wood or finds concealed in a plastic bag in a roadside ditch? What if we are sitting here in another few days or weeks, facing these cameras again, talking about Harry in the past tense?

I am filled with a burning impulse to tell the journalists that Harry is out there right now, somewhere in Truro, and that I saw him. Or rather *heard* him.

But of course who would believe me?

Even Jon does not believe me.

Everyone is staring at us, like we are strange new exhibits at the zoo. I want to growl and snarl, maybe scratch under my arms like a chimpanzee, give them something really startling to stare at, not just this lost little woman and her husband.

Jon would kill me.

I begin to be glad of Emily's reassuring presence at the back of the hall, her eyes steady on my face too, but friendly, non-judgemental. Jon is sitting close beside me, of course, his knee touching mine, our hands linked on the cloth-covered table top. My husband. The father of my child. But there's so much tension coming off him, it's more like sitting next to a man with a bomb than a supportive husband. So I lock my throat shut and stare past the terrifying rows of journalists and photographers and cameras, focusing on Emily instead. She is a safe place in a room of dangerous, bristling . . .

Jon squeezes my hand, and I realise that I have been making little sobbing noises under my breath.

I swallow the sobs, tighten my lips and slip my hand out from under his. It suddenly makes me feel ill to have him touch me. That tiny shift should be barely noticeable to the watching journalists, I hope, but will be enough to make my feelings plain.

Rebellion. Of a kind.

Emily does not smile, but seems to nod slightly, both hands clasped about the strap of her shoulder bag, her flowery blouse rucked up, light-brown hair a bit windswept.

My friend.

People can surprise you at times of crisis, I find myself thinking, having previously dismissed Emily as a bit of a flake, frankly.

I feel my breathing start to calm down. My mind settles on the comforting knowledge that, if I did hear Harry today, and didn't imagine the whole thing, then he is alive. That whoever that grey-haired woman is, and for whatever reason she has taken my son away, she must at least be looking after him, perhaps even making sure he is getting his medication.

Suddenly, I hear my name, and glance at DS Dryer to see him looking back at me expectantly. The room is silent.

He has just introduced us.

'Good afternoon,' Jon says, leaning forward to the microphone. 'Thank you all for coming. My wife and I are very grateful. And we hope that, as DS Dryer outlined, by making ourselves available to questions at the end of this session, we will be allowed some privacy at our home during this very difficult time.'

He sounds surprisingly cool and detached, I realise, more like another policeman than the father of one of the missing babies. His training as a lawyer, I suppose.

I ought to be grateful that one of us at least is not falling apart.

But for some reason his ability to stay calm is having the opposite effect on me. I look at my husband's face and resent him. Resent his cool demeanour and high-handed assurances that Harry will be found, and particularly his arrogant belief that I must be going out of my mind for having claimed I could pick Harry out of a crowd *just by his cry*.

But you are going out of your mind, an inner voice tells me. *And everyone here knows it.*

I keep my eyes on Jon's face, listening to the blood beating in my veins. I feel faint and have to cling on to the table top to stay upright. He is begging whoever has the stolen babies to return them, and if they have Harry, to return him to us, explaining that our son has a serious condition, that he needs constant medication. Hands go up in the audience at once, and voices call out for more information, but he ignores them.

He turns to me, his face very serious. 'Anything you want to add to that, Meghan?'

To my own amazement, I nod.

'Yes, yes, I do,' I reply in a voice that does not tremble as badly as I had feared.

Several journalists at the back shout that they can't hear me, and I stop, momentarily thrown, not sure what to do.

'Speak into the mic,' DS Dryer tells me.

'Right, thanks.' I lean towards the microphone, and look deliberately at Emily. Focus on her so I can't get distracted by everything else that's happening. She pushes her glasses back along her nose, then gives me a quick thumbs-up gesture, which is somehow more reassuring than anything Jon could have said to me.

What do I want to say to the press?

That's easy.

Jon discussed the plan with me before we sat down. Show emotion but keep calm, talk about Harry and how much he means to us, use his name as often as possible, let the kidnapper know they have the power – and hope they will use it for good by releasing him.

'I love my darling little boy very much,' I begin, slowly and clearly. 'And I want to say to . . . to whoever has taken Harry that . . . that . . .'

As I hesitate, a few cameras start going off, flashes blinding me; the heat from the arc lights they've set up feels suddenly overwhelming. There's sweat on my forehead, trickling into my eyes. I stare blindly through the journalists, some of them standing now, and realise I can't see Emily anymore.

Has she gone?

She seems such a shy little creature at times, and a bit kooky, not quite with it. But then I remember her unexpected response outside the pub, saying what she would do if she had a baby and someone stole him. Emily was transformed for that instant from a kitten to a lioness. A lioness who would rip out the throat of anyone threatening her child, and think nothing of it.

I lick my lips, my throat dry, then continue, 'That if you don't give me back my son safe and well, I'm going to hunt you down and kill you.'

Chapter Twenty

Outside the room where the press conference is being held, in a narrow corridor that smells vaguely of drains, we find a handful of people waiting for us. A man in a flat tweed cap and a woman, who both look to be in their early forties, and two other women, one clearly younger than me, the other older and dressed very differently, though they share the same square jaw and slightly bulging blue eyes. Sisters, perhaps?

DS Dryer murmurs in my ear, 'Some of the other parents.'

I throw a questioning look at him.

'Of missing babies,' he elaborates.

I examine their faces more carefully. Perhaps I'm expecting them to be waving pitchforks. I'm guiltily aware that I did our cause little good back there, and no doubt they know it too. Someone may have told them what I said, the stupid threat I made. Perhaps they were even watching on a monitor, or standing at the back of the room, behind that intimidating forest of cameras and mics.

'Jon,' I say urgently, plucking at his sleeve. 'I'm feeling tired. Especially after what happened at lunch. Perhaps we should go straight home.'

DS Dryer frowns. 'Something happened at lunch?'

Jon puts his arm around my shoulder, smiling at the policeman. 'Nothing. It was nothing,' he says. His lawyer voice. 'We were at Lemon Quay. You know how busy it gets there. Babies in buggies, the noise of the carousel. Meghan *thought* she heard Harry crying, that's all.'

'I didn't *think* anything. I definitely heard him.'

'Now, darling, you know it's impossible for anyone to pick out one baby's cry above all the others in such a large public place. Do be sensible.' He looks down at me searchingly. 'Perhaps you aren't up to meeting anyone right now. I could do it alone.'

'No,' I say quickly.

'Then maybe Dr Shiva should see you again. You had a good day yesterday.'

Yes, I think grimly. *When I was drugged up to the eyeballs.*

DS Dryer meets my gaze. 'Can you tell me about it, Meghan? Where exactly were you when you had this sighting? Perhaps we could find some CCTV footage.'

'I never actually . . . That is, I didn't see him for sure.' I look at both men, and my voice falters. 'There was a middle-aged woman with a red buggy. She walked through the covered market off Lemon Quay. Grey hair, blue jacket. I didn't see her face. Or the baby's. But I heard his cry.' Since he appears to be taking me seriously, I add more firmly, 'It was Harry. I swear it.'

'I'll get DC Gerent to sit down with you later and take those details,' he says, nodding. 'Then we'll see what we can find out. And do please call me Paul.'

'Thanks, Paul.'

Jon glances at the people waiting to talk to us. The other parents. He makes a face, and mutters in my ear, 'God, do we really have to do this right now? I need a drink.'

But it's too late to retreat. DS Dryer is already shaking their hands and muttering words of comfort before turning expectantly back to us.

'This is Jack and Serena Penrose,' the detective sergeant tells us, his air suitably sombre as he introduces the other parents.

Only four others though.

I think of the body in the field, and can't imagine how that baby's parents must be feeling. The pain and loss must be indescribable.

'Their son, Tom, was taken a few weeks ago,' he continues. 'Jack, Serena, can I introduce Jon and Meghan Smith to you? Baby Harry only went missing on Friday. I expect you heard the press conference just now.'

He waits while the four of us shake hands, then smiles at the two other women, who have been waiting patiently to one side. 'And this is Heather Mackie, Poppy's mum. And Heather's aunt, Kate. Poppy was taken shortly before Tom.'

All four of them look slumped and exhausted, their faces drawn in pain, like life has taken a stick to their backs. Fleetingly, I wonder if that's what we look like too. And we have only suffered a few days of this torment. What will it be like if this ordeal is dragged out for weeks or even months, as it has been for the Penrose and Mackie families?

'Hello,' I say with a weak attempt at a smile, shaking Heather's hand, then Kate's.

Heather is wearing a loose orange T-shirt and a hippyish pair of red tartan trousers that sit low on her slim hips. She looks about twenty, maybe. Kate is older, her dark skirt and white blouse more sober and conventional. She is supporting her niece, a protective arm about her shoulders.

'Excuse me, I have to speak to a colleague,' DS Dryer says, and hurries away down the corridor, leaving us alone with the other parents.

Jack Penrose is frowning heavily when I turn back. 'I'm sorry to be rude,' he begins, looking directly at me, not Jon, 'but why did you have to say that? That you'll kill whoever's taken your baby?'

His wife bobs her head in agreement. 'Yes, you shouldn't have said that about hunting them down. That was crazy talk. What if it makes her angry?'

'Her?' Jon repeats.

'Or him, then.' Serena Penrose shrugs. She and her husband both have strong Cornish accents, and I guess by his tweed jacket and her dark-green overjacket, marked with dried splashes of mud, that they are farmers of some kind. 'It's usually a woman though, isn't it? When it's babies. That's what I've been told.'

'I've heard that too.' Poppy's mother, Heather, is nodding. She has a round, slightly flushed face, and jagged-edged hair. Did she cut it herself? I can tell that she is as annoyed with me as the others are. But her voice is softer, less emphatic. 'I was speaking to a psychologist at Truro College last week. She thinks it's probably a woman who's taken them. Unless it's a couple, with one egging the other on. That's how these things work.'

I stare at her, and wonder for the first time if it could be a couple behind Harry's abduction. Hard to believe though. Surely one would get cold feet and give themselves up to the police in the end? But then I remember Myra Hindley and Ian Brady, their fierce loyalty to each other, and shudder.

Perhaps a couple is actually worse, if it leads to obsession.

Her aunt speaks at last. 'Either way though,' Kate says, her disapproving look aimed at me, 'I don't think it was a good idea to antagonise them. They've got our babies, remember? They could do anything they like to them.' Her eyes fill with tears. 'You know, out of revenge for what you said.'

'I didn't mean to say it,' I tell them, feeling awful. 'Honestly, it wasn't rehearsed. It just came out.'

Jon loops his arm about my waist, as though in support of my statement. 'What my wife means to say is that she's very sorry. She was angry and scared. And because of that, she made a mistake.'

He looks round at them all, then settles on Jack Penrose's face. Maybe he thinks he's the leader, if there can be such a thing in this dubious club we've joined.

'I'm sure you can understand that,' he continues smoothly. 'When somebody's frightened, they often say things they regret afterwards. All those journalists, the cameras . . . It's only human to be a little knocked off balance.'

Heather exclaims, 'Absolutely,' instantly sympathetic. She turns to me with a forgiving smile. 'I felt the same when I did my appeal. If Kate hadn't been there . . .'

Her aunt squeezes her shoulder and Heather falls silent.

'It was quite an intimidating experience, I have to admit,' Kate remarks. 'But Heather and I got through it with a little careful preparation. It's just a question of staying calm.'

'I'm sorry,' I say, and wish Jon had not made it so obvious that I had not apologised before. It wasn't very helpful, as they now look at me without much interest, as though my apology has lost all validity by not being given at once. 'I'm not very good at being calm under pressure. I've always been a bit . . .'

'Hare-brained,' Jon supplies with a wry smile for their benefit when I hesitate, and Jack Penrose gives a grudging laugh.

'I was going to say easily panicked,' I mutter, but nobody is listening.

'Well, I suppose that's some kind of excuse,' Serena Penrose is saying, and everyone looks at her instead, taking the attention off me. I should probably be relieved by Jon's intervention, but instead I feel ridiculous and unimportant. Like a child who has misbehaved in the company of adults. 'It was still potentially damaging though. As Kate here says, this sick person who's taken our children can do whatever she likes to them. And we can't lift a finger to stop her. So using a press conference to threaten her life is the very worst thing you could have done.'

Her husband adds deeply, 'Look at what happened to that other poor boy.'

'Charlie,' his wife whispers.

'That's right, Charlie Pole. The remains they found in the field.'

My stomach clenches.

I'm going to hunt you down and kill you.

Jon is looking horrified. 'God, yes. That was appalling. We saw it on the telly, but we didn't know his name. The police wouldn't tell us.'

I remember driving out there like a lunatic. The cold stretch of the fields, the sea in the distance, the mud, the creaking gate . . .

'The Pole family want to keep things quiet while they arrange the funeral. The press have respected their privacy so far. Not sure how long that will last, of course. You know what those vultures are like. I expect it will be all over the papers in another day or two.' Jack shakes his head. 'But everyone knows locally, of course. Such a lovely young family, Cornish born and bred. And now they've lost their baby son.'

'That's right,' his wife agrees. 'And we don't want to lose ours. You know what I'm saying?'

'I'm sorry,' I say again.

Heather Mackie puts a hand on my arm. 'Don't worry,' she says hesitantly, but I can see it's costing her an effort to be kind to me. 'Meghan, is it?'

I nod silently, on the verge of tears.

'Let's go and get a coffee together, Meghan. I don't agree with what you said. But it's done now, and there's no point crying over spilt milk.'

'Well put,' her aunt says loudly, and even smiles at me and Jon in a restrained fashion. 'I think a quick coffee is an excellent idea. Jack, Serena, will you join us?' She pauses, glancing round at the others. 'After all, nobody else can understand the hell we're going through. So it makes sense for us to stick together.'

Chapter Twenty-One

I hear the slam of the front door early the next morning, and scramble out of bed and to the bedroom window just in time to see our car disappearing down the street.

Bewildered, I glance at the bedside clock.

07.10.

Stumbling downstairs, I find Jon's briefcase and overcoat are both gone. He's also taken the files and documents he was working on in the lounge last night. I open the front door pointlessly and peer out. The neatly shorn grass of our lawn is sparkling. The street is quiet, as it usually is at this hour. It is raining lightly, little dark speckles beginning to appear on paving stones and car windscreens, but the sun is shining at the same time.

Perhaps there will be a rainbow later.

He must have gone to the office early, I decide, and hope that by the time he returns from work this evening, he will be approachable again. Not the cold creature who dismissed me last night without any sign of love or affection.

Day four without Harry.

Whoever took him must have run out of medication by now.

The thought makes me despair.

I trudge back upstairs to the bathroom, but cannot find the energy for a shower. After a restless night, my hair needs brushing. Detangling, even. I stare at it helplessly, not sure where I left my comb.

I thought he was going to stay home from work until . . .

The faint sound of a telephone ringing makes me stop and listen. Not ours, of course, not loud enough. Next door's, then. And being semi-detached, that means Treve and Camilla's landline. Vaguely, I recall raised voices from last night, car headlights over the bedroom ceiling. I assumed they were having a row. But has something more serious happened, perhaps? I imagine a sick relative, a late-night mercy dash, and now more news, the phone ringing early before either of them has left for work.

The telephone stops ringing. I hear nothing more.

This is how sad my life has become, I think, gazing at myself in the bathroom mirror. Trapped in the house, living for other people's phone calls.

I decide to get dressed for the day, not stay in my pyjamas on the assumption that nothing is going to happen. Then at least if *my* landline rings, or my mobile buzzes, and it's news of Harry – good news, perhaps, that he has been found and is waiting for me – then I will be able to leave the house at once.

Today is the first day I do not bother with a nursing bra. I select one of my pregnancy bras instead, and am depressed to see that it fits, if a little tightly, the cups not quite big enough. Soon I will be able to wear my pre-pregnancy bras. The upside is that I can select a top that does not need to unbutton easily or is large enough to lift discreetly for feeding.

I wriggle into one of my old T-shirts, and consider myself in the mirror.

Not too bad.

Apart from my little pot-belly, you would never guess I have recently had a baby. Strange how easily that harassed, shuffling, earth-mother look can be shed, once the reason for it is gone.

As I am pulling my jeans on, I hear voices below in the street. I push the wardrobe door shut, and wander to the window.

It's the gold Volvo again. Double-parked two doors down, someone at the wheel, the engine running. I can hear it, a low humming in the quiet morning.

I stare, my breath catching in my throat.

The number plate.

But I cannot see it, not from this angle. There's a hatchback in the way, parked on this side, facing the opposite way.

I run downstairs, throw open the front door, and charge outside barefoot.

It's raining more heavily now, a spring shower that has left the path gleaming. I ignore the feel of slippery stone under my bare feet and fling myself out of the gate just in time to see the Volvo accelerating away down the street. Not with any particular urgency, but it's already too late. The car is too far away for me to see the number plate. Not even a single letter or digit.

I run after it anyway, though it is pointless. Perhaps if the car stops . . .

The driver signals right as he or she slows for the crossroads ahead, and I wish for heavy traffic to keep them there a few moments, for engine trouble, a miracle. But I am not so lucky. I have only run a hundred yards towards it when the car turns slowly, methodically, towards the road out of town and disappears.

'Fuck it.' I stop dead where I am, my feet wet, and look up, suddenly aware of the rain pelting down. I'm gasping, struggling to get my breath back; it must be months since I went to the gym. I bang the nearest gate with my fist, and it shudders under the blow. 'Fuck it, fuck it.'

'Hey,' someone shouts at me from the doorway of the house. 'Hey, don't hit gate. Get lost, crazy bitch.'

It's one of my neighbours, a strange shambling sort of man who never speaks to anyone. Except apparently now.

I look round at him. He's standing on the doorstep, as barefoot as I am, but in a creased grey flannel dressing gown. He has a dark, shaggy beard with grey streaks in it and long hair that reaches his shoulders; his age is somewhere in his forties, at a guess. His hair is usually tied back, but he looks wilder than usual today. Probably because of the early hour, or perhaps because he has found some woman thumping his garden gate.

It may be the look in his eyes, or his dishevelled demeanour, but I imagine a man like this has a bottle of pills on his bedside table just like the ones Dr Shiva prescribed for me, only he takes his instead of throwing them in the bin.

'Sorry,' I say, only now realising where I am and what I am doing. I step back, raising my hands to indicate I have finished my attack on his gatepost. 'Sorry.'

But he is not satisfied with an apology.

'Get away from here, you crazy bitch,' he tells me, spitting out the words, really getting himself wound up. His beard flaps as he shouts, the hairs long and straggling. I hear an accent that isn't Cornish. Some kind of Eastern European lilt. He may even be Russian. 'I see you with that baby.'

'What?'

'No baby today, huh? Maybe you too mad to have baby.'

You crazy bitch.

'It was you,' I say suddenly, staring at him. A moment of terrible revelation burns itself into the inside of my skull. 'You're the one.'

He only lives a hundred yards or so from us; he must have seen me out with Harry many times since we brought him home from the hospital, wheeling him up and down the street in the buggy.

'What's your name?' I demand unsteadily, advancing on him down the garden path.

His eyes widen and he steps back inside his hallway. 'I told you, go away, crazy bitch,' he repeats, and starts to shut the door. 'Get lost, I call police.'

I reach the door before he can close it, and push back. Hard, with all my strength. He's not going to get away with this. 'What's your name? Let me in. I want to see inside your house. Who else lives there?'

'Get lost, get lost, get lost,' he begins to chant, his voice deep and panicked, and puts his shoulder to the door.

I lose the battle for the door, and it clicks shut in my face. He's strong and well built, and I'm barefoot; I can't even stick my foot in the gap. I hear him locking the door against me, bolting it too, top and bottom, then putting on a rattling chain.

Like Fort Knox.

The door has been painted black at some time in its history, but is very dusty and scratched now. The step is chipped too, and covered in leaf debris and bits of rubbish. The place has a general air of neglect; I wonder if he is a tenant rather than an owner. I can't believe I have never looked at him properly before today, that he has been living here for months without me taking the smallest notice. But as I recall, he does not come out of the house very often, and when he does, it's only to walk to the one-stop shop, probably for the cigarettes I see him smoking in his front garden sometimes, wearing a black cap, his neck wrapped in a red-and-black scarf against the cold, like a throwback to the Bolsheviks.

I bend and peer through the caged letterbox. But someone seems to have covered the cage on the other side with some dark cloth to stop people seeing into the hallway.

I shout through the letterbox, 'I know it was you.'

'Crazy bitch.'

171

'I know it was you!' I scream at him. 'You've been watching us. You took my baby. And I'm going to tell the police.'

He says nothing more, but I hear him breathing harshly behind the door. Then he shuffles away and an internal door slams.

I hop across into his garden – plain concrete with a few over-grown pots – and rap on the front windows with my knuckles. The windows are filthy; it looks like nobody has cleaned them in years. I shout again, and bang on them with my fist; the glass shudders in the frame, just like the gate. I try to peer inside, cupping my hands against the glass, but the windows are so heavily curtained, I can see no gaps anywhere, and can hear nothing.

I return to the door.

'Harry,' I shout through the letterbox, and listen for a few minutes before calling his name again, though of course I know he's a baby and cannot answer me. But perhaps if he is in the house, he will hear my voice and know that I'm nearby. Or perhaps if I wait here long enough, I will hear him cry, and then I could use one of the old plant pots to break in through one of these downstairs windows . . .

But there is nothing. No sound at all.

I straighten up, crying bitterly. The rain has stopped but my hair and clothes are soaked and I am shivering. I feel so helpless on my own; if only Jon had not gone into the office today.

Crazy bitch.

Anger floods me. I have to get home, call the police, let them know . . .

But when I run back to the house, I see Treve coming along the road wearing a black hooded pullover and jeans. He is carrying shopping bags from the local one-stop shop. His head is down, face hidden, hood still up against the rain, even though it stopped raining several minutes ago. He seems intent on his own business; he has not noticed me yet.

'Treve,' I say, running up to him before he reaches his own front gate. 'Treve, I need you.'

He looks up then, a startled expression on his face. He was listening to music, I realise. He pulls an earplug out of one ear and stares at me. 'Meghan?'

'I think I've found him,' I gasp, and then lean forward, trying to get my breath back. I want to sound at least vaguely coherent.

He pulls out the other earplug, then turns off his iPod, eyes narrowed on my face. 'What?'

'Just down the road here. Quick, will you help me?'

Briefly, I explain the situation while Treve listens, his gaze fixed on me. He does not protest or suggest I am mistaken, which is a relief, for even I am beginning to worry that I may have overreacted again. He takes a few minutes to put his shopping inside his house, then locks up again.

'Camilla's at work this morning,' he explains, then shoots me a quick smile. 'Do you think you should put some shoes on first?'

I glance down, taken aback, and only then realise that I'm still barefoot. 'Oh God, yes. Sorry, you must think . . . I ran out without shoes, you see.'

I can see from his expression that he is concerned for my mental state, so decide not to explain about the Volvo. And now that I think about it, I can see how insane that would sound anyway. Why would a child abductor come back to the place of the abduction and just double-park there in plain view? It makes no sense whatsoever.

'Of course,' he says, nodding. 'Look, you pop inside and grab some shoes, then you can show me which house you mean.'

I hesitate.

'I'll keep an eye on the street,' he reassures me. 'Your Eastern European friend isn't going anywhere. Or not without me spotting him.'

'Thanks.'

I feel so much better with Treve on my side. But when I step into the empty house, I find myself hating the cold mockery of its silence more than ever. The front door was left wide open; I didn't even pick up my keys on the way out. Anyone could have wandered in, helped themselves to my handbag, to our televisions and our audio system, even to my laptop, sitting on the side in the kitchen.

I check everything is still where I left it. Then, feeling foolish, I take the stairs two at a time to my bedroom, pull on some socks, wriggle my feet into my trainers, then kneel to lace them up.

Glancing at myself in the floor-length mirror, I'm horrified by my appearance. I treated that bearded man contemptuously because he looked so unkempt, like someone on the fringes of society. Yet my own hair is all over the place, damp fringe plastered to my forehead, my eyes wide, my face pale and strained without any makeup. My clothes are soaked, my T-shirt clinging to my skin in a way that is almost obscene.

I look frankly mad.

I drag off the wet T-shirt, and grab a pink sweatshirt instead, one of the ones I used to wear to the gym before I fell pregnant, and pull it over my damp bra. Using my fingers, I try to tidy my hair as best I can. Then I hesitate, and slick on some sugary pink lipstick as an afterthought.

I'm presentable again. Just about.

I hurry back downstairs, pick up my keys from the hall table, and find Treve waiting patiently by the gate, studying his smartphone with apparent absorption.

'Treve, I've been thinking,' I say, feeling shaky and not sure that I want to go back to that house. 'Perhaps we should just call the police.'

Slipping the phone into his back pocket, he considers that suggestion. 'Better go round there first, talk to this guy, don't you think? If, after that, you still have a reasonable suspicion that he's got Harry hidden away in there, that would be the time to call the police. Otherwise, you risk . . .'

'Looking stupid,' I supply, finishing his thought.

He says nothing, but lifts his shoulders in a quick, ironic shrug.

'Right,' I mutter.

I shut the front door and check that it's locked, then pocket my keys. I smile at him. He is very polite and does not comment on my change of clothes, though he must have got a good eyeful of my nipples when I was doing my Miss Wet T-shirt impression. It's good to have his company. Now that I am not alone, I feel much calmer, more rational.

I say, 'We'll knock on the door and ask if he's seen Harry, shall we?'

'No harm in that,' he agrees.

We walk together down to the house. It is spitting again now but the rainclouds are drifting over to the west of the city, and the sun has come out again. In the distance, a bright streak of colour above the rows of rooftops and satellite dishes shows me the rainbow I was eager for earlier. I look up at it dully now, and say nothing.

We get to the gate, and I come to a halt. 'This is it,' I say reluctantly. 'This is the place.'

The curtains are still closed. The front door is shut. I imagine the man inside, how he will react when we knock on the door, when he sees me again. *You crazy bitch.* Is that what I've become?

Treve looks at me, his eyes sharp on my face. 'So what made you suspect this guy in the first place?'

You crazy bitch.

'No particular reason,' I lie, and see at once that he does not believe me.

He raises his eyebrows. 'That's not much to go on.'

'I . . . I thought I heard a baby crying inside the house,' I say, this second lie even more ridiculous than the first, and then grimace at what's happening to me. 'No, I didn't hear a sodding thing.'

He keeps looking at me, waiting for more.

'He mentioned seeing me with Harry, then said I was too mad to have a baby. I just got a bad feeling about him. A sudden suspicion. Do you know what I mean?'

'Absolutely.'

Now I do not believe him. He thinks I am completely round the bend too. How could anyone not, given what I just told him?

But I force a smile, and say, 'Shall we knock, then?'

'And run away?'

It's meant to be a joke. Actually though, running away is precisely what I want to do. However, we're here now, right in front of the house with the black door, and if I don't go through with it, Treve will have his suspicion confirmed that I am crazy.

I march down the path and knock on the door. There isn't a bell.

Nobody answers.

'He's not going to come,' I say, staring at the shut door.

'Okay, you want to call the police?' Treve has his smartphone back in his hand, thumb poised over the screen as though ready to dial.

I look at him, and his phone, then shake my head.

He locks the phone without comment, then pushes it into his pocket. 'You want to go back to the house, then?' he asks mildly. 'Maybe sit down, have a proper think about what to do next?'

I nod.

He takes my arm. 'For what it's worth, that man doesn't speak English very well. I tried to talk to him about the recycling collection once, and it was pointless. We ended up agreeing that it was good weather. He probably didn't have a clue what you were on about.'

As we walk away, I glance back at the house. I remember the way I yelled through the letterbox, the awful things I said, and shame runs hot into my face.

'Poor man. He must have been terrified.'

'Probably,' Treve agrees, which does not help much.

'If anyone should be calling the police, it's him,' I point out bitterly. 'To arrest the crazy lady from down the road.' A thought strikes me. 'Oh God, perhaps he has already called them. That would be the icing on the cake.'

'Don't worry, I won't let them drag you off to the cells without a fight.' His flippancy is so warm and reassuring, his Cornish accent so strong, it's hard not to smile. Though I only realise I am smiling through my tears when Treve reaches into his pocket and produces a clean, folded tissue. 'Here, take this, and cheer up. Could have been worse.'

'How could it have been worse?'

'You could have run amok, attacked him with a rolling pin.'

'I don't have a rolling pin.'

'Really?' He makes a wry face. 'Camilla has a large ceramic rolling pin. She's always threatening me with it.'

'I don't make pastry.' I blow my nose. 'Don't know how. Never learnt.' Then what he said becomes clear to me. I remember the tension between them on the night Harry went missing. 'You and Camilla, are you two okay?'

He looks sideways at me, hesitates, then pushes a clump of dark hair back from his forehead. There's a look of frustration on his face. 'To be honest, things haven't been brilliant for a while. You know what I mean?'

I do know, and want to squeeze his arm, to show friendship and solidarity. But I don't know Treve that well, and I am not sure if he would understand – or even appreciate – the gesture. Men often misinterpret things like that, I have to remind myself.

'I understand.'

We are nearly at my front door. I reach for my keys, wondering if I should ask him in for coffee. Jon probably wouldn't like that. Not when he's at work. Treve isn't exactly good-looking, but he does have something about him. He's also our neighbour though, and he just helped me out in a very difficult situation. I don't want to seem ungrateful.

Treve pauses. 'I thought you would,' he says, then adds slowly, 'We hear things sometimes.'

I feel an icy cold at my core, spreading outwards.

'Wh . . . what?'

'The walls in these houses are too thin for secrets.'

He turns his head, looking at me intently. We are standing so close. Everything inside me feels jumbled up, chaotic, hurting.

I don't want to meet Treve's eyes. 'I don't know what you mean.'

Close up, I see he has tiny creases at the corners of his eyes and mouth. Tanned face, tanned throat, his body well built but sinewy, like one of these oaks you see stubbornly rooted in a Cornish hedgerow, too large for the space but enduring nonetheless.

'Yes,' Treve says, 'you do.'

My eyes widen, catching on his. I'm finding it hard to breathe again, my heart beating against my ribcage like a wild bird.

What does he know?

Chapter Twenty-Two

Whatever Treve is about to reveal, he never gets the chance.

A car pulls up beside us with a sharp squeal of brakes, just squeezing into the space in front of Treve's house, and I hear a shout.

Shaken, I turn and see Jon striding towards us.

Instinctively, Treve and I moved apart at the first sound of the car pulling up. But now I push the door open, the house keys still swinging in the lock. I suppose my first impulse is to get inside before Jon loses his temper . . .

But it is too late.

'Fuck's sake, Meghan!' he exclaims on reaching us. 'Have you been out somewhere? I've been calling and calling. Why the hell didn't you answer the phone?'

I stare at him, my heart beating fast, my back pressed awkwardly against the door frame. 'Why, what is it?'

But Jon is looking at Treve, frowning as he takes in the pair of us together, our general air of conspiracy, and my pink sweatshirt, an old, tight-fitting favourite. Now there's a note of suspicion in his voice. 'Treve? Why are you here? Has there been a problem?'

Too late, I see him glance at my face. His eyes narrow on my mouth.

I haven't worn lipstick except for special occasions in ages. I gave up make-up in early pregnancy because the faint scent of the cosmetics made me feel sick, and simply haven't started up again properly since Harry's birth. I think the first time I made an effort with myself was the dinner party.

And now I'm with Treve, and wearing lipstick.

'Meghan?' The threat in his lowered tone is implicit, though perhaps only to me.

Or perhaps not.

I see a flicker of apprehension on Treve's face, but also something else as he straightens, turning to face Jon, shoulders back, an almost martial glint in his eyes.

Treve wants to hit him.

I'm shocked at the realisation, and then secretly gratified. Then horribly, horribly guilty. Jon is my husband, for God's sake. And he's no match for Treve, physically at least. This could be disastrous.

And it's my fault. I've caused this conflict, and for no good reason. So it's up to me to intervene. 'I totally lost it with that guy down the road this morning,' I tell Jon quickly, almost babbling, trying to distract him. 'You know, the big Russian, or whatever he is. The one with the beard.'

Jon is still staring straight at Treve. Thinking, brooding, perhaps even speculating about what we've been doing while he was at work.

Desperately, I add, 'I'm not sure I know why, or what on earth I was thinking, but I suddenly decided he was the one who took Harry.'

Jon's head swings back towards me. '*What?*'

'He isn't the Cornish Snatcher, of course. I just went crazy. It was awful. I was yelling at the poor man, and then I ran back to call the police.' I take a breath, slowing down now that I have his full attention. 'Luckily, Treve was just coming back from the shops. He persuaded me to drop it, and not jump to stupid conclusions.' I see his eyes narrow again, and add, 'I was desperate for someone to blame. And that guy . . . Well, he's different, isn't he? So I blamed him.'

Much to my relief, Jon finally seems to have understood. He looks grudgingly at Treve. 'Thanks.'

'No problem. Look, I'd better go. I've left my shopping in the hall.' With a casual air, Treve smiles at us both. 'See you later.'

Once he's gone, I look round at Jon, suddenly seeing the wild intensity in his face, the slight flush on his cheeks. Oh God, I think, does he suspect me of having an affair with Treve? I remember the last time he thought I might be interested in another man. How could I forget?

'What is it?' I ask, no longer sure if I want to go inside the house with him. I don't like the look in his eyes. 'What's happened?'

'You need to come with me right away.' Jon grabs me by the shoulders, and I freeze, a statue in his arms, staring up at him. 'They've found her,' he explains. 'I got a call at work about twenty minutes ago. I came straight home to fetch you.'

'Found her?' I wish his hands weren't gripping me so tightly. 'Found who?'

'The baby snatcher.'

The Cornish Snatcher – as the papers insist on calling her – has been based all this time in some isolated farmhouse south of Truro. The police have been examining CCTV footage, piecing together different descriptions, and finally identified a suspect. Then they found a possible address, and sent a car out to investigate.

'I don't know what the police have found there,' Jon tells me, 'and all I got from DS Dryer's mobile was his answering service. But the journalist who called me said we should probably get out there asap.'

Jon drives. I can see how much this news has animated him, made him hopeful that this may mean the end of our ordeal – for better or worse. His face is intent and frowning at the same time, his hands constantly moving: twisting the wheel, slamming the gearstick up and down through the gears, tapping restlessly on the window frame in the sunshine.

I watch him as I listen, and share some of his excitement – and his fear at what we may find when we get there.

The call he got was not from the police, I discover, but a freelance journalist. This is not what I expected, and makes me wonder why the police have not been in touch.

Jon is wondering that too, it seems. 'The reporter didn't give his name, just wanted to know if Harry was still alive. He sounded surprised that I didn't know yet. That's when he told me about the snatcher.'

The farmhouse is set deep in the woods, within sight of an inlet of the River Fal, the kind of rambling old place that those with a little money might hire for a family holiday, or buy as a second home. As we drive out there with guidance from our dashboard satnav, Jon relates what the anonymous caller told him, which is that several reports from the public had led the police there. To make enquiries at first, but later with growing suspicion. A patrol car was dispatched early that morning, but failed to gain access. Another police car followed it, and however it happened, maybe one officer taking matters into his own hands, maybe permission being given for a forced entry, a window was broken and they got inside.

I ask, 'So a journalist told you all this on the phone? I hope it's not a hoax.'

He stares at me sidelong, then looks back at the road. We are leaving Truro, heading out into open countryside, woods and fields on either side. 'I didn't think of that,' he admits, and the relentless pace of the car slackens. 'Shit, it never even occurred to me. He sounded totally on the level.'

'But didn't give his name?'

Jon blinks, then says with fresh conviction, 'Actually, I didn't ask. But he did mention one or two papers he works for. I can't recall which ones. Maybe *The Times*?' He shrugs, and the car picks up pace again. He has done with feeling guilty and is already rewriting the situation in his head, making things acceptable again. 'It doesn't matter. We get there and nothing's happening, we'll know for sure it's a hoax.'

I hang on to the handgrip as he corners at speed, my heart beating fast. I want to ask him to slow down, but dare not. Not when he's in this dangerous mood. Mania, I think they call it. He might do anything. Even crash the car.

I try not to think about what is waiting for us at our destination. But it's impossible not to allow myself at least a tiny flicker of hope. Within less than half an hour, I could be holding Harry again, kissing his soft cheek, snuggling him against my chest, breathing in his gorgeous baby smell.

But perhaps all that lies ahead is his cold, stiff body.

I put a hand to my mouth, everything in me rebelling against that image, but not before a sob escapes.

Jon glances at me, misinterpreting my gesture. 'I'm telling you, it's not a hoax. Look,' he says, and points ahead. There is a police car coming towards us along the woodland road, no sirens, no lights, but at a good pace, the driver looking determined. 'See, I told you.'

I watch the police car in my wing mirror until it disappears. I feel ill and have to battle against a sudden light-headed sensation, like I'm going to faint.

Everything is about Harry now.

I focus on the road ahead, the woodland trees, the strips of sunlight and shade the car is passing through, one after the other, flash, shadow, flash, shadow.

I need to be strong, to think of Harry and not myself. What I feel is unimportant, because what happens to me doesn't matter, not even if I end up ripped apart by this hope and fear, their terrible alternating highs and lows.

The relentless trees part for a few seconds.

A sunlit meadow flashes past.

I turn my head, momentarily blinded. I suddenly remember lying in a field as a child, tearing petals from a daisy. *He loves me, he loves me not; he loves me, he loves me not.*

The black-and-white chequered flag pops up on the satnav screen. According to the display, we are due to arrive at our final destination in three minutes.

He's alive, he's not alive; he's alive, he's not alive.

There are police cars on the road ahead. A track leads to a small, dirty-looking farmhouse, a glimpse of water through the trees. A bird flies across the road right in front of the car bonnet. Sturdy brown tapering wings, and the hint of a sharp beak.

I stare after it until the bird vanishes into the trees.

A falcon?

Jon slows to a crawl as he approaches the turn. I hear him muttering under his breath, 'Yes, this has to be it. We're here.'

He's in his work suit, but the tie is askew, his top button undone. That's not like him, even on a warm day like this. I imagine him getting that call in the office, his face filled with elation, then rushing for the lift, tearing at his top button, loosening his tie . . .

'Did he call you on your mobile?'

'What?' He is opening his window; a male police officer is flagging us down, trying to stop us turning into the farmhouse track.

'The journalist. You were at the office when he called, weren't you?'

Jon hesitates, frowning. 'Yes.'

'So did he call you on your mobile or on the office phone?'

'Mobile.'

'How did he get your number?'

'No idea.'

'Can you call him back?'

'Number withheld.'

The police officer looks in at us, assessing who we are, public or plain-clothes police service. I do not know him. He's a young man, friendly smile, but clearly unwelcoming.

'I'm sorry, sir, madam,' he says politely, presumably having satisfied himself that we are members of the public, 'but you can't stop here.'

'I need to get down to the farmhouse,' Jon tells him, that crisp lawyer's authority in his voice, the kind that makes me shrink when he uses it on me. 'It's urgent.'

The officer studies us both again. More suspiciously this time. 'Press?'

'No.'

'I'm afraid you can't come down here,' the officer says, then glances at my face. 'Do you have any connection to the owner?'

Jon is frowning. 'Of course not. Look, I need to speak to whoever's in charge.'

'I can make a call for you. But you'll need to park up and wait. I have to tell you, it could take an hour or more for anyone to get back to you. There's a bit of a situation in hand down there. If you could turn your vehicle and park over there . . .'

The officer points back the way we've come, then spots a scruffy-looking man trying to sneak past him with a camera. 'Hey, hang on

185

there, I've already told you no,' he shouts, and turns away to deal with the photographer.

While Jon has been wrangling with the officer, I have been watching all the people milling about by the farmhouse. There are so many cars, police vans, even an ambulance, it leaves me with a cold feeling of dread.

From where we are, I can only see the gable-end of the house. It's a dirty off-white, mud-splashed at the base, presumably from the track that runs around it. No windows, just a blank wall. I can see people congregating beneath it, discussing things, pointing at outbuildings, exchanging information. The entrance must be round the other side, I guess; a steady number keep heading that way, then returning for more pointing and discussion.

Two men are standing apart from the rest. One is a tall man in a suit and duffle coat, with silvery hair – DI Pascoe. He's on his phone, talking earnestly. The other man is DS Dryer.

'There's Paul Dryer,' I say promptly.

Jon revs the engine, then pulls away from the policeman without waiting for him to come back. 'Bloody jobsworth,' he mutters.

He is driving too fast, no doubt to make it harder for the policeman to chase after us. Not a good idea. The car bounces up and down through deep mud ruts, their contours made worse by all the traffic this track must have seen today. Once we are nearer the place, I can see more fully what's happening. The front door to the farmhouse has been wedged open for easier access, and people are traipsing in and out with bagged items and boxes of equipment.

There's one old car parked opposite the farmhouse. Not a gold Volvo but a battered Land Rover that looks like it's nearing the end of its useful life. Its greeny-grey body is smeared with dust streaks after the recent rain, perfectly in keeping with the farmhouse and its surroundings. Both doors and the back door are open, and a man in blue overalls is peering inside, chatting on the phone to someone.

A second ambulance is parked nearby, its back doors also flung wide but nobody is inside. A couple of dogs are being released from a large specialist police van, a spaniel and a German Shepherd, both dogs alert, both wagging their tails for their handlers. Forensics are there too, with bags and cameras, their all-white suits making the place look like the scene of a nuclear disaster.

But it's not the Land Rover or the farmhouse that is attracting the most attention. It's one of the outbuildings, its far edge just visible from the track. There are police in what looks like heavily padded riot gear ranged outside, crouched down behind cars as though expecting resistance, perhaps even a shoot-out, which frightens me.

What the hell is happening in there?

Jon pulls sharply to a halt, parking up on the muddy grass bank, maybe thirty yards from the house itself. The car tilts at an angle, but seems stable enough. Besides, there are already several other cars parked along the bank and nobody seems bothered by our arrival.

'Right, let's find out what's going on.' Jon jumps out without waiting for me, and slams his door shut behind him.

I follow more slowly.

My mouth is dry and my hands are shaking.

Not good.

I should be like Jon, full of nervous energy and thankful that something is being done at last, that progress has been made on my son's disappearance. But I'm not.

Instead, it feels like my insides have been hollowed out with a spoon.

Because something is wrong here.

Very, very wrong.

Chapter Twenty-Three

My gaze has been moving restlessly across the scene the whole time. I have seen police cars and police vans, and their uniformed occupants wandering about the place. I have seen plain-clothes police officers directing activities. I have seen two ambulances now. I have seen paramedics in their distinctive green jackets standing outside the front porch of the farmhouse. I have seen the sniffer dogs and their handlers. But I have seen no sign that there are any babies here. Nobody is cradling a bundle, or tending to a crying child. And we are the only people here who look like parents of a missing child. Surely if the babies had been found, there would be other parents here by now, looking lost and fearful like us, asking questions, demanding information.

Which means one of two things: either the police were mistaken and this is not where the Cornish Snatcher has been hiding out, or they are in the right place – and all the babies are dead.

I shut myself off from that thought at once. Shield my mind from it, like someone sheltering behind a wall during a controlled explosion.

I can't afford to flake out, I tell myself.

Not again.

And particularly not here.

DI Pascoe has finished his phone call. He speaks briefly to Dryer, who bends his head to listen to the reply, hands clasped behind his back, nodding like a courtier listening to a king.

Then Dryer turns and gestures in the air, a circular motion like a cowboy indicating, 'Round 'em up, boys!' in a Western. There is sudden movement, everyone in the waiting crowd moving forward at once, but with precision rather than confusion. Several of the officers in protective gear are carrying rifles, I realise.

Nobody seems to have noticed us.

Jon has stopped, staring at the police marksmen. 'Fuck,' is all he says, but then holds up a hand when I try to follow them. 'Don't be stupid.'

Again, I look at him sideways, but say nothing.

This isn't the time.

I decide that I rather like being stupid though.

Slipping round behind his back, I cross quietly to the other side of the single track and scramble up on to the opposite bank. Then I balance along the uneven slope of the bank, not caring whether Jon has seen me or not, and pick my way across the mud and tangled roots until I reach the entrance to the farmyard. There's no gate here, only a wire boundary fence that stops on either side of the track. The fence is roughly waist-high, rickety and sagging between posts, with plastic bags and newspaper fragments trapped between the wires in places. I guess it was put up once upon a time to stop livestock wandering, but the livestock is long gone.

I walk round the edge of the fence, staring.

Dryer is marching towards the outbuilding, flanked by the other officers. He's not as smartly turned out as the last time we saw him, his grey suit a little more tired, his shoes and the base of his trousers not surprisingly showing mud flecks.

I study his profile, trying to gauge the seriousness of the situation from his expression. But he's tight-lipped and grim, almost blank in his determination; it's hard to draw any useful conclusions from that. I am more worried by the fact that guns are apparently required. It makes me wonder who on earth is in that building, and what might happen to any babies also inside there.

The outbuilding they have surrounded looks like an old barn, probably built a little later than the farmhouse. It has another high gable-end angled towards the road, only this time with one large window in the end nearest us, perhaps where it once stood open to the weather. The outside walls are in a serious state of disrepair, the wooden frame decaying and sagging towards one side, partially repaired with what looks like straw and mud. Its steeply sloping roof has a large number of slates missing, with some kind of plastic sheeting to cover the gaps. But the plastic sheeting has torn and come loose, flapping limply in the breeze, as though whoever did the job was not a professional. Either that or it was done a long time ago, and never intended to be a permanent arrangement.

The whole structure looks like it might blow away in the next big storm. Though at a guess I would say it has managed to withstand even the most violent gales for at least the past two hundred years. Maybe longer.

Some kind of order is given. Then I hear shouts. And what sounds like a gunshot from inside the barn.

I stop dead, my heart thudding violently.

A small group of officers in protective gear, at least two of them with rifles raised to their shoulders, suddenly rise up and charge the double doors to the barn. The doors are thumped open with a hand-held battering ram, then the men flood inside, shouting hoarsely.

Others rapidly follow, heads down, charging in. More marksmen wait behind the parked cars, their rifles trained on the building.

There is a lot more shouting inside, though all I can hear is a deep voice yelling, 'Get down, get down, get down on the floor!' Like a crazed DJ shouting instructions to clubbers. I wish I could see what is happening inside, but I can't seem to move, my feet rooted, my pulse racing.

DS Dryer goes in last, striding towards the barn with several others beside him, presumably other plain-clothes officers.

A moment later, the police drag a woman out of the barn. Her glasses are askew, one lens cracked, and her ankle-length dress is dusty from where they made her lie on the floor. She looks half-mad, wrestling against her captors, repeating something in a thick Cornish accent, a streak of dirt on her cheek.

An officer is following them with some kind of weapon in his gloved hand. An air rifle, by the look of it.

I stare at her as she passes, and my stomach heaves in shock.

It's the woman from the supermarket. The thick-set woman with black hair and glasses. The one who wanted to make a complaint against me.

The one who tried to touch Harry.

I can't help myself. I start towards her, my hands outstretched.

'I knew it was you,' I shout at her, shaking and wild with rage, my body flooded with useless adrenalin. 'I knew it, I knew it. Where's my son, you bitch? I hope they lock you up and throw away the key.'

I realise with surprise but a sense of rightness that I intend to kill her. That I *want* to kill her. Then suddenly I find myself being restrained by officers, my flailing arms captured and pinned behind my back.

It doesn't stop me screaming after her, 'Where's my baby, you fucking psycho? Where's Harry?'

They are dragging the woman towards a waiting police van, her dirty Wellington boots trailing in the mud. She turns her head, staring back at me through her cracked glasses with what looks like blank astonishment. Then she smiles.

She fucking smiles at me.

'You bitch,' I sob loudly, rocking against the police who are struggling to hold me back. 'You fucking bitch.'

I have forgotten Jon, forgotten DS Dryer, forgotten the police twisting my arms painfully behind my back now, forgotten everything except this burning need to get my son back. And this is the woman who knows where he is.

I can hardly get the words out, I am so incoherent with grief and fury. 'Where is he? Oh my God, what have you done to my boy? What have you *done*?'

Chapter Twenty-Four

To my amazement, I am not arrested and thrown into the van with the baby snatcher. But no doubt the police can see that I am half-dead with exhaustion, and not likely to be a danger to anyone – except possibly myself.

It takes nearly fifteen minutes and a plastic mug of lukewarm tea, administered from DI Pascoe's own flask, for me to recover enough composure to start asking questions. By then they have driven the black-haired woman away, and are now methodically searching the farmhouse and outbuildings.

I am led to one of the ambulances, and persuaded to sit down on the back step. Jon joins me there after a minute, his face taut with fury. But he says nothing, of course. He would never do that, not in front of other people.

It is obvious that DS Dryer is not happy to see us either. But at least he has not yet sent us away, perhaps understanding that I will do anything, even break the law, in order to be here for when they find Harry.

'Detective, have you found the missing children yet?' I ask.

Dryer shakes his head, his look pitying. 'Not yet,' he admits, and I see guilt in his face. 'But we will. I'm certain about that.'

That's something at least, I think. Too late to help us though.

Jon has turned on his heel and is staring up at the front of the farmhouse. Its gloomy upper windows reflect the mass of rainclouds once more gathering overhead.

'I don't understand what's taking so long in there,' he mutters. 'It's a big house, yes, but no more than four or five bedrooms, at a guess. Your team should have finished searching by now.' He sounds strained again, like he's only just holding it together.

'How did you hear about this place?' the detective asks Jon without replying, his tone curt but not unfriendly. 'You shouldn't have come out here, you know. It was very dangerous. You saw she had an air rifle in the barn with her; even fired it once, to try and keep us out.' He looks from Jon to me, shaking his head. 'One or both of you could have been killed or seriously hurt. How would that have helped your son?'

While Jon is explaining about the anonymous tip-off, I turn my head to survey the farmyard. Thanks to the recent rain, there's mud everywhere, officers pulling on boots to avoid the worst of it, people slipping in it, walkways being constructed from loose planking. Despite all this chaos, there's an air of organisation now the longed-for arrest has been made. As though everyone knows where they are supposed to be, and why.

To find the missing babies.

Overhead, I hear the growing hum of rotor blades as a helicopter approaches fast from the direction of Truro, no doubt heading for this farmhouse. As it nears us, the treetops sway, beginning to flatten out.

'You should go home.' DS Dryer sounds irritated. I turn to look at him, see the pinched look about the detective's mouth. Again I feel that sickening lurch in my stomach. The sense that he is withholding information from us. 'We haven't called the others,' he adds, almost as an afterthought.

Jon frowns. 'Others?'

'The other *parents*,' I tell him, since DS Dryer is gazing up at the helicopter, too distracted to explain what he meant.

I ask, 'Was it the gold Volvo I saw in the street? Is that how you found her?'

'No.' Dryer looks back at me sharply. 'One of my officers found that Volvo, and spoke to the owner. It's a local car. We're satisfied there's no connection.' The detective runs a hand through his hair, looking weary again and frustrated. 'Look, I need you both to go home.'

'Do you think our son is here, Detective?' Jon interrupts him. 'That's all we want to know. And don't give me that *not possible* crap. We're Harry's parents, we have a right to know, regardless of . . .' He pauses, then finishes, 'Regardless of the circumstances.'

He means, *regardless of whether Harry is alive or dead.*

The helicopter pilot appears to be looking for somewhere to land. Perhaps there is a field somewhere behind the farmhouse. The noise is horrendous. And most of the police officers seem to have moved away from the barn, I realise. The double doors are still wide though, one door leaning off its hinges at an awkward angle where it was battered open.

'A simple yes or no.'

'I can't say for sure. We have to follow due process. You know that.'

'But you could have got here sooner,' Jon argues. 'Who knows what that maniac may have done to our children while you lot were following procedure, doing everything by the book?'

'We've got her in custody now. We'll find the babies too. Just go home, give us time.'

DS Dryer is looking up at the sky again, raising his voice to be heard above the mad whine of the helicopter as it hovers above the trees.

Neither of them is looking at me.

I can't bear this anymore. Waiting, and not knowing. Expecting to be sent home again at any moment, without what we came for.

Without Harry.

I slip away, not checking if they have seen me go or not, and make my way round a departing police car and towards the barn.

⌣

The farmyard is less crowded than it was even five minutes ago when we first arrived; I'm guessing quite a lot of the preliminary work of bagging up evidence and dusting for prints has already been completed, and many officers are now on their way back to the station. Whatever the reason, fewer people are about, and none of them do more than glance in my direction, too busy with their own jobs to bother wondering who this random woman in jeans and pink sweatshirt is, picking her way across the mud. And I suppose most would assume I have legitimate business here, having got past the officer at the top of the road.

The helicopter must have landed. I can hear the blades slowing, the noise lessening.

Suddenly, I hear shouts from the barn.

Excited barking.

Then a series of metallic bangs.

I take another few steps towards the barn, then stop again, fearing that I will be spotted and sent away if I get too close.

'Guv?' A uniformed policeman peers out of the barn a moment later, looking round at the other officers in the farmyard. 'Detective Inspector Pascoe still here?'

'Gone back to the station,' someone replies.

'What about DS Dryer?'

There's some hurried conversation, and soon DS Dryer runs past me without a word and through the double doors into the barn.

It's starting to rain again, just lightly. The first drops are like icy fingertips tapping on my forehead and cheek. The sun has been well and truly buried. All I see now are grey clouds in grey skies, and a metallic grey stretch of water below us through the trees. An inlet of the Fal estuary, meandering and branching off into little gulleys along this rural stretch between Truro and the sea.

On any other day, this part of Cornwall might be scenic. Idyllic, even. Today though, it strikes me as cruel and depressing.

I don't want to be here, but I have to be. I owe it to my son.

Despite being almost speechless with terror, I make my way to the open door of the barn and look round it.

In the rain and the chaos, nobody seems to notice me.

Five or six men, including DS Dryer, are bending over a trap-door in the floor, staring down into some kind of pit below. Like an inspection pit for a car, I think at first. Then I realise from the resonance of the men's voices, standing above it, that the hole must be much larger than that. An underground space, possibly running the whole length of the barn. The ancient carpet that must have been concealing the trapdoor has been rolled back unevenly, sitting humped beyond the edge of the hole like a dusty pink tongue furred with dirt. And there's a German Shepherd beside it, right at the end of its leash, dragging on its handler and barking hysterically, desperate to get inside.

There's a horrible smell coming up out of the pit. A smell like rotting meat. A smell that leaves me stunned.

'Oh God,' I whisper, staring.

Harry could never survive in a place like this. Since he came home from the hospital, I've scrubbed and disinfected everything he touches. His immune system could not possibly cope with such a filthy, unkempt environment.

One of the policemen runs to the police van, and comes back a moment later with a large, heavy-duty torch. He glances at me in passing, recognition in his face.

'You can't be here, sorry.' I've seen him before, possibly on the night of Harry's disappearance, one of the officers who searched our house and gardens from top to bottom. He calls over his shoulder to the other police waiting in the yard. 'Could someone escort Mrs Smith out, please?'

He passes the torch to DS Dryer, who has not taken his eyes off the pit below. 'Here you go, sarge.'

'Thanks.' Dryer has his foot on what looks like the top rung of a ladder. There's a brief discussion – I guess it's about forensics, and whether they should wait for gloves and plastic shoe covers – then he seems to come to a decision, and begins to descend the ladder, his feet clanging with every step.

A hand descends on my shoulder. 'Mrs Smith? This way, please,' a young police officer says, his expression sympathetic, and tries to lead me away from the pit.

'No,' I say, pulling away from him. 'Not yet. Wait.'

I do not notice myself moving forward. Yet somehow I am suddenly there, standing alongside the hole with the others, looking down and hoping, hoping to God, just like them, for good news.

'I'm sorry, you need to leave.'

'One minute, for God's sake. My baby could be in there.'

It's black and formless down there, just as I imagine death must be, and the bouncing torch beam as Dryer descends picks out dust in the air, then support beams, metalwork, what looks like concrete. The pit has been specially built, then hidden with the carpet, kept concealed and probably soundproof.

The smell is unbearable. I remember Charlie Pole, whose pathetic remains they found in the field, and I cover my mouth with a hand that will not stop shaking.

'Down here,' comes the shout, and my heart seems to fly down into the black hole with its echoes, desperately seeking out whatever he has found, so I can know the worst, and know it as swiftly as possible. 'Down here, quick,' Dryer repeats, and then his voice seems to alter. 'Bring more light.'

Then, just as my horrified brain is trying to dissect his tone for intricate layers of meaning, peeling back words to expose the nuances beneath, picking over what sounded like fear in his voice but could as easily have been excitement, a wholly unhoped-for sound splits the air in the barn and renders us all suddenly, wildly, ecstatic.

A baby's cry.

Chapter Twenty-Five

It's not Harry.

I know that even before the echoes have died away from that first wonderful cry, and the baby has drawn an angry breath, ready for its next demanding wail.

But it is a live baby. A live baby in a dusty hellhole.

A miracle, in other words.

Dryer shouts out of the darkness, 'Paramedic!'

'Shit,' one of the men mutters.

'And fucking hurry with it, would you?' Dryer adds savagely.

'You got it, sarge.'

'I need one helper,' he adds. 'George, you up there?'

The young officer next to me says, 'Sarge.'

'Get down here, would you? Everyone else stay put for now. We'll need forensics down here too.' He pauses. 'After the paramedics.'

George glances at me, unsure. Then shrugs and starts climbing down into the pit too.

Everyone else round the edge of the pit seems to move at once. The next few minutes are chaotic, not helped by the thin cries from below that torment my ears, demanding our help, urging our love. Two of Dryer's plain-clothes team scramble back to their cars for more torches. One of the uniforms, a young man who only looks about twenty, runs in search of the paramedics. The police around me become suddenly busy, talking on the radio, making phone calls, putting their heads together in discussions over what happens next.

We wait in silence, then I hear someone ascending the ladder.

A head emerges. It's Paul Dryer.

He's holding a baby in his arms. A baby in a dirty blue sleepsuit.

It's not Harry, of course.

I already knew that, from the cry alone. But I had still hoped . . .

My heart contracts in pain, yet I allow myself a smile for the survivor. One mother at least will not be hurting tonight. One mother will hold her baby tonight. One mother will not cry herself to sleep.

Is that Tom?

He is a very young, chubby-faced baby, though balding on the back of his head like an old man. His hair is wispy and gingerish. His eyes are wide and dark blue and utterly gorgeous. I can't imagine what the poor little darling has been through. Or rather, I refuse to allow myself to imagine it, or the imagining alone would break me. And I need to stay sane and whole.

'Paramedics are here,' someone shouts.

A man and woman in green jackets come running into the barn. They are carrying rolled-up silver hypothermia blankets and a hefty bag of equipment between them.

Paul looks relieved to see them. 'Here,' he says, still cradling the baby boy close to his chest.

The paramedics both stop to examine the baby, blocking my view for a moment, then the woman bears him swiftly away to the waiting ambulance.

Paul Dryer talks to the male paramedic for a moment. Their voices are quiet, the conversation too low to be overheard. Then they start to climb down into the pit, the paramedic first, Paul watching him descend before putting his foot on the top rung too.

I watch them, the hairs on the back of my neck prickling in horror.

No urgency, no haste.

'No,' I say thickly, and call Dryer's name. When he turns back, staring at me, I say, 'He's my baby. Please, I have to be the one to pick him up. Not someone else, not a stranger. I can't let someone else . . .'

'Meghan, no,' he says, shaking his head with sympathy.

'He's dead, isn't he?'

I am sobbing.

DS Dryer looks at me but says nothing.

———~———

This time I allow one of the officers to lead me out of the barn, all my sense of purpose gone. I wander outside into the rain, but there is no sign either of Jon or DC Gerent. I explain how we arrived.

'Wait here with PC Hannah. I'll find your husband,' the woman officer who escorted me out of the barn says, and leaves me with another policewoman while she traipses away across the mud.

PC Hannah smiles at me tentatively. 'Coffee?'

I shake my head.

Police are going about their business all around us in the farm-yard. This is how a ghost must feel, I think, gazing back at them without much interest. Trapped on earth, unable to be seen or to communicate with the living. I am aware of the rain falling steadily now, soaking my hair and face, but am too stunned and exhausted to seek shelter.

I am not there long before DS Dryer emerges from the barn again, looking fairly exhausted himself. He runs a hand across his forehead, then spots that I'm still there, and comes straight across to me.

'I thought I'd sent you home. Where's Jon?'

PC Hannah says helpfully, 'Someone's gone to find him, sir.'

'I see.' He studies me, frowning. 'You're soaked.'

I laugh, then cry.

'Who cares?'

'Meghan,' he says, then puts a hand on my arm. 'I wanted to wait to speak to you both together. You and Jon. But since he's not here . . . It's not your boy down there. It's not Harry.'

I stare at him.

He hesitates. 'Turns out the baby who survived is actually Poppy. And the other baby down there is much younger than Harry.' He closes his eyes briefly. 'Poor little sod.'

I gasp, and clap a hand to my mouth. 'Oh my God. You mean, the baby that died was . . . Tom?'

He nods grimly. 'I have to speak to Jack and Serena Penrose straightaway. That's why I've come out. Look, please don't say a word to anyone. I shouldn't have told you, by rights. Not before them.' His mouth twists. 'But I could see the state you were in.'

My heart is galloping. 'I need to tell Jon.'

'Of course,' he agrees. 'I'm sorry, I'd take you home myself if it was up to me. But DI Pascoe has gone back to the station to oversee the interview process, and I'm needed here. Someone has to run this awful bloody circus.'

'It doesn't matter.'

'We'll go over the details of Harry's disappearance again tomorrow, if you can bear it.' He looks beaten. 'I'm beginning to think we've missed something really important. I thought Harry would be here with the others. I'm so sorry.'

'It's not your fault.' At least he's not here and dead, like poor Tom. I remember Jack and Serena after the press conference, their scared faces, the hope still in their eyes. 'His parents, oh God. I can't bear to think of it, it's too horrible.'

The detective trudges away, and I get out my phone. I have to get hold of Jon. But his mobile rings out, then goes to voicemail.

'Jon? I don't know where you are, but please come and find me. I'm near the barn.' I pause, a sudden rush of emotion clogging my throat. 'He's not here. Harry's . . . not here.' I take a breath, try to sound more in control. 'So we're back to square one. Please come quickly, I need you.'

I hug the phone against me, staring back into the sinister, dark hole of the barn.

If Harry's not here, then where the hell is he?

Everything inside me had been screwed up tight to confront his dead body, and now I feel like a broken spring, all my nerves jangling and uncoiled.

Harry was here in this vile place. He must have been here. She spotted him first in the supermarket, maybe followed us home that day, bided her time, then took the opportunity when it arose. The dinner party in the garden. The empty house. The front door that I must have left unlocked. She would have brought him here to join the other babies, her illicit treasure trove of innocence. So where is he now?

What did that insane bitch do to my son? It's hard not to think of the baby in the field. But I try all the same.

There's still hope.

I think of Jack and Serena again.

There's always hope, until the very last possible second.

Long minutes pass, and still no sign of my husband. Finally, PC Hannah gets on the radio, then comes back and tells me haltingly that Jon appears to have driven home without me.

'What?'

'Your car's no longer on site. I checked its description with the officer at the end of the farm track, and he says he saw that car head back towards Truro about twenty minutes ago.' She looks at me sympathetically. 'I'm sorry.'

I stand there, aghast, and can't meet her eyes. Why on earth would Jon have left without me? We're miles out of town here, in the depths of the Cornish countryside. How on earth am I supposed to get home?

I feel so alone and humiliated, I don't know what to say. But the big question running through my head is, what have I done to make him treat me like this?

'If you like,' PC Hannah says, 'I can organise a lift home for you.'

'No, please don't bother. I'm going to call someone to pick me up. A friend.'

At least I hope she's a friend.

'Okay,' she says, then adds, frowning, 'Don't forget this is a crime scene. If you could keep what you've seen here to yourself—'

'Of course.'

I take out my phone. For a moment it seems the call will go unanswered. Then I hear a tentative, 'Hello?' at the other end.

'Emily? Thank God.' I swap the phone to my other ear and turn my back on PC Hannah, aware that she is listening intently. 'I was wondering, are you free to come out and pick me up?' I explain the situation as discreetly as I can, and give her the directions. 'I'm sorry, it's quite a long drive from town. I'll give you the petrol money.'

'It's fine. I'll be there as soon as I can.'

'Thanks, Em,' I say huskily.

PC Hannah looks at me expectantly after the call.

'Half an hour,' I tell her.

She waits with me at the end of the track until Emily turns up, both of us sheltering under a large police umbrella. I suspect she doesn't quite trust me not to try to sneak back to the barn, where dozens of police and white-coated forensic officers were milling about as we left the site. While we wait, I make a series of increasingly frantic calls to Jon on my mobile, including several to our landline at home, which rings out each time until finally going to answerphone.

I hesitate, decide not to leave a message, and then call his mobile again. This time it does not ring at all but goes straight to voicemail, the automated message telling me that the mobile I am trying to reach is turned off.

I leave a breathless message, telling him I'm on my way home and asking him to call me. 'Jon, I need to know where you are,' I say at the end, then add, 'urgently.'

Which really means, why did you leave without me, you sod?

Finally, Emily pulls down the track, waving at me through the half-open window. 'Sorry it took so long. The traffic is crazy.'

I lean down and smile at her with relief. She looks even more like a hippy than usual, in a patchwork-style dress with trainers and no socks, and a navy-blue waterproof coat over the top. No make-up, no jewellery. Like she dressed in a hurry to come out to me.

'Thank you so much for doing this,' I tell her.

'No problem.'

I climb in and Emily drives straight off again, barely glancing at PC Hannah or down the track to the farm, even though yet more police vehicles are now parked up on the verge. But her hands are clenched on the steering wheel, and I can see she is looking pale again. It may be my imagination, but she seems to be holding herself stiffly, as though her stomach hurts.

'Still feeling unwell?' I ask, concerned.

'It comes and goes.'

'Nothing serious, I hope?'

'Women's problems,' she says enigmatically, 'as Simon likes to call them. He can be a bit squeamish about . . . physical stuff. Bodies, you know.'

Bodies.

I swallow, and look away. 'Jon's not much different.'

'So old-fashioned though, don't you think? Honestly, I thought we'd got past all that crap.' She runs a hand through her hair, which is looking messier than usual. 'Where is Jon, by the way?'

I tell her what happened at the farm. The basics. I leave out the part about the babies they found. I don't have permission to share that kind of sensitive information, and besides, Jack and Serena ought to be first to know about their son's death.

'He just drove off and left you there? That's appalling.'

'I'm not sure what happened. One minute he was there, the next . . .' I frown, thinking. 'Perhaps he got an urgent call.'

'From work, you mean? But why not tell you he had to leave? And why not take you back into town with him?'

I shrug, helpless and still too hurt to trust myself to discuss it.

She glances at my face, then brakes suddenly. Pulling into the side of the road, she parks the car precariously on the grass bank. 'You look bloody awful.' She lurches sideways, grabbing her phone from the handbag at my feet. 'I'm going to call Jon myself. Find out exactly what he thinks he's playing at.'

'I've tried. No answer.'

I wait though, watching as she dials. Then she shakes her head and ends the call.

'No answer,' she agrees.

I bury my face in my hands. 'Christ.'

'You want me to drive you to the office? See if he's there?'

It's tempting.

But I sit up and shake my head. 'No, I need to go home. Clear my head.'

'Of course.'

She pulls straight back on to the road. Then glances at the dashboard. 'Damn, I need to stop for petrol.'

Guiltily, I rummage in my handbag for a twenty-pound note. 'This is so good of you, Emily. Especially given you're not feeling one hundred per cent. Please, let me pay.' I point ahead as we join the main road back into Truro. 'Look, a filling station.'

There's a queue at the fuel pumps, so we have to wait. It's still raining, but I wind the window down once we're under the canopy. My chest feels tight and I need the fresh air. All the stress, I expect.

'Stay here, I'll do it,' she insists when I try to get out.

Watching in the mirror as she pumps fuel into the tank, I see how bloodless Emily looks. There are signs of strain about her eyes and mouth, like she too is labouring under some enormous stress. It makes me feel doubly awful for having dragged her all the way out to pick me up.

'Thanks,' I say again, and hand her the money through the window.

Emily disappears into the filling station to pay.

Almost as soon as the sliding doors have closed behind her, her phone begins to ring. Down in her handbag. At my feet.

I look through the rain. Emily is at the back of the queue. I can't answer someone else's phone. Whoever it is can call her back later, that's all.

But what if it's Jon?

I resist for about five more seconds. Then I lean forward and drag her phone out of her bag. The screen is lit up. *Incoming call.*

As I suspected, it's Jon's number.

Fumbling, I answer the call quickly. 'Hello? Jon? It's Meghan. Where are you?'

There's a short silence.

I can hear him breathing. Thinking.

'Jon?'

Then the line goes dead.

I close my eyes, my heart beating hard. My husband does not even want to talk to me, and I have no idea why. What the hell have I done?

I look round. Emily is nearly at the front of the queue. I hesitate, then slip her mobile back inside her handbag. I don't need to tell her it rang and I answered it. She would only be shocked that Jon refused to speak to me, which would be embarrassing. And she might well be offended that I took her phone out of her bag without permission.

My fingers brush hard plastic as I release the mobile. A small box of some kind, lodged in the bottom of her handbag. I glance down, curious, and my breath stops.

I feel oddly disconnected from what I'm seeing, unable at first to understand it fully, to put it in its proper context.

It's a baby's dummy.

Brand-new and unopened, still in its see-through plastic display case.

My hands begin to shake again.

It's blue.

Chapter Twenty-Six

I thank Emily, then wait until she's pulled away before turning to the house. I don't know what to make of the baby's dummy in her bag, but I can't afford to draw far-fetched conclusions. There could be any number of logical explanations. Maybe she was planning to give it to me as a present at the dinner party, but then forgot. Or maybe she bought it because she wants a baby so much herself, and just wanted to feel like a mother, even if only for thirty seconds while choosing it.

That I could understand. If I'd only been allowed to hold Harry in my arms for thirty seconds before he was taken from me, I would never have let go of that incredible feeling. Never. That's how powerful it can be, even a taste of motherhood. Is that how she felt too?

No, I'm being ridiculous. Emily has been good to me. She's becoming someone I can turn to in need, exactly as I did today, and I want to cling on to that. Not destroy our newfound friendship with needless paranoia. And Simon is a respected lawyer, not to mention Jon's best friend. He would know for sure if his partner was somehow involved with Harry's abduction.

Reaching the front door, I find it slightly ajar.

Camilla's car is parked outside next door. No sign of Treve's work van. I glance up at their house, and see the bedroom curtain twitch.

The rain is persistent now, drumming noisily on the pavements and car roofs along the street. I run a hand through my wet hair, suddenly self-conscious. I must look like a drowned rat, and I can't shake off the impression that Camilla is watching me. More paranoia that I can't afford.

Frowning, I push the door and walk inside.

'Jon?'

There's a shuffling noise, then Jon emerges from the lounge. The light is not on in there, even though the persistent rain is making the whole house dark.

'Home at last?'

He has been sitting there in the gloom, waiting for me. And judging by his expression, he has had ample time to work up a temper.

He hasn't changed, still wearing his work suit, though it's looking a little creased now. He's taken the tie off, the collar and two shirt buttons undone, which is unusual for him. Normally he changes into jeans and a T-shirt as soon as he comes home. I wonder if he came home only recently, or perhaps has been napping on the sofa while he waited for me to arrive. It's just something about the rumpled state of his hair, a slight sheen to his skin.

'Where did you go?' I ask, my voice uneven. 'I looked for you, and the police said you'd gone. That you'd left without me. Without even finding out if Harry was there.'

'I knew he wasn't there.'

'What? How?'

'I was waiting for you by the car. That was what the police told me to do. They wouldn't let me go into the farmyard to find you. Then your voicemail arrived, telling me Harry wasn't there. So I left.'

211

'Without me?'

He shrugs.

I turn and go into the kitchen, if only to put some distance between us. I don't know why he's angry with me, but I can feel it, and it puts me on edge.

He follows, saying nothing.

I put the kettle on and turn to face him. 'Even if the police wouldn't let you through to find me, you could have rung me. Replied to my message. I would have come to find you.'

'I didn't think of it.'

'Well, I was going out of my mind, wondering where the hell you were.' I wait, but still he says nothing. 'They found two babies at the farm. In a pit under the barn. DS Dryer went down there. He found Poppy alive. She looked well. But the other . . . He was dead. The youngest one, Tom.'

A muscle jerks in his jaw. 'Shit.'

'Jon, what's going on?' I burst out. 'You drove off without me, you bastard. And I've got no idea why.'

'Haven't you?'

'Of course not. I'm not psychic. Why leave me there, Jon? It was a crappy thing to do. Is it because you blame me for Harry's disappearance? Because it wasn't my fault. I swear, I locked the front door after Emily left that night. I checked several times before we went outside to eat.'

'It's not about Harry.'

'Then what?'

'It took me a while but I finally worked it out,' Jon says, as though answering my question. 'With hindsight, I'm amazed I didn't see it before now. I suppose the business with Harry distracted me.'

Bewildered, I study his face for clues.

'I don't know what you're talking about,' I tell him frankly.

'Seriously, is that the best you can do?' His mouth tightens. 'Come on, drop the innocent look. It doesn't suit you.'

'Sorry?'

'I caught the two of you earlier today, remember?'

I hear the sneer in his voice, the barely disguised hostility, yet can't seem to register his meaning. The kettle rumbles and hisses behind me.

'Jon, you've lost me.'

'Enough bullshit, just come out and admit it.' When I don't respond, he adds with deliberate exaggeration, 'You and Treve.'

My eyes widen on a discovery. It's not me who is mad, it's him. 'You think I've been having an affair behind your back? At a time like this?' Then I focus on the name, and it feels like he's slapped me. '*With Treve?*'

'*With Treve?*' He mocks my tone. 'Yes, with our next-door neighbour. The classic bored housewife's choice. You've been going next door to borrow a tool.'

The image he has conjured is lewd and ludicrous at the same time. Me in bed with dark, thick-set Treve, whose physique always reminds me of some kind of beast? I have often secretly wondered what Simon would be like as a lover, his lean body so like Jon's, and his sleek blond looks undeniably head-turning.

But never Treve.

You've been going next door to borrow a tool.

He's serious.

'You've got it wrong. I'm not having an affair with Treve or anyone else. You came home today to tell me about the Snatcher, found me with Treve on the doorstep, and totally misinterpreted what you saw.'

'Which is what, exactly?'

The kettle has almost reached the boiling point. It's shuddering and churning, steam constantly escaping, dampening the side of the kitchen cupboards overhead.

'A kind man trying to help his neighbour out.'

He shakes his head, and one corner of his mouth lifts in a disdainful smile. Treating me with contempt again. 'Darling, you must think I'm so naïve.'

'No, I think you're distraught,' I say sharply. 'Either that or stupid.'

The smile drops straight off his lips.

He comes round the breakfast table, his gaze locked on mine. There's a sudden air of menace about him that makes me want to shrink away. But I refuse to move, willing myself not to show fear even when he stops right in front of me and stares down into my face.

It has stopped raining at last. I can no longer hear its noisy, restless patter against the windowpane. The kettle comes to the boil, and clicks off.

I do not move to make the tea though. I dare not break eye contact.

The kitchen settles back into silence.

'I know what a woman looks like when she's lying,' he reminds me. 'And don't forget, I happen to know what you look like after sex.'

'No.'

But I am remembering how I must have looked earlier, when he drove up and caught me with Treve on the doorstep. Flushed, dishevelled, a little wild, perhaps. But like a woman in love? I suppose it's possible. It could have looked to a jealous husband like we were coming out of the house after a secret tryst.

No wonder he was so aggressive towards Treve.

Jon sees me thinking, and his eyes narrow. 'Now, time for truth, please. You've never been to bed with Treve?'

'No.'

'Has he ever tried to get you into bed?'

'No.'

'Hinted that he wants you?'

'No.'

'Behaved suggestively, touched you, made any kind of—?'

I interrupt him with an angry, 'No.'

'And you don't find the man attractive?' Jon continues, watching me intently. Ever the lawyer, his voice softens, becomes persuasive when I do not answer. 'Not even a tiny bit?'

For a split second of idiocy, I allow myself to take that question seriously. To consider Treve in those terms, not just as a next-door neighbour and Camilla's husband, a man who likes to keep his garden scrupulously clean, but as a potential lover. I think of his patient smile. The generous way he fills a space. His large hands and blunt, neatly trimmed fingernails. The unexpected frisson of intimacy I felt when he stood close to me earlier today, and how I had become aware of him physically . . .

'No.'

Jon's hand explodes out of nowhere across my face and sends me staggering backwards into the wall.

'Liar.'

Chapter Twenty-Seven

'Liar,' he says again, barely a second after his blow knocks me backwards into the kitchen wall. 'You lying, adulterous bitch.'

I tumble sideways, ending up on the floor, half-supported on my elbow.

He stands over me, his mouth tight, fists clenched like a prize fighter. Like he's going to slug it out with me.

Except I never hit back, and he knows it.

'Jon?'

Crouched on the kitchen lino, I look past him, gasping with shock, my heart thumping, ears still buzzing with the effect of his blow.

Camilla is standing in the kitchen doorway.

'The front door was open. I heard raised voices, and I thought . . .'

At her voice, Jon turns his head in surprise. Even in profile, I see a change come over his face. Like a mask being hurriedly pulled down to hide the ugliness beneath.

Too late.

Camilla looks at me, clearly stunned. 'M . . . Meghan, are you . . . Do you need any help?'

I say nothing.

This is not her fight, not her business.

'Get out of our house,' Jon tells her, his voice like a whip.

But Camilla does not leave. She hesitates, then takes another step forward, as though to see me better, ignoring his angry movement.

'Meghan?'

I clamber to my feet, gripping on to the kitchen surface for support.

It was more of a slap than a punch this time, across my cheek and into the hairline. Designed not to leave a mark, or not one that cannot be hidden later by strategically applied blusher. But still hard enough to make my eyes moisten and blur; it's not always something I can control, much as I hate crying in front of him, and even less now Camilla is here. Not a default, more like a reflex action.

'Go,' I agree. 'I'm . . . fine.'

Hysterical laughter rises in me, and I have to suppress it.

Fine?

Who am I kidding?

Camilla stares at me, then Jon. For a second, I think she is going to refuse. But then she nods and stumbles away. I hear the front door closing quietly.

So here we are again. Back to zero.

I don't know why I'm surprised that he's started hitting me again. My pregnancy changed us as a couple; softened some of the hard edges between us, made our marriage feel different. But then we discovered that Harry was special, and everything shifted again, became more dangerous, less predictable.

There was a temporary lull in hostilities while we tried to find a place for ourselves in this new, three-person dynamic. I even fooled myself that it was going to work. But now he's thrown aside that uncomfortable mask of good husband and father, and fallen back

217

on his petty hatreds and feuds, the iron control he likes to wield at home when the outside world is not going his way.

I stare up at him and see that he is still boiling over with anger, still looking for a fight. He's not angry at me though. Not really. Jon's anger is at the world, at destiny, at the haphazard and not always one hundred per cent accurate way human DNA seems to work. He's angry with life for having thrown us this unexpected curveball, a child who is not perfect. He cannot understand why these things have happened to us – or more pertinently, to him, to perfect Jon. He sees it as a personal affront. An attack on who he is and what he stands for. As far as Jon is concerned, there always has to be a reason for the shit in his life, and a range of people he can blame for it – and punish, as often as possible. I fall deep into that category.

But sometimes there's no reason. Nobody to blame. Shit just happens.

And now our imperfect child is probably dead.

It deadens me inside even to think that. But I have to be practical. Kept so long without medication, in God knows what kind of conditions, how could he still be alive? At some point, you have to give up wishing for the impossible, you have to abandon hope.

Is this the day when I finally reach that point?

'You blame me, don't you?' I meet his eyes, suddenly furious too. 'For the whole thing. For Harry.'

'Shut up.'

'Because it would be easier for you if he never came back. And you can't bear admitting that, even to yourself.' I rub my aching cheekbone. 'I hate you sometimes.'

'I know you do.'

'But I'm not having an affair with Treve.'

He hits me again.

I'm not expecting that, and it takes me by surprise.

I try to dodge the blow at the last second, and he catches me fuller than he intended. My head snaps back and I gasp.

'Don't say his name.' He's more aggressive now that he's hurting me, not less. 'I saw you together on the doorstep.'

His voice thickens. 'Was he coming out or about to go in though? How many times has he been here? Jesus Christ, in my own home.'

'You're so full of shit.' I straighten, my cheek throbbing, my eyes stinging with tears, and push past him.

'Hold on, where are you going?' he demands, catching at my arm.

Jon thinks I'm trying to run away, that I'm scared of him. He's wrong. I just needed to get out of that corner.

I swing round to face him, shaking off his hand.

Then I hit him.

It's a full-on punch, close-fisted, knuckles first, pushing through his face and beyond it. There's a muffled crack as bone meets bone.

Jon reels back against the kitchen cabinets, caught off guard, his look one of blank astonishment. His hand flies up to his face and comes away red with blood. He stares down at it, speechless, then grabs the nearest tea towel and clamps it to his face. From the way he is swearing under his breath, it would seem that it hurts.

'You sadistic bastard,' I hiss, both fists still clenched, as though ready to hit him again. 'How do you like it?'

He stares at me over the top of the blood-stained tea-towel, but says nothing. It looks like I've broken his nose. Or done it some serious damage, at least.

Adrenalin has kicked in, like a Class A drug injected straight into my bloodstream. I can barely feel the pain. Not like before. My knuckles are tender where I hit them, but really, it's nothing. And the throb in my face is like a badge of honour. Yes, that's where he hit me. But you should have seen what I did to him.

I glance at my face in the reflective glass door of the microwave. I look wild, flushed, exhilarated – and like I'm going to develop a black eye.

'Get out and don't come back,' I tell him unsteadily.

He lowers the bloodied cloth then, staring. 'You must be joking. This is my fucking house.'

'Then you'd better get yourself a good lawyer. It shouldn't be too hard,' I tell him. 'Just ask around the office.'

'You're out of your mind.'

'Maybe I am, but I still want you to pack a suitcase. You have one hour.' I point to my swelling cheek. 'Or I'm taking this to the police. Is an assault charge crazy enough for you?'

Without waiting for a reply, I leave the kitchen and hurry upstairs. I drag his favourite suitcase out from one of the fitted wardrobes, toss it on to the bed and unzip it. My heart is thudding and I can't stop my hands from shaking. But it feels good to be in charge of the situation for once.

Then I hear him coming up the stairs. Swiftly, I run into the small bathroom and slam the door behind me, turning the key to lock it.

The lock doesn't look very strong. I hope he doesn't decide to kick the door down.

I stare nervously at the key. The window blind has been lowered, and it's dim and gloomy in the bathroom. I don't have my phone, so can't check the time. But I guess it must be early evening. I hadn't realised how much time had passed while we were arguing downstairs. But with Jon, when he's angry with me, everything I've done is dragged out for appraisal, everything has to be examined and pored over.

I click on the light so I can see what I'm doing. He goes into the bedroom first, and walks about for a bit. Then comes back out and hesitates on the landing. I know he's not going to give up that easily. He'll want to try to wheedle me out of my decision. I'm not stupid though. I've won this round. And I'm not going to give him the chance to hit me again.

'Meghan?' He knocks on the bathroom door. A tentative rap, almost respectful. 'Are you okay?'

I hold my breath, and say nothing.

'May I come in?' He tries the door handle, finding it locked. 'I'm not going to hurt you. I just want to talk.'

I stare at nothing, waiting.

'I'm sorry I hit you. I don't know why I did that. I just . . .' His voice turns pleading. He rattles the door handle again. 'Meghan? Please, darling, let me in.'

I trace the swelling on my cheek with one exploratory finger, and wonder how bad it will look by tomorrow morning. I may need to find some concealer.

Jon waits another moment, bending down to the bathroom keyhole as though trying to look inside. But the key is in place on my side. He won't be able to see a thing. I hear his breathing though, deep and rapid, right on the other side of the wood panel. Like having a wild animal prowling about outside your door.

'Fuck you,' he finally snarls, then goes into the bedroom and slams the door. A moment later, I hear the scrape of drawers noisily opening and closing.

I hope he is genuinely packing and not trying to trick me into coming out.

Shaking with reaction, I turn my back to the door, then slide slowly down it until my bottom hits the cold lino. I draw up my knees and hug my arms about them, turning my hurt cheek upwards and resting the other against my knee.

I cry then, but in as near-silence as I can manage, muffling the sobs against the back of my trembling hand. I taste salt on my sore lip, and remember how I cried the night Harry was taken. Only a few days ago, yet already it feels like another century. Like a time far in my past, when I was still a child and thought nothing could be worse than walking into his nursery and seeing that cot standing empty.

I wonder about Tom's parents, how they're coping; how anyone copes with the death of a child. Not just their death, but murder. I don't believe in God, but find myself praying anyway. I need to hold my baby again. Just one more time. Please, please.

I rock back and forth. It's like being a little girl again, hiding in the bathroom after a terrible row with one of my friends. Except I don't have any friends to argue with. Not anymore. I lost them all, or left them behind when I got married.

Now it's just me and Jon.

And Harry.

Only Harry's gone. And soon Jon will be too.

He takes his time packing, as I feared he might. He is not going quietly either. I catch violent expletives as he moves about the bedroom for what feels like hours, rattling coat hangers, knocking stuff to the floor, and even mysteriously ripping up papers at one stage. Credit card receipts? Bank statements? Old letters?

'Selfish, ungrateful bitch,' he shouts from time to time. 'Is this what Harry has to come home to now? A single-parent family?'

I silence the angry words in my head. He is not ready to hear them anyway.

'You stopped being any good in bed years ago,' Jon throws at me through the dividing walls. His voice is sneering now, deliberately cruel. 'I had to fake enjoying it.'

Ditto, I think coldly.

I hear the bang-bang-bang of his suitcase down each stair about two hours later, then the jarring thud of the front door behind him.

Letting out a deep breath, I decide to give it another half an hour, just to be certain. I know Jon and his ways. But there's no sound.

I don't know what the time is. But it's getting dark outside; the light has faded against the window blind.

At last, I decide it must be safe to move. I clamber up unsteadily and stumble across to the sink. My legs and feet have gone numb with pins and needles. I stare at myself and suck in my breath in disbelief. The classic battered-wife look. Straggling hair, wide eyes, pale, waxen face, and a dark, shoehorn-shaped bruise across my cheek, exactly like I have walked into the proverbial door. This is what everyone is going to see tomorrow. This is what he's done to me.

What I have *allowed* him to do to me, I correct myself. Over too many years, and behind too many discreetly closed doors.

I desperately want to phone my mum, tell her what's happened. She can't help, but she could comfort me, at least. The problem is, she would panic and tell my dad how badly things are going, and I can't stand to think of him getting upset. Not with his angina. She would also insist on flying home to England to stay with me, and while I love them, I'm not ready for that stress right now. Having to worry about my dad's heart as well as Harry.

Not until I know for sure if my son is still alive.

Wearily, I strip and step naked into the shower cubicle. I turn on the hot water and stand beneath it with head bowed and eyes closed, letting everything sluice away from me like blood: the stress, the unhappiness, the terrible grief, even the rage I have been feeling towards my husband.

Fifteen minutes later, I rinse off, every inch of me shiny and smooth and ready for life, and stand under the dripping shower-head for a few moments in contemplative silence. I am clean again at last. But all the time, I'm aware of this tiny black seed in my heart, purpling and growing like a cancer, threatening to kill me.

Harry's absence.

I have to believe he's still alive, I decide. If I allow him to be dead in my imagination, then his chances of being alive in reality will diminish too. More than ever, I need some purpose to cling to, something to believe in. Besides, it feels like a kind of betrayal to assume he is dead.

Harry isn't dead, I tell myself firmly. My baby is alive and well, and I'm going to find him and bring him back home.

I step out of the shower cubicle and reach for a clean towel from the rail. Which is when I hear it. A tiny, barely perceptible noise from below. A creaking sound, like someone opening the front door.

Chapter Twenty-Eight

I stand perfectly still, my hand on the towel rail. What the hell was that? But the creaking sound does not come again, and after a few seconds, I begin to breathe more easily.

How ridiculous. It's ages since Jon left the house. How likely is it that he would come back without announcing himself and start creeping around downstairs? If he had forgotten something, he would hardly be behaving so covertly. He would stride back in, bang about furiously, and then leave again.

It's more likely I'm jumpy because I'm alone in the house.

I'm suddenly aware of my nakedness, my hair dripping coldly down my back. It's not the most comfortable position. I am just beginning to wrap the towel around me when something happens that takes my breath away.

The bathroom light goes out.

And I stand there in the darkness, my heart thudding under my breastbone.

Don't panic, I tell myself. But it's too late, I'm already panicking. I try to stay calm and think logically. There's probably a simple explanation.

Maybe the bulb is dead.

I try to recall when the bathroom light bulb was last changed. Maybe it's not been changed since we first moved in. I stare down at my feet in the darkness, hoping to see light under the door. But there is nothing.

I struggle against the tide of fear rising inside me. If I just wait a few more seconds, my eyes will adjust to the dark, and then I should see a glimmer under the door.

The darkness continues to mock me, black and stifling.

My hand hesitates on the key, not turning it. Some internal bat-squeak of caution warns me to stay put another few seconds.

Then I hear it.

It's the creaking sound I heard before, only now it's like a foot pressing down on a loose stair board, then releasing it. It's louder too, closer at hand. One creak, then another, then a long pause, and then a third.

Like someone coming up the stairs as slowly and quietly as possible.

I withdraw my hand and take a step back from the door. The floor creaks under me too. My heart gives a jolt, then shudders on, beating hard.

Someone is outside on the landing. I can hear them breathing.

I almost say, 'Jon?'

But my brain tells me it's not Jon even before the word forms on my lips. I know what Jon sounds like in the dark and this is not his light, easy breathing. It's harsher, deeper, faster . . .

It's a man though, I'm sure of it.

A strange man is standing outside my bathroom in the dark, breathing as he listens. But listens to what?

To me, breathing.

My free hand curls into an instinctive fist, nails biting into my palms. The other grips my towel at my breasts, as though he can see me through the locked door.

Stay calm, stay calm. Don't give yourself away.

The listener outside the bathroom shifts. Tries the door handle.

I can't move, my whole being rooted in horror.

Then I hear a creak to my right. Whoever it is has gone into my bedroom. But only for a few seconds. Then they're on the landing again, passing the bathroom and going into the nursery.

My eyes widen at a scuffling and rustling from Harry's room.

Are they touching my child's things? Taking them away?

I tense up, trying to make sense of the little noises I can hear. Is this the same person who came in and stole Harry from us? Or is this intruder some kind of accomplice to the Snatcher, perhaps? But why come back to the scene of the crime? Why not wait until the house is empty? Unless they didn't know I would be here?

But then why cut the lights?

To frighten me.

The door to the nursery clicks shut.

I hear the breathing again as they pass the door. Then another tiny creak, this time at the top of the stairs. Then another, further down, softer.

They are leaving.

Something snaps inside me. How dare somebody come in here and abduct my child? Then come back and terrorise me when I'm on my own? What kind of fucked-up person is this anyway, taking a baby away from his mother, wandering about my house in the dark, scaring the shit out of me?

I lean into the steamed-up door panel and scream, 'Where's my son, you fucker?' I bang on the door, then kick it, barefooted. 'Hey, you bastard. I want Harry back. I want him back right now. Or I'm going to kill you.'

I fumble to unlock the door and stumble out on to the landing, clutching at my towel, my hair still dripping, my body wet.

It's pitch-black. I can't see a thing.

'You hear me?' I yell down the stairs, and hear the ghostly thud of the front door below. 'Yeah, you run. Because I'm going to fucking kill you.'

I step back and hear a tiny crunch underfoot. Pain shoots through my heel, and I cry out.

I bend down and feel about on the carpet. There are two or three small objects there, plastic by the feel of them, sharp and hard. Broken too, judging by the pain in my foot. I want to see what I've trodden on, but when I grope along the wall for the light switch, it doesn't work. No power.

The possibility strikes me that it's a power cut. Pure and simple. Even so, that would not explain my intruder.

I make my way down the stairs, limping, grimacing, holding on to the banister. At least there's a vague glow from the street lights in the hall at the bottom. None of the light switches downstairs seem to be working either. I stand there in the glimmering darkness and listen, feeling foolish now that it's all over. The silence in the house is thick and oppressive, but I do seem to be alone.

I hear a car start up somewhere nearby, and see the faint trace of headlights through the frosted glass of the door. I nudge my way outside, still wearing nothing but my bath towel, and limp to the garden gate. The car has gone by the time I get there, but at least there's light outside, a gentle rain falling, and I don't feel so shut in.

Our car is still parked outside.

That surprises me. It's Jon's car, not mine. I'm the one who uses it most, but only because of Harry. Now that Harry is not here, I assumed Jon would have taken it.

Perhaps he walked into town instead. Or used his mobile to ring for a minicab.

I realise that I have no idea what the time is. Dinner time, maybe.

There's a light on downstairs next door at Treve and Camilla's. I see its gleam through the lounge curtains. So it's unlikely that the whole street has lost power.

I hesitate.

There's nobody about. Nobody to see me.

I run down the garden path and ring the doorbell.

A long, excruciating moment goes by while I stand there, shivering in my towel, balanced on my toes, then I see a light go on in the hall.

Definitely not a power cut.

The front door opens and it's Treve in the doorway, tartan slippers on his feet, staring at me. He's in faded blue jeans and a tight-fitting black T-shirt, and for the first time I can see the tattoos on his upper arms close-up. I'd spotted the tattoos before, of course, but I've never seen them up close.

Snake-like, Celtic-looking, the strange, dark, matching patterns writhe about both biceps, accentuating the muscular bulge below the short black sleeve of his T-shirt.

I remember Camilla telling me Treve used to be in the navy, years before he met her. No doubt that's when he got them done. At least, I seem to recall that tattoos and the navy go together. Which makes sense: Treve's such a quiet, domestic type, he doesn't strike me as the kind of man who would go in for tattooing otherwise.

'So sorry to disturb you,' I begin, but he interrupts me.

'Meghan?' His brows jerk together in a frown, and he looks me up and down, making me very aware that I'm wearing nothing but a bath towel. 'Are you okay? What on earth's happened?'

Chapter Twenty-Nine

'Nothing, I'm fine. It's just the power has gone down next door,' I tell him hurriedly, 'and I think someone . . .' It seems ludicrous now, not quite believable somehow, yet I finish anyway. 'I think someone was in the house.'

'*What?*'

'I heard someone creeping about upstairs. While I was in the shower.'

'Fucking hell.' He sounds really shocked, which makes me feel better. Less like I'm losing my mind. His eyes narrow on my face. 'Where's Jon?'

I feel heat come into my cheeks. 'Gone out.'

To my relief, Treve does not question my explanation. He turns and grabs his house key, then nods at me to go first. 'Right, better take a look, then.'

'But your slippers,' I protest, glancing down at his feet. My own feet are bare and very uncomfortable. 'It's wet out here.'

'Don't worry about that.'

'What about Camilla? Shouldn't you tell her where—'

'She's gone to her mum's for the night.' Treve's face seems to close up, his mouth tightening. 'Dot's had another bad turn. She needed someone to sit with her.'

I remember then that Camilla's mum has been struggling against breast cancer for the past few years. Dot used to come round quite often, and sit out in the garden with them when the weather was good. Now she's in and out of the local hospice, poor woman. Such a horrible disease.

'I'm so sorry.'

He manages a thin smile as he closes the door, but says nothing.

I lead the way next door and push our front door slowly open. Everything is dark and silent, just as I left it. I was lucky the door did not swing shut while I was gone, I realise, as I forgot to take the key with me; it's still on the hall table. I can see the metal glinting in the faint light from the street.

Treve tells me to wait by the door, then feels along the wall for the hall light switch. He flicks it on and off a few times. Nothing happens. Methodically, he moves further into the house, and does the same with the light switch in the lounge.

'Have you checked the fuse box?' he asks, coming back into the hall.

The fuse box.

In my panic, that had not even occurred to me. I feel stupid as I shake my head.

'Where is it?' he asks patiently.

'Up there,' I say, and point into the dark space behind the front door where a closed box hangs about six feet up the wall.

He hesitates. 'There's a torch in the kitchen, isn't there?'

'Should be one in the drawer here too.'

I reach into the small drawer under the hall table and grope about for the slim, metal cylinder of the torch. Of course, it is still in there. As it always is, waiting for moments like these. But my brain never thought of it, nor the one hanging behind the back door in the kitchen. That's what fear does to you.

I check that the batteries are still working, then hand him the torch.

'Thanks.' Treve tries to close the front door, but it won't shut. He frowns, bending. 'What's this?'

He holds something out to me, and I take it. He shines the torch over it.

'It's a sock,' I say blankly.

Then I remember Jon banging downstairs with his suitcase. I don't know what to say. Clearly Jon dropped it in his hurry to get out.

'I imagine that's how your intruder got in. The door wasn't shut properly.' Closing the front door, Treve reaches up to the fuse box in the corner behind it. He opens the cover, then runs the torch beam across the confusing rows of fuses. 'Ah, as I thought. The trip switch has gone.'

He pulls the large red switch down with a heavy clunk. Lights go on at once throughout the house. The fridge starts up again with a whirring hum. He closes the fuse box, then clicks off the torch and returns it to the drawer.

'There you go, all sorted.'

He's smiling.

'Thanks,' I say, suddenly very aware that I'm wearing nothing but a towel. I can only imagine what Jon would say if he could see me now. Alone with Treve.

'You're welcome.'

I see his gaze studying my face, and look away, a little awkward. The bruising from Jon's handiwork must be pretty obvious.

'So why did the trip switch go off?' I ask, hoping to distract him.

He shrugs. 'Plenty of things can throw a trip switch. Did you have anything electric on at the time?'

'Nothing unusual.'

'You said, you were in the shower . . .'

'I'd finished and turned it off by the time the lights went out.'

'Right,' he says thoughtfully. 'Then I'm afraid it sounds like somebody tripped the switch deliberately.'

I shiver.

He studies my face again. 'That looks painful.'

'I fell over. In . . . In the dark.'

'Right.'

I can tell he does not believe me, and feel my cheeks grow warm. No doubt Camilla has told him all about the appalling scene she witnessed in the kitchen earlier.

He looks up the stairs without comment though, one hand on the wooden newel post at the base of the banisters. I keep remembering how it felt to be standing up there in the dark, utterly terrified, wondering if I was about to be attacked.

The stairs are lit now.

Everything looks ordinary, reassuringly so.

He asks, 'Want me to check the house over before I leave?'

God, yes, absolutely.

Mutely, I shake my head though. Jon may not be here to see us together, but I still feel awkward. Not least because, although Treve is not my type, he is very attractive. And I know from the way his gaze keeps running over me that he is not immune to me either. We are both married though, and we know it.

He nods slowly, his eyes very dark and thoughtful. Like he can tell exactly what I'm thinking. 'I'd better get back home, then. If you're sure that you're okay.'

I hesitate, feeling very far from okay, and see Treve glance down at my feet. I've been absentmindedly rubbing my sore heel over my other foot all this time.

'You're bleeding,' he says sharply.

I look down. My bare foot is streaked with fresh blood. 'Shit.' I turn my other foot up and hold on to the banister for balance. There's a small cut on my heel; it's seeping blood and looks messy.

'How did you do that?'

I am bewildered, then suddenly remember. 'There was something on the carpet at the top of the stairs. I trod on it when I came out of the bathroom.'

'*Something?*'

'Small and hard. Made of plastic, maybe. I couldn't see; it was too dark.' I pause; my heel is stinging now. 'Whoever came into the house must have dropped it.'

We both glance up the stairs.

'That's it, I'm going to check the house,' Treve says grimly, pushing past me and starting up the stairs. 'Every room, up and down. I'm sorry, Meghan, but I'm not leaving you alone here when there could be an intruder on the premises. If this was Camilla, and I was out somewhere, I'd expect Jon to do the same.'

I start to protest, but he's already halfway up the stairs. He stops at the top, and bends to pick something up.

I follow him upstairs, limping awkwardly, trying not to touch my bleeding heel to the carpet. 'What is it? What have you found?'

He straightens and holds out a piece of broken plastic. 'This.' He watches as I turn it over in my hand, frowning. 'Some kind of toy?'

I feel suddenly icy cold, my stomach tight with apprehension. It's part of a tube of rigid plastic, with numbers marked along one side.

'Jesus.'

'What?' Treve is staring at me. 'Meghan, talk to me. You've gone completely white. You look like you're going to be sick.'

'That's because I probably am,' I say faintly.

'Come here.'

He helps me limp back into the bathroom, but I am not sick. I refuse to vomit, to collapse, to allow these disasters to take me over.

I sway instead, beating off the nausea, and lean forward slightly, my forehead against the steamed-up tiles.

The room is spinning.

I try to focus on the moment, to think what needs to be done, but it's impossible now. All I can think about is Harry, lying on the changing mat in his nursery, chubby legs kicking, blue eyes widening as I handle his regular morning and afternoon injections.

Regular injections he can't manage without, or not without becoming very, very ill. Medication that my baby needs to survive.

Treve bends down and checks the sole of my foot. His hands are cool and gentle, the very opposite of Jon's.

'Here.' He grabs a handful of baby wipes and cleans my cut heel, then leans across to throw them in the bathroom bin. 'You need some antiseptic cream on that.'

'I'll be fine,' I tell him.

'Let me get you a plaster, at least.'

I nod towards the bathroom cabinet, and wait in silence as Treve rummages in there, returning a few seconds later with a tube of antiseptic cream and plasters.

'Sit down,' he tells me, pointing to the toilet.

I put the lid down and perch on the edge of the white toilet unit, then close my eyes as he kneels down before me and squeezes a small amount of antiseptic cream on to my foot. The smell is sharp in my nostrils, almost unpleasant. It makes me think of hospitals, and Harry's diagnosis, his long stay in the incubator as a newborn. But not for long. Treve's fingers are careful, rubbing the cream into my skin with tiny, circular motions while he cups my heel. I look down at his dark head, and become aware of a creeping sensation of warmth, a flutter of sensuality trying to get my attention, and fight against it.

He opens a plaster and covers the cut with it, smoothing down the corners. 'There,' he says calmly, glancing up at me. 'Better?'

I nod. 'Thank you,' I say huskily.

'You need something for that too?'

He is looking at my cheek. It must look badly bruised.

'I told you, it's fine.'

He does not release my foot, still cradling my heel. His dark eyes lock with mine. 'So?'

'So?'

'What was it?' He glances down at the piece of plastic still clenched in my fist. 'The thing you trod on.'

I hesitate, then relax my fist, letting him see. The piece of plastic rolls over, then settles in my palm. 'Part of a syringe.'

'I don't understand. You seem so upset. What's the significance?'

'Harry's sick,' I remind him wearily. 'He needs daily injections. The hospital supplied us with syringes and medication.'

'So?' he asks again.

'So, some medication was taken with Harry. But not enough. Whoever took him must have run out by now.' I stare down at the broken syringe, remembering the creaking footsteps on the landing, the rustling sounds I heard from the nursery. 'So they came looking for more tonight.'

His eyes widen. 'But that's fantastic news, Meghan.'

I stare at him.

'It means Harry's still alive,' he points out.

My heart jerks violently at those words.

'Yes,' I stammer, 'of course, you're . . . you're right.'

My head clears abruptly, the sickness abating, and I am flooded by a sudden sense of urgency. 'I need to call DS Dryer straightaway. That woman, the Cornish Snatcher . . . She must have an accomplice. That's who's got Harry.' Understanding hits me, and I stiffen. 'That's why he wasn't in that pit under the barn. Because there's someone else involved. And whoever that is, they came here tonight to get more of Harry's medicine.'

His fingers have circled my bare ankle and are now stroking upwards, light and unemphatic, as though he is not quite aware of what he is doing.

'I heard you two earlier,' he says suddenly, still gazing at my bare ankle and shin.

My attention snaps back to him. 'Wh . . . what?'

'You and Jon. You were arguing again. Then . . .' He looks up, nodding at the bruise on my cheek. 'You didn't fall over in the dark, did you? Jon hit you.'

Heat floods my face. 'That's none of your business.'

'It's not the first time he's hit you, is it?' He releases my foot and stands up in one strong, lithe movement. His gaze is on my face. It's hard to look away. 'Camilla told me what she saw. You're right, it's not our business. But for God's sake, Meghan, you can't let him hit you.'

'I don't,' I stammer, horribly embarrassed. 'When Camilla walked in on us . . . That was unusual. That was down to stress over Harry's abduction.'

I see pity in his face. 'Meghan, if you don't want to tell me, that's fine. But don't lie to yourself.'

I don't know what to say.

He holds out his hand. 'Come on, let me take a quick look round, then I'll get out of your way.'

I balance the broken piece of syringe on the sink surround, then let Treve help me up. Though he's right, I'm feeling much less faint now. I don't really need his help. But I do appreciate him being here. Knowing that he and Camilla have been discussing what goes on in this house is not pleasant. But at least he is not judging me. And he's here, which is more than my husband is.

Perhaps it's time I admit what Jon is like. Not just to myself, but to others. It's hard though. It would feel like admitting that I've failed in some way.

Once he's satisfied that I'm okay to walk about, Treve checks the bedroom very briefly, then glances around the nursery. The room looks much as I left it, still quite a mess. But with the light on, I can see that more of Harry's medication has gone. And one of his blankets.

'Someone has definitely been in here,' I say.

'You should tell the police.'

'Yes,' I agree.

Yet I don't seem able to move.

I stand over the cot instead and stroke my hand along the wooden rail, then set the mobile dancing. 'I can still smell him in here,' I whisper, and see Treve watching me. 'I know it sounds pathetic. But if I close my eyes and breathe in deep, I can almost pretend Harry's still here.'

Briefly, I tell Treve what happened out at the farm. The appalling things I saw and heard. How Jon left me there to cope with it alone. I don't mean to but I start to cry. I bow my head, close my eyes, and let it out, all the horror and stress and naked fear of the past few days since Harry disappeared.

'I just want him back,' I sob.

Treve comes up behind me. 'Of course you do,' he tells me. 'You're a good mother, Meghan. Don't let anyone tell you different.'

'I have to get him back, Treve. Whatever it takes.'

'Whatever it takes,' he repeats after me.

I hear an odd note in his voice, and turn, only to find Treve standing close behind me. So close that I can see hazel flecks in his eyes, stubble on his chin. So close that I realise the situation has become suddenly – and quite unexpectedly – dangerous.

He grabs me by the shoulders, then leans forward.

I need to move away, I think.

Too late.

Chapter Thirty

For a split second after he kisses me, I'm too bewildered to react. This is not what I was expecting when I invited him back here.

Or was it?

I stand still while his mouth moves persuasively against mine. Then my lips part under his, almost by accident, though I can't rule out the possibility that I secretly want this to go further. His tongue slips inside my mouth at once, gentle, exploratory. I feel his body moulded against mine, hard and urgent, and realise how little I'm wearing, the incredible intimacy of the situation, alone upstairs with my neighbour, practically naked . . .

Suddenly, I'm burning up for him, incandescent with desire. I press against him with a sigh that becomes a moan, and his kiss deepens. He strokes my bare shoulders, then drags at the front of the towel, anchored above my breasts.

I resist for a few seconds, then let it go.

The towel drops to the floor.

'Meghan,' he groans, and buries his face in my neck, kissing my skin, my hair still damp from the shower, while his hands cup my breasts. 'God, you're so beautiful.'

I think of Jon hitting me. His rage, his sudden bursts of violence. I think of him in the bedroom, his long months of neglect punctuated by sudden bursts of excitement that take me by surprise. His occasional odd taste for role-play. A touch of domination. Then back to a coldly turned back most nights, so that I can't work out what he wants or how to give it to him.

Treve's lovemaking is a thousand years away from that. He is tender, almost tentative. Though I can feel him growing in confidence.

My fault, I realise. For not pushing him away immediately. For not slapping his face, or shouting abuse, or whatever it is married women are supposed to do when their next-door neighbour tries it on.

How can I push this man away though? And why would I want to? He is not my husband, but he is turning me on. Clever fingers stroke my nipples. His tongue works in my mouth. His touch brings me back to life.

Why should I fear what Jon would think? He's hardly the best husband in the world. And he doesn't want me like this. He doesn't touch me like this anymore. Like I'm a real person, with feelings and a human body. To Jon, I'm a mere thing these days, a ragdoll, a sexual object to be used as he likes and forgotten about afterwards. And now I don't even have the comfort of my child to keep me sane.

I touch Treve back. And enjoy it.

'Yes,' he mutters, and pushes me against the wall.

I remember how Jon fucked me in the shower cubicle the day Harry disappeared. How the water cascaded down over his thrusting body, the cold tiled wall against my back. The shock of his unexpected sexual interest, and how quickly it faded once our guests arrived.

Yes.

His breath coming fast now, Treve lifts my body to meet his. To raise me to the right level. Then I feel him fumble at the fly of his jeans.

240

He is going to have sex with me. Right here, right now.

Fuck.

Lost in the blind urgency of the moment, I do not even consider objecting. Instead, I let him touch me, manhandle me, and even touch him back. He may be shorter than Jon, but he's broader too, more substantial. The difference is electric. I enjoy the feel of his still-clothed roughness on my naked body. The waistband of his jeans rubbing against me. The warm snub-head of his penis butting against the apex of my thighs, making it obvious what he wants.

What I want too.

I clutch at his broad shoulders, urge him on. I don't care anymore. 'Yes,' I repeat after him, and open my legs for him.

But as he adjusts my position, cupping my bare buttocks, we shift awkwardly sideways, and my hip bangs into the wooden side of the cot.

My son's cot. My missing son's empty cot.

Then it strikes me what I am doing.

And where I am doing it.

'Shit.' Reality comes flooding back, and the tide of sensuality is pushed back beneath it. In that instant, I change my mind, and push hard at his shoulders, his broad chest. This all feels wrong. Horribly wrong. 'No, I'm sorry, Treve. I can't.'

'What?' He buries his face in my neck, panting. 'But . . . you want it.'

'I can't,' I say again.

Treve raises his head to stare down at me. There's a hard flush in his cheeks, his eyes glittering. 'You're kidding?'

I look away, too embarrassed to meet his gaze any longer, and he mutters something under his breath.

I turn back at that hoarse whisper, catching a flash of what looks like fury in his eyes. 'Sorry?' Is he angry with me? He started this, after all. And he's married too.

241

'Nothing.' He grimaces. 'Forget it.'

Treve lowers me until my toes touch the carpet. Like a dance partner after the dance is finished. Then, with horrible incongruity, he turns away to zip up his jeans.

I apologise again, not sure what else to say. Perhaps I'm being too apologetic. I think of Camilla, and try to imagine her reaction if she knew what we had just done. This has been one of the more serious mistakes of my life, I decide. A moment of madness brought on by a spectacularly stressful situation.

But it's over now.

Except I know now that I want Treve. And he wants me. Which changes things. The relationship between us is no longer what it was only ten minutes ago when I invited him into my house to investigate a power cut.

Hurrying into the bedroom, I grab my dressing gown from the back of the door and belt it round my waist, the thin material covering my body down to my knees – though it's a bit late for a display of modesty. Treve comes to the bedroom door and watches me, his hands shoved into his jeans pockets. He looks brooding.

Downstairs, the telephone starts to ring, the shrill insistent sound breaking the silence. But it's a welcome relief, as though the outside world has intruded just in time to stop me from making a complete fool of myself.

Treve mutters, 'I'd better go.'

I don't argue, but follow him downstairs in silence.

The phone keeps ringing.

Fleetingly, I wonder if it's going to be Jon on the line. Maybe ringing to apologise. Not that he's very good at apologising. But he has made a habit of hitting me, then apologising, and swearing it will never happen again, and then one day hitting me again out of the blue. His vicious little pattern.

My lips are tingling from having been kissed so thoroughly. Jesus, we came so close. I'll never be able to look at Treve the same way again.

As soon as the door bangs shut behind him, I pick up the handset. My hands are shaking.

Guilt makes my voice husky. 'Hello?'

It's not Jon.

It's DS Dryer, sounding weary and a little on edge. 'Meghan, it's Paul Dryer. I'm sorry to be calling so late.'

My heart jolts in shock, all thought of Treve put aside. I stare at myself in the oval hall mirror opposite. I'm pale, hair damp and curling, eyes suddenly wide. I look ill. Maybe even a little unbalanced.

'Why are you ringing?' I have to force myself to say the words, suddenly breathless. 'Is it about Harry?'

'Are you and Jon able to come to the station?'

'Tomorrow?'

'No, tonight. In the next hour. I wouldn't ask if it wasn't important.'

I wet my lips, ridiculously nervous. 'Jon isn't here.'

'Can't you call him?'

'I could ring his mobile, I suppose. But I don't want to. That would be too . . .' I close my eyes, and blurt it out. 'You see, he's gone. Left.'

In my hurry, the words come out thick and tangled, probably the wrong way round. For God's sake, what am I saying? His silence on the other end of the phone feels like an accusation.

'Me,' I add carefully. 'He's left me. Packed a bag and gone.'

'Meghan, I'm so sorry.'

I have been holding it together so far, but his sympathetic tone makes the tears come. I can't say anything more for a moment. Or nothing coherent. I just gasp, blinking away the tears, struggling against the desire to sob aloud.

'Look, it's okay,' he continues when I say nothing, but I can hear frustration in his voice. 'You sound really upset. You don't need to come out tonight if it's too much.'

I glance at myself in the mirror again. Is that terror in my eyes? Yes, maybe I do need some support. And outdoor clothes would be good too.

My hand drops to the thin belt of my dressing gown, which is hanging loose and open, one of my breasts showing in the mirror. I have a sudden flashback to Treve pressing himself against me in the nursery, kissing me, touching my breasts, the horrible incongruity of that encounter, and wonder if I have lost all sense of perspective.

It's like I'm clutching at anything and anyone who might help me through this sense of loss, distract me from the gnawing fear of what lies ahead. But there's no avoiding it. Not anymore.

'Meghan? Are you still there?'

'Yes, I'm fine. I'll do it.'

'Very well.' He sounds relieved, not arguing. 'Thank you, I'll send a car to pick you up.'

'There was someone here earlier,' I tell him before he can hang up. 'An intruder. I think they were looking for Harry's medication.'

'*What?*' He sounds astonished. 'Why didn't you call me?'

'Whoever it was hit the trip switch when they came in, knocked the lights out. I was in the shower. My next-door neighbour turned the lights back on for me. I was about to ring you, honestly.'

'And you think whoever it was had come for Harry's medication?'

'Most of it has gone.'

'Right, I'm going to send some officers round. Don't touch anything, okay?'

'But what about the police station? You said you needed me to come over there.'

'They can check out the house while you're at the station. If that's acceptable.'

'Yes.'

'I have Jon's mobile number. I'll ring him too.'

'But what's this about?'

'She wants to speak to you,' Paul admits at last. 'The woman we arrested at the farm. She's not denying anything. But she won't tell us a damn thing about Harry.' He sounds almost embarrassed. 'She's insisting that she wants to see you first. That she'll only talk to you, in fact.'

'Me?'

I am shocked. My skin creeps with sudden cold. It feels so personal.

'She's been following the news. Child abductors usually do. She admitted that she caught part of your press conference. Then, of course, she saw you at the farm today. They like that kind of thing. To watch their victims squirm, see how much pain they've caused.'

'Oh God.'

'You won't be alone with her, don't worry. We'll be there with you the whole time.' DS Dryer draws a deep breath. 'Look, I know this is a hard thing to hear. The hardest thing for any parent. But I'm afraid you may need to prepare yourself.'

'Prepare myself?' My heart starts to race, my palm suddenly clammy, slipping against the handset. I already know the answer before I ask the question. 'For what?'

'For the fact that, whatever she wants to tell you, it's unlikely to be good news.'

Chapter Thirty-One

She's sitting at a table in a brightly lit interview room at the police station. The Cornish Snatcher, as the newspapers continue to refer to her. I recognise her at once, though she looks less intimidating here, as though she has shrunk since her arrest. The ankle-length dress has gone. The police must have taken her clothes for forensic investigation, I guess. She's wearing a shapeless white outfit like a jumpsuit now. Her pudgy face is pale, her black hair unkempt, cracked glasses smudged with fingermarks. She is staring straight ahead at the wall, wedged tight against the table with the wooden rim pressing into her large belly, both elbows resting on the table top.

The man in the creased grey suit next to her is presumably a lawyer. He is talking to her quietly as we walk in, but looks up and falls silent when DS Dryer announces my arrival. I glance at the lawyer briefly, and see pity and resignation in his face. It makes me wonder what she has told him. Nothing good, by the look of it.

The woman straightens, adjusting her glasses to stare at me.

I turn to Paul Dryer. 'Where's Jon?' I ask in a whisper.

'I couldn't get hold of him,' he replies, also in a whisper. His gaze meets mine. 'I'm sorry. He's not answering his mobile.' He hesitates. 'You okay to do this alone?'

I hesitate.

She may have Harry stowed away somewhere, perhaps with an accomplice. What if I say the wrong thing and make her angry?

We could lose Harry forever.

My heart begins to pound as the enormity of this meeting hits me.

Paul is waiting. 'Meghan?'

'It's fine,' I say, with more conviction than I feel. 'I want to do this.'

Paul Dryer told me when I arrived at the station that he could not tell me the Snatcher's real name. For legal reasons, apparently. But he said they had agreed to refer to her as 'Chrissie' during tonight's meeting.

Chrissie.

It seems like such a nice, ordinary name. Not the kind of name you would give to a woman who abducts and murders babies.

The small interview room is crowded with police officers. DC Gerent is there, standing against the wall opposite, hands clasped behind her back, watching the proceedings with an unreadable expression. DI Pascoe is there too, following us in with some manila folders that he hands to Paul Dryer with a shrug, as though he does not think they will be much use.

'My client needs a rest,' the lawyer begins, a slightly aggressive tone to his voice, but the woman interrupts him.

'Not yet.' She is looking at me keenly. 'I want to speak to her first.'

I do not like to meet her gaze.

DI Pascoe looks round at me. 'Right, I think we should make a start. Would you like to sit?'

There are two blue plastic seats on our side of the table. I choose the one nearest the wall, opposite the lawyer, perhaps because I do not like the idea of looking directly into the Snatcher's face. I feel cowardly at once, and wonder if I have made a tactical error. That she knows now that I am afraid to face her.

But it's too late to change. Inspector Pascoe has sat down next to me, facing the woman, and put his hands flat on the table.

'Well, this here is Meghan.' I hear tension behind the warm Cornish accent and am oddly comforted by it. It matters to him too, that we find Harry alive, and find him soon. He is doing his best for us. They all are. 'She's come to talk to you, Chrissie, exactly as you requested. Much against my better judgement, I have to tell you. But she's here. So I trust you're going to be more cooperative now.'

'I have been cooperative,' she tells him sourly.

'Not about the whereabouts of baby Harry.'

'Baby Harry,' she repeats, seeming to savour the words. Then she turns her head and smiles at me. The same cloying smile she gave me in the farmyard. The same vile 'I know something you don't' smile.

'Now, Chrissie,' DI Pascoe continues, his bushy eyebrows contracting fiercely, 'is there something you'd like to say to Meghan? She very much wants to be reunited with her baby son, and I know you can help us with that.'

'Can I?'

'I'm sure your lawyer has explained the benefits to you. That it could serve you well later if you can show that you helped us find Harry.'

Chrissie shrugs, still looking at me.

I force myself to hold her gaze. It's horrible. My skin is creeping, and what I actually want to do is lean across the table and force my thumbs into her eye sockets. But DI Pascoe is right. She holds the key to Harry's whereabouts. I have to do this, for his sake. There's still a fleeting chance that he might not be dead. I have to hold to that, not give up hope. I owe it to Harry to believe he's still alive.

'Please,' I say, beginning with a plea, keeping my voice soft, as instructed by Paul Dryer before we entered the room, 'if you know where Harry is, tell us. Tell me. Please, I'm not angry. I just want him back.'

She stares back at me without speaking, her mouth still curved in a half-smile, the light reflecting off her dirty glasses.

'Please,' I say again, softening my voice even more, 'where is Harry? He's sick. He's a very sick baby. He needs constant medication.'

Still she says nothing, just watches me avidly and with keen interest, like someone watching a beetle trying to crawl up the slippery walls of a trap.

'But you already know that, don't you?' I say, my gaze locked on hers. It's like staring straight into hell, into dark, smoking pits of turbulence, into madness. 'You took enough medication to keep him alive for a few days. Then you sent someone back for more.'

I swallow, seeing a flicker in her eyes. 'Please tell us. Talk to us.'

But she has her mouth closed; she is not going to say anything. This is pointless. She has brought me here to gloat over my pain.

'How did you know he was sick? Was it when you came to the house and saw the syringes? Or did someone tell you?' My voice hardens. 'Did you follow us home from the supermarket? How long were you watching us before you decided to take him?'

Her eyes flicker again. 'The supermarket,' she says wonderingly.

DS Dryer bends forward and whispers something to Pascoe, who listens intently and then nods.

'Yes, we'd like you to tell us what happened in the supermarket,' Pascoe tells her. 'Was that the first time you saw Harry?'

The lawyer glances up from his paperwork, surveying our faces, then speaks quietly to his client behind his hand. But Chrissie ignores him, waving the man away.

'You were in the supermarket,' she says, staring at me with what appears to be surprise. 'Yes, I remember. That was . . . Harry? The baby in the buggy?'

'Of course it was.'

I do not know what else to say. Does she not remember our encounter that morning? Or is this part of some elaborate plan to spin this out? To take so long to reveal Harry's location that he dies before the police can rescue him?

It's hard not to want to rip out her throat.

Pascoe has turned his head, studying her face. 'Are you saying you didn't choose Harry because you saw him in the supermarket?'

She ignores the detective inspector's question. 'What's wrong with your baby?' she demands, staring at me. 'Tell me, if you want me to help you find him.'

'It's a very serious condition.'

'How serious?'

'Please, just tell us where he is. What difference can it make to you now?'

'How serious?' she repeats.

'You must know how serious. You took the wall chart. And some medication.'

'Did I?'

She is smiling again.

My hands are trembling, so I shove them out of sight, under the table. Fear? Rage? Whatever it is, I don't want her to see my weakness and exploit it. Before they let me in here, the police took half an hour to explain how I should speak to this woman, what to say, and what not to show on my face, including anger and desperation.

I say humbly, 'Please, Chrissie—'

'My name isn't Chrissie.'

'Have pity on him. He's only a baby, and he's very ill. There's a real chance he could die without his medication.'

'So let him die.'

Fury surges through me again, and I struggle for a moment against its red mist.

Out of the corner of my eye, I catch DC Gerent staring at me, her thin brows frowning. Perhaps she can read my thoughts. Perhaps they are written on my face. All I can feel is a desire to kill. Is that so very wrong, under the circumstances? If we were left alone in this room for five minutes, me and the Cornish Snatcher, I would almost certainly try to kill her. I might strangle her, perhaps, squeezing that chubby neck until all life is extinct. Or beat her head against the interview room wall until her skull fractures and her brains spill out.

But I can do nothing to hurt her, and this smug bitch knows it.

I stare at her, sitting so meekly opposite me, triumphant in her protected status as the accused, examining her fingernails with apparent fascination. I feel nothing but rage and helplessness, the one fuelling the other.

For the first time, I realise the officers in the room may be there for Chrissie's protection as much as my own.

'We're not getting anywhere with this,' DI Pascoe says suddenly. He stands up. 'I'm going to suspend this interview until you are feeling more cooperative.'

'No!' the woman exclaims, and stands up too, knocking her chair backwards. Her belly looks enormous, straining against the white outfit they have given her to wear. 'No, I want to keep going.'

Her lawyer looks up at her, startled.

DC Gerent and a male constable grab the woman from behind, and force her to sit down again, while I stare, my heart thumping violently in my chest.

DI Pascoe has not moved from his seat. 'If you want to keep talking to Meghan here,' he tells her calmly, 'then you have to give us some useful information about her son. You have to tell us where you've hidden him. That was the deal.'

Her small mouth is pinched. It quivers as she looks from his face to mine, then shakes her head. 'I can't,' she says, and her voice is bitter. 'I can't tell you.'

'Can't or won't?' I demand.

She turns her glare on me. 'And if I say I won't?'

I realise that I have got to my feet and am leaning over the table towards her in an aggressive way. I feel the police looking at me with disapproval, and clear my throat, then sit down again slowly.

The woman seems amused by my aggression rather than intimidated. She folds her arms across her large chest. 'Well?'

'I'm sorry, I didn't mean to speak to you like that.'

'Oh, I rather think you did,' she contradicts me, that sour note back in her voice. She resettles her glasses on her nose, then folds her arms across her chest again, fixing me with that same hostile look I remember from the supermarket. 'In fact, I think you want to kill me.'

'No,' I say hurriedly.

'There's not much point denying it. You said as much in your press conference.'

'*What?*'

'Have you forgotten already what you said?' Her mouth twists in a smirk. 'Well, I haven't, so let me refresh your memory. You said, on camera, that if you didn't get your baby back alive, you were going to kill whoever had taken him.'

I instantly recognise my own words, and stare back at her, too shocked to speak for a moment. She's right, of course. I did say that at the press conference, or words to that effect. Because I was insane with anger, and desperate to get my son back. But now, at this very delicate moment, the truth is a slap in the face. And an accusation I can hardly deny. My own stupid mistake, my own arrogance, come back to haunt me. To stab me in the back.

If I do not take care, I am going to lose this fight.

And Harry with it.

'I did say that, yes,' I agree.

Her smirk broadens, becomes gloating. 'So you admit it, do you?'

I long to wipe that smile from her face, crush her under my heel until there is nothing left of her but dust. But I have to sit here instead, frozen with impotence, and let her say what she wishes. Do whatever she wishes. Let her destroy my life, and my son's life too, and then walk away, laughing.

Because she holds all the power, and I have nothing in my heart but fear and pain.

'Admit what?'

'That you're a killer too.'

Chapter Thirty-Two

Paul Dryer mutters something behind me, but I ignore him. This is my time, not theirs. The police brought me here to talk to this woman, to persuade her to give up my child, and that's what I intend to do.

I count silently to ten before answering her question. I'm angry, but I owe it to Harry not to lash out at her.

'I admit to saying that,' I tell her calmly, though I hear the quiver in my voice and know she must be able to hear it too. 'And I'm sorry if it upset you. But I didn't mean it like that. I've never killed anyone, and I don't want to kill you.'

'Is that so?'

'It was a stupid thing to say and I'm sorry,' I say again. 'But in my defence, when I said it, I was scared.'

Her eyes widen behind the thick-rimmed glasses, and her lips twist in a horrible way. She looks at me almost hungrily, as though eager to hear how much she has tortured my soul these past few days.

'Scared?'

I hesitate. 'Terrified.'

'Go on,' she says urgently, reaching out to me across the table. I look down at her hand, at the dirty fingernails and the deeply creased knuckles, but do not touch it. 'Please, tell me more.'

So now it's her turn to beg.

I glance at DI Pascoe, who hesitates, then nods silently.

She wants to hear about my pain and heartbreak. Not in general terms, but in gruesome, closely described detail. Like she wants to *feed* on it. And if I want to see Harry again, I must give this vampire what she wants.

'I wanted my baby back so badly, you see. I still want him back. My little boy. I don't want Harry to suffer anymore.' Somehow I jerk my lips into a tiny, humourless smile. 'You can understand that, surely?'

'Yes,' she agrees, her voice like a hiss in the dark. 'I understand. You missed him.'

I swallow past the lump in my throat, nodding my agreement.

'Tell me about *that*,' she urges me, and leans forward, her eyes on my face, her voice dropping low, as though we are confidants, alone together, and no one else can hear us. Her request feels acceptable, though inside I'm screaming at her to shut up, to leave me alone. 'How has it made you feel, being without your little baby?'

'It's been the most awful time of my life,' I whisper, holding her gaze. I feel tears roll down my cheeks, but do not raise a hand to wipe them away. I want her to see my pain. To witness it. 'Every day, I wake up and remember that Harry's gone, and it's like part of my heart has been torn out.'

'And your husband?'

'He's been out of his mind with worry too.'

'So where is he?' She looks about the interview room, then glances briefly under the table, as though she expects him to be hiding down there. 'If your husband cares so much what happens to his son, why isn't he here?'

My palms are damp with sweat. I clasp them together out of sight, staring at her. It's almost as though this bitch is psychic, like she can read my deepest thoughts. Or a witch, someone with powers none of us can understand or control. The idea terrifies me, and I have to tell myself firmly not to be so superstitious, that she is just a woman, and an evil one at that.

Witch or not though, she understands my pressure points, knows how to needle me with just the right question.

If he cares so much what happens to his son, why isn't he here?

'I . . . He . . .' My heart thumps violently as I lie to her, trying to look and sound casual. 'The thing is, the police told me you only wanted to speak to me. So Jon stayed at home tonight. In case . . .'

'In case?'

'In case there was any news.' I unclasp my sticky hands and rub them on my jeans. 'One of us had to stay at home. In case Harry was found.'

'So your husband doesn't hope he's already dead?'

'*What?*'

'Oh, I'm not judging him. A sick child. Who wants that in the family? Better to put the little runt out of his misery.'

The woman places her hands flat on the table in front of her. She takes a long, deep, contented breath, her broad chest rising with it. Her smile is so sweetly cloying, I feel physically sick and lift a hand to my face, almost retching behind it.

Is this creature even human?

She leans closer and her voice drops, conspiratorial now. 'I expect that's the *real* reason your husband didn't turn up tonight,' she adds. 'Because he secretly thinks it would be rather useful if his firstborn never came home again.'

'No.'

'And that's what you secretly think too, isn't it?'

'God, no,' I gasp.

The woman looks across at me and smiles. With untarnished happiness. As though I have made her life a little brighter just by agreeing to let her torture me.

'You devil,' I say, choking on the words.

DI Pascoe stands up. 'That's enough. I'm terminating this interview.'

DC Gerent puts a hand under the woman's arm, as though about to drag her away. Back to the cells for the night, I presume. Back to her deliberate silence. I can't allow that to happen.

'No!' I exclaim. 'Wait. I have one more question to ask. Please.'

'What is it?' The woman looks across at me with pleased expectation, her head tilted to one side, like a dog hoping for a treat. She's enjoying my desperation. 'I want to hear Meghan's question.'

I hate her using my name.

DC Gerent glances at DI Pascoe for permission, then releases the woman's arm. The policewoman stays beside her though, waiting impatiently for the interview to finish, her lips pursed with disapproval.

'Who is your accomplice?' I demand, staring at her, my whole body trembling with the effort not to leap across the table and beat the truth out of her. 'Who's been helping you?'

'I don't have an accomplice.'

'You're lying.'

'No, I'm not. I don't need no fucking accomplice. I've never needed no one.' Her voice sharpens, turns cruel. 'Do I look helpless? Don't tar me with your own brush.'

'But there was someone in my house tonight. Somebody came back for more of Harry's medication. I heard them.'

'Nothing to do with me.'

'And I saw her. At Lemon Quay.' When she does not react, I add, 'The middle-aged woman. Grey hair. Blue jacket. She was pushing Harry in a red buggy.'

She shrugs, looking blank.

'Look, you must have run out by now,' I say desperately.

'Run out of what?'

'The medication you took from his room.' I swallow. 'Please, Harry needs those injections every day. Or he could get sick and die.'

'I didn't take nothing.'

Rage flares inside me. 'You took *Harry*,' I almost shout at her.

'No, I didn't.'

There's an abrupt silence in the interview room. I hear someone breathing heavily, almost panting, and realise with a shock that it is me.

She is shaking her head at me. 'It was fucking hilarious,' she says into the silence, 'that interview they showed on the news. The way you threatened to hunt down and kill whoever took your baby. Like *you're* the one in control. After I saw that, I had to meet you close up, listen to you beg me for your baby. *Please, please, I just want my Harry back.* You sad, sorry bitch.'

'Don't say another word,' her lawyer tells her sharply.

'I was tempted when I saw him in the supermarket, yes. Just for a minute. But then you said he was sick.' She grimaces. 'Hate sick babies, can't stand to be around them. All they do is bloody scream the place down.'

'But you told the police—'

'One more name on a list of missing babies. What difference does it make to say, yes, all right, I took that one too, when I didn't?' She takes off her glasses and cleans them on her white sleeve. Then puts them back on and smiles her horrible, cruel smile at me again. 'And saying yes meant I could meet you like this, face to face. It's been a real treat, thanks for that.'

'Jesus Christ,' Paul Dryer says hoarsely.

I feel the blood draining from my face, my body turning to ice. I stare at her, trying to make sense of what she's saying.

'I don't understand.'

'I never took your baby, you stupid bitch.' She leans across the table, her gaze locked on mine, speaking slowly and clearly. 'Never went to your house, never took him away with me, never laid a finger on the little bastard. That clear enough for you?'

My chest is tight again. I'm breathing fast and shallow, like I'm about to have another panic attack. Even this place feels claustrophobic, the walls of the interview room closing in on me. And her words are going round and round in my head, alien, utterly incomprehensible.

'But if you didn't take Harry,' I whisper, 'then who did?'

Chapter Thirty-Three

I wake next morning with Emily's image in my head.

Emily, turning up late for our dinner party, looking pale and unsettled throughout the meal.

Emily, staring after Harry as Jon carried him back into the house. That look of longing on her face, as though forced to give up something precious.

Emily, putting dangerous words in my mouth at the press conference. Then mysteriously disappearing.

Emily, hiding a baby's dummy in her handbag.

Emily, forever texting and calling to ask how the investigation is going.

Emily, who has been trying unsuccessfully for a baby for – I don't know how long. Months? Years?

With these thoughts confusing my head, I wander down to the kitchen in my pyjamas, and am just filling the kettle when my phone buzzes with a notification.

It's Emily again.

You free for lunch?

I hesitate.

The Cornish Snatcher has categorically denied taking Harry, and the investigating team seemed tired and uncertain when I left the police station last night.

Maybe it's up to me now.

I meet Emily for lunch at a pub a few miles outside Truro, along the road to Falmouth. It's an old country inn, set back from the main road beside the meandering River Kennal. We order our meals at the bar inside, then carry our drinks out into the sunshine. We're both driving, so we've ordered non-alcoholic drinks: a pine-apple juice for Emily, an iced coffee for me. The pub gardens slope gently down to the waterfront, and we choose a picnic bench-style table right beside the river itself.

Emily is wearing a trouser suit that looks like it's come straight out of the Seventies: dark-brown check, with a bright-orange blouse. Another of her eye-catching outfits.

I'm in jeans again with a loose gypsy-style top. I didn't put much thought into my outfit this morning, just threw on what I could find in my wardrobe. I did spend some time on my make-up though, trying to hide the bruise from last night's argument. And I'm wearing heels. A concession to my femininity that makes me feel a bit better about myself.

She brushes away a few gnats from around her head. 'So hot today.'

'I love this place.'

'But the river attracts the flies.' She turns in her seat to look across the river. The sun reflects off her glasses as she tilts her head back, an almost blinding flash of light. 'It is beautiful though.'

'Thanks for asking me to lunch,' I say, watching her closely. 'I've not been very good at replying to your messages, I'm afraid.'

'You're upset and probably run off your feet too. Which is hardly surprising. And for what it's worth, I don't believe a word Jon says about you.'

'What's he been saying?'

'You know.' She shrugs. 'That you're not yourself at the moment. That you imagined seeing Harry that day at Lemon Quay.'

'I didn't imagine anything. I'm sure it was Harry. I was sure then, and I'm still sure now.'

Emily is smiling, perhaps because of my vehemence. 'It's okay, Meghan. I've never known you to be fanciful.'

'Thank you.' I pause, thinking it over. 'Did you tell the police that?'

'Nobody asked me.'

'Well, thanks for being so supportive anyway.' I hesitate, unsure how to go about questioning her without letting on that I'm suspicious. 'I don't want to get you into trouble though. Are you missing work for this lunch?'

'Day off. I'm on part-time at the moment anyway.'

'And how are you? You've seemed unwell lately.'

She grimaces. 'Endometriosis. You know, where womb tissue grows outside the uterus. Causes cramps and abnormal bleeding . . . Well, it's been quite bad this past year, though they say it sometimes gets better on its own. I take anti-inflammatories for the pain during a flare-up.' She pauses. 'That's what's stopping me from falling pregnant.'

'I'm so sorry.'

I believe her. But is it possible her condition has made her desperate for a child? So desperate that she could countenance stealing *my* baby?

'Did the police ever find that woman?' she asks, adroitly changing the subject. She takes a sip of juice, watching me over her glass. 'The one you saw with Harry that day.'

'No, though I got the impression they didn't look very hard. Frankly, the police think I'm a flake. Seeing Harry in every baby's face.'

'Idiots.'

'Well, it probably didn't help having Jon undermining my story the whole time. You probably saw the way he was with me before the press conference. He thinks I've lost it. That I need psychiatric treatment.'

'Have you heard from him yet? I was so shocked when he rang.'

I pause. 'He rang you?'

'Last night,' she admits, and glances away again, her expression distracted. 'He spoke to Simon, of course, not me.'

'And what did he tell Simon?'

'No details, only that you and he had argued. Are you sure splitting up over a row is the right move? Especially now, when you need each other more than ever. I'm sure it must be all this stress over Harry's disappearance that's causing any arguments.' Emily turns her head, looking at me sharply. 'Please don't think I'm interfering, but the two of you always seemed so close, so deeply in love. I thought you had the perfect marriage.'

I feel uncomfortable under her sudden close scrutiny. I was supposed to be the one grilling her at this lunch. Instead, she's making me question myself. I look away, and take a long swallow of my iced coffee. It tastes great, cold and pungent, just right for this hot weather.

'Appearances can be deceptive.'

'Not always.' She pauses, and I take another drink of iced coffee, wondering exactly what she means by that. Has her appearance – as a friend – deceived me? 'Did Jon do that?'

I look up, taken aback. I'd hoped my concealer had reduced last night's bruise to a dark smudge, barely visible in the dim light of the bathroom mirror this morning. But we're sitting in full sunlight, right opposite each other, and it's obvious Emily can see the discolouration for what it is. The after-effects of a marital dispute that got physical.

'Things became a bit . . . heated,' I mutter, touching my cheek.

'God, that's appalling.' Her voice hardens. 'If Simon ever hit me, I wouldn't hesitate. I'd call the police. Even if we had a child together.'

I try to steer her back to the topic of Harry's disappearance. But subtly. So she does not see where I'm heading.

'So Jon called. Did he stay with you last night?'

'No, though he asked if he could. I got the spare room ready for him, but he never showed up. And Simon says he's not at work today either.'

'Are you sure?'

'Simon's been calling his mobile on and off all morning. He says the call goes straight to voicemail, that Jon must have turned his phone off.'

I stare at her blankly, thrown by this information.

Paul Dryer said he tried Jon's mobile last night too, and couldn't get hold of him. It did not seem strange at the time. But during the daytime?

'Meghan,' she murmurs, 'do you think Jon would ever . . .'

'Ever what?'

She shrugs, looking awkward. 'Just something Simon said. That Jon is a little neurotic. Takes it very personally when the firm loses a case.'

'So?'

'Simon wasn't sure if Jon might perhaps be the kind to overreact in a situation like this. You know, with Harry missing, and then the two of you arguing.' She bites her lip. 'Simon wondered whether Jon might hurt himself.'

Taken aback, I say, 'Jon? Are you kidding?'

I think of my husband's carefully concealed temper, the way he has raised both his voice and his hand to me, always behind closed doors where I am the only witness, and have to bite back a laugh. I should tell her, really. Explain how bad things have become between me and Jon, particularly since Harry was taken. But I'm not ready yet to admit the truth about my marriage.

Besides, I didn't come here today to talk about me and Jon.

'No,' I say firmly.

'That's good to know.' She knocks back some fruit juice, then puts the glass down with a snap. 'But look, what about you? And the investigation? How's it going?'

I study her face. She seems so genuine, but I can't shake my suspicions. I'm still unsure that Emily is innocent, that she didn't take my child. But innocent or guilty, she's right about one thing. I have to focus on Harry now, and push Jon to the back of my mind.

Briefly, I explain about my interview with the Cornish Snatcher, avoiding the worst details and trying not to dwell on my emotional response to the woman, though I imagine my expression of disgust must give it away.

'Anyway, I thought it was all over,' I finish, 'that we were going to find Harry at last. Only now she claims she didn't take him.'

Emily stares, clearly shocked. 'But she must be lying.'

'Maybe.' I shrug. 'Maybe not.'

'She admits to having taken the other babies though?'

I nod. 'But not Harry.'

'God, how awful. I'm so sorry, Meghan. You must be going crazy.'

That's one way to describe it.

The meals arrive, and for the next few minutes we eat without talking. But I am going through her words in my head.

Even if we had a child together.

'Emily?'

She looks up from her meal, smiling. 'Yes?'

'I've got a confession to make.' I put down my knife and fork, and look at her directly. 'When you gave me that lift home, and you went into the garage to pay for fuel, your phone started ringing. It was in your bag.'

I see a change come over her face. Her lips part, her eyes fix on mine, but I continue regardless. 'It was Jon. He wouldn't speak to me, just hung up. But when I was putting the phone back in your bag, I saw . . .'

She is staring. 'What?'

'The baby's dummy.' My heart is beating furiously, a deep, erratic thud. 'The blue dummy in your bag. In a plastic box. And I wondered if . . . That is, I thought it might be you who did it.'

'Me who did what?'

'Who took Harry.'

Her eyes widen with incredulity. Then she laughs. 'Is this a joke?'

I shake my head.

'Okay,' she says, and her smile fades. 'Look, I had that dummy in my bag because . . . To be honest, I meant to give it to you as a little gift. That night at dinner. Only I got sick and couldn't stay. Then afterwards . . . Well, it wouldn't have been appropriate anymore. So I hung on to it.' She pauses. 'I'm really sorry if seeing it upset you.'

She reaches across the table, her fingers brushing my hand, and I jerk back as though I've received an electric shock.

Emily sits back too. She looks stricken. 'Meghan, this is me. I thought we were friends. Or becoming friends, at least. You really think I could steal a baby? Your baby? Take Harry away from you?'

'I don't know.'

She shakes her head vehemently. 'Not me.'

I study her face in silence for a moment, trying to read her expression, then nod. I'm still unconvinced. There's something about her defensiveness . . . I can't put my finger on it. But I'll take it up with Paul Dryer after lunch. There's no point pressing the point with Emily herself.

'Sorry. When I saw that dummy, I thought . . .' I shrug. 'I shouldn't have accused you like that. I'm not thinking straight at the moment.'

'Forget it.'

But I can hear the hurt and anger in her voice.

'I'm really sorry,' I repeat.

Emily looks away, her lips pressed tightly together.

Nerves flutter in my stomach. Fuelled by paranoia and lack of sleep, I spoke without thinking, and have inadvertently caused a crisis between us. If I'm not careful, I may lose her friendship. And I could do with a good friend right now. I need Emily.

I reach out and touch her hand. 'Please, will you forgive me? That was a crazy thing to say. I know it wasn't you who took Harry. And I should never have intercepted that call from Jon. That was what made my imagination start to work overtime. Though you did seem very taken with him at the dinner party.'

There's horror in her eyes now. 'The dinner party? No, it was nothing like that. I would never touch someone else's husband.'

'What?' For a moment, I'm confused. Then I realise her mistake. 'No, I meant Harry. You seemed so taken with Harry.'

'Oh.'

I see her look away, a slight tinge of red in her cheeks.

A sudden, horrible suspicion strikes me, and I stare at her averted profile. I force myself to say the words, though my lips feel numb. 'Christ, I've hit the nail on the head. You're having an affair with Jon, aren't you?'

Now she looks sick. 'Absolutely not.'

I hear truth behind that fervent denial. Maybe even a hint of repulsion. She doesn't like Jon. *Really* doesn't like him. Which makes me instantly suspicious.

'Emily, what do you know?'

'Nothing.'

'Please don't lie to me.' I stare at her across the table. 'Is Jon having an affair with someone behind my back? Maybe someone at work?' I see her smile freeze in place, then begin to fade. 'Please tell me if you know. I'm his wife, for God's sake. Don't I deserve the truth?'

She swallows, then puts down her knife and fork. 'I don't know anything,' she insists, but her voice is weaker now, the certainty gone from her expression.

'But you have . . . suspicions?'

'It's only a few things Simon has said. I don't have proof.'

I think back over the past year, remember the phone calls and texts, the repeated excuses about missing dinner because of a demanding legal case. 'All those times he said he was working late . . .'

'I can't be sure.'

I push my plate away, no longer hungry. I don't know why I feel so hurt. Perhaps because I've had suspicions before, when he's stayed out late after a big case, or disappeared off at weekends on professional training courses, but decided to give him the benefit of the doubt. Or perhaps because I stupidly thought, after Harry's birth and the discovery of his auto-immune condition, that Jon was concentrating on us as a family at last.

I allowed him to trick me, that's what hurts.

'Who is she?'

'Honestly, I don't know. And Simon would never tell me who it is, even if he knew. He and Jon are thick as thieves.' Her lips tighten, and she looks away towards the river. 'Sometimes I think he prefers Jon's company to mine.'

'I know the feeling.'

'I thought if I tried hard to have a baby, that Simon would look at me differently. Ask me to marry him. But he's not that kind of man, I suppose. Nothing's as important to Simon as making partner at that damn law firm.'

'You could be talking about me and Jon.'

'Except Jon married you.'

'I'm sure Simon will marry you,' I tell her.

Turning her head, Emily gives me a sad little smile. 'To be honest, I'm not sure that I want him to. Not anymore.' She frowns, then adds, 'Look, I know this won't make a lot of sense, but since we're talking about your husband, I keep asking myself where Jon went last night, why he's suddenly disappeared too.'

'What are you saying?'

'I'm not really sure.' Emily raises her gaze to my face, her look troubled. 'But it feels like there's a pattern to the way Jon's suddenly gone AWOL. Or a connection, at least. And we're just not seeing it.'

'A connection to what?'

She stares at me. 'To Harry's disappearance, of course.'

Chapter Thirty-Four

After lunch, we hug and say goodbye in the pub car park, then I wait until Emily has driven away before hunting through my bag for my mobile. I am determined to try Jon again, now that I've calmed down after our argument yesterday evening. I don't want him back, but he needs to know what the Snatcher said. He can't just walk away and pretend none of this is happening, that his son is not missing, that our marriage has not fallen apart.

I keep asking myself where Jon went last night, why he's suddenly disappeared too.

I don't believe Jon is connected to Harry's disappearance. Not even remotely. But I am beginning to worry that something may have happened to him. I was angry and hurt when I thought he might be with someone else, though I was not sure it was true. Now I am a little uneasy as well.

Could there be anything in what Emily said?

I try Jon's mobile again. All I get is a generic voicemail message, exactly as before, telling me to leave a message. This time I speak more urgently, hoping this will prompt him to get in touch.

'Jon, it's me again. Please call me back at once. It really is very important.' I hesitate, then add, 'There's been a development with Harry.'

I feel a little deceitful for saying that. But it's important that he gets in touch.

I stop, staring down at my phone. A voicemail notification is lit up on the screen.

My heart jolts.

Jon?

Hurriedly, I retrieve the message and put my ear to the phone, frowning as I listen. I don't recognise the number it came from, but it has a Truro prefix. So perhaps it is Jon, and he's calling from his hotel. That would be a relief, at least.

The message begins.

Nobody speaks.

I hear a long echoing silence, like whoever recorded the message was standing in a large, empty space. There's a faint rushing sound in the background, like a train passing through a tunnel, punctuated by a few high-pitched noises.

Birds?

Then I hear a baby crying.

I almost drop the phone, my hand shakes so hard. 'Harry?' The message is recorded, but I can't help myself.

It's him; it's Harry.

It's like that awful moment on Lemon Quay, when I heard a baby crying and knew it was my son, but couldn't see where he was in the crowd.

I know my own baby's cry, and this is Harry. I want to reach through the phone line and grab hold of him, hug him close forever. But all I can do is stand there helplessly and listen to him cry.

'Harry,' I sob.

To my relief he sounds hungry, a little petulant, perhaps, but – thank God – not hurt, not screaming in pain or for medication. He's not being tortured, then. And he's still alive. I cling to that idea with all my strength.

My baby is alive.

I wait, still listening, expecting to hear some kind of ransom message following his cry. But the message ends, and I moan out loud, rubbing the phone against my cheek, utterly distraught.

'No, no. Where is he?' The phone is silent. So I shout at nobody in particular, at the air around me, at the blue sky. 'Please, for God's sake, where is he? Where's my baby?'

An elderly couple getting into their car opposite cast doubtful looks in my direction.

Turning my back on them, I thumb the keyboard and listen to the message again, this time memorising the telephone number it came from.

I close my eyes, listening to that familiar cry again. A cloud moves over the sun as it finishes, chilling me. I can't keep listening to the same message again and again, I realise. I need to act.

Hurriedly, I scroll through my recent call list for Paul Dryer's number. I hit it, and wait, tears running down my cheeks, my heart hammering loudly.

The detective answers on about the fifth ring, sounding tired and impatient. 'Dryer here.'

'I just had a call on my mobile,' I gasp, leaning against my car for support. 'It was Harry. I heard him.'

There's a short silence.

'It was only a few minutes ago,' I add. 'Please, you have to find him.'

'Slow down, Meghan. You're not making any sense.' He pauses, listening as I gulp. 'Deep breaths, yeah?'

'Sorry.'

'Don't worry, it's okay,' he says calmly. 'Now, where are you? No, hang on, let me get a pen. Okay, tell me everything. Start at the beginning.'

Briefly, I tell him about my lunch with Emily, and explain where I am. He recognises the pub name at once. Then I describe the voicemail message, trying not to get too emotional about it. 'It was Harry, I'm convinced of that. I'm not sure how to play it again while I'm on the phone to you,' I say shakily, 'but I can tell you the number it came from.'

'Right, give it to me.'

He takes down the telephone number I have memorised, and I wait while he keys it into his computer.

'You need to hear this message,' I insist.

'I intend to,' he agrees. 'I have to do an interview in a few minutes, but come over to the station in an hour or so. Bring me the phone, I'll sort it out.'

I close my eyes. 'Thank you.'

'But listen, you're absolutely sure it was Harry?' He pauses again, as though he's reading. I wonder what the computer screen is telling him. 'It could have been a crank call. Maybe some other baby you heard crying. There are some sick types out there, the kind who take pleasure in tricking people in your situation.'

'I'm sure.'

But I know from his tone that he's remembering the Lemon Quay incident, and Jon's dismissal of my maternal instincts.

'I'm not mad,' I add firmly. 'It was Harry. I'd swear on my life.'

Paul clears his throat. 'Right.'

I decide to change the subject.

'Have you heard from Jon yet? I've been trying his phone but there's still no answer.'

'Same here. Apparently it's been turned off.'

I frown. 'Why would he turn off his phone? It doesn't add up.'

'Don't worry, I've just sent one of my sergeants round to his offices. We'll run him to ground soon enough.'

'He's not there. Or that's what I was told.'

'Not there?'

'He didn't show for work today.'

'Huh,' is all he says, a note of surprise in his voice, then falls silent.

I have a horrible suspicion there's something he's not telling me. 'Paul, what is it?'

'That phone number you gave me. It's coming up as a public call box.'

'In Truro?'

'Truro, yes,' Paul Dryer agrees, and I hear that odd note in his voice again. 'In fact, it's the number of the public call box at the end of your street.'

'What?'

For a few seconds I feel wild elation. That means Harry must be close at hand, probably still in the same street. Maybe one of my neighbours took him. I think of the large Russian and how I shouted through his letterbox. Was I wrong to walk away that day, to let Treve persuade me I was losing my sense of perspective?

Then I remember the background sound in the voicemail message, and shake my head. 'No, wait, that's not possible. On the phone, it sounded like he was in a large space. The room was echoing and . . . I thought I could hear some kind of rushing noise too. Like a train, perhaps.' I frown, briefly closing my eyes as I try to recapture the sound in my head. 'Or maybe an airplane going over.'

'I'm telling you, that's the call box number.'

'And I'm telling you, that's impossible. I know what I heard.'

'Then perhaps it was a recording, made elsewhere and played down the phone line to you. From the box at the end of your street.'

'You mean . . .'

'I mean the recording you heard of Harry crying – if it even was Harry, which isn't certain – could have been made at any time. Not necessarily today.'

I feel sick and dizzy as the realisation hits me. Of course he's right. There was no ransom demand made, no voice spoke on the line. All I heard was my child crying.

That's not evidence that Harry's still alive.

It's a taunt.

'Do you think the Cornish Snatcher was telling the truth?' I ask. 'That she doesn't have him?'

'I don't know what to think. Not yet, not until we've had time to go through every word of her statement and check the farm more thoroughly for any DNA that could link her to Harry.' He pauses. 'I don't want you to give up hope, Meghan.'

I say nothing, staring across the pub gardens at where the river threads noisily through the valley bottom.

'We're doing our best to get your son back, do you hear me?'

'I hear you.'

'Now I need you to bring me your phone. Are you able to do that straightaway?' He hesitates. 'Or I can send someone out to pick you up.'

'No,' I say. 'I'll bring it to you at the station.'

'That's the spirit.' I can hear the forced cheerfulness in his voice. 'Try not to worry about Jon. I've got people looking out for him across town. We'll find him soon enough, and let him know what's happening.'

'Thank you.'

'Everything's going to be all right,' he tells me.

Again, I say nothing.

'Meghan?'

'I'm on my way.'

I end the call and climb into the driver's seat, trying to remain optimistic. *I don't want you to give up hope.* It's hard not to fear the worst though, and somehow hearing Harry's cry has made everything feel a thousand times more urgent and dangerous.

As I'm closing the door, my hand knocks clumsily against the steering wheel and I drop the mobile somewhere between my feet.

'Shit.'

Shakily, I climb out of the car again and crouch, fumbling for my mobile under the driver's seat. Something plastic comes to hand first, a wrapper of some kind, and I drag it out, frowning.

It's a condom wrapper. *Ribbed for extra sensation*, it says.

I stare in disbelief. My hand trembles as I turn the plastic wrapper over in my hand, examining it. Torn across in a hurry, empty now, the condom itself gone. The inside of the packet is still a little greasy with lubricant.

Recently used.

I force myself to grope about under the seat for the actual condom itself. To my relief I find nothing else under there except my mobile, which I throw on to the passenger seat in disgust.

But the empty wrapper is incriminating enough.

We don't use condoms. I had a coil fitted at my six-week postnatal check, though we'd not had sex since before the birth. And before that I was pregnant. The only possible reason for Jon to open a condom packet would be to have sex with someone else.

So he's had sex. With another woman. In our family car.

The same car I take during the day when Harry and I are doing the weekly shopping trip, or to go for a drive in the country, or for one of his scheduled hospital appointments. On longer journeys, I have often had to stop and change Harry's nappy in the back.

Without thinking, I glance automatically towards the back seats, and imagine some late-night encounter, all the windows steamed-up, with Jon and some unknown lover writhing about in the back of our car, while I was waiting at home for him with Harry . . .

'Oh God,' I choke, and rock back and forth. 'Oh God, no.'

⌣

When I've stopped shaking enough to concentrate, I decide to drive home and check today's post before heading to the police station to hand over my phone. Since Harry's disappearance, a few handwritten letters have arrived every day, some from anonymous crackpots, others from concerned friends and well-wishers. I have been putting aside the letters from well-wishers, to be answered later, when I have more time and emotional strength. But now we know the Cornish Snatcher did not take Harry, I think the police ought to study the ones that sound a little crazy, in case any of them hold a clue to his whereabouts.

Glancing at myself in the rear-view mirror, I'm horrified to see thick, black smudges of mascara under both eyes. That's what crying does to you.

'Shit.' I lick my fingertips, trying to wipe away the smudges one-handed while I drive, but only manage to make things worse. 'Wonderful.'

I look like a panda.

Definitely a good idea to go home before taking my mobile to the police station. Then at least I can spend five minutes in front of the bathroom mirror making myself look human again.

I turn into our street, and slow down as I pass the phone box.

That's where the call came from.

I clutch the wheel, staring at the empty phone box as if it can answer all my questions. It looks innocent enough: an ordinary phone box.

Who used it today to send that recording to my phone?

I remember my confusion as I listened to the echoing silence. The dead air. Then I noticed that faint rushing sound in the background. I'm still not sure what it signified, but perhaps the police will be able to clean it up and pinpoint the location where the call was recorded.

A flash of gold further up the street catches my eye.

I stare.

It's the Volvo again.

The driver is manoeuvring out of a tight space a few doors up from our house. I drive forward, very slowly, practically a crawl, keeping my eyes on the rear window of the car.

DS Dryer told me to ignore this car. That they'd checked it out and it did not belong to anyone suspect. Yet I saw the same gold Volvo out of the window on the afternoon of the day Harry went missing. It was parked further along the street, someone clearly at the wheel. Not getting out of the car, not moving about, not doing anything. As though they were waiting.

Waiting for what though?

For a phone call?

For someone to alert them that the coast was clear?

I strain to see the driver, and catch a glimpse of grey hair as their head turns. I'm not one hundred per cent sure, but in profile it looks rather like a woman.

I stare, suddenly finding it hard to breathe.

Could it be the woman from Lemon Quay who was pushing the red buggy?

Assuming it even *is* a woman behind the wheel.

I continue to crawl forward, holding my breath. I am about a hundred yards away when the driver finally negotiates his or her way out of the space, and drives off, heading inexorably away from me, making for the crossroads at the far end of our road. It's the same direction the Volvo took last time, when I chased so hopelessly after it, a mad woman, panting and barefoot in the rain . . .

All thought of going home disappears in a sudden, wild impulse to give chase. I find the accelerator and press down hard. My car leaps after the gold Volvo.

'Gotcha.'

Chapter Thirty-Five

I keep my distance, not wanting to alert the Volvo driver to the fact that he or she is being followed. All the same, I can see that there are two people in the car this time, not one. I am more sure now that the driver is a grey-haired woman, while the one in the front passenger seat looks like a man, though it's hard to tell without getting closer.

And if I get too close, I might spook them.

So I hang back, trying to drive casually. But all the time my brain is firing, remembering things, making connections.

How many times have I seen this car now? Too many for it to be ignored, given that the owner does not live in our street and I have not noticed it here before. Though perhaps it's simply someone who is often visiting one of my neighbours, but has changed their car recently. I have made enough mistakes lately for that possibility to worry me. I don't want to look like an idiot for chasing another ludicrous lead.

Yet the driver does seem undeniably similar to the older woman I saw in Truro city centre that day, pushing my son in a buggy.

If only I could have got closer, seen her face clearly, been sure that it *was* Harry in the buggy.

I glance at the phone beside me on the passenger seat, tempted to call Paul Dryer, ask him exactly who owns the gold Volvo. He must know, after all. He told me plainly that he had checked out the car, and it was not relevant to his inquiry. Yet all my instincts tell me that whoever is in the gold Volvo knows *something*, however small, however remote, about my son's disappearance.

Should I try to make a call while driving? Not very safe, and certainly illegal. Yet if I stop, I am bound to lose them.

The gold Volvo turns right at the crossroads, exactly like last time, and takes the road that eventually leads out of Truro into the surrounding countryside.

After they have gone, I move up to the stop sign in my turn, watching covertly as the occupants pull away into the traffic. I do not like being so close behind them, but staying too far back would look equally suspicious. To my relief though, neither of them look back at me, and the driver does not appear to be checking her mirrors.

Nonetheless, I stay crouched behind the wheel at the crossroads, trying to make myself as small and inconspicuous as possible, and hope they did not spot me.

It's busy as always on the main road, people going about their daily business, moving in and out of town. I have to wait for a break in the traffic before I can pull out, tapping the wheel in frustration, afraid that I will lose them.

The main road system around Truro is a complicated one, often shifting direction, east to west, then swinging abruptly back again. But I manage to keep them in my sight for most of the time, and eventually catch up with the Volvo about a mile out of town, heading due west along the A30.

It's a dual carriageway, and I am afraid of being noticed. So I hang far back, trying to stay out of sight behind larger, slower-moving vehicles like vans or trucks. But of course there are numerous turn-offs, and it eventually strikes me that, if I fall too far behind, they might leave the main road without me noticing. So after some judicious overtaking, I settle into a comfortable and relatively safe position three vehicles behind theirs in the inside lane.

We are doing a brisk fifty miles per hour. The sun is glaring in my eyes. I lower the sun visor, and hope it will help to obscure my face, and that whoever it is does not know my vehicle.

I am sweating, too hot in the enclosed metal box of the car. It soon gets like a sauna on a warm day like this. There's no sunroof, so I open the driver's-side window all the way down and lean my bare arm out in the sunshine. The refreshing wind ripples through my top. It lifts my hair, whipping it across my face.

I feel exhilarated and free for the first time in years. Free of everyone and everything. Doing my own thing, making my own choices, however crazy.

This is an adventure.

And maybe I am going to find Harry at the end of it.

Or maybe it will lead only to embarrassment and apologies and another dead end. To a muddy field and a bad taste in my mouth.

The gold Volvo eats up the miles ahead of me, and I follow it with renewed caution, keeping out of sight, not getting too close. Belatedly, I check my fuel gauge and am horrified to see how low it is. I am not sure how much fuel is available to me once the arrow hits the last mark on the gauge, which is where it is hovering. Enough to get me to wherever they are going, perhaps.

Unless they are going all the way to Land's End.

I struggle to recall how many miles it is between Truro and Land's End, the very westernmost tip of Britain. After Land's End, as the name suggests, we would plunge into the sea if we kept going. There's nothing at Land's End itself though, except a large tourist attraction with rides and exhibitions and a small zoo. Surely they wouldn't be going that far? But what if they are? What if I need to stop to refuel? I would lose them then, for sure.

I lean across and grope around for the mobile on the passenger seat, intending to make a call to Paul Dryer, to warn him what I'm doing. But my hand meets nothing but empty space.

I glance down. The phone's not on the seat anymore.

'Shit.'

At some point while I've been driving, presumably during one of my wilder turns, the phone has slid off the passenger seat and on to the floor.

I crane my neck, keeping the wheel as steady as possible, but can't even see the mobile in the footwell. It must be under the passenger seat.

I grip the wheel with clammy hands, and try to stay focused.

The mobile is no big loss, I tell myself. It was running low on battery charge anyway. And if the battery is dead when I finally retrieve it from under the seat, I can always stop at any phone box or service station and call the police from there.

Assuming I haven't run out of fuel by then.

'Shit,' I say again.

But at least I can still see the gold Volvo. It's five cars ahead now, moving briskly but staying mostly in the inside lane.

———

We have been travelling about half an hour on the A30 when we reach the large roundabout to St Ives. The driver of the gold Volvo abruptly shifts lanes, signalling to turn off towards the coast.

The change is so sudden that it takes me by surprise.

I pull into the same lane behind the Volvo, my heart racing. I'm completely exposed, our two cars maybe two hundred yards apart, nothing between us but sunshine.

I brake hard, desperate not to be too obvious.

The vehicle behind me swerves past me in the nearside lane. It's a blue van, a local business with a large white logo painted on the side, driven by a thick-set man with a beard. He sounds his horn and makes a rude gesture at me as he passes, then accelerates erratically away.

I continue to brake, thankful that no other cars are close behind me.

We are only a few car lengths apart now. Suddenly, the grey-haired woman glances at me in her mirror as she swings off towards St Ives.

Has she seen me? Recognised the car, perhaps?

My palms sweating, I decide to drive round the roundabout a second time, swinging past the A30 to Truro and heading on towards the St Ives turn. On the second approach to the turn-off, I overdo the pace in my anxiety, and heave my car round the bend, clipping the dusty verge to my right. The car bumps up and down in a cloud of dust, then settles back on to the tarmac with a thud.

My foot slips off the accelerator, but I find it again. I grip the wheel hard and keep driving, but painfully slowly, staring straight ahead through the dust cloud.

'Stay calm,' I mutter to myself. 'Stay calm, you idiot.'

At first I don't see the Volvo. But by the time I reach the next roundabout, I see the gold flash ahead.

'You're not getting away from me.'

All the same, I make sure I take no more risks. No sense alerting them to the fact that they are being followed.

It was easy on a major road like the A30 to merge anonymously with the other traffic. But out here in the scrubby Cornish countryside, even with the peak of the tourist season just around the corner, cars are far less numerous.

To my surprise, when we reach the next junction, the Volvo keeps bearing left, well away from St Ives. I follow, very aware of the emptiness of the road, until the car branches off down a leafy lane signposted to an obscure hamlet.

After a moment's hesitation, worried that I am being too obvious, I signal and turn down the same lane in pursuit.

I need not have worried about being spotted though. When I round the first bend, they are nowhere in sight. By then I am committed, and have no choice but to keep driving. The trees begin to thin out. The leafy lane becomes a narrow, winding road in full countryside, with straggling hedgerows and overgrown verges that go on for miles in every direction, and no signs that mean anything to me. It's all Pol-this, Pen-that, and fields of sheep.

It is just as I realise that I must be heading towards the sea that my mobile begins to ring.

Chapter Thirty-Six

The phone is set to vibrate, so all I can hear is a faint buzzing sound coming from under the front passenger seat. I glance down at the passenger-side footwell, gauging the distance between the floor and my seat. I don't have a particularly long arm, but perhaps . . .

The phone continues to buzz.

As soon as I release the wheel with one hand, and bend from the waist, stretching out towards the underside of the passenger seat, I can no longer see where I'm going. On the A30, it might be possible to do this for a few seconds without incident. But on a narrow Cornish lane, with a tight bend every few hundred yards, many of them blind, it's tantamount to suicide.

Struggling to steer a straight course down the centre of the lane, I lunge over as far as my body allows and grope for the unseen phone.

All I feel under my fingertips is the edge of the rubber floor mat, and parts of the metal mechanism that slides the seat backwards and forwards. The vibrating buzz of the phone sounds louder now that I'm closer. More urgent and accusing.

Answer me, answer me.

In desperation, I stretch a little further.

The car lurches sideways, and the wing mirror strikes the verge, greenery whipping against the passenger window.

'Shit.'

I straighten up, and sit in seething silence, listening to the rhythmic *buzz-buzz-buzz* from below the seat.

Ten seconds later, the phone stops ringing.

Another few bends without any further sign of the Volvo, and I start growing anxious. The unanswered call on my mobile distracted me. Have I missed them? Did they park up somewhere out of sight, or turn off without my noticing? I drive faster, hoping that nobody is coming in the opposite direction. It would be just my luck to meet a tractor.

Another three minutes pass.

Then I catch the tell-tale flash of gold cresting a slope in the near distance, the Volvo climbing slowly between a cluster of gnarled old trees before descending invisibly the other side.

Tractors or no tractors, I am determined to catch them.

I put my foot down.

Round the next bend, the road begins to climb. For a moment, it's cool in the shadow of the trees on either side of the road. Then, as I reach the top of the slope, the trees abruptly vanish, and a panoramic view opens up across the Cornish landscape: a patchwork of green and gold fields, woodlands and hills, and beyond them, the wide blue expanse of the Atlantic Ocean.

I brake hard as I descend the hill. The Volvo has disappeared again. At the bottom of the slope, another tight curve forces me almost to a crawl in case of oncoming traffic.

Beyond the bend, the road widens out briefly. I catch a glimpse of grey slate roofs rising above the banked hedgerows. A minute later, I pass them on my right. Old whitewashed walls, chimneys, narrow windows beside each front porch. Three modest dwellings built low into an earth bank centuries ago, hunched against the sea winds.

A row of old fishermen's cottages, perhaps?

The sea is bright here, dazzling on the horizon, the coast only a short distance away now. I can smell salt on the air, and the breeze has grown sharper, chilling my skin, whipping my hair about madly.

The road ends without warning thirty yards later in a small turning area perched high above a stretch of windswept beach, part rock, part sand.

There's a small space for car parking beside the gate that leads to the coastal path. Room for maybe five cars. It's really a glorified verge, overgrown with thick, coarse grasses and gorse bushes, and the odd determined dandelion. The road broadens here though, presumably to allow any drivers who have come this way by error to turn around and escape.

There is only one car parked beside the gate today.

It's not a Volvo.

It's a bright yellow Fiat with a Cornish flag bumper sticker.

I get out, leaving the engine running, and peer up and down the windswept coastal path. The cliffs look very steep and jagged along this part of the coast. Far below in the sandy cove, I can just see an old man in a grey jacket and woollen hat staggering up the path from the foreshore, his arms full of driftwood. Almost certainly the owner of the yellow Fiat.

NO OVERNIGHT PARKING, the council sign by the gate tells me cheerfully. PLEASE TAKE YOUR LITTER HOME WITH YOU.

I climb back into the car and sit there a moment, staring out at the bright, wind-flecked waves of the Atlantic Ocean. On any other day it would have been a beautiful sight. Now though, it simply looks bleak and empty.

Where the hell did the Volvo go?

I must have missed something between the cottages and here. A small turning area, perhaps, or a gate into one of the fields on either side of the road. Any place where the Volvo could have pulled in, and then turned round and driven back the way they had come after I passed by. But that would suggest they had seen me. And I am fairly confident they had no idea I was following them.

I lean over the passenger seat and finally locate my lost phone. One missed call.

One new voicemail message.

I straighten up and thumb through the screens to my phone message centre. The missed call was from Paul Dryer. Presumably the voicemail message will be from him too. I press to dial my message service, but it refuses to connect.

No bars, no reception.

I am in the middle of nowhere, so no surprise. But I had hoped for at least one bar. Enough to send a text, perhaps. But the phone is effectively useless. No chance of making a call, let alone retrieving my voicemail. And the battery is low too. Right in the red, like the fuel gauge. If I leave the phone turned on, it'll probably be dead soon.

I take the difficult decision to turn the phone off completely. Better to leave power in the battery, and hope for better reception later, than to let it die without even being able to make a call. I shove it down into the front pocket of my jeans, where it makes an uncomfortable bulge, then slam the car in reverse and back up the lane about fifty yards.

I stop again, frowning.

There's a rough track off to the left, so narrow and muddy that I discounted it in passing, assuming it must be a farmers' track, a way for sheep or cattle only.

Does it lead to a house?

I jump out and stare down the farm track. The air is sharp and salty so close to the sea. I get the impression that a vehicle has driven along there recently. The deep mud ruts on the other side of the narrow, gated entrance look freshly cut, and one of the puddles near the roadside is still cloudy and disturbed, as though car tyres splashed through it only a moment ago.

I can't see beyond the first bend in the track. But it must lead somewhere or it wouldn't need to exist.

To an old farm, perhaps?

There's a dirty wooden sign half-buried in brambles beside a leaning gatepost. Trying to avoid the worst of the mud, I pull the nearest brambles gingerly aside, and slowly decipher the faded, hand-painted lettering.

PRIVATE ROAD: TIDE HOUSE

I have no way of knowing for sure, but instinct tells me the Volvo went this way.

I clamber into the car, back up a short distance, then turn the wheels and ease the bonnet through the muddy gateway. The lane is narrow but more or less passable. I reach the first bend without serious incident, and spot what look like farm buildings ahead through a cluster of low, gnarled trees.

Suddenly, without warning, the car judders to a halt.

I try to restart it.

The engine remains silent.

I try again.

Same deal.

That's it, then. No more diesel.

'Bloody hell.'

I'm in a single-track lane with steep, straggly hedgerows on either side, and muddy, unpassable fields beyond them. There's nowhere to turn off, nowhere to stow the car, no space for anyone to get past my vehicle. I am vulnerable here, a target, not to mention an immovable obstacle if the Volvo should come back. Not that I am afraid of a confrontation with that grey-haired woman. But that's not what I intended when I first started following the Volvo. I originally had in mind a stealthy approach, maybe keep her in my sights while I remain unseen, scope out the place from a distance, decide whether to call the police . . .

Don't panic, don't panic.

I grab the car keys, clamber out of the car, and after a moment's hesitation, lock it behind me. I rather like the idea that nobody can hit me over the head, then drive off and leave me here. Not without towing my car out of the way first, at any rate.

My phone in my pocket, I set off down the muddy lane.

I can see the Atlantic, a glittering expanse stretching beyond the buildings ahead, and recall the cliffs I saw on either side of the beach below. If Tide House stands on a clifftop, I might be able to get a mobile signal from there.

Cautiously, I hug the rough hedgerows over the final few hundred yards, ignoring the scratches from the brambles and spiky hawthorn branches. Though I am still not sure what on earth I am going to do, even if I do find Harry in this house. Am I going to break in without being seen, steal him back, and run cross-country with him in my arms? The very idea is ludicrous. I'm not that kind of person, even if I did drive out here today on impulse.

If only I could have answered the phone when Paul Dryer rang.

It looks like a farmhouse, several hundred years old, probably about the same age as the fishermen's cottages down the road. There's a cluster of palm trees on an island bed in front of the house, looking a little sad and gnarled, their long palm leaves tattered by sea winds. The rest of the gardens are gradually turning to wilderness, weeds choking the flower beds, the empty drive overrun with coarse grasses.

I can't see the Volvo yet. Or any cars or people at all, in fact.

Oh God.

What if I'm in completely the wrong place?

I try to suppress my panic. The driveway leads round to the back of the house. Perhaps the Volvo went that way. It's worth pursuing, at least.

I creep round what looks to be a disused workshop, its one window furred with dirt, the narrow interior empty and festooned with cobwebs. Then I stop dead on the corner, staring round into the sea-facing yard.

There's a car parked at the back of the house.

It's the gold Volvo.

The car is angled away from me, the boot open, as though someone has been taking out the shopping. The back door to the main house also stands open in the bright sunshine, and I can see someone moving about inside the house. The passenger-side back door is also open, and as I watch, my heart thumping, a woman in late middle age comes out of the house and heads straight for the car.

I stare at her, eyes wide, unable to move.

The woman has grey hair.

She's dressed casually, rather like me. Flat pumps, neatly ironed blue denim jeans and a plain blue T-shirt, with a denim overshirt to hide a less than perfect figure. Despite the large chest, she's trim and light on her feet, and walks as though she has somewhere important to go.

It's the same woman I saw that day, wheeling my baby son around Truro in a buggy. I study her face, seeing it clearly for the first time. A little fleshy around the mouth, perhaps, but with a long, narrow nose, and a pinched, determined air.

She reaches into the back of the Volvo. Straightens up, smiling, exclaiming happily, holding something in her arms. Or rather, someone. An animated bundle in blue that kicks and moves with her, held aloft in the sunshine.

A hungry shriek splits the air.

I stiffen, staring at the kicking baby in her arms, barely able to suppress my gasp.

Harry.

There's no doubt in my mind. I hear his cry and know it's my son just as I know my own reflection in the mirror.

My baby. And he's alive.

Relief and excitement flood my heart, and my eyes fill with tears.

I knew Harry was still alive. I knew it!

My first instinct is to run to him. But I force myself to draw back, clamping a hand over my mouth to suppress my sobs of relief. This woman thinks she's safe here, that nobody in the world knows where she is or what she's done. Her body language is relaxed, even happy.

All that will change as soon as I try to take Harry back.

I am alone.

With no working phone and no weapon.

I have to think, to come up with a plan.

Perhaps if I sneak unseen to the cliff edge in search of a mobile signal, I can call Paul Dryer, tell him exactly where I am and how to find me, and that I've found Harry.

That's Plan A.

I hope there's a signal. Because I don't have a Plan B.

The grey-haired woman ought to have taken Harry inside the house by now. But I hesitate, deciding to be ultra-cautious. I don't want to be seen. I count up to ten in my head, taking my time.

One-one-thousand, two-one-thousand . . .

Finally, I shuffle to the corner of the workshop again, staying so close to the wall that my shoulder and hip rub against the rough whitewashed stone. Then I look round the outbuilding.

Straight into the cold, hard eyes of my next-door neighbour.

Chapter Thirty-Seven

'Hello, Meghan,' Treve says, looking back at me without any sign of surprise. He is unsmiling. 'How nice of you to join us. Not part of the plan, unfortunately. But not to worry, I expect we can sort something out.'

I back away, too shocked to reply.

What the hell is Treve doing here? Was he the unseen passenger in the gold Volvo? And what's his connection with Harry?

A terrible possibility flashes through my head at that instant. But I shake my head, feeling like I must be going insane. The explanation for his presence is so bizarre and outrageous, so obscene in its monstrousness, that I can only reject it.

Was it Treve who took my baby?

'Leaving already?' he asks, watching me back away.

My heart starts to race.

He follows at a lazy pace, but his broad shoulders are hunched, head jutting forward, as though he's about to tackle someone at rugby. I take another few steps backwards, staring at him. I want to speak, but my throat is too dry.

'I'm afraid I can't allow you to leave,' he says. 'Not that way, at least.'

I stumble over a loose rock, and clutch at the wall for support. My heart is thundering in my chest, my breath strangled. But I decide to stop and hold still, facing him. Even if I run, Treve would catch me in a moment. He's too fast and too strong. And whatever this is about, I can't run anyway. My baby son is here, and I have no intention of leaving without him.

Treve comes to a halt too, watching me speculatively. He flexes his large hands, betraying some inner turmoil, and I am suddenly very afraid.

I'm afraid I can't allow you to leave. Not that way, at least.

What does he mean by that?

'I saw you about ten minutes ago from my bedroom window,' he tells me casually. 'Followed us from Truro, did you? I told her not to park so close to your place. But she never listens, silly bloody woman.'

Silly bloody woman. Who the hell is she, that grey-haired woman who was at the wheel of the Volvo?

'That was impressive, I have to say. I didn't even notice you behind us until we turned off to St Ives. By then, it was a little late to try and shake you off. Though we made a good effort through the lanes. I thought we'd succeeded, until I looked out and saw you trying to blend into the hedgerow along the drive.' His mouth twists in a mimicry of a smile. 'You're not very good at subterfuge.'

He looks so bloody normal. I've seen him often enough before in that black T-shirt and burgundy V-neck sweater, the dark-blue denims, though he's wearing boots instead of trainers today. Scuffed old black boots, the heavy type he might wear for digging in the garden. There's even dried mud on them. Everything about him shouts *ordinary*.

'Treve, I don't understand. What are you doing here?'

Something in his face makes me fall silent, then a bunch of wild, incoherent thoughts tumble over and over in my head.

I repeat, slowly, '*Your* bedroom window? This is your house?'

'My mother's. Not much of a grand estate these days, I admit. Most of the place is falling down, or leaking, or subsiding, and it doesn't even have power anymore. But it's very isolated, off the beaten track, as you have no doubt realised. And that suited our needs very well just recently.'

'I don't understand,' I say again.

He shoves his hands in his jeans pockets, inhales the salty sea air, and then glances about at the run-down, overgrown grounds and outbuildings with a wry expression.

'You want a proper explanation,' he says flatly.

'I want my son back.'

He makes a face. 'I'm sure you do. But sometimes we can't have what we want, and that's just the way life is.'

'Treve—'

He interrupts me. 'I used to come here every holiday as a boy. These gardens were stunning in the summer time; people would come from miles around to admire them. The winds can be harsh in winter. But the summers are mild, and my grandfather had green fingers.' He unfolds his arms and points behind me, but I don't turn to look, keeping my gaze firmly on his face. 'He used to sit under that tree in the shade and watch me play.'

'Why is my son here, Treve?'

But Treve is not listening. 'My grandfather was an amazing man, Meghan. But he was dead by the time I hit my teens.'

'Does Camilla know you took Harry? Is she here with you?'

'Oh yes, my wife is here. I made damn sure of that.'

I catch that strong Cornish accent again on the end of his words, its humble warmth strangely at odds with what he's saying. He pauses, his long lashes hiding the expression in his eyes. I remember how charming he can be, and how he kissed me, held me, made me feel something for him. Not love, but desire.

I shudder.

'None of this would be happening if it wasn't for Camilla,' he continues. 'You could say she's been a catalyst for the whole business. So I couldn't let her miss any of the fun.'

My teeth grind together. '*Fun?*'

His heavy gaze lifts, meeting mine directly. 'No, you're right. Fun is the wrong word. Justice is more like it. Perhaps retribution. An eye for an eye, that's what the Bible says.'

'Is that why you took Harry from me. For retribution?'

'Yes.'

I stare at him, bewildered. 'Retribution for what though?'

'Adultery.'

I catch my breath, staring at his face.

Oh my God, no.

'Adultery?' My voice drops to a whisper. I can barely force the words out. 'Whose . . . Whose adultery?'

He makes a rough noise under his breath. His dark eyes never leave my face, a flicker of disbelief in them. 'You're telling me you didn't know about them?'

'I don't have a clue what you're talking about.'

It's a lie, of course. But how can I tell the truth when it might condemn my son to death?

He turns his head and spits vehemently on to the gravel path beside the workshop. It's a gesture of hatred, of utter contempt. 'Ha.' The sound he makes is not laughter, not speech, but an angry explosion of breath. 'Ha.'

I take another step backwards.

'So hearing Harry cry didn't work as I'd hoped,' he says, turning to look at me again. 'Disappointing.'

My eyes widen. 'You sent the voicemail.' When he nods calmly, I ask, 'But why do that to me? Were you trying to torment me?'

'Quite the opposite. I thought by sending you that message, I was demonstrating that Harry was still alive. That there was still a reason to hope. I was sure you'd stay in Truro then, waiting for the police to analyse the recording. You could have avoided what's coming. But I hadn't reckoned on your instincts as a mother.' He makes a face. 'You've been like a bloodhound ever since we took him. Tracking us down, sniffing out your baby.'

It occurs to me that he may be mad.

It's not a very comfortable thought. There's no reasoning with a madman, after all.

'Us?'

He says drily, 'My mother's never much liked Camilla. It wasn't hard to persuade her to help me. Not once I told her about Jon. But then, she's like me. She doesn't easily forgive that kind of betrayal.'

My senses tug at me. For the past few minutes, there's been some faint engine noise in the distance. A thick, guttural chugging in the sky that is growing louder all the time.

Treve glances upwards, brows contracting in a frown.

I turn, staring upward too.

It's a light aircraft, wobbling slightly on its approach, its wings lit up by the sun behind us. It's coming in low towards Tide House and the cliffs beyond, one of these very small planes that carry the pilot and one passenger. I calculate that it will pass overhead in about thirty seconds, heading for the open sea.

Treve looks back at me, and his eyes widen as he realises my intention.

'No.'

He lunges forward, making a grab for my arm.

Too late.

I break away and start to run, back the way I came, past the workshop, past the overgrown network of paths, towards the island bed with its ragged palm trees. I kick off my cumbersome heels, and run even faster.

'Hey!' I shout, waving my arms wildly over my head and jumping up and down as the small plane begins to pass low above the house.

I shout as loudly as I can. 'Hey, down here! Stop, look down! Help me!'

Chapter Thirty-Eight

The small aircraft keeps flying straight, the engine noise almost deafening now. I stare up at it, straining my arms as high as they will go, still waving frantically. The plane passes over me, a winged shadow that blocks out the sun for a few brief seconds. I catch a flash of light reflected from the cockpit, and the vague shape of a head inside that might be the pilot. The propeller is a blur. The palm leaves seem to flutter in its wake, or is that just the wind?

There are markings and numbers written large on the underside of the plane, I almost catch them as it soars overhead, begin to read them . . .

But then it's passing over the house, noisy and intent on the Atlantic Ocean ahead, a metal beast in the air, uninterested in the tiny scurrying figures below.

I keep staring upwards, shielding my eyes from the sun as I turn.

The small aircraft continues on across the short stretch of land between the house and where I imagine the cliffs to be, and into the glittering light that is the sea.

My arms fall back to my sides.

I want to cry.

I must have been mad to think I could get their attention from the ground. Perhaps the arm-waving was not entirely pointless, though probably too late to be spotted once they had started their approach. But how could any pilot hear someone shouting from below with that noise in their ears?

A second later, Treve tackles me to the ground. I don't hear him coming, not after the noise of the plane, but I get the wind knocked out of me by the impact.

'You stupid bitch.'

He pins me to the grass around the base of the palm trees, half-squatting on my back, his weight crushing me. I struggle to turn over, to wriggle out from under him. But he's too strong and heavy; I can hardly move my arms, let alone the rest of my body. My chest is still labouring to breathe after that flying tackle.

I rest my cheek against the cool grass and try to get my breath back. It feels like I've been hit by a car.

'You ever do anything like that again,' he mutters, close to my ear, 'I'll kill your baby. I don't want to hurt him, Meghan. I'm not a monster. But if you force my hand, I swear to you, I'll break his neck myself.' He is breathing hard. 'Now, do we understand each other?'

I nod.

'Good.' He jerks me to my feet, then drags me back towards Tide House, gripping my arm like he wants to break it. 'After that stunt, I can see it's time for a little reunion. I've tried talking to you. But it's clear you've already made up your mind about me.'

He sounds so angry, I'm terrified he will kill Harry.

'I'm sorry.'

'Nobody asked you to follow us here, Meghan. You weren't supposed to do that, to come here, to be any part of this. You could have walked away. But no, that would have been too simple. So don't blame me for what's about to happen. Because you've brought this on yourself.'

'No, please,' I stammer.

'Your problem is, you couldn't accept that you'd lost him. You couldn't let Harry go.' His voice is thick with contempt. 'So here you bloody well are, with victim stamped through you like *Cornwall* through a stick of rock.'

He drags me barefoot across the gravelly yard, ignoring my cries of protest, past the gold Volvo, and through the back door into the sunlit hall.

Dazed, I stare around at the painted walls and high ceilings. The ceilings are almost twice the height of our own, giving an impression of airy grandeur, and the stairs are broad, the banister ornate dark wood that looks like someone may have polished it recently. Tide House is not in good repair though. The stained wooden floorboards in the hall are warped and uneven. There's a powerful smell of damp everywhere, of musty old furniture and mildew. And from what I saw of the front, with its cracked timbers and missing slates, I imagine that the roof must leak in places.

Treve pushes me towards the stairs, and I stumble, knocking into a small side table. As I try to right myself, the table falls with a clatter.

No doubt startled by the noise, his mother appears in the open doorway of one of the ground floor rooms.

She's holding Harry in her arms.

My heart jolts.

Harry is lying against her chest, dressed in a sky-blue romper suit that ends at his knees, leaving him bare-legged despite the cool interior of the house, only a pair of white knitted bootees covering his toes.

'Harry, oh Harry.' I stare at my son, hungrily devouring him with my eyes. 'My gorgeous, darling boy.'

Treve's mother seems shocked to see me in her house, her mouth dropping open, eyes widening in surprise and alarm.

'What the hell is she doing here?' she demands of her son.

Treve says nothing.

Did he fail to tell his mother that I'd found them? Or perhaps he assured her that he was going outside to get rid of me. Now here I am, still on their land, in their actual house, still very much a threat. I wonder what her son might have in store for me now that I've discovered their secret hideaway.

Nothing very pleasant, I expect.

Harry is not crying anymore, thankfully. But he looks pale and lethargic, his head tilted against her shoulder as though he's too tired to hold it up on his own. His blue eyes are dull as he glances around the hall, his gaze barely pausing on my face.

I struggle to hold back my tears. Forcing a smile to my face, I say lightly, 'Don't worry, sweetheart. Mummy's here now. Have . . . Have you missed me?'

Treve's mother's face hardens, looking from me to her son in silent accusation. She whisks Harry back into the room, then slams the door. I hear him start to cry again, a high piercing wail of despair, and it makes me want to kill her.

'Please don't hurt him,' I call after her. My voice trembles with rage and I try to suppress it, to beg for mercy instead of threatening her. 'I'm sorry if I made you angry. I didn't mean to. Please don't take it out on Harry. He's not to blame.'

Treve twists a hand in my hair and hauls me up the uncarpeted stairs like I'm a piece of furniture, my bare feet and shins banging against each stair.

Tears start in my eyes at the pain, but I ignore them.

'Please, please, please don't hurt him,' I call out to her again, staring back down at that closed door. 'He's only a baby.'

I know she must be able to hear me.

Whatever Treve has told her, whatever insane lies he has spun to get her on his side, surely she can't blame a tiny baby for her son's problems? She's a woman, and a mother too, and she seems to have been doing her best to look after Harry since his abduction. Perhaps even if I can't make her empathise, I can at least make her understand.

'Shut up,' Treve tells me roughly.

'But Harry's sick, can't you see that?' I'm shouting the words like a crazy woman, struggling against the pain of having my hair practically ripped out. 'He has a serious condition. He needs urgent treatment. Has he had his medication today?'

'I said, shut up.'

He turns me towards him like a rag doll, then slaps me round the face.

My eyes sting and blur. The sheer force of the blow shocks me into silence, and he drags me the rest of the way up the stairs without any resistance. All I can think is that, if he can hurt me like this with so little provocation, how much harm could he do to Harry if things get any more out of hand?

At the top of the stairs, I get my breath back.

My mouth is numb where he caught me hard with the back of his hand, yet somehow I still manage to mumble, 'I'm begging you, please take Harry to a hospital. Before it's too late. Whatever I've done to upset you, I'm really sorry. You can do whatever you like to me. Have whatever revenge you want. I won't try to stop you. But please, let your mother take him to a hospital first.'

Treve stops on the landing, releasing my hair, and jerks me round to face him. I can see frustration in his face. 'I've always thought of you as an intelligent woman, Meghan. But you still don't get what's going on here, do you?'

'Explain it to me.'

'I thought I had been explaining it.'

'Please.'

'I've got a better idea.'

He throws open the bedroom door to his right, and pushes me inside.

'I'll show you instead.'

His shove is so hard, I end up sprawling on the floor. There's an old fleece partially covering the wooden floorboards near the door. It stinks. The smell is so bad, I almost retch.

What is that stench? Urine?

Choking, I look up and see a bed. Or not so much a bed as a bare mattress. A bare mattress in an old wooden frame, no sheets, no pillows, no covers.

Lying on the mattress is his wife, and she's staring at me.

Camilla has been placed on her side, facing the door. She's dressed in a short, tight skirt and strappy top, as though for a night out, and is still wearing a pair of red high heels, open-toed with a thong-style ankle fastening, very glamorous. But her make-up is tired and smeared, her mascara dried in streaks down her cheeks as though she's been crying. Her beautiful blonde hair, usually so flaw-lessly straightened, is matted and tangled, and there's a strip of silver tape across her mouth and binding her hands and ankles.

Her eyes are fixed on me, wide open and terrified.

'Oh my God,' I gasp.

Then I realise she is not the only person in the room.

Slumped in a chair near the old-fashioned wardrobe is a man in a crumpled shirt and grey pinstripe trousers, his jaw dark with stubble.

There's a dark stain at his groin. That explains the stink in the room. But not what he's doing here in the first place. His eyes are closed, his feet bare, his mouth stuffed with what looks like a balled-up blue tie. He looks unconscious. His handsome face is covered with cuts and bruises.

It's my husband.

Chapter Thirty-Nine

'Jon.' I lurch forward, and my hair is almost torn out by its roots as Treve twists his fingers, dragging me back. 'Shit, you bastard. That hurts.'

'Then stay where you are.'

'But he's hurt. He's bleeding.'

'So what?'

'How can you be so callous? Look at the state they're both in. Your own wife too, for God's sake. Why the hell are you doing this?' I glance at Treve sideways, and see the conflict on his face. 'You said, *retribution*. Is this it?'

'Yes,' he agrees, his cold gaze fixed on his wife. 'For adultery.'

'Adultery.' I look from Camilla's scared face to Jon's bloodied and unconscious figure. 'Between your wife and my husband.'

'You didn't seem to know about it just now. But now you don't sound so surprised.' He jerks on my hair, his voice rising on a bitter note. 'Were you lying to me, bitch?'

'No, I didn't know about them. Of course, I'm not blind. I saw the way things were going between me and Jon. I suspected . . . something.' I swallow, aware of a deep sense of hurt and betrayal filtering through the fear. 'But not this. Not Camilla.'

Camilla's eyes widen even further at her name, and she starts to tremble. As though she thinks I have been brought here to be her judge.

I ought to be furious, I think, staring back at her. I remember her knowing looks and smiles, the way she and Jon were together, the times I saw them glance at each other. I thought it was friendship. Neighbourliness. A memory comes back to me, of seeing her in the front garden with Jon, her arms around my husband, comforting him after Harry's abduction, as I thought.

How she must have laughed at my ignorance.

No wonder Treve tried to seduce me. It was not physical desire, as I thought at the time, but a deliberate act of war. He wanted to get even with my husband, to enjoy Jon's wife as Jon had enjoyed his.

Yes, they played us for fools. And Jon does deserve punishment. But the humiliation and financial punishment of a divorce, not this kangaroo court. Right now all I feel towards Jon and Camilla is numbness. My fury is directed towards Treve's mother. The woman who is holding my baby son prisoner. Perhaps even torturing him.

I have to get back downstairs.

Unfortunately, I have no idea how to do that without incurring Treve's wrath myself. And I will be no good to Harry if I get myself killed.

'So now you know the truth,' Treve is saying hoarsely, 'do you understand why I had to take your son? Why all of this was necessary?'

'No, I don't. Why hurt a baby?'

'Because hurting Harry hurts his father too. Like this does.'

Treve drags me across the room and kicks Jon between the legs. With the reinforced toe of his boot.

Jon gives a stifled grunt of pain, then blinks and raises his head, abruptly returning to consciousness. He stares at Treve, then sees me and seems to stiffen, something new in his face. He groans incomprehensibly against the tie stuffed into his mouth, and rolls his eyes towards the door.

'Yes, I have your wife too,' Treve tells him, seemingly entertained by the faces Jon is pulling. 'But she's not here to save you. She's here to watch you die.'

He kicks Jon in the knee, and stands watching as he writhes in agony.

'After I left you last night, I found the two of them together in some woodlands off the Falmouth road, shagging like teenagers in the back of her car. Silly bitch didn't realise I'd stuck a GPS tracker under the driver's seat.'

I feel sick.

'He was so proud of himself for fathering a baby,' Treve explains to me. 'As if any fool wasn't capable of that simple act. He deserved the pain of losing his child. I lost my wife to him. Why shouldn't he lose his baby to me?'

'But why not take me instead? You said, *an eye for an eye.*'

'He didn't care enough about you,' Treve points out coldly. 'It had to be Harry. You were never love partners.'

You were never love partners.

I think back to those heady days after the wedding. The lovemaking, the excitement of learning about each other's bodies, the sadness of being apart, even for a few hours. But even then I was aware that the emotion was more on my part than his. From the start, Jon had not wanted a girlfriend. He had wanted a wife. A woman to keep house and help with the mortgage and raise a family. And I had come along at exactly the right time.

'No, he loved me once,' I insist. 'If things went wrong between us, and he turned to Camilla for comfort, it . . . it was my fault.'

'You still want him? After everything he's done?'

I have to lie. If I don't, he's probably going to kill us all.

'He's my husband.'

'I hope you'll enjoy being a widow, then.'

'Treve, you can't be serious.'

'Give me your phone,' he demands, yanking on my hair again.

'I don't have one.'

'What's that, then?' He points to the bulge in my front jeans pocket. 'Do you want me to kick him again?'

I fumble the mobile out of my pocket and offer it to him. What difference does it make now? My situation is not particularly good, and there's no signal anyway.

'Turn it on,' he orders me.

I do as he tells me.

'Now show me the last few calls.'

I thumb through the screens, then show him the list of calls. He points to the last missed call, which is from DS Dryer.

'What's that?'

I hesitate, wondering whether to lie. But he could easily find out by using another phone to call the number back. 'The police.'

'You missed the call.'

'I was driving and couldn't reach the phone.'

'Show me your outgoing calls.' He studies the list of calls. There are several made recently to Paul Dryer's number, I've been in touch with him so frequently this past day or two. 'Do the police know you were following us? Do they know about this house?'

'Yes,' I lie, 'and they're on their way.'

His hand whips up and he slaps me round the face again. My vision blurs and I stagger backwards, dropping the phone.

'Liar,' he says, a vicious note in his voice. He hits me again. Another explosion of pain, this time behind my nose, and more blurred vision. I overbalance against the mattress, landing on my back next to Camilla, who moans behind her gag and draws her knees up to her chest.

'If they were on their way, they'd be here already.'

'I couldn't give them the exact location.' I sit up slightly, leaning on my elbows, watching him. Blood is running down my face. 'But they know the rough area. They'll be searching houses around here. It's only a matter of time.'

'Time, yes.' Treve lifts his booted foot above the phone, then brings it down. Smashes the phone to pieces. 'And it's just run out for you.'

He marches to the window and lifts a corner of the yellowing net, staring up at the blue sky, scouring the air in both directions. 'No sign of any helicopters,' he comments, and then lowers his gaze to the driveway. 'No sirens. No flashing blue lights. If they're even in this area, which I very much doubt, it's going to take the police a while to find this house.'

'As soon as they see my car, they'll know where I am.'

His face tightens, and he glares down at me. 'You think you've been clever, Meghan, don't you? That you can force me to abandon my plan. But you're wrong. Yes, it's an annoyance. But I don't have to give up, sorry to disappoint you. I have to move more quickly than planned, that's all.'

He pauses, studying me on the bed. 'You know, when you turned up here, I thought it would be a wonderful twist to shag you in front of your husband. After the way you responded to me last night, I expect you'd enjoy that, wouldn't you?'

Jon makes a noise behind his gag. Despairing and enraged at the same time.

Treve ignores him.

'But I guess that can't happen now,' he continues coolly. 'You've spoilt my plan. So now I have to think of an alternative.'

I struggle up off the bed, but stay out of his reach. I need to keep Treve talking for as long as possible. Because the police aren't coming.

Which means I am the only person who can get my son out of here alive.

'You were going to rape me? Is that your idea of *an eye for an eye?*'

He says nothing.

'When you found out about their affair, why take Harry? Why not come straight round, tell me to my face?'

His look is one of disgust and incredulity. 'Openly admit that I can't keep Camilla happy in bed? That your husband is banging my wife every chance he gets? I don't fucking think so.'

'So all this, Harry's abduction, Jon and Camilla, whatever comes next . . . It's all about your personal pride? Your manhood?'

'There are worse sins than pride.'

'What, like murder? Jon screws your wife. So you steal his son. That's just charming. How did you manage that, by the way, given that you were sitting with us at the dinner table the whole evening?'

'Not the whole evening. It only took a couple of minutes, and it was easy to slip away for that long without drawing attention to myself. You and Jon were so wrapped up in your own little world that night, I could have stolen your baby a thousand times over and you wouldn't have noticed.'

Guilt boils over inside me. Is he right? Was it my fault that Harry was taken?

'I locked the front door. I'm sure I did.'

'Yes, you locked it,' he agrees calmly.

'Then how—'

'I went back inside on some errand for you, acting the helpful dinner guest. Then I slipped into the hall and unlocked the front door. My mother was waiting outside in her car, as arranged. I gave her the signal. She ran upstairs, took Harry from his cot as quietly as she could, then went back out the front door. I closed it behind her, and rejoined you in the garden while she was driving away. It

took a maximum of two minutes, I'd say.' He smiles. 'Not particularly difficult.'

'You bastard.'

'The only issue she had was when she saw the chart on the wall.
All Harry's medicine. She knew he wasn't a sturdy child, but she
wasn't expecting him to need so much care.' Treve makes a face.
'She's a soft touch, my mum. I think Camilla told you she used to be
a nurse. I suppose old habits die hard, because she grabbed some of
the syringes and the chart. Took them with her when she stole him.'

He looks at me wryly. 'I expect she has some fantasy about
keeping your boy, raising him like her own grandson. But of course
that's impossible.'

I hate him so much, I don't care if he hits me again.

'I thought you were such a nice bloke when we moved in,' I spit
at him. 'Someone kind and generous, someone we could trust. The
man next door who was always there for us. But now I see you for
what you really are, Treve.' I pause. 'A fucking psychopath.'

He shrugs.

I wipe the blood from my face on to my jeans, my hands sticky
with it. 'If you kill us, you're going to spend the rest of your life in
prison. Or do you expect to make it look like suicide?'

'Why not? The cliffs are very dangerous along the Atlantic
coast.' His voice thickens, and he pauses for a moment, clearing his
throat. 'Beyond the trees, it's a few hundred feet to the cliff edge.
There's no chance anyone could survive that fall. No one's survived
it before, at any rate.'

My eyes narrow on his face. There's something in his voice.
'Someone you knew fell from the cliffs and didn't survive,' I hazard.

'My grandfather.'

'Did he fall from the cliffs?' I hesitate. 'Or jump?'

'He had lung cancer. Terminal.'

'I'm sorry.'

'It was his choice.' He's snarling now. 'But there has to be retribution. Some decisions can't go unpunished. Not forever.'

He pounces on Jon, drags him to his feet, holding him upright by the front of his shirt.

Jon sways, clearly in agony from his hurt knee, staring wildly from me to Treve. There's terror in his face now.

He kicks the bed. 'You too, get up,' he orders Camilla, no emotion in his voice whatsoever. When she moans and shakes her head, he looks at me. 'Help my wife off the bed. We're all going for a little walk along the cliffs.'

My heart starts thumping violently, my palms damp with sweat as I realise he's not kidding. 'No, no.'

He pushes Jon towards the door. 'Don't argue, Meghan, don't be stupid. You'll only make me angry with you too.'

'I'm not going to help you throw us all off a cliff.'

'All?' He shakes his head. 'I'm no child-killer; I'm not a complete ogre. And you were never even meant to be here. Look, you want to survive this? You want Harry back alive?' He looks at me hard. 'Then do exactly as I say.'

I don't believe he's planning to let us go. But what choice do I have?

I take a deep breath. 'Treve, stop and think about this. The police will never believe it was an accident. Or suicide. It's right next to your house, for God's sake.'

'I don't care what happens to me afterwards. Neither does my mother. We just want to see justice done,' he says flatly. 'Now get Camilla on her feet, rip that tape off her ankles, and let's go.'

Chapter Forty

His mother is waiting by the back door as we head down the stairs. Harry is nowhere to be seen. 'Well?' she asks her son brusquely.

'It's time,' he tells her.

Her eyes widen, then she nods. 'I'll get the baby,' she says ominously, and disappears back into the downstairs room.

A moment later she emerges with Harry clutched to her chest. He's still in his blue romper-suit, looking even drowsier than before, his eyes barely open. Perhaps he's been given a bottle feed while we were upstairs. Or perhaps the woman has drugged him. I have to suppress an instinctive desire to snatch my child away from her. But Treve and his mother would overpower me in an instant if I did that, and might well hurt Harry in revenge. Or even kill him.

I have heard enough today to know that's a very real possibility. I need to be careful. To take this one wary step at a time.

'Let's go,' Treve tells us, authority in his voice. 'And no stupid moves, Meghan. You can still walk away from this. You and Harry. But only if you do exactly what I tell you.'

I don't believe that, not for a minute. He's going to kill me. And probably Harry too. Tidying up loose ends, that's how he will justify our deaths to himself. It's probably true that he doesn't care what happens to himself after he's achieved this self-styled goal of retribution. But I doubt he would leave his mother to face a likely prison sentence. Which means the two of us will also need to be shuffled off, in case my version of events fails to tally with theirs. And whatever he says, I'm sure Treve has a cover story already concocted for when the first police car arrives at Tide House.

For now though, I have to play along. I don't have much choice.

We follow the path through the overgrown grounds of Tide House, past a cluster of wizened old trees bent into eerie shapes by the prevailing winds, and make for the headland beyond. Jon is limping badly, so Treve walks behind him with a hand on his shoulder, pushing him constantly forward. Behind them comes his mother, carrying a limp Harry in her arms, no coat or blanket over him, despite the sea winds.

I bring up the rear, my gaze on the top of Harry's head. I'm supporting a weeping Camilla on my arm, who keeps shaking her head and groaning through her gag, as though she thinks I can understand what she's saying.

I try to ignore her. I don't want Camilla to die. I don't want anyone to die. But it's hard to be one hundred per cent sympathetic towards the woman who's been cheating with my husband behind my back.

Not that I care much about Jon right at this minute. Now that I know the whole story, I realise that my husband is the one who is to blame for all this. If he had not misjudged the strength of his neighbour's emotions, and started this disastrous affair with Camilla, we would not be here now, limping across rough ground towards some horrific death.

I believe Treve when he says he did not want to take Harry. Despite all evidence to the contrary, I can only hope he's not the kind of man who would ever harm a child, let alone a sick baby.

315

But I saw the look in his mother's eyes when she went to fetch Harry, and it chilled me to the bone. She used to be a nurse, he said. But that was the look of someone who has made up her mind to do something utterly appalling, to perform an act of such atrocity that nothing can ever excuse it, where the only recourse is to harden the heart and stop off all emotion.

It was the look of a baby-killer.

Treve stops us a few feet from the edge of the cliff. He pushes Jon down to his knees, then stands looking out to sea.

His mother turns to me and Camilla. 'On your knees,' she tells her daughter-in-law. Her voice is devoid of emotion.

Camilla looks at me for help.

I don't know what to do. I avoid her glance, concentrating hard, looking around for a weapon. But there is none.

There's nothing out here on the headland but rough grass and rock outcrops dotted with gorse. Further away from the edge are brambles, and odd clumps of cow parsley, plus the occasional low-creeping plant, clinging to jagged crevices among the rocks. Not surprising, I suppose. The wind blows in hard from the Atlantic below, leaving no chance for anything taller than a small shrub to get established. Anything higher would simply be uprooted in the winter storms they must get here, and be blown away.

So no trees. Which means no sticks lying about. And the rock is all rising out of the cliff itself, not lying about loose as shale or pebbles.

The best I could do is tear up some grass and throw it in Treve's face.

Hardly promising as a weapon.

Besides, his mother is perilously close to the edge of the cliff, which means Harry is too, still clutched in her arms, crying weakly now.

'He's cold,' I tell her.

She looks round at me sharply. 'Mind your own business, bitch.'

'He's my son. How can it not be my business?'

'Shut your ugly face.'

Her aggression is worrying. Not for me, of course. I have ceased to care what happens to me. But she's holding Harry. One misstep and she could fall. Or toss him over the cliff edge if she gets angry enough. If I make her angry.

I say nothing, carefully lowering my gaze to the ground.

'That's right,' she says, nodding with satisfaction. 'And you keep it shut. My son will deal with you soon enough. First, the others have to die. Your husband and his whore.'

'Mum,' Treve says quietly, and she falls silent.

I don't want to look at Camilla, who is on her knees now, still crying and trembling. The sun is beginning to set to the west of us, and it's bloody chilly in the direct path of the sea winds. Camilla is dressed for a nightclub, not a cliff edge, and her arms and legs are bare, covered with goose pimples. She's shaking with cold now as well as fear.

There's nothing I can do for Camilla at the moment. And if I try to console her, I may incite that woman's anger.

I shift my gaze to Jon instead.

My husband is pallid with terror, the cuts and bruises standing out against the paper-white of his face, purplish-black and vivid red. He's a mess. I try to remember the man I married, the man I thought that I loved up until a week or so ago. But all I see is the man who betrayed our marriage, and brought us to this moment, to this cliff edge on the Cornish coast. I'm horrified by my own calmness, contemplating his imminent death.

Then I realise that it's shock. I'm not callous. I'm merely in shock. My hands are shaking, and my eyes are blurred with tears. My body knows what's happening, even if my emotions are having a tough time catching up.

Treve seems to be praying. At least, his head is bent and he's muttering something under his breath.

The reality of what's happening suddenly hits me.

This is an execution, and I have no way of stopping it.

I consider running for my life. I doubt Treve would bother coming after me. But they still have Harry. It would almost certainly mean his death if I run.

'I'm freezing,' his mother says sourly.

Treve nods, still staring out to sea for a moment. He seems to come to a decision. Maybe his prayers are finished. Or maybe he's getting cold too. 'Bring me Camilla,' he says at last, to no one in particular.

His mother looks at his wife, then gestures to me. Like I'm their lackey.

I shake my head.

Treve looks round at us both. 'Bring me Camilla,' he repeats.

'Treve, please,' I say, 'think what you're doing. There's no going back from this.'

'I made my mind up weeks ago. This is how it has to end, Meghan. This brings justice for you and me. My cheating wife dies. The lawyer dies. This is what needs to happen.'

'Treve, you can still change your mind.'

'Bring me my wife,' he enunciates clearly. 'It's her or the baby. Can I make myself any clearer?'

God damn him.

Reluctantly, I look round at Camilla, meeting her eyes.

She looks terrified. She's trying to say what sounds like Treve's name behind the gag. Only it's reduced to an incomprehensible grunt that she repeats again and again, more and more frantically.

Treve suddenly grows tired of waiting.

'Get the bitch up on her feet,' he shouts, his face contorted with rage. 'Bring her to me. She has to die first.'

Camilla's eyes bulge at this pronouncement. She makes a terrible choking noise behind her gag, and then throws herself face-down on to the grass like she's having a fit of some sort. I step hurriedly backwards as she rolls violently back and forth near the edge of the cliff, shaking and kicking her legs. She seems to have gone mad. There's grass caught in the tangled blonde mess of her hair. The noise resonating out of her is primitive, a kind of deep guttural yowl that's somehow rising from her chest and stomach rather than coming past the gag over her mouth.

It's the sort of noise a feral cat might make, caught in a trap.

Treve tries to approach her from behind, ducking down to grab at her leg, but she kicks out and catches him with her stiletto heel, still making that appalling noise.

'Fuck!' he exclaims, clearly hurt. 'Right, you fucking bitch. Let's see how you enjoy watching your lover die first. Then I'm coming back for you.'

He marches towards Jon, who is staring wide-eyed at Camilla, and drags him to his feet.

'No, please, don't!' I shout at him.

But it's too late.

Treve pushes Jon to the very edge of the cliff, holding on to his shirt, then rips the tape away from around his wrists.

Jon struggles, but Treve is too strong. He overbalances, his arms flailing.

I gasp, 'Jon, no.'

There's an eerie second where Treve reaches out, as though to grab him back, and I suddenly think he must have changed his mind. That it's all been a trick, a way of frightening Jon as a punishment for his adultery.

But he is only reaching for the tie in Jon's mouth, ripping it away. Maybe he wants to hear Jon beg for his life. Or scream as he's falling.

Who knows what goes through the mind of a psychopath?

Jon mouths a desperate, 'No,' through gaping, swollen lips. But gravity is against him. He is already toppling backwards as he reaches out, missing Treve's arm. His bare scrabbling toes lose contact with the loose stones and grass at the edge. Then there's nothing but air at his back, no chance of recovery.

For a split second, Jon stares back at us blankly, as though he cannot quite believe what is happening.

He stares at Treve's hand, just out of reach now, the creased blue tie trailing between his fingers, flapping in the wind.

At Harry, who stares back at him with idle curiosity.

At me.

Then he drops backwards out of sight, his long cry silenced with a thud as his body hits the rocks below.

The silence afterwards is appalling.

Treve stands there without moving, staring at the place where Jon had been a few seconds before. His hand drops to his side, still holding the blue tie.

Even Camilla stops shrieking and rolling about, and sobs into the grass instead.

I look at Harry, horrified.

His mouth twitches and trembles. The corners turn down, and his eyes screw up. Then he begins to cry, a terrible plaintive wail, as though he knows what he has lost, that life will never be the same again.

I take three long paces past Harry. Past the woman holding him, who is not looking at me but is smiling down at Camilla, as though enjoying her reaction to her lover's death. Past the place where my husband was kneeling only a moment before, the coarse grasses still flattened in two semi-circular patches where his knees rested.

I shove Treve from behind.

One good hard push, both hands planted firmly in the middle of his back.

He is not expecting it. He never even gets a chance to turn round. His arms flail upwards in surprise, his trunk plunges forwards like a heavy statue being pushed from its plinth, and he falls without a word, the tie still in his hand.

I stagger back, then turn to face his mother's wrath.

She screams.

Then drops Harry. Just drops him to the ground and rushes past me to the edge of the cliff.

'No!' she shrieks, staring wildly over the edge. There is no sound from below but the rhythmic crashing of waves on to rocks. 'Treve? Treve, are you there? My boy, my precious boy. Oh God, oh God . . .'

I return to Harry and fall to my knees beside him. He is lying on his back in the thick grasses, as though in a cradle. I think at first he must have cracked his head. I expect to see blood, maybe to find him unconscious.

Miraculously, he seems unhurt. He stares up at me, his blue eyes wide and shocked.

'Harry,' I murmur, and gather him up, clutching him compulsively to my chest. He cries a little then, perhaps crushed by my embrace.

I am laughing and crying at the same time. My husband is dead but my son is alive. I want to kiss his puckered-up little face, hug

321

him to me, burst into tears. But there's no time for any of that. We are still both in danger, and we have to get out of there.

I need to get Harry to safety.

I struggle to my feet and begin to lope away, blood dried on my face from where Treve hit me, but otherwise unhurt.

Then I hear that strange muffled noise again from behind me. The feral noise.

I turn, startled, just in time to see Camilla charging towards Treve's mother. Blonde head down, like a maddened bull charging at a red cloth. Her wrists are still tied together with silver tape, her mouth gagged.

The woman half-turns, sees Camilla coming towards her at a run and cries out, 'No!' She throws up an arm to defend herself, crooked at the elbow. An instinctive defence, but on a crumbling cliff edge, it only serves to knock her off-balance.

Treve's mother lurches sideways, and disappears, falling at exactly the same spot as her son.

I watch in horror, sure that Camilla can't stop in time, that she too must fall to her death. Yet somehow, with a massive physical effort, she manages to throw herself on to her knees right at the edge of the cliff. The momentum jerks her sideways, but she does not fall, lying along her side, mere inches from open space.

Raising her head, she stares down towards the rocks and sea below. Then she lowers her forehead to the ground, and begins to beat it against the rock. She is keening and choking behind her gag now, her whole body trembling.

At first I think she's mourning her husband. The man who would have murdered her. Then I realise this is for Jon.

I hesitate, then take a few steps back towards her.

'Camilla?'

She starts violently at the sound of her name, and jerks round, turning a tear-stained face up towards me. I get the feeling she had almost forgotten about me. There's fear as well as defiance in her eyes now. Perhaps she thinks I've come back to kill her, to exact revenge for her secret affair with my husband.

But I'm too tired to think about revenge.

All I want to do is call the police and get Harry to a hospital. His body is so much lighter than it was the day he was abducted, and I can feel how chilled his skin is in this wind. He may have been medicated, but I suspect he has been severely underfed. He is still crying, but feebly, more of a whimper, as though he has very little strength left for anything but surviving.

I know how he feels.

'Come away from the edge, Camilla,' I tell her, and somehow manage a thin smile. 'You don't want to fall too, do you?'

She stares at me warily, then nods and shuffles a few feet away from the cliff edge, hands still bound together. My dead husband's lover. I wonder for the first time if she truly loved Jon. When I realised they had been having an affair, I assumed it was all about the kicks for her, the peculiar twist of adulterous sex. I didn't think she was capable of caring much about anyone. But then I remember the keening noise she made when she stared down at the rocks below, and the way she beat her head against the rock as she wept.

The human heart is a strange place.

I crouch beside her, Harry still whimpering in my arms, and struggle to tear the silver tape off her wrists.

Camilla holds them out to help me. She keeps her gaze fixed on me the whole time, as though afraid I may be trying to trick her in some way. Treve had wound the tape round her wrists several times, so tight it had cut off the circulation, her hands cold and bloodless, the skin deathly pale.

It is not an easy task to remove the tape one-handed, and takes me several minutes of concentrated effort.

Afterwards, I straighten up, exhausted. She can remove the gag on her own.

I wonder where the nearest phone is, since there's no power at Tide House. Perhaps someone in those whitewashed fishermen's cottages on the steep road back to St Ives will have a landline, or a mobile at least. Any phone will do to call the police.

DS Dryer needs to know that I've found Harry.

I am not looking forward to the other explanations though.

Nor to confessing to knocking Treve to his death.

Then I hear Jon's ghostly voice in my ear, smooth, arrogant, almost cocksure. The lawyer's point of view. *Self-defence, darling. No jury in the land would convict you.*

I did the right thing.

The only thing.

All the same, I wonder what the police will make of the three bodies they are going to find at the foot of this rocky cliff.

Jon, Treve, and his mother.

'Let's get out of here,' I say, and hold my baby close.

Epilogue

'Jon!'

Someone is shouting his name in the distance, an urgent cry.

'Jon, for God's sake!'

Slowly, the terrible dream begins to recede.

My eyes snap open to bright sunshine, salt air, and the rush of the tide.

What the hell?

I struggle up on to one elbow, staring about myself, disorientated. Then I remember. I'm at Widemouth and it's a gorgeous summer afternoon. The famous Cornish bay, smooth golden sand with a deep shelving beach, popular with local surfers and holidaymakers. It's high season. There are hundreds of people around me in shorts and swimsuits, some walking down to the sea, making sandcastles or playing beach volleyball, others lying back on their towels, asleep in the sunshine. Just as I was a moment ago.

'Jon!'

I stare, shielding my eyes against the sun's glare.

A young woman in a bikini is standing in the surf, hands on slim hips, shouting out to sea. Jon is a teenager on a blue body-board, half-hidden by the white-crested rollers, his hand raised to acknowledge her.

'Jon, you coming out yet? We're ready to leave.'

I close my eyes. My racing heart begins to slow.

How long have I been asleep?

I sit up properly and rummage in the cool bag for my water bottle, then take a few swigs, gazing around me. The sunlight dazzles on the water beside a series of jagged black rocks, half-submerged by the tide. I stare at them as reality returns slowly. It was the same appalling dream again, the one I can't seem to shake. I was there, back on that high clifftop, watching as my husband was thrown to his death. I saw his terrified face, his eyes . . .

Then I heard Jon's name and it felt so real, like it was happening all over again.

I shudder.

'Look, Harry,' says a familiar voice higher up the beach, 'that's Mummy over there! Do you see her?'

'Mummy!'

I hear a squeal of delight from behind me, and turn my head, smile firmly back in place. 'Who's that? Who could that possibly be?' I hold out a hand to him. 'Darling, come to Mummy!'

It's Harry, rushing precariously towards me over hot, uneven sand, looking perfect in his white beach shorts and T-shirt, sunhat tied round his chin, one sandal strap flapping loose.

He trips over a stone and almost falls, then recovers his balance, still grinning.

'Careful,' I say, though I can see he's fine.

Emily follows more slowly, one hand on her swollen belly. In a bikini, her pregnancy looks even more enormous, though she still has another three months to go. She and Simon are very happy now, which is lovely to see. I suppose the shock of what happened to us must have brought them closer together. Certainly after they finally married last year, and Emily underwent successful IVF treatment, their relationship settled into a permanent loving bond, the kind of intimate warmth I never really experienced with Jon.

I don't know if they ever talk about Jon and Treve though.

I try not to.

After the police concluded their investigation, and the Crown decided not to charge me and Camilla for the deaths of Treve and his mother on the grounds of self-defence, we were finally able to get on with our lives. As far as that has been possible, with the memory of that day still hanging over us.

Camilla was far less affected by what happened than I expected. I thought she would be devastated – both the men she loved dying so suddenly and violently. But when I saw her at the inquests, she seemed calm and remote. She never came back to live next door though. No doubt the memories were too much for her. She took what she wanted from the house, sold the rest, and the last I heard she had found a flash new boyfriend and moved to Rome with him. A very long way from Cornwall, was what I thought.

I won't miss her.

Harry will be three this November. He's grown into a lovely boy, if a little impulsive and headstrong.

I talk to him about his daddy sometimes, but I'm not sure how much he understands. He is unlikely ever to remember the events at Tide House, Dr Shiva says, and I am deeply grateful for that mercy. One day I shall have to tell him the whole story, of course. Lies and pretence will do neither of us any good. But right now, he is beaming and flushed and has smears of vanilla ice cream round his mouth.

I hug my boy close, then reach for a tissue and wipe his face clean.

'Ice cream,' he tells me proudly.

'Sorry, Meghan.' Emily eases herself into the empty deckchair next to my beach towel. 'We tried hard, but not all the ice cream made it into his tummy.'

'Oh, don't worry. He's always been a mucky pup. Thank you so much for taking him to the café for me.'

'It was good training for later,' she says with a wink, and rubs more sun cream into her gleaming belly. 'I'm glad you got a chance to relax. Harry seems much better these days, doesn't he? Stronger, healthier.'

'He is,' I agree. In fact, his ANC has never been higher, and those awful days of long courses of injections are a distant memory now. 'Dr Shiva says we may be over the worst of it.'

'That's fantastic news.' She looks at me curiously. 'So, did you think any more about Simon's offer?'

Her husband has offered me a job at the law firm once Harry starts nursery full-time. He thinks I need to start living again. And he's right, I've been keeping my son wrapped up at home for too long. And myself. It's time we both opened up to the world again. See what it may bring us, for better or worse.

'Yes, and I think I'm going to accept.'

Harry struggles free from my arms and lunges for his yellow plastic bucket.

'Harry, wait.'

His fair hair flops over his eyes as he glares back at me in a bull-ish fashion. He looks so like his father in that second, it takes my breath away. Then he beams again, and rattles his bucket, and the illusion is gone.

'Want water,' he announces, and sets off across the sand towards the sea, his short, sturdy legs moving at a trot, bucket swinging by his side.

'Wait for Mummy!' I call after him, and hurriedly clamber up.

Emily smiles and shakes her head, watching him run. 'He's a handful, that boy,' she comments, and closes her eyes.

I don't even have time to grab my own sandals, but run after him barefoot. My heart is in my mouth at first, my gaze fixed on his bobbing figure ahead. Then I realise I'm not as scared of letting go of Harry as I once was, of letting him behave like a normal toddler. Even last summer, I would never have brought him to sit on a public beach like this for fear of exposing him to unknown germs and bacteria. Let alone entertained the idea of letting him paddle in the Atlantic Ocean.

That's how much our lives have changed.

I chase after my son, easily catching up with him as he nears the water's edge. Harry looks back, sees me a few steps behind, and gurgles with excitement, almost dropping his bucket in the frothing surf.

I take his hand and study his face, smiling.

If Harry was affected by the horrors we saw on the clifftop that day, I can't see a trace of it in his fearless gaze and happy little grin.

He's a born wriggler though.

'Come on,' I say, 'there's a good boy, hold Mummy's hand properly.'

'Swim!' he insists, trying to pull away from my grasp.

'Not today, darling.' I kneel at the water's edge to fasten his sandal strap properly, and look into his sand-encrusted, glowing face. 'Maybe next summer, when you're bigger.'

He does not seem too bothered by the restriction.

'Love you, Mummy,' he says, and blows me an inexpert kiss with his chubby fingers.

I pretend to catch it, and then kiss his flushed cheek in return. 'Love you too, baby.'

Acknowledgements

As always, many thanks to my agent, Luigi Bonomi, for his unflagging support and encouragement. Thanks also to my editor, Jane Snelgrove, and to Gillian Holmes, Hatty Stiles, Sammia Hamer and all the fantastic team at Amazon Publishing for their hard work and inspiration.

My thanks too to my readers, to whom this book is dedicated, many of whom stay with me even when I shift genre, which is lovely to see and very encouraging. Thank you all, and I hope you enjoy this latest offering.

Lastly, as ever, but most important of all, to my husband, Steve, and my kids, who now do the dishes for me so I can keep typing. I couldn't do it without you!

About the Author

Jane Holland is a Gregory Award–winning poet and novelist who also writes commercial fiction under the pseudonyms Victoria Lamb, Elizabeth Moss, Beth Good and Hannah Coates. Her previous book, *Girl Number One*, hit #1 in the UK Kindle store in December 2015. Jane lives with her husband and young family near the North Cornwall/West Devon border. A homeschooler, her hobbies include photography and growing her own vegetables.